He'd told her he loved her, so how could he leave her?

Annabel stared at him, feeling completely bewildered by his rapid speech as she tried to organize thoughts that were spinning around her head. "London is so far away, Jevan," she said slowly, shaking her head in protest. "You can't go."

Jevan looked distraught. "Believe me when I say that I don't want to. I want to stay here and be with you."

"Then stay," she said bitterly, sitting up and attempting to retrieve her clothes.

Jevan's arms tightened around her and he pulled her close again.

"Let go, Jevan," she said irritably, "I want to get dressed."

He ignored her requests as he held her tighter than ever, resisting all effort to push him away. "Don't cry," he said with a broken voice, although his words only seemed to have the effect of making the tears run faster.

"I'm really cold, I want to get dressed," she insisted, prizing his hands from her and, although the air had chilled her, her body felt frozen from shock.

Jevan sighed heavily and reluctantly released her. He pulled on his clothes as she scrambled to do the same. It was only a distraction.

Annabel felt as if someone had hit her and the contents of her insides were slowly making their way up her throat. She thought she might actually be sick, as the evidence of what they had just done was seeping through the thin fabric of her clothes. She thought about the complete intimacy they just shared, and how, with a few spoken words, Jevan had ripped her apart. He might as well have taken that knife and plunged it deep inside her, as her death would have been a welcome release from the ordeal she was now experiencing.

Annabel Taylor, a beekeeper's daughter, grows up wild and carefree on the moors of England in the late 1860s, following in the footsteps of her mother, a beautiful witch. Annabel's closest friend is Jevan Wenham, the son of the blacksmith, who lives his life on the verge of destruction. His devotion to Annabel is full of twists and turns as brutality melds with deepest desire. But when Jevan is forced to travel to London to receive an education, Annabel is devastated.

Then Alex—heir to the Saltonstall legacy and son of Cerberus Saltonstall, the wealthy landowner of the foreboding Gothelstone Manor—comes into her life. Alex is arrogant and self-assured, but he cannot stop thinking about the outspoken girl he encounters on the road to Gothelstone. Not only is he bewitched by Annabel's beauty, he feels drawn to her by something he can't explain. Alex and Annabel are socially worlds apart, but that doesn't stop him from demanding her hand in marriage. When Annabel refuses, she is forced into an impossible situation. Jevan believes she has betrayed him, regardless of the fact that her decision saves him from the hangman's noose.

As a devastating love triangle unfolds, disturbing revelations thrust Annabel into a startling reality, where nothing is as it seems. Now both her life and Jevan's are in danger, and her fledging powers may not be enough to save them…

KUDOS for *The Beekeeper's Daughter*

In *The Beekeeper's Daughter* by Jane Jordan, Annabel Taylor is the daughter of a beekeeper in 1860s England and, like her mother, has special powers. Annabel and Jevan Wenham are childhood friends and inseparable. But when they are teenagers, Jevan is forced to accompany his mother to London. Annabel is devastated and hurls angry words at him. He is gone for over four years, and when he finally returns, Annabel is being courted by Alex Saltonstall, the local noble's son, a situation that becomes dangerous for Annabel and Jevan alike. The plot is strong and complex, full of twists and turns, and the character development is superb If you like historical sagas, *The Beekeeper's Daughter* is a must read. ~ *Taylor Jones, Reviewer*

The Beekeeper's Daughter by Jane Jordan is the story of love, pain, and betrayal. Set in England in the late 1860s, the story revolves around Annabel Taylor and Jevan Wenham. She is a beekeeper's daughter as well as a witch, and he is the son of a blacksmith. Soul mates, the two grow up together and are joined at the hip until Annabel turns sixteen. Then Jevan is forced to leave and journey to London with his mother, who wants to live with her sister and brother-in-law, who is quite wealthy. Annabel is broken hearted, sure that Jevan will forget her and marry some high-bred city girl. They fight and harsh words are said. Jevan leaves before Annabel comes to her senses and can apologize. When he finally returns, four years later, the local rich boy wants to marry her and Jevan's life is in danger. Annabel is caught up in a web of lies and betrayal, with only one way out. *The Beekeeper's Daughter* is a complex, intriguing, and suspenseful romance/thriller. Filled with interesting and well-developed characters, this fast-paced story is a great read. ~ *Regan Murphy, reviewer*

The Beekeeper's Daughter

JANE JORDAN

A Black Opal Books Publication

GENRE: HISTORICAL THRILLER/PARANORMAL ROMANCE

This is a work of fiction. Names, places, characters and incidents are either the product of the author's imagination or are used fictitiously, and any resemblance to any actual persons, living or dead, businesses, organizations, events or locales is entirely coincidental. All trademarks, service marks, registered trademarks, and registered service marks are the property of their respective owners and are used herein for identification purposes only. The publisher does not have any control over or assume any responsibility for author or third-party websites or their contents.

The Beekeeper's Daughter

Prologue

*T*he natural world is full of extremes, and not everything has rhyme or reason. If the mind is open to possibility, then a witch can bend reality and create magic. For the sake of love, some are willing to open Pandora's Box. After all, evil is a point of view, and what may be acceptable to one, will repel another.

Dark magic does not follow the path of the wise. It is a corruption of the craft—except that, when faced with adversity, sometimes the rules have to be broken.

Chapter 1

Gothelstone Village

1698:

The crowd surged forward, straining their necks to get a better view. Venomous whispers carried ominously through the air, and the words on their lips were full of condemnation. Most of the villagers played their part in this madness. Only a few saw through the falseness. They prayed silently and held back tears of sorrow. This small number hoped their presence might be of some comfort. They had not come to gloat or gain satisfaction at the spectacle. They came to witness the injustice.

Morning dew was still evident. With the earlier mist nearly gone, weak sunshine penetrated through low-hanging clouds, throwing a subtle light across the young woman's face. Her breath came in sobs, clearly audible to the people closest to her. She could not control the trembling of her body or the cold stark fear that caused sweat to run down her brow. Long dirty streaks, caused by earlier tears, marked her cheeks. Long, matted hair obscured her face further. Her eyes darted amongst the villagers as disbelief invaded her mind.

There was no justice in the world, and she could not depart on these terms. Lifting her head higher, she shook the hair out of her eyes and stared at the restless crowd in defiance. Reality was before her and fear numbed any more emotion.

From the back of the crowd, a figure pushed through to stand before her.

Coward. She thought, as his eyes refused to meet hers. After a few moments pause, a sudden hush came over the gathering. Then her accuser's voice filled the cold stagnant air with terrifying prose as he read from the indictment.

Accusing murmurs mounted, and bile rose in her throat. She stared blindly into the mass, unable to believe they so easily succumbed to the lies. These people were neighbors and friends. She had known them all her life, yet, even their betrayal paled into nothingness compared to her mounting hatred for him.

His voice was booming in her head, drowning out any other noise or sensible thought, his intention to intimidate and threaten. It was incredible that he appeared to be a complete stranger to her now. No longer the man she once loved. As more lies spilled from his mouth, the gnawing sickness of moments before vanished. With his provocation enraging her further, something altered. Her mind let go of the fear and replaced it with pure unbridled hatred.

Instinctively, she pulled harder against the chains. They were unyielding, just as before. In the mob, a few called upon their God to have mercy. It was an illusion. Their pious cries did nothing to conceal the suspicion in their eyes.

Another man approached. His identity was of no consequence. Her gaze tore from her accuser and rested upon the fiery torch the other man held. He came closer. The breath caught in her throat. Terror rendered her body rigid as he bent and lit the pile of faggots beneath her.

Blood coursed through her veins, making her feel light-headed, and her heart pounded so heavily that it brought physical pain. Tears found renewed energy and streamed down her face. The heat seeped up, slowly at first. Then faster, surrounding her legs as the faggots smoldered for a few moments before catching alight.

A terrified gasp escaped her lips, as the first wisps of smoke invaded her nostrils. She twisted her body, fighting against the chains that bound her to the stake. The metal links were unrelenting. They cut deeper and deeper into her flesh. The heat intensified, engulfing her torso and making her cough. The fire took hold quickly and crackled ominously beneath her. Her tears, now a steady stream, clouded her vision. She felt the first tiny shocks of pain, as the flames licked her soles.

"God save me!" she screamed, panic besetting her.

Frantically, she searched faces in the crowds, still believing someone would show compassion. Somebody would speak up and free her. As her eyes burned into theirs, she saw no reprieve. Instead, the crowd grew quieter and settled down. They watched in morbid fascination as her flesh seared and pain surged through her.

Summoning courage, she tried to withstand the pain, but terror thwarted her spirit. The fire began to spew the sparks that caught hold of the hem of her ragged clothes, and an uncontrollable force made her shake violently. Smoke began to billow from the pyre, forcing the congregation to move backward. Only her accuser stood his ground.

"God will not save you!" he cried, "for thou shall not suffer a witch to live!"

A faint murmur of agreement rippled through the crowd. She was unable to look at them anymore. Terror had a firm hold on her psyche as flames beat at her feet and lapped her legs. She screamed again, a terrible sound that rang through the village square. The torture was unbearable. She could no longer stand it. Blinking the oppressive breath of the fire out of her eyes, she prayed for the end.

Death was not far away. Suffocating slowly, and unable to scream anymore, she was slipping into unconsciousness from the agony. She managed to lift her head one final time and silently beg God for a merciful release. The smoke cleared for a few seconds in front of her face and, quite by chance, she caught his eye. It took only a second to register that he was actually smiling.

Rage pulsed through her. She battled against the constriction of her throat and the creeping, burning agony that was melting her flesh. Her heart pounded so violently against her ribcage that she feared it would surely burst from her chest. Then on the verge of death, her unbroken spirit gave her the power to raise her voice once more.

It was surprising, shocking even, that her words rang so clearly across the gathering. The God-fearing peasants clutched at each other, seeking reassurance, afraid of her words and the unnatural power she appeared to possess. With her final scream echoing through their heads, they watched the hungry flames engulf her body. Some cried out in pity, others uneasily marked themselves with the sign of the cross. Only one looked on in satisfaction.

The witch was dead.

Chapter 2

The Bee Charmer

Many Years Later:

At first, the humming was barely noticeable, until the incessant noise invaded her mind, and little by little chased away the vivid images of the dream. As intellect gained clarity, Annabel roused into wakefulness and opened her eyes to the sunlight streaming into the room. Shape-shifting shadows fell across the bed, while a light breeze caressed her skin, and sheer white curtains billowed away from the window. She lay perfectly still with her hands tightly clasped over her stomach. She breathed in the soothing scent from the lavender, which grew in a pot on the night table. Then she looked toward the noise that woke her.

Lured through the open window by perfumed flowers, a honeybee hovered for a moment before descending. Annabel watched in fascination and slowly shifted position onto her stomach. The bee vibrated its body over each bloom and hummed a ceaseless song. It was in no particular hurry, meticulously inspecting every flower spike in turn. Already fine yellow pollen covered its legs and back.

It was oblivious to the scrutiny. After several minutes, the bee became still, as if tired from all of this early morning exertion.

Annabel saw her opportunity and leaned closer until her

face could almost touch the flower stems, then she held out her hand.

"Come to me, little bee."

The bee stirred at once, this subtle encouragement was enough to tempt it from the flowers. Its tiny legs tickled Annabel's delicate ivory skin, as the bee moved down the length of a finger and onto the palm of her hand. She caressed the bee's back with slow stroking movements and felt the velvety coat bristle with enjoyment. She marveled at the tiny legs and whispered admiration of the fragile gossamer wings. The minute eyes seemed to gleam with understanding and intelligence. She increased the pressure of her finger by a fraction. In response, the bee wriggled its little body and waved tiny antenna as if in pleasure.

Curling her fingers around the bee protectively, Annabel rose from the bed and made her way along the hallway. She stepped down the uneven wooden steps, taking care not to tread on the splinters from the edges of the rough wood. With her free hand, she clutched at the handrail so she would not trip over her long nightgown. When she reached the bottom, she went to her father who was sitting at the table reading. He looked up and a smile transformed his face into an expression of delight.

"Ah, Annabel, what do you have there?" he asked, peering at her outstretched fist.

She uncurled her fingers to show the bee resting, perfectly content. Her father's smile widened as he saw the creature, then he patted his daughter on the head and smiled into her big green eyes.

"My little bee charmer," he said, smoothing back her long red curls.

He looked up and caught the eye of his wife standing in the doorway. She too had a mass of long curls, only hers were dark. Lilith's hair was not the only thing that drew his admiration.

Even after years of marriage, he could not help to marvel at her striking image. Her pale skin had remained unblemished by the sun. Her long dark lashes concealed the magnetism of green irises that lay beneath and bordered her exotic almond shaped eyes. Although, it was her smile that reminded him of how much he loved her, and quite suddenly, he had an urge to rip the clothes from her slender body. Even now, she still had that distracting effect over him. He felt his color rise, and all of a sudden, the cottage felt particularly warm. He looked back to his little daughter, still hovering by his side, and gestured toward the door.

"That's a very fine specimen you have found. I'm sure she will be happier outside. Go into the garden and put her on a flower."

Annabel smiled back at him, looking more like a miniature version of her mother, and headed toward the door.

She walked into the sultry air of the warm summer's morning, and although the stones on the path were sharp against her bare feet, she paid no attention, too intent on the task her father had set. She stopped halfway down the path and looked about the garden. It was a riot of colorful flowers. Thinking back, she remembered the bee liked the lavender on the nightstand. It now made perfect sense as to which flower it would prefer. Annabel turned and made her way to the clump that grew under the kitchen window.

The long stalks nodded their purple heads approvingly in the breeze. She uncurled her fingers, and, as if inspired by their heady perfume, the bee instantly roused and flew from her hand. Within seconds, it was busily collecting nectar again. Just then, Annabel's mother's soft exclamation carried through the open kitchen window.

"It's a wonder the child has never been stung!" Her voice carried some concern, even so, there was a hint of admiration as she continued. "She has your ways, Josiah, for I am certain that she could charm a whole swarm to give up its precious hive."

Her father laughed lightly before he spoke. "That maybe so, Lilith. She is a beekeeper's daughter, although, she has your ways too, a child of nature and grace."

That year was 1866 and Annabel was five years old.

Chapter 3

An Enchanted Wilderness

Honeymead, the moorland cottage, was as enthralling as any picture book could describe. Annabel grew up surrounded by heather-clad moors, dense woodlands, and fields that made up the landscape of North West Exmoor. Her views were mostly uncultivated. Early explorations taught her to understand the natural world and respect the dangers of living in such an untamed place. As a young child, she played in the gardens and orchards, exploring only the gentle slopes and neighboring fields. As she grew, she discovered craggy outcrops that led to jagged cliffs, which plummeted from great heights down into the sea. In this landscape, trees overhung steep, precarious ledges and stood in defiance against the relentless westerly winds and ferocious winter gales.

Being an only child and given the freedom to roam where she pleased, she felt in tune with the wilderness and preferred to keep her own company. Occasionally, she had wished for a playmate, although from an early age she had the impression that local children were dull and constrained by morals and rules made up by adults.

Lilith and Josiah had an altogether more natural way of childrearing. Something she grew to be extremely grateful for. Instead of a playmate, she befriended many wild animals, bringing them into the cottage to nurse when they were injured or sick. Most of all, she adored her Welsh mountain pony, April. That admiration stretched farther. The bees that lived in the orchard were fundamental to her life. Her connection with them was curious and instantaneous.

The bees came to know all her secrets. They learned of every new discovery she made and appeared sympathetic when she related the most recent cuts and scratches that marked her skin—often caused by her falling on the serrated black and slippery rocks, which the waves constantly drenched as they broke against the shoreline.

Exmoor was a land of extremes, enchanting and beautiful or harsh and unforgiving, and for Annabel, the passing of each season brought familiar rituals to her life. In autumn, she went whortleberry picking with her mother. Then her fingers were stained with the purple juice, which stayed under her finger-nails for days. New colors would then appear in the landscape, the glorious brilliance of the golden gorse that grew in great clumps and the changing of leaves from greens to reds and oranges. Wild animals were also more abundant at this time of year, and sighting a deer herd or Exmoor ponies that grazed on the higher slopes delighted her.

With spring came the first flowers, heralding the reawakening of nature, and a time when the cold dark hours of winter gave way to lighter and warmer days. The primroses broke through the carpet of brown leaves and lit up the banks of the ancient woodland streams. Annabel searched the bark of the ash, rowan, and oak to discover the creatures that lived on them. She studied the fascinating forms of lichen and picked armfuls of wild flowers. Later, came the bluebells with their gently drooping heads, adding their own touch of brilliance amongst the green. They littered the woodland floor, so densely in places that she could not help stepping on them.

Not only the seasons changed the landscape, each day brought new wonder. Deep mysteries surrounded the curious standing stones and burial mounds. Her imagination ran wild as she splashed in the sparkling streams or rivers that meandered through this harmonious landscape. Walking along the riverbanks, she followed the current to where the water chased its way under ancient stone bridges and tumbled down rocky ledges to become scenic waterfalls. She would follow the la-

menting call of the raven when she was up on the high slopes
and roam amongst the sheep that had long shaggy coats and
ebony faces. They were everywhere, dotted amongst the countryside and grazing on grasses on the moors and in the valleys.
Twilight brought the bats from their roosts, swerving between
the trees, before they dropped down into the valleys on their
nightly pursuit of prey. Dusk enticed the badgers from their
dens to forage upon the woodland floor. Sitting with her father
in a makeshift hide, Annabel watched entire families going
about their nightly activities.

Honeymead was nestled in a wooded combe, but there was
still enough elevation to allow a view of the Bristol Channel,
even though the cottage was roughly a mile from the water's
edge. On a clear day, the shimmering water gave the impression of a million diamonds dancing in the sunlight. By contrast, the dense mists could rise dramatically and change the
landscape into a mysterious entity that blotted out the sea entirely.

Gardens surrounded the cottage on three sides. On the east
side was a wide cobbled path, which led to a narrow road. A
dry stone wall bordered a small orchard. The annual harvest
brought forth a bounty of apples and plums. Beyond the hedge
at the far end of the orchard were the skeps that housed the
bees. From there, numerous pathways led through the woodlands and out onto the moors. The road that led to Honeymead
was also the only road from Gothelstone village. On a clear
day, the imposing Gothelstone Manor house, rose majestically
from out of the landscape, presiding over its vast estate.

Annabel's parents were hard workers, always industrious,
most of all, they were happy together. Annabel, saw the attrac-
tion between her mother and father. She felt loved as a child,
and as such, her world felt idealic.

Josiah had inherited the cottage and a few acres from his
father years before. Back then, it had been little more than a
crude stone building, thrown together out of necessity, and
topped with a thatched roof. The roof overhung the walls to
protect the structure from the extremities of the weather.

Josiah, being of a practical nature, had vastly improved the comfort of the cottage, however, the windows still did not fit properly and the glass was undulating, making the view outside a little distorted. Well-constructed wooden boards acted like shutters on the outside. They were kept shut in the winter months when blusterous gales, whipped up by wicked winter storms, blanketed the countryside in sweeping rain showers.

In the summer months, the cottage was delightful and warm, the windows and doors flung open to allow the scent of the roses to waft through. A robin or sparrow would perch on the windowsill, begging for tidbits from the kitchen. Lilith would be up with the sun, stoking the fire, even in summer. For a time, it was the only cooking facility available when Annabel was young. Later on, came a modern stove that fed greedily on the wood supplies. In the winter months, the cottage took on another feeling entirely, dark and draughty, and the heat from the fire did not throw enough warmth into all the extreme corners.

On those many dark winter evenings, Lilith would sew or read by the glow of the firelight and candles, or rush lights, which she made from peeled rushes dipped in mutton grease when she could get it. The cottage was cozy. It was comprised of four rooms, two up and one large downstairs area, which was partially divided into two. The two floors were connected by a spiraling wooden staircase. Annabel's bedroom consisted of a bed and a nightstand, while her parent's room was larger but just as sparsely furnished.

Downstairs were a table and four old chairs; a dresser, displaying various items of china; and a high-backed settle, strewn with colorful cushions. Everything centered on the fireplace, as old iron pots and jugs hung from the inglenook and served as a kitchen. Water came from a well in the garden. Josiah had built it out of old bricks and covered it with a thatched roof to match the cottage. Attached to a chain was an old wooden pail. A winch lowered the pail deep into the well. Josiah, forestalling any accident, installed a wooden cover when Annabel was young to ensure that she would not fall into that dark hole.

Annabel was a curious child. She thought deeply and took

in every detail of what happened around her. As much as she thought she knew her mother, Lilith intrigued her. Over the years, Annabel asked many questions, often sensing that Lilith was reluctant to talk about her past. As Annabel grew, she finally understood the anguish her mother had suffered.

Lilith had come from a good social background in Ireland, and her family had been of some importance. With the outbreak of the dreadful cholera, which devastated whole towns and villages, Lilith's family suffered greatly. The disease nearly wiped them out completely, and Lilith fled Ireland with an aunt. On their arrival in England, they faced only fear and condemnation, forced to move from village to village and driven away by locals, for fear of contamination. They had survived by foraging for berries and wild plants and, eventually, they reached Rookwood, a large village lying two miles beyond Gothelstone.

A kindly doctor and his family, who saw that they had no symptoms of the illness, took them in and provided them with food and shelter in his stables. Soon after, and at the good doctor's word, the community finally accepted them. After a while, they found suitable lodgings in a nearby house and began to build a new life.

Lilith's social importance along with any money was gone. She had to find employment and found a position as a ladies' maid at Gothelstone mansion. Although, anyone who met her instantly recognized that she had an uncommon refinement. Her ability to read, write, and entertain with conversation delighted the mistress of the house. Nevertheless, Lilith never elaborated on her life back then, and Annabel knew no other details.

Instead, she told her daughter how she met Josiah—stories about their married life and of the improvements they had made to Honeymead. Then she spoke of her contentment after such tragedy. She did indeed seem to be happy, having resurrected old practices of her homeland that had been handed down to her by her own mother. Lilith knew how to heal using herbal remedies. With her education, she was highly regarded. Over the years, many villagers came to her with their various ailments. Her tinctures and creams helped many people. Josiah's father handed down the craft of beekeeping. Honey was a valuable commodity, and in leaner times, the bees made sure that they did not starve.

There were twelve skeps, in total. They were made of wood with straw roofs, which gave them the appearance of tiny thatched cottages. The bees were most content in their picturesque homes. As the colony's life pattern was dependent on the flowers within its flight range, the spring flowering orchard was invaluable to the colony, as well as hawthorn and sycamore trees bordering the heather-filled moorland. The swarm did not often need to stray as far as the moors, as the white clover in the small pasture and wild flowers meadows provided ample pollen.

Lilith was exceptionally resourceful. She made beeswax candles to sell in the nearby village of Rookwood. Later, she learned the properties in making beauty products to sell to the wealthier women of the village. Royal jelly being a favorite in their bid to stave off aging and keep themselves looking young. On occasion, and if the mood took her, Lilith spoke of growing up in Ireland and, through those stories, Annabel was transported to a faraway magical place, where fairies and leprechauns inhabited enchanted woodlands and vast emerald forests concealed all manner of mystical beasts. She imagined her mother as a beautiful, sad heiress, banished from her own land.

From Lilith's description, Annabel could picture the beautiful old house she grew up in and the great gardens she had played in as a child. She imagined her mother walking in the most beautiful rose garden, dressed in the finest silk with her long dark hair falling to her waist. She wondered what her mother's life would have been like had a handsome suitor on a white horse whisked her away to a safer place. Those thoughts only served to make Annabel unhappy, knowing that she would not exist, and Josiah would not be her father. It shamed her to know, deep down, she felt glad that her mother's family tragedy forced her to leave Ireland.

The few acres of land that Josiah farmed he also owned,

and he sold the produce to local grain merchants. Each July, he would be extra busy with the harvest and, at these times, all the surrounding fields were a hive of activity with men, children, and horses harvesting mainly wheat and barley that grew in the neighboring fields. Annabel could have also gone to the fields, although she preferred to spend time delighting in the creatures that shared the garden, making friends with the warty toads that lived at the base of the old stone wall, or following the silvery trails of the snails, was a far more agreeable pastime.

By far, the company she preferred to keep was the bees, and, from her father, she learnt the art of beekeeping.

He had an uncommon connection. Perhaps it came from the fact that Josiah had never killed a swarm, as was often done. Instead, he would remove the bees by shaking them gently into an empty box. The bees seemed to understand his method and tolerated his management and, since Annabel always accompanied him, the bees accepted her. In her childish world, she engaged with them on another level. She understood social issues that dictated the politics of the colony. Being a welcome observer, she learned all the personal grievances that beset their society. She watched and listened until she deemed the necessary course of action for the disruptive culprits.

Sometimes that meant removing them from the hive for a while, or sometimes, just a severe chastisement would resolve any issues. Annabel showed no fear of these creatures, and the bees would not sting her. On the days that the whole colony was harmonious, Annabel would tell them stories. They appeared to listen and absorb her every word. More often than not, she would hear Lilith's voice calling to her. Then, forced to step back from this minute world, she returned to the reality of her own.

One summer morning, something surprising happened. Josiah was stung several times. Puzzled by the sudden aggressive change in their behavior, he spoke of destroying them and looking for new swarms. It was the first time in Annabel's life, thus far, when she truly felt afraid, and she pleaded with him not to kill the bees.

"If they have gone bad, Annabel, then it's only a matter of time before they turn on you as well," he said, trying to make her understand the danger.

"No, Father, they do not bear you any ill will. It's just they can only have one master—" Annabel bit her lip, hesitating for a moment. "—and they have chosen me."

Annabel saw the odd look on her father's face. He did not respond to her comment, although deep down, he reluctantly submitted to her and her observation. Right from the beginning, Josiah saw the peculiar bond between the bees and his daughter, a curious thing to observe. He still believed in his own ability. It was just that her persuasion seemed suddenly so much stronger. He masked his sorrow and smiled. She was an accomplished bee charmer. More than that, as young as she was, the bees *had* chosen her.

Chapter 4

The Boy in the Ivory Tower

Eventually the bees calmed and after Annabel's words of warning, they did not sting Josiah again. Even though he continued to tend the bees, from that moment on, he was noticeably more cautious around them.

Annabel's carefree years of early childhood flew by. Her life changed significantly when she found herself enrolled at school in the village of Rookwood. She was horrified at this terrible turn of events, and even more so, when she found herself standing in a schoolroom full of other children. Some, she recognized some from the hamlet of Gothelstone, although there were others she had never set eyes upon before.

The teacher, Miss Gatchell, looked down her disapproving nose at Annabel's long hair, which had all, but escaped the confines of the ribbon that held it in place. Miss Gatchell looked austere. Her hair, secured in a severe bun, pulled her skin so tight that it made her veins protrude unnaturally. Her eyes were small and set deep into her pale face, and she appeared to wear a constant sour expression.

Even her clothes looked ugly. The dove gray dress she wore was so tightly buttoned that it made her neck look abnormally thin. Miss Gatchell was engaged in conversation with Annabel's mother for a few minutes, and then Lilith turned to Annabel.

"I will be waiting for you after school," she said, fixing

Annabel with her lovely eyes and one of her irresistible smiles.

Annabel could not help, but notice the marked difference between the two women before her. She had a feeling of overwhelming pride at her mother's gentleness and beauty compared to the other woman. The feeling disappeared when she caught Miss Gatchell's harsh stare.

"I don't want to stay, please let me come home. I can come to school another day," she pleaded with her mother.

"No Annabel, you have to stay, and it's not good for a girl to be so uneducated," Lilith answered firmly.

"I don't want to be educated," Annabel insisted miserably.

Even though she was the tiniest bit curious about school, she refused to let that show, instead, she protested again, this time more loudly. The other children turned to stare. Annabel glared back at them defiantly, not caring she would be the talk of the class. Again, she caught Miss Gatchell's disapproving eye. Her mouth was set in a firm line, and a tiny muscle had started to twitch in the side of her face.

"Come along, Miss Taylor," she said abruptly, "we don't have the time for this behavior."

She took a firm hold of Annabel's arm and led her to a small desk and chair. Annabel looked back at her mother. To her dismay, Lilith was already gone. Annabel was alone with the room full of strangers. Miss Gatchell placed a copybook before her and then barked instructions. Annabel suddenly felt afraid. She had a strong urge to run from the room, and then she heard the door shut with a loud click. It suddenly seemed like a long way to the back of the schoolroom. She could feel all eyes upon her and stared miserably at the book before her.

It felt like the worst day of her life. She closed her eyes in misery and imagined herself banished from her homeland and thrown into this prison cell, where the jailor was an old hag. Annabel felt betrayed and angry that her mother could have done such a terrible thing. It made her remember her parent's recent conversation, the one that she was not supposed to overhear. Her mother had talked about the school, but her father seemed not to care either way. He would have been happy for her to be out in the woods or on the moors, enjoying the countryside. Lilith insisted that she was becoming too wild, and much to Annabel's disappointment, Josiah finally agreed that school might be a good thing after all. Although, that initial day was really the worst, as the days that followed were not quite as bad as Annabel first imagined.

The village schoolhouse was built of rough red sandstone and topped with a gray slate roof. Inside there was one single long room with several wooden desks arranged in rows. From her mother, she had learned her letters, although, it was from Miss Gatchell that she soon learned arithmetic and the loathsome weights and measures. Object lessons taught geography and sciences, and Miss Gatchell occasionally read out tiresome poetry. While these things certainly expanded Annabel's knowledge for the better, school was the setting for one of the most important events that would happen in her young life.

Many of the children who attended school came from Rookwood, including Jevan Wenham, the blacksmith's son. He was tall for his age, and much taller than Annabel. He was nearly three years older, but classes were of mixed age groups and, although she was nine at the time, there were children even younger. Annabel knew of Jevan. She'd seen him mainly at a distance, and from her father, knew that, when he was not required at the forge, he disappeared for hours at a time. Up close, Jevan had a peculiar force about him. Perhaps it was just the effect of his startling dark eyes and nearly black hair, which was long and untidy. Jevan attended school infrequently and even more reluctantly than her.

The very first day she encountered Jevan at school, he walked into the schoolroom ten minutes after the bell sounded and sat down heavily at a desk across from Annabel. Miss Gatchell showed predictable outrage at his tardiness. She lectured him about punctuality, and he mumbled a few words of apology. Somewhat satisfied, she went back to the front of the class. Curiosity got the better of Annabel and she discreetly gazed at Jevan. As if sensing her look, he deliberately turned and stared straight at her.

There was menace in his eyes, as if he was daring her to

continue, because she would be sorry. For a moment, she was stunned. Heat flushed her cheeks and she promptly stared down at her work. Even so, she felt his intense stare through the curtain of hair that hung down her face. She continued to feel oddly intimidated, so much so that she did not even hear Miss Gatchell's question. Suddenly, it seemed that from out of nowhere, her name rang shrilly across the classroom, making her jump.

"Are you deliberately ignoring me?" shrieked Miss Gatchell.

Annabel looked up, feeling flustered. "N—no," she stammered, "I didn't hear you."

"Then perhaps you are deaf. Or my words are not important enough for you to pay any attention."

"No, I am not deaf," Annabel said boldly, meeting the older woman's gaze straight on.

"Don't be insolent," barked Miss Gatchell. Annabel resisted the urge to answer back. The teacher's eyes narrowed fractionally. "What is the capital city of France?"

Annabel's mind was blank. The schoolroom was in silence, only the tick of the clock indicated how many long seconds were passing. Annabel dreaded saying the next words. Somehow, she found the courage. "I don't know."

Miss Gatchell's eyes narrowed further. "Perhaps you're stupid as well as hard of hearing," she said angrily. "We went over capital cities only yesterday?"

Annabel stared at the woman's small ugly eyes. She loathed her shrill penetrating voice and her stupid capital cities. Most of all, she hated Jevan and his concentrated black eyes that had the effect of driving every normal thought out of her head. Miss Gatchell huffed in disgust and turned from her. Suddenly Jevan's voice sounded loudly next to her.

"The capital city is Paris, I thought everyone knew that."

Annabel stared at him in dismay. His arrogant smirk caused her eyes to open wider in anger. His conceited look dared her to react as the blood rushed to her cheeks and she felt her face grow even warmer. She did not answer. Instead, she looked back at her book. She refused to look at Jevan again and became silent. Then for the rest of the day, he mainly ignored everyone, refusing to participate in any more of the lesson, and seemed locked away in a remote place where no one, certainly not Miss Gatchell, could even begin to infiltrate.

Jevan made an impression, one that Annabel could not forget, and she vowed that, one day soon, the walls of his ivory tower would come tumbling down.

ℯↄℯↄ

One morning in early spring, Annabel accompanied her father to the blacksmith. April needed new shoes and having walked into the forge, they found the blacksmith forging a piece of metal. When he saw his visitors, he put his tools down and greeted them with his usual warmth. Annabel liked Jophiel a lot. He occasionally came to the cottage, as he and her father were good friends.

He was tall and dark, like Jevan, although *his* eyes were blue and full of laughter. However, Annabel was surprised to find Jevan at the forge that day. By the looks of things, he was helping Jophiel shoe a large stallion. At their intrusion, Jevan gave her a longer than necessary stare and then sullenly turned away. He went and sat on a stool at the back of the forge and began polishing a harness.

At first, Annabel politely listened to the exchange of pleasantries between her father and Jophiel. She viewed the various tools in the forge with a small amount of interest, even if her attention was elsewhere. She looked back at her father, still in deep conversation about seemingly mundane matters, and so she turned and walked to where Jevan sat. He looked up at her with a small amount of surprise. In the dim light of the forge, his eyes seemed even blacker, and there was suspicion in their depths, which she found unsettling.

Not at all concerned by his manner, for Annabel had neither forgotten nor forgiven him for the incident in the schoolroom, she smiled mischievously. "Hello, Jevan."

Jevan's stare became even darker, as if daring her to utter another word. Annabel let the smile fade and stared back at him, challenging him at his own childish game. Suddenly, Jevan rose abruptly from the stool and left the room, banging the heavy wooden door loudly after him.

Jophiel made her jump when he spoke, having seen the exchange between them. "Don't take it personally Annabel." He hesitated for a moment. "Jevan's a loner, always has been," he said, smiling warmly at her and turned to Josiah. "I sent him to school, but I am at that school more often than he is. He doesn't want to learn," he remarked, slightly exasperated, "he just seems so isolated, always in a world of his own."

Annabel's father nodded in understanding. "He just needs time, he'll come round."

"I hope so, Josiah. At the moment, he spends all of his time with the horses or out on the moors."

Annabel looked at the doorway that Jevan had disappeared through moments ago. She saw the daylight vanish through the large crack in the wood. The door was a couple of inches off the floor, the light beyond was still visible, all apart from the area where the hovering shadow could easily be seen.

She could feel him watching her. The schoolroom rebuke still smarted, and his behavior today irritated her greatly. She turned squarely toward the door and stared hard at the split in the wood. Josiah looked down at his side and saw his daughter's fixed stare, as if in a trance. He turned and looked behind him. He could not make out what she looked so intently at. "What are you looking at?"

"Oh nothing," she said, "that door just looks extremely dense, don't you think?" Annabel caught her father's strange look as she turned to smile sweetly back at him. Then she glanced back at the door, and the daylight was already back.

That night, she thought about how Jevan might react to that candid observation in his father's forge. She reassured herself that he would not even be at school the next day, although the following morning as she walked to school, she felt butterflies in her stomach. In the schoolroom, the bell sounded and everyone took a seat. Annabel breathed a sigh of relief. Jevan was absent.

"Coward," she mumbled triumphantly under her breath.

Almost instantly, the schoolroom door opened. She didn't
need to look up. She knew Jevan stood in the doorway. There
was an odd sort of premonition that he would sit at the desk
behind, even before he made his way across the room.

He sat noisily down, scraping his chair across the floor. It
felt as though he purposely moved his desk closer to the back
of her chair. She did not react. She was certain that his eyes
were fixed upon her. It felt as those dark hostile pools of malice burned through her cotton pinafore and seared her flesh.
She could not help squirming in the seat, getting warmer by
the second, as she tried to concentrate on the lesson.

Miss Gatchell's monotonous voice filled the air as she
droned on about the names of rivers written on the blackboard.
Her words seemed hazy, and Annabel's mind became too distracted by something that would happen, it was just a question
of when.

"Open your copy books," Miss Gatchell barked sharply,
swishing the birch rod in her hand several times. She strolled
back and forth a few times and, satisfied that her pupils were
studiously complying with her demands, sat down at her own
desk.

Annabel had just been given a clay pot filled with ink and
placed it above her copybook, which was full of smudge
marks and in a general sorry state. She picked up the pen,
dipped the nib in the ink, and slowly scratched the words from
the blackboard. Suddenly something tugged her hair, just hard
enough to jerk her head back. Without a moment's hesitation,
she turned and narrowed her eyes, her temper growing as she
saw the look of satisfaction in Jevan's eyes.

"Don't pull my hair," she hissed between clenched teeth.

"Annabel Taylor!" Miss Gatchell's sharp voice made her
jump. "Turn around this instant." Annabel turned forward,
with her face burning. "You will pay attention in my class,
Miss Taylor," the teacher continued. Annabel looked back
down at the paper and took a deep breath, willing her temper
to calm. Miss Gatchell turned back to the blackboard and began to write more names.

A few moments passed and then, just like before, came another tug on her hair. This time Annabel had just dipped her pen in ink, and the unexpected pain made her drop the pen. She stared down at the huge ink splodge on the copybook. Rage suddenly possessed her. In one quick movement, she turned, grabbed Jevan's inkpot, and neatly tipped its contents over his head.

Jevan eyes flew open in shock. He gave a cry of anger as he scrambled to his feet and seized her wrist, twisting it firmly, as he pulled her to her feet. His black eyes stared wildly as she cried out in pain while the black ink dripped down his face. It seemed to reflect his dark character.

"Let go!" she yelled in protest.

"No," he said fiercely, and she felt his grip tighten.

Instinctively she raised her free hand and viciously dug her nails into his arm, trying to inflict as much pain as possible, or at least match the pain he was exerting on her. He stifled an angry cry and swung her round, pushing her forcibly back against the wall. She was pinned there, unable to move. It was as if no one else existed in that room, her anger was so concentrated on Jevan. And then, she was suddenly aware that Miss Gatchell was screaming at them both.

Their eyes left one another and they stared at Miss Gatchell. She was livid, so much so that her veins appeared to be protruding excessively, and her skin was flushed with anger. Jevan released Annabel abruptly and even though Annabel dearly wanted to hit him, Miss Gatchell was already between them. Instead, Annabel had to make do with scowling darkly at him, infuriated that he overpowered her so easily.

"Annabel Taylor and Jevan Wenham get to the front of the class, now!" Miss Gatchell cried, shoving them both forward.

They stood facing the whole class and Annabel could feel everybody's eyes watching. She did not care. Her only thought was how much she hated Jevan. Only Miss Gatchell's penetrating voice forced her attention as she said her name. Annabel stared at her, shocked by her tone. Miss Gatchell's eyes were wide with rage. She bristled with anger as she looked from Annabel to Jevan and then back to Annabel again.

"What on earth possessed you, you're a wicked girl, I will

not tolerate such terrible behavior," she said grabbing her arm firmly and turning her to face Jevan. "And how am I going to explain his ruined clothes to his father?"

Her voice sounded close to breaking and Annabel stared back at her in a sort of strange delight, wondering if she might break into hysterics or even faint.

"Well speak, girl!" the teacher barked, her eyes gleaming fiercely. "Tell me," she demanded shaking Annabel's arm firmly.

Annabel could not be certain what stopped her from blurting out, "It was his fault."

Something made her hesitate. Perhaps, it was the sight of him covered in black ink, or knowing that Jophiel was already at his wits end with him. She did not want to be the cause of more worry for him. She had despised Jevan only moments ago, except that feeling had gone. Instead, she felt oddly drawn to him. She pursed her lips thinking of something to say and caught Jevan's eye. He watched her with curious speculation.

"It was an accident," she said at last.

At those words, she quite thought Miss Gatchell might explode. She shook in frustration, and her voice was more strident than ever.

"You're a disgrace to your parents, with such wicked lies. How can it have been an accident?" she demanded, staring at Annabel as though she were deranged.

Annabel stayed silent, staring steadily at Jevan. He stared back, evidently surprised.

Miss Gatchell was running out of patience as she directed her next words to Jevan. "Well, why did she do this?"

Jevan's eyes had not left Annabel's and, even though the ink staining one side of his face made him look comical, she did not smile, but kept her mouth set in a straight line.

"It was an accident," he said, turning his gaze to the teacher.

Miss Gatchell had heard enough. She picked up the birch rod. Annabel saw what she was about to do and hastily tried to pull her hand away. She was not quick enough, and Miss

Gatchell struck her with it twice. Annabel cried out in pain. As it was raised it for a third time, Jevan suddenly caught hold of the rod. Miss Gatchell gasped.

Jevan leaned closer to the teacher and fixed her with a threatening stare. "If you hit her again, I will break it," he said icily.

Miss Gatchell shrank back at his words, looking as though she might burst with anger. Jevan was already tall enough to be on eye level with her, and his look was intimidating.

Miss Gatchell reluctantly lowered the cane. "Get out of my classroom, both of you," she hissed through gritted teeth.

They did not need further prompting and quickly left the schoolroom. When the door shut behind them, Jevan leaned against the doorpost. Annabel turned to him.

She looked at the black stain covering his face and neck, although it had already blended with his naturally dark hair. "You should wash that off before it dries," she said quietly and sat down on the stone step.

Jevan stared down at her as she cradled her sore hand. It was already starting to show signs of swelling from where the wood struck.

"Why didn't you tell?" he asked.

She thought for a moment, then shrugged her shoulders. "You're already in enough trouble."

ഗഗഗ

Miss Gatchell wasted no time in reporting the incident to their parents, and they were mildly scolded for their behavior. Even so, Annabel secretly believed that they were actually more amazed, firstly that she had done such a thing, and secondly Jevan had forgiven her and consequently attended school more frequently. Because of this incident, Annabel and Jevan became the best of friends, and Jevan never pulled her hair in class again.

Jevan was very troublesome and, much to Miss Gatchell's dismay, all too soon, Annabel copied his every move, becoming just as disruptive and disobedient. They often caught mice and insects and let them loose in the schoolroom to create havoc, or spent lessons composing secret messages to one another. Occasionally, Miss Gatchell caught them, but, despite these antics, she never caned Annabel again. Instead, Miss Gatchell made her write line upon line of meaningless quotations and passages from the bible. Perhaps she believed she was saving Annabel's soul from the devil, except she was completely wasting her time, because *he* had already captured it.

Jevan's willfulness was a much stronger enticement than scripture and, like Annabel, he longed to be free, for their spirits resided far from the constraints of school and moral conduct. They belonged wholly to the wild countryside that surrounded them. Miss Gatchell made long and elaborate reports to their parents, even suggesting that they keep Jevan and Annabel apart, lest their character and moral fiber be completely undone. Much to Annabel's relief, their parents did not seem to put much stock in Miss Gatchell's words, or perhaps they just knew their children well enough to realize that neither demand nor request would have kept them apart.

Jevan soon began to lure Annabel away from school completely with the promise of some tantalizing new find, a bird's nest or molehill that he discovered. She was happy to follow him wherever he went, and they spent many happy days upon the moors tracking down the wild ponies who inexplicably allowed Jevan to touch them.

School it seemed was a brief interlude in their life, only instrumental in forging their unbreakable bond because as Jevan and Annabel grew older, not only did they become more adventurous they became inseparable.

Driven on by each other's willfulness, they often sneaked into the vast gardens and orchards of Gothelstone mansion, where they would catch the exotic fish that swam in the pond. They wandered about the walled kitchen gardens, stocked with all sorts of unusual vegetables and fruit trees.

Jevan spent more and more time at Honeymead. It was as if he was a part of the family. He had seen the skeps on several occasions and often witnessed Josiah tending the bees.

One morning as he and Annabel were in the orchard, she suddenly turned to him. "Are you hungry?"

"Yes," he replied, thinking they would go into the cottage.

She smiled coyly at him, took his hand, and led him to the far end of the orchard. When they reached the nearest skep, she pulled off the roof and reached into the hive. She looked back at Jevan with a playful gleam in her eye. "Are you afraid?"

Jevan stared at her for only a moment before answering. "No."

She smiled and withdrew her arm, and the large chunk of honeycomb along with a few bees. They were unperturbed and flew back into the hive. She broke the honeycomb in two and offered a piece to Jevan.

He took it and looked at her admiringly. "Have you ever been stung?"

"No, never," she answered, grinning back at him. "The bees understand me, just like you and animals."

Jevan nodded and smiled a rare smile, understanding her meaning completely. She saw what others didn't. He had a way with wild creatures not easily explained. "People," he said, "can never fathom me, but animals are different. You can tell them your darkest secrets, and they listen. I don't know if they understand, though it's as if I understand them."

"I know," she replied slowly, "other people just don't get it. Everyone knows Josiah is a beekeeper so they accept that I can be around bees also." She watched him closely. "But, if they knew what I could really do with them, how a quiet suggestive power allows them to land on my skin and never harm me, people would say I was evil. I would be an outcast." She shrugged lightly. "Even more than I already am."

Jevan shook his head. "You're not, it's just you don't fit in with them, any more than I do." He hesitated. "You and I don't need them. We don't need their society or rules, we make our own."

෨෧෨

On the days they were absent from school, which was

many, and when it was too cold or wet to ride far, they often went up into the old hayloft above the stables of the forge. More often than not, they were discovered. Then Adella, Jevan's mother, would lecture them about education and suchlike. Jophiel was a skilled farrier and blacksmith, just like his father and grandfather before that. Jevan often argued with his mother that he already knew the trade, riling her further by asking exacting questions as to why he even needed school.

Adella was always infuriated at his lack of concern and reminded him that she wanted more for him than the life of a blacksmith. At this ongoing opinion, Annabel often saw the gloomy look on Jophiel's face, and they would listen patiently until Adella finished her speech.

Annabel saw the logic in Jevan's question, even if his mother didn't. He was already an adept blacksmith and talented in handling horses. Jevan often demonstrated his skill to Annabel. She watched as he controlled the molten metal he forged in the fire and cleverly shape the metal over the anvil. He made many horseshoes and expertly fit them to the horse's hooves. Jevan's complete lack of fear when he was around the horses reassured them, and they allowed him to do anything with them.

One morning, Annabel watched as he helped his father shoe a particularly large chestnut stallion. The horse stamped his feet and shook his head. Jophiel did not share Jevan's confidence. The animal's display troubled him.

"Be careful with him, Jevan, Sultan is a brute of a horse, a bit like his master," Jophiel added, winking at Annabel.

"Who is his master?" she asked, intrigued by his comment.

"Cerberus Saltonstall of Gothelstone Manor."

She knew the name well enough and caught the distinct dislike in Jophiel's tone when he said the name.

Cerberus owned much of the surrounding lands and many locals were in his employ. The general opinion seemed to be that he was a harsh and unforgiving master. When he came into Rookwood, everybody preferred to avoid him. She encountered him on one occasion. She had been about to leave the Rookwood Apothecary, just as Cerberus was walking in the door. An odd expression of shock passed across his face, and he quickly stepped back as if to avoid touching her at any cost. His eyes traveled down the length of her body before he turned from her. Even though he did not speak, she felt insulted by him and, as she walked farther away, she felt certain that he watched her.

Jevan smiled, regardless of his father's words of warning, and as always Annabel watched him with admiration. Sultan really did seem to calm under his touch, and, as Jevan whispered in his ear, she could believe that the horse trusted him completely.

Jophiel skillfully shod Sultan and tied him to the post at the side of the forge. He disappeared inside, leaving them alone. Jevan waited a few minutes and then grabbed Annabel's hand and quietly un-tethered the horse. She did not protest. Her confidence in Jevan did not falter, even as he lifted her quickly onto the horse's back and immediately swung up behind. However, Sultan took instant dislike to this imposition and reared, attempting to unsaddle them. Jevan held onto Annabel and the reins firmly, and she clung tightly to Jevan's arm and Sultan's mane.

"Whoa." Jevan's voice was soft, although commanding, as he pulled on the reign firmly. He dug his heels in and they set off at a rapid pace. The horse was wild. He was fast, powerful, and less than happy about his unfamiliar riders. But, little by little, Jevan brought him totally under control, cementing Annabel's belief that he really could work his magic with anything.

They rode carefree and recklessly fast across the moors. Only when the light started to dim did they head back toward Rookwood and, by this time, Sultan had resigned himself to their company and seemed as docile as any pony they had ever ridden. Annabel was just happy to be with Jevan. He made her feel safe and protected. He was the brother she never had, the playmate she had longed for. Most of all, he was the one person she loved more than anyone else.

An hour or so later they rode into Rookwood and toward the forge. Jophiel had been watching out for them and came storming out the door. He was clearly furious as he pulled Jevan roughly from the horse and Annabel firmly after him.

"Are you stupid boy? You could have both been killed," he shouted irately and glared angrily at her for a moment. "I should beat some sense into the pair of you." With those words, he pushed Jevan roughly toward the door and took Annabel to the waiting trap. "I'm taking you home," he stated briefly, glancing at her, "and I'll deal with you later," he directed menacingly toward Jevan, making his meaning very clear.

Jophiel was silent as the pony trotted compliantly toward Honeymead. He was angry. In fact, Annabel could not remember seeing him this furious before, and she could feel the tension in the air, as she turned beseechingly to him.

"Please don't beat him," she said earnestly. "He—he didn't mean any harm."

Jophiel did not respond. His face was set in a rigid expression.

She took a deep breath. "Beat me instead."

Jophiel's head turned and stared at her with something like an incredulous look, then she saw his face soften. "That's your father's obligation, not mine," he said, clearly trying to hide his evident amusement. "Jevan is older than you and should have more sense," he added.

Jophiel did not speak again until her mother opened the door to Honeymead. Lilith was uncharacteristically angry.

"Don't you know they hang people for horse stealing?" she said, glaring at her daughter. "And of all the horses you could have taken, why did you have to pick his?"

"We didn't steal the horse—we—we just went for a ride," Annabel stammered, feeling frightened by her mother's words.

Her father did not say anything and certainly did not beat her. Much later when she was in bed, she heard them talking in low voices. Although she could not make out much of the conversation, she managed to hear a few words.

"Don't worry. Jophiel has covered for them. And what do you expect, Lilith? She is just like you were."

"And that is what I am so frightened of, Josiah."

ᏜᏜᏜ

Annabel slept badly. She dreamed of hanging with Jevan on the end of matching nooses, and all the while Cerberus Saltonstall watched with a twisted smile on his lips. Her imagination was working overtime. Even so, the powerful dream haunted her for days. Time went by, the fear duly passed, and accordingly, this incident only served to bring Jevan and her closer. They believed they were invincible to the whole world because, despite what anyone thought, Jevan and Annabel knew exactly what they were doing.

"Life is not worth living, if you can't take risks," Jevan said. "To feel alive, there has to be some danger."

Annabel agreed wholeheartedly. They both understood what others didn't, or perhaps the wildness of the place affected them deeply. It was in their blood.

On their own and alone on the moors, they were free from any social burdens or expectations. They did not have to learn anything other than what they needed in the moment.

Perversely, they did not even have to be nice, not even to each other, and, at times, there was a powerful urge that drove them to distraction. At first, these moments were moderate, then, as time went by, Annabel would leave deep scratch marks over Jevan's skin, while hers displayed numerous bite marks. Her head would hurt from where Jevan pulled her hair so hard that her neck would be sore for days. But despite these odd moments, she never felt in any real danger. Regardless of the lack of control or the complexities of youth that drove them, they were totally committed to each other. If someone had demanded, Annabel would have willingly hung by a noose with Jevan, rather than ever be apart from him.

Chapter 5

To Pay the Devil on the Bridge

The river Barle ran from northern Exmoor and was carried southward to join the river Exe. Long before it reached this meeting point, the fast-flowing water ran through a hidden place, concealed deep within a wooded combe. Here, several unordered stone piers spanned the breadth of the river, upon which rested rough stone slabs known as clappers, each being roughly eight feet long and about four foot wide. This clapper bridge was a surviving relic from history. At certain times of high water, the river flowed furiously downstream, where the undercurrent churned the transparent substance into a turbulent mix, as it continued its journey over rocks and boulders to create a series of small rapids. It then calmed to become a meandering river again, and at this slower pace, it wound its way through the extensive woodlands.

Jevan called it "The Devils Pass" and first took Annabel to this secret place on a particularly overcast and misty day. With a predominantly sinister gleam in his eye, he informed her that the devil could often be seen sitting upon the bridge.

Even though she had laughed at the ideology, she approached the bridge with a certain amount of apprehension. She tentatively looked through the encroaching woodland, searching for any dark figure that might be resting on the ancient stones. The flow of water was fast as it ran between the pillars, lapping several of the lower stones and making them glisten darkly. A light breeze rustled the leaves, making the trees whisper and sigh, although it was not especially sinister.

"I don't see anything," she said, turning back to Jevan, who was now standing behind her. He leaned closer, so that she might hear the disturbing edge in his voice.

"The devil will take payment if you dare to cross," he remarked, trying to unsettle her as he slipped his arm around her waist and pulled her toward him.

She pushed him away and fixed him with a look of defiance, before stepping onto the first stone. The mist was streaming through the trees in light layers and she shivered as the air felt heavy and oppressive. She continued forward, slowly picking her way across the clappers and feeling her shoe slide a little on the slick surface. Precariously balanced on the ragged edge, feeling the force of the fast-flowing water beneath her feet, she looked back at Jevan. He was still on the bank, and watching her progress with interest.

"Are you coming?"

"No, I am waiting for him to appear."

Even though his words sent a chill down her spine, she refused to humor him. Devil or not, she would not let Jevan's words intimidate her. She shrugged indifferently and turned to continue. As she picked up her right foot, the left one slid under her and she slipped heavily into the cold water. The water was not very deep, and she instinctively grasped the nearest clapper trying to steady her body in the quick current.

The cold fingers were so sharp and unexpected that she jumped, the shock stunned her for a second, then as the nails in the murkiness ripped through her flesh and painfully clutched at her leg, she screamed in horror. Panic-stricken she pulled and twisted her body to loosen the hold, although the hand beneath the water had no mercy. It was dragging her down to the terrifying shadowy underworld.

All at once, Jevan was hauling her out of the river. The nails dragged down the length of her leg, and Jevan pulled hard, making the hand release her. A moment later, Annabel stood shivering in his arms. Fearfully, she looked back to the water and half expected to see the demon's hand reaching out. Instead, beneath the water she saw the fingers of jagged sharp rocks, which had held her foot fast. Blood ran down her entire leg. As the shock subsided, a severe stinging sensation ran through all the severed flesh, and she could no longer hold back the tears.

Jevan quickly swung her up in his arms and carried her back to the bank. He carefully lowered her onto the grass, knelt down, and gently wiped away the blood. Anger replaced her fear.

"It's your fault," she said, glaring angrily at him, "you shouldn't have tried to scare me."

Jevan kept his eyes upon hers without answering for a few moments, and then he turned his attention back to the long jagged cut on her ankle, which was still bleeding profusely. He removed his shirt and tore a length of material from it, then he wrapped that tightly around the wound. "Does it hurt?"

"Yes," she answered abruptly, still feeling cross.

Jevan pulled her to her feet. The movement made her wince, so he swung her up in his arms and carried her back to Jess.

Although Annabel did not show it, she was glad that he took control of the situation. She was badly shaken and frightened, as thoughts of what might have happened, had Jevan not been there, flittered through her mind. Jevan lifted her onto the horse's back and turned Jess toward home. They rode in silence for several minutes, and then Jevan's arm shifted and tightened protectively around her.

"I wouldn't have let anything happen to you," he said firmly.

She looked up at him, as his eyes fixed her with a penetrating stare.

"I know," she answered lightly and leaned back against him, allowing the warmth of his body to take away the chill of hers. All her previous annoyance suddenly vanished.

❧❧❧

Despite that episode, they continued to visit the clapper

bridge. At every approach, Annabel always searched for an elusive dark figure. The imagery in her mind was just too great, it was impossible to banish it completely. There were times when she could have believed that his dark shape lurked just beyond her focus, and the apparition quickly vanished into the shadows of the trees at their advance. Such was the addictive lure of the sparkling water on a summer's day, it soon chased his demonic image far from her mind.

Even a loud rustle in the undergrowth, or a dark shadow covered the sun—even if it had no substantiality—made her anxious, as did the feeling of a watcher in the woods. Jevan laughed at these suspicions and vivid thoughts and drew her attention to him instead.

They occupied their time jumping off the stone slabs and enjoying themselves swimming in the cool water. They attempted to catch the little fish carried by the current, or they sunbathed on the stones and stared up at the patterns made by the leaves on the trees. They listened to each other, the natural surroundings, and the constant flow of the water beneath them. The birds would drift from tree to tree softly twittering, and they watched the occasional butterfly that invaded their paradise as it flapped lazily by. They watched, enthralled by the playful antics of the squirrels as they chased each other up and down the tree trunks. Lying together, it felt as though this delightful archipelago rising out of the river was theirs to claim alone.

One summer's day toward the end of August, they had been lazing in the water for some time and starting to feel cold. Annabel climbed onto one of the larger stone clappers. She lay down and stretched her body luxuriously like a cat, before fanning her long hair out in all directions, hoping the dappled sunlight might dry it quicker. She had long since discarded her cotton dress on a nearby rock and only her wet chemise, which had become almost transparent, covered her nakedness. Jevan wore no clothes. He pulled himself out of the water and sat close beside her. Even though Annabel's lids remained closed, she could feel the heat of his gaze over her skin. She smiled and opened her eyes.

He leaned closer. His hair dripped cold water onto her body that sent tiny shocks through her nerves. His hand absently stroked her arm for a few moments and then he moved it low onto her stomach. He bent his head close and brushed his lips lightly across hers. It seemed like the most natural thing, and she did not put up any resistance. Her heartbeat increased and a warmth seemed to radiate from inside. Their lips touched again, and Annabel closed her eyes.

They listened to the sound of the river as it flowed sedately beneath them. Jevan's hand caressed lower, and with that intimate touch, she felt a fluttering sensation in her stomach. She moved her head fractionally and their lips parted. Jevan was watching her with an expression that she had never seen before. She stroked his shoulder, and her hand traveled slowly down his back seemingly of its own accord. He was breathing more rapidly. His skin was soft and yet the tone of the muscle was hard and addictive to her touch. Hypnotized by his gaze and unwavering caress, she no longer felt in control of her own body.

A sudden screech overhead made her jump. They both looked up. The raven flew low through the tree branches, and the spell was broken. Annabel sat up and casually brushed his hand away. She was certain that the color had risen dramatically in her face and, feeling self-conscious, turned her head away. Confused by these new feelings, and as a distraction from the odd situation, she steadily ran her fingers through her hair, trying to dislodge the tangles. After a few moments, Jevan stood and retrieved his clothes. Annabel glanced warily at him. His tall powerful body naturally tanned by the elements, except today just the sight of his naked skin sent unfamiliar sensation through her body and she could not help remembering how it had felt under her touch. His hair hung down covering his face as he bent forward.

He suddenly raised his eyes and caught Annabel's look. "We should leave. It's getting late," he said indifferently.

He reached down, picked up her dress, and held it out for her. She took the dress and Jevan leaned against a tree watching her. Annabel glanced in his direction a couple of times, and when she removed her damp chemise, his face was expressionless. Neither one of them ever had a problem with modesty before, especially when they were younger. Now, she felt oddly aware and uncomfortable, as his eyes lingered on her bare skin.

ᗒᗏᗕ

The weeks passed and, although Jevan and Annabel remained inseparable, something between them had changed. She felt it in the way he looked at her, or the way his hands grasped hers. Then he would suddenly remember something, and it was as if her skin burned him, for he would abruptly release her. His words were often harsh or even sarcastic as if he were purposely trying to provoke a response.

With the end of summer looming, they knew that the visits to the clapper bridge were ending. In winter, it promised to be a cold, forlorn place, as the icy water froze and the trees were stripped bare of any adornment. Already, the days felt crisp and the fresh smell of autumn hung thickly in the air. Even the leaves had started their gradual decline and were turning all shades of gold and orange, while others already littered the woodland floor.

They had been riding for hours. They had started out early on the moors and unhurriedly made their way along the coast, only stopping to allow Jess a short break from the burden of riders. They had walked for a while and then continued on horseback down the valley sides and through the thickly wooded combes and, inevitably, they ended up at The Devil's Pass.

Annabel was more than glad to dismount and took a few moments to stretch her limbs and recover from sitting for so long. Jevan left her with Jess and walked ahead to the clapper bridge. Annabel stroked Jess's head for a few minutes and then tethered him to the usual thick branch. Then she went to find Jevan. He was standing on one of the larger clappers near the middle of the bridge.

She made her way to where he stood and then began to step

past him. As she did so, he caught her arm firmly and turned his body, blocking her way across. She looked up at him in surprise.

"You'll have to pay the devil to cross," he said darkly.

She narrowed her eyes and pretended to be affronted. "And exactly what am I supposed to pay him with?" she said impatiently.

Jevan grinned, his black eyes gleaming dangerously. "A kiss."

At first, she widened her eyes in indignation and then bit her lip as she smiled seductively up at him. His grip relaxed and his hand moved to her waist. He bent his head and closed his eyes and she placed her hands lightly on his chest. His lips found hers, at the same time she pushed him hard, catching him completely off guard.

Jevan fell heavily backward into the water with a huge splash. Annabel turned and ran back across the bridge, laughing. She watched him flailing around for a minute, trying to get his breath and scramble to find his footing. She laughed harder, although there was no amusement on his face as he hauled himself out of the water.

"Come here, Annabel," he demanded angrily, shaking the water from him.

"No." She faltered. "No way."

She saw his furious look and thought that perhaps she had gone too far this time. Not waiting to see what he would do, she turned and ran through the woods.

"Annabel."

His voice was sharp, which made her run faster. She could hear him close behind, and soon the thick brambles blocked her path. Jevan was behind her and she turned.

The dark shadows cast out by the trees suddenly made his presence feel dangerous, and she saw the madness glinting in his eyes.

"You think this is funny?" he roared. "Look at my clothes!"

"Since when did you care about clothes?" she answered, feeling unnerved by both his tone and close proximity.

With his hair still dripping, he shook his head slightly, sending water droplets over her skin. He reached forward and roughly pulled her toward him.

Their eyes locked. She did not see the water running down his face, or the expression he wore. She could only think about his lips on her skin and his eyes that seduced her in their concentration. His kiss was powerful and then his grip tightened painfully, which had a startling effect. Annabel wildly pulled his wet shirt away from his skin and raked her nails down his bare back to draw blood. In retaliation, he dug his nails into the exposed flesh of her arms and neck. She tried to cry out in pain. Even so, his kiss became fiercer. When he eventually surrendered her mouth, she drew back and let her kiss trail down his neck. Then she bit him. Hard.

From his throat, he made a noise of anger and firmly pushed her before him to the ground.

"Let go," she demanded breathlessly, as his weight pinned her down.

"No," he said, taking a handful of her hair and winding it tightly around his fingers. His breathing was rapid and his eyes stared insanely into hers. "I could really hurt you," he said, and as if to prove the point, he gripped her neck with his free hand and exerted pressure, "or I could do anything I want with you," he continued, "even kill you."

She saw the malevolence in his eyes and heard the wicked inclination in his words.

"Hurt me then," she taunted breathlessly.

Jevan saw the rebellious look in her eyes and heard the passion in her voice. For a long moment, he just stared at her. Then he released his grip and roughly pulled her to her feet.

"No," he said sharply.

He turned and walked away.

Annabel had been confident that her words were enough to unnerve him, and she had been certain that he wouldn't have really hurt her. She could not deny that she felt oddly disturbed, because somewhere deep in her conscience, she had really wanted him to.

Chapter 6

The Watcher in the Woods

They visited the Devil's Pass once more that year. The days were short and leaves had nearly gone from most of the trees. It would be spring before they came back. Annabel and Jevan stood together on the clappers, watching the fast-moving water, swollen from recent downpours. Annabel breathed in the clean air. Bird song intermingled with the torrent running beneath he stones.

"Do you want to walk for a while?" Jevan asked, turning toward her.

She looked up and nodded. They stepped across the clappers, and, as they reached the bank, Jevan pulled her round to face him, his face bathed in filtered sunlight. He wore an odd expression as he bent down and pressed his lips to hers. She needed no persuasion to respond to his deep sensual kiss, and, as he pulled her closer still, his breath came heavier as his hands moved over her clothes.

The water and natural noises faded and became distant background noise, as his lips left hers and traveled to her neck. Caught up in the moment, she couldn't think why she felt strangely nervous—until a sudden snap of a twig breaking underfoot made her jump. Startled, they looked across to the edge of the woods to find a familiar figure step into the small clearing.

Aidden Murray was the same age as Jevan. He had attended their school, and he was the son of the Rookwood vicar. A bitter twist just clouded their perfect day, as he and Jevan had many quarrels in the past. Aidden was normally condescending and righteous as was his father and he made no secret about the fact that he disliked Jevan intensely.

In recent weeks, Annabel had been on the receiving end of his spiteful tongue, to which Jevan had responded accordingly and punched him. Aidden, not one to turn the other cheek, fought back and a full fight had ensued It was only broken up by passersby, who feared they might inflict serious injury to each other.

Aidden eyed them disdainfully. "Back here again, so soon?" he said smugly. "Did you think you were alone up here?"

"What's it to you?" Jevan said coldly and stiffened as he took Annabel's hand.

Aidden thought for a moment and narrowed his eyes. "This is not the first time I've been here, fishing's good up river," he said, gesturing behind him. "I've seen you before, in the woods."

"You have been spying on us?" Annabel said sharply, her outrage evident as she realized that perhaps he was the watcher she had imagined. "How dare you?" She was not scared of him, not with Jevan by her side.

"I am not spying on you," Aidden said contemptibly. "I just happened to see you." He paused briefly. "And again today, cavorting sinfully about the woods. Wait till my father hears. He will make sure your parents know what goes on up here."

Annabel saw the spite in his eyes. She knew he would waste no time in spreading damaging gossip about them, not that she cared too much, save for—she knew Aidden well—he could and would say all manner of things that were not true. She let go of Jevan's hand and stepped forward.

"What goes on up here?" She laughed lightly. "Don't you know? We call up the devil, we dance around naked with him, and we make spells over people like you."

Aidden looked horrified and quickly made the sign of the cross over himself.

Jevan smirked as he also moved closer to Aidden. "Why don't you run back to your father? Tell him what you want. No one will believe your malicious tongue," he said. "And what does it say about you, that you come up here to watch us?"

"You don't belong in decent God-fearing society," Aidden said pointedly at Jevan. "And she," he said, glaring at Annabel, "she is a heathen!"

Jevan made an angry noise in his throat, and before Annabel could stop him, he flew at Aidden. Jevan struck him hard with his fist and knocked him to the ground. Aidden staggered to his feet. He swung his arm up to return the punch. He missed, and Jevan hit him again with a powerful blow to the side of his head. Aidden tumbled backward, catching his head on a low boulder. Then he was still.

Annabel heard Jevan's sharp intake of breath, as the world seemed to stop moving. Nothing stirred, not the water or the birds. Even the trees, it seemed, were motionless. They watched as blood seeped from Aidden's head and onto the ground. Jevan glanced nervously at her, and she saw disbelief in that look that must have mirrored her own. Jevan knelt by the body, and placed trembling fingers lightly on Aidden's neck. He took a deep breath and lowered his head onto Aidden's chest. Jevan turned his head and looked up at Annabel.

Annabelle caught her breath and covered her mouth with her hands. Jevan's pallor was white, and his look terrified her. She felt sick. Her knees buckled and she fell onto them, shaking her head, unable to comprehend the situation. Everything had happened so fast. Ten minutes ago, they had been happily watching the water. Now they were staring at a dead body. Wanting reassurance, she felt for Jevan's hand.

"We must bury him, in the woods. No one will ever know!" She said the words quickly. They seemed horrifying. The implication of them was terrible. Even so, there was no other choice, no one would believe it had happened this way, and Jevan would go on trial for murder.

Jevan snatched his hand away. "What am I going to bury him with?" he said, glaring at her. "Someone will find out!"

His sharp words made tears well up in her eyes. The sight of them brought Jevan to his senses. He saw how frightened she looked, and *he* had to protect her. She was right. They had to cover this up. No one must find out. He stood, pulled Annabel to her feet, and wrapped his arms around her.

Every inch of her was trembling. She no longer felt like a carefree child. She felt burdened with the horror of what this could mean for them both. Prisons and nooses flashed through her mind.

"Not in the woods," Jevan said calmly. She looked up at him. There was determination in his eyes, and he suddenly seemed much older. "We will put him in the river. If someone finds him, they will think that he fell, hit his head, and drowned." He looked at her uneasily. "This has to be our secret. No one can ever know, ever!"

She saw the haunted look in his eyes, a fear she had never seen before. "No one will ever know, Jevan."

⁂

It was a shock for Annabel to realize how much a dead body weighed, and Aidden had not been slight. He was of stocky build. She pushed any squeamish notions to the back of her mind, as she noted his body still had warmth. Between them, they carried him to the water's edge.

"We need to get him into the middle, otherwise the current won't lift him," Jevan said, wading in first. Even though Jevan had the torso, Aidden's legs were so heavy that Annabel struggled to hold them up, and the shock of the icy water made her shiver even more. They made their way to the middle of the river. The water was now waist high and the current stronger. Together they cast Aidden's body into the water. The current carried it slowly away from them, downstream. They kept it in sight to be sure there were no obstacles that could hinder its progress, and as they watched it move farther away, they clambered back to the clapper bridge. Annabel could not stop shaking, partly from cold, partly from hauling a dead body around. She had never seen a corpse before, let alone touched one, and the whole horror of the afternoon suddenly hit her with full force. She wished they had not come here today.

Jevan was silent, he too suffering from the shock. They scrubbed the bloodied boulder, and, with their bare hands, scraped up fresh earth to bury the blood on the ground. Then they felt the burden lift a little. They needed no words. There was a mutual understanding, an affirmation of their beliefs. Only it had taken this awful happening to confirm they could overcome anything.

The sun had warmed the clappers a little, so they removed their clothes and wrung the excess water from them. They sat huddled together, Jevan's arms wrapped around her, and little by little, her shaking stopped as the heat from his body warmed hers. It shouldn't have been a sensual moment, but their nakedness and the raw emotion of what had occurred made it so. When Jevan kissed her, she felt the longing in him. When his hands moved over her body, she experienced such an intense feeling that she began trembling again. As strong as their passion felt, the sun was setting, the autumn air was crisp, and they would freeze if they didn't move soon. With only sopping clothes to wear, they knew they had to get home fast.

Over the following days, they spent as much time together as possible. Neither wanted to talk about the incident, although, one way or another, their conversation came around to it. Jevan hoped it would be many weeks before anyone found the body. He hoped that wild animals might at least devour a portion, so no suspicion could fall upon anyone. There was, of course, much talk in the village of Aidden's disappearance. Several villagers went out to search the surrounding woods and moors.

Annabel and Jevan were on edge and fearful as they waited for any news, and Jevan did his best to reassure her that everything would be all right, even though he felt suffocated by the burden of this terrible secret. The incident brought a strange sense of reality to her life. Jevan had killed someone. She thought about all the times she had goaded him and felt the danger in him, however, she had never really believed he was capable, until now.

❧

The search party came back with no news, so Annabel and Jevan relaxed for a few more days. She tried not to wince when her mother and father spoke of it. The bees, of course, were the only ones she could tell this dark secret to, and they soothed her as they flew around and landed on her skin, seeming to reassure her that everything would be all right.

The vicar, convinced by this time of foul play, set up an extensive search, even enrolling her father as part of it. A new fear spread through Annabel's heart, which increased tenfold when, four days later, the search party returned with Aidden's remains. From Jevan's point of view, it was a good thing that time had passed, and the body had been in the water for a while. The only logical explanation that people wanted to believe was that Aidden had, in fact, drowned. Even though the vicar tried to rally villagers to his belief that it was the work of the devil, the body having been found not so far from the ancient clapper bridge. He told anyone who would listen, "Aidden could swim well, and the devil must have had a hand in this deed."

Thankfully, no one took the vicar seriously or even suspected the truth. The villages were content that Aidden had drowned in a tragic accident, and as much as they could, Annabel and Jevan went back to a normal life.

Chapter 7

The Blood Binding

The orchard at Honeymead was brimming with fruit, and Annabel picked up the last of the windfalls to add to her already full basket. It was precisely one week before her sixteenth birthday, and she contemplated her mother's promise of a new dress for the occasion. Although she had never before given much thought to clothes in the past, the innocence of childhood had disappeared and been replaced with an undeniable awareness of more mature feelings. Now she coveted something prettier than the practical, but plain, plain day dresses she wore—which, in all probability, had more to do with Jevan than she would have credited.

Abruptly pulled from these idle thoughts by the sound of a loud whiny, she spun around to find Jevan on horseback, watching her from beyond the orchard wall.

She picked up the fruit basket and smiled brightly, as she hurried to the wooden gate that marked the boundary to the orchard. Annabel let the gate slam firmly shut behind her as Jess walked closer.

She reached out her hand to Jess which he investigated with interest before giving a snort of disgust when he found it empty. Laughing, she plucked an apple from the basket and offered it by way of an apology.

Jess, easily appeased, chomped noisily on the fruit while she steadily stroked his sleek coat and looked up at Jevan. "I thought that you would be working in the forge today," she said, giving him an inquiring glance.

Jevan hesitated for a moment before answering. "I wasn't needed, after all," he said simply.

She drew closer to him. There was a marked surliness about him, and the dark shadows beneath his eyes told her that he had not slept well. In fact, he looked decidedly ailing. Annabel was alarmed at the sight. Jevan had never been sick, not that she could remember.

"Are you all right?" she asked, searching his eyes for some clue.

His mouth turned up for a fraction of a second, resembling something of a brief smile. "Ride with me?" he asked quietly, ignoring the question.

Annabel did not wait to for him to ask twice. She nodded and quickly deposited the basket inside the cottage. She shouted to her mother that she would be back later. If Lilith replied, Annabel did not hear because she was already out the door. Jevan reached his hand down and pulled her up to sit before him, then Jess set off at a steady walking pace.

The pressure of Jevan's hand resting just below her waist invoked all too familiar sensations, which reminded her vividly of the incident by the bridge. The color rose in her cheeks as she remembered how it had felt in his passionate embrace. Suddenly the day seemed warmer than ever. Jevan leaned forward, so that his head was close to hers and she could feel his breath against her cheek.

"You smell of flowers," he said approvingly.

"I've been in the garden picking lavender and roses," she answered.

Jess trotted quietly along and, on the surface, it seemed a perfectly idealic afternoon, although the longer they rode, the clearer it became that something was troubling Jevan. He was never usually this quiet.

"Where are we going?" she asked, trying to break the silence, and turned her head to look at him.

Jevan avoided her gaze and moved his arm even tighter around her body while, at the same time, he encouraged Jess to canter, forcing her to turn back to the original position.

"We're going to the oak tree," he said after a while and then lapsed into silence again.

This time, she could feel an uncommon barrier between them, as his sullenness really did seem to engulf him completely. Annabel thought that he had probably been in trouble at home, or maybe there had been talk of Aidden. She quickly pushed that thought away. No one knew. No one ever would. She didn't question him further. He would tell her eventually. He always did.

Jess had taken them past the orchard, through the woodland, and onto a rough steep path that ran through the trees and down to the rocky beach. The dense coastal woodland shielded them for a while and then the land rolled up again to the patchwork of the heather and gorse of the higher moors. Before them now was the vast land and seascape. The woods stretched out along miles of cliff face. They continued on, heading toward a gentler part of the cliff where the trees swept evenly down onto golden sandy shores.

They were heading for a very particular place on the perimeter of this ancient woodland, where an old oak tree perched precariously close to the edge of a jagged cliff. It was easy to believe that the wickedness of the wind and the onslaught of the sea eventually would take its toll. It was possible that one day, this cliff face and their beloved tree would topple into the ocean and be lost forever. Right now, the oak was their sanctuary, their special place to come. Like them, it felt apart from all other things and living on the verge of destruction.

On the other side of the tree, long grasses ran down a slight incline to a copse. This vantage point commanded views over the moorland, woodland, and the sea. They dismounted and Annabel walked up the incline to the thick trunk of the oak. She ran her hands lightly over its bark, smiling at the familiarity of the old tree.

Jevan tethered Jess to a smaller tree, lower down the slope, and walked to where she stood. He looked out across the sea for several moments before he turned to her. The wind had notably increased its power and whistled dramatically. The air felt charged by its strength as Jevan's long hair whipped across his face, making it seem remarkably pale, and his eyes darker than ever. The wind shifted and caught her hair in its grip. It streamed out, almost horizontally toward. Jevan. He reached forward and pulled her to him.

Instinctively, she moved even closer, so that she might feel his reassuring warmth through the thin material of his clothes. Their eyes locked in an unspoken connection and her throat tightened as she clasped his hand in hers. There were no words to say, just a longing to be in his embrace. Her thoughts were hazy as she rose up and kissed him. The wind, now ferocious, was in danger of knocking them off balance. Even so, Jevan's dark eyes were unwavering as she placed her hands around his neck and felt his arms tighten about her waist. They fell into the long grass, where they were somewhat sheltered from the relentless wind. Their kisses became more urgent, as their yearning intensified. Jevan pulled urgently at the restrictive laces and buttons of her clothes. She did not want to resist her body's willingness to surrender to his touch. With most of her skin exposed to the elements, Jevan abruptly froze.

Annabel watched his face tentatively. "What's wrong?"

Even though his eyes did nothing to conceal his desire, she heard his voice falter. "Annabel—" he began.

"Shh—don't say anything, not now," she said, silencing him with another long kiss. She felt him relax. His lips moved to her neck and then farther down her body. "Just don't say anything," she repeated and sighed in satisfaction, seduced by his touch.

Despite the obstacles of buttons and laces, they soon discarded most of their clothes, Annabel's skin felt electrified under his kisses and his dominating strength covered her as her body responded and willingly submitted to his.

"I love you," he whispered softly in her ear, as he pierced her flimsy resistance and his body pushed farther into hers.

She drew her breath in a half-stifled gasp and shuddered in a mix of pleasure and pain. The world stopped turning around them, the landscape disappeared from view. Even the vicious winds no longer bothered her. They were in a vacuum where nothing and nobody else existed. Together they were one, not just their bodies, but their consciousness. Jevan's embrace was unyielding. Annabel felt secure in the idea that Jevan stood between her and the rest of the world. Nothing could harm her with him by her side.

When the reality of what they had done struck her, it seemed a natural conclusion of all the previous intimate moments they had shared. Jevan and she suddenly made sense in a way that she could not find words to describe. Annabel moved so that she might look into his face. Something in his expression betrayed his feelings, because she did not see her own mirrored there. Rather, a deep concern or grief was reflected in his eyes. She frowned.

"Are you all right?" he asked, his eyes glowing darkly in the light of the setting sun. A small tremor was evident in his voice.

"Yes," she said.

His expression changed subtly, and he closed his eyes, steadily stroking her skin and arousing her sensuality once more, while being lured in the security of his unwavering touch. They remained this way for some time until Jevan rose up and pushed a wisp of hair from her eyes.

"I shouldn't have done that," he said with a note of regret.

"Why not?" She sounded hoarser than usual and she suddenly felt fearful. "Together we can do anything." Her voice was losing momentum, and she felt oddly afraid of his reluctance. "Jevan?"

He did not speak. Instead, he rose up farther, pulled his clothes toward him, and began rummaging amongst them, before producing his pocketknife. He hesitated for only a moment before opening it. The silver blade hovered over her in the fading light. She did not protest when he took her hand and turned it, exposing her palm to the sky, or even think to resist when he held the blade inches from her skin and looked at her oddly.

"Do you trust me?" he asked.

She gazed into his black eyes, not understanding his intention. Jevan could have talked her into anything at that moment. Even so, at those words her throat went dry.

"Yes," she whispered warily.

There was a kind of exhilarating terror as he placed the edge of the blade against her skin, with his other hand he held her firmly.

"Don't cry sweetheart," he said, fixing her with a penetrating stare and quickly made a deep cut across the delicate surface of her skin.

She immediately cried out in pain, and the tears pooled in her eyes, as she tried to make sense of what he had done. Then just as quickly he made a similar cut across his own hand. He then clasped their blooded hands together tightly, and she looked up into the dark mirrors that gleamed with danger.

"Now we are joined by blood. You and I are connected forever, no matter what happens." His statement was dramatic, laced with promise, and, given the tone of his voice, it sent her mind reeling.

"What is going to happen?" she whispered, trying not to be distracted at the sight of the blood running down her arm.

"Annabel—I—" His voice, tinged with pain, halted.

She could not mistake the anguish etched on his face and got a sudden sinking feeling in the pit of her stomach as he looked away and shook his head despairingly.

"Jevan, tell me what is wrong!" she demanded, feeling suddenly very afraid by the distinctly sinister atmosphere he had created.

Jevan looked back to her and took a deep breath. "I have to leave, Annabel," he blurted out quickly, anticipating a reaction as she instantly felt his hold tighten.

She stared at him blankly, unable to comprehend his meaning. "Leave—what do you mean?"

"My mother is going to stay with her sister in London. You know she has not been well and treatment would be easier in a big city. My aunt married very well," he said, almost in one breath, continuing hastily and avoiding her eyes. "My mother will stay with her for a while, and Father will not hear of her going alone, so I am to accompany her. My aunt, having no children of her own, wants to finance an education for me in London."

Annabel stared at him, feeling completely bewildered by his rapid speech as she tried to organize thoughts that were spinning around her head. "London is so far away, Jevan," she said slowly, shaking her head in protest. "You can't go."

Jevan looked distraught. "Believe me when I say that I don't want to. I want to stay here and be with you."

"Then stay," she said bitterly, sitting up and attempting to retrieve her clothes.

Jevan's arms tightened around her and he pulled her close again.

"Let go, Jevan," she said irritably, "I want to get dressed."

He ignored her requests as he held her tighter than ever, resisting all effort to push him away. "Don't cry," he said with a broken voice, although his words only seemed to have the effect of making the tears run faster.

"I'm really cold, I want to get dressed," she insisted, prizing his hands from her and, although the air had chilled her, her body felt frozen from shock.

Jevan sighed heavily and reluctantly released her. He pulled on his clothes as she scrambled to do the same. It was only a distraction.

Annabel felt as if someone had hit her and the contents of her insides were slowly making their way up her throat. She thought she might actually be sick, as the evidence of what they had just done was seeping through the thin fabric of her clothes. She thought about the complete intimacy they just shared, and how, with a few spoken words, Jevan had ripped her apart. He might as well have taken that knife and plunged it deep inside her, as her death would have been a welcome release from the ordeal she was now experiencing.

When Jevan pulled her to her feet, she backed up and leaned against the tree for support. Her hand hurt and she looked at the dried blood that now stained the skin. She tentatively touched the wound and it stung intensely.

"Why did you do that?" she asked, not taking her eyes from her hand.

Jevan moved closer. "Our scars will be a permanent reminder of our commitment," he said.

His touch was very gentle as he took her hand, and she stared at him for a few moments, not knowing what to do.

"Don't leave Jevan," she said, with alacrity, the desperation so obvious in her voice.

Jevan sighed heavily. He could not have imagined that this would be so difficult. "I have to. I told you why. My father insists that I accompany her, and he will not rest easy unless I am with her. She is adamant that with her ill health she cannot manage alone…" His voice trailed off as he felt the impact of his words. "How can I say no?"

"You'll forget me," Annabel said miserably. "And how can you leave now after what we've just done?"

"I could never forget you, how can you even say that?" He looked wounded at the suggestion. "And I will come back, Annabel."

She heard the grief in his voice and saw the anguish on his face, his suffering still felt insignificant compared to hers. "When will you come back?" she said, sudden hope springing to mind.

He pushed the hair from his eyes and shrugged lightly. "I don't know," he answered. "How long does it take to get an education?"

"But…you've been to school, and you're far too old for that now."

"No Annabel," he said. "This will be an appropriate education, fit for proper gentlemen." And then he laughed lightly, even if there was no indication of humor. "My mother hates the thought of me becoming a blacksmith, you know," he added. "And with my aunt's good connections, and me a proper gentleman, my mother thinks she can climb the social ladder."

"You are already a blacksmith, and you can do that job with your eyes closed." Annabel felt sudden animosity toward Adella. Jevan's mother was not sick, although she suffered with her nerves, which was compounded by the fact that she was far from satisfied with her life. She had always hated the country. Even when Annabel was younger, she had sensed that

Adella and Jophiel's marriage was not a happy one. Although Jevan had never spoken of their relationship, it was obvious Adella certainly had higher expectations than her husband did. Perhaps Annabel could have understood that, though, Adella wanting to impose them on Jevan was not something she would ever understand.

"That's the irony. I already have a trade that I want," Jevan said, interrupting her thoughts, "and I care nothing for becoming a gentleman, the city, or the wealth I might find there. Apparently, what I want is not good enough," he said bitterly, "not for my mother at least." Annabel failed to understand Adella's reasoning, and Jevan's words did not seem to make sense.

"How can your mother climb socially? Because, regardless of her sister's public connections, even she cannot deny that her own husband is a lowly blacksmith."

Jevan seemed not to hear the sarcasm in her voice, or perhaps he just ignored it.

"You don't know my mother very well, Annabel. Exmoor is such a great distance from London. I am certain that my father's name will not even be mentioned, and, to her, his existence will be all but forgotten."

As his words slowly sank in the realization struck her.

"What about me?" she said slowly.

They were inseparable. Everyone, including Adella, knew that. He started to turn away from her, but she caught his arm. "What about me?" she repeated, "am I not good enough either and to be forgotten?"

Jevan looked defeated, and briefly closed his eyes. "Annabel, my father loves you, you know that. My mother…" He shook his head irritably "What does she know, anyway?"

A mild sinking feeling in the pit of her stomach lurched even lower. "What does she think, Jevan?" she demanded, her voice higher pitched.

Jevan shifted uncomfortably. He could tell that she was not going to let this go.

"Jevan, tell me," she ordered again, her eyes burning into his.

"That surrounded by London society, I could make a better match," he blurted out. "You know that's not my thought, Annabel," he added quickly. "For me, there is only you."

Annabel narrowed her eyes. A hundred words came to mind and she would have accused Adella of being devious and scheming and hurled vicious insults, if Jevan had given her the chance to speak.

"My mother has always wanted to be something that she is not, and she is very much mistaken if she believes she can manipulate me to love someone because they have a better social standing."

Annabel shot him a look of distain. "She is already manipulating you, Jevan," she said with resentment.

"No," he replied instantly. "I am going only because it is my father's wishes, not because of her. Despite her callousness, my father still loves her and will ultimately do anything to make her happy. Deep down he knows that he has already lost her. He knows that I will return."

"You really don't have to go Jevan. You are eighteen, I am almost sixteen. We could run away together," Annabel said eagerly, a plan forming in her mind.

Jevan looked skeptical and shook his head. "And what will I keep you with? I don't have any money, and I can't give you a home, or even put food in your mouth."

"I don't care, I'd rather starve than be apart from you," she said passionately.

Jevan smiled briefly, it was not a happy smile. He wiped away another of her tears and bent to kiss her. "I would not see you starve," he said sadly. "We will be together again. I promise you. Annabel. You are my life, without you my world doesn't make sense."

Jevan couldn't have guessed the effect his words would have upon Annabel, because, to her mind, it seemed he had already accepted his fate.

Caught up in the emotional aftermath of what had just occurred between them, and the more she listened to his defeatist words, the angrier she felt.

"If that was true, you wouldn't leave," she burst out indignantly, pushing his arm away. "I hate you for doing this. Just go and leave me alone!"

"Annabel!" His voice betrayed his own anger, although he reached out in an effort to pacify her.

Her own emotions were running too high, and she would not listen to any more of his words. She screamed at him in frustration, wanting to rant and rave at him. She felt so desperate for him not to leave her, and she now knew exactly how Miss Gatchell had once felt, she thought miserably.

She was, in this moment, definitely in danger of becoming hysterical.

Jevan was trembling. His eyes widened as he grasped her firmly and shook her hard. "Annabel, stop it."

"No," she cried, giving him a defiant glare and forcing his hands from her. She backed away from him. "You don't care how I feel. I am surprised you even bothered to tell me." She paused for a long moment, collecting her thoughts. "Oh of course—" The realization dawned on her. "—you wanted one more thing before you left, didn't you? I'm such a fool, I should have known that."

Jevan glared fiercely at her, his own rage vividly apparent. "How can you say that, even think that?" he roared. "You and I belong together, and it wasn't my sole intention. I never realized that saying goodbye to you would be so hard, or that you would act in such a way as to rip my heart into pieces."

"And so you thought you would ruin my reputation instead," she countered mockingly, "after which you would leave me alone to face the consequences."

Jevan fixed her with a darkly penetrating look and took a step closer. "Are you mad?" he snapped savagely. "Your reputation is quite safe with me, and who in hell is going to know?"

"I know. I will know what you've done."

Jevan stiffened as though she had hit him. "You make it sound as if I have done something horrific, and we both know it wasn't like that," he said coldly. "Why are you being this way? None of it is my fault, and I thought you, of all people, would understand, sympathize even, but you are crazy, and a fool, if you believe that you are the only one who is suffering." He took a deep breath. "You have always known what you mean to me, although right now—I feel as if you truly hate me."

Jevan was right, she did feel hateful and vengeful and at this moment, she didn't care what he thought. Right now, she wanted to hurt him more than anything else. At one time, she would have used her nails and fought him. That time was over, she had found a new weapon, a spiteful tongue, and she stared back at him full of contempt.

"Perhaps I do," she agreed "and we both know that you are capable of something horrific, and I should consider that I've had a lucky escape. You've merely been an amusement, and taking all things into consideration, you really mean nothing to me, after all."

Jevan's look turned into a disturbing trancelike gaze and a veil of darkness fell across his eyes. Annabel felt the nausea rise in her stomach, and any other words she might have spoken lodged in her throat. She felt appalled by her words, but once said, she could not take it back.

Jevan suddenly grabbed her shoulders roughly, his nails digging into her flesh. "Tell me that's not true!" he roared, his eyes wide with rage.

She stared willfully back at him. She felt the anger and malicious wrath of his heart, which told him to strike her. She saw the brutality in his eyes as he shook with emotion and fought to control a violent urge. Suddenly he released her, too aware of his capability. She could not conceal her spitefulness. It was like an infection eating away at her mind

"What do you care?" she demanded bitterly. "Nothing! You don't care at all, because very soon you are to be gone from this place. You will go to a new life and forget your old one."

His eyes were brimming with pain, and his mouth set in a firm line. "You're tearing me apart, Annabel," he said with a shake of his head. "Tell me what you really feel." The fierceness had gone from his voice.

"No," she said venomously and turned away from him. She

ran down the little slope, and his voice reached her at the bottom.

"I will come back," he said bitterly.

His words echoed through her head. She did not stop. She refused to hear any more words from his lips and wanted to run far away from everything, especially him. Propelled forward by grief alone, she ran as fast as any wild creature fleeing for its life. Tonight, the moorland seemed harsh and unforgiving as she stumbled more than once. She could not stop. She felt oddly unhinged, uncertain of anything anymore, and as though she had taken leave of all senses. Her body could not take the punishment for long and forced her to slow down as her breathing felt laborious. She was tired from the exertion. Still, she pushed herself to move as fast as it was possible, even if her grief was inconsolable and the tears still poured down her face. She could not forgive herself for the hatred she had displayed. A nagging voice inside her head insisted it was justified. After all, she'd willingly given herself to Jevan, body and soul, and, in return, he had shown his true character and cruelly betrayed her.

The world Annabel knew felt as if it was fragmenting all around her. Fears bombarded her mind, and to confound her understanding further, her reason insisted that she could not survive without him.

Annabel put a considerable amount of distance between herself and the oak tree, before she was compelled to look back. She could just about make out his dark silhouette still standing beneath its sprawling branches. There was no doubt about it. He was still watching her. His grief had been unmistakable, but perhaps that was just an act on his part. Surely, if it was real, then he should have followed her, begged her to forgive him, or sworn his undying love, as she would have done in his position.

She wanted to go back, tell him that she loved him, and feel his arms wrapped about her. The void between them was too great. She could not turn around now. Either pride or stubbornness bade her continue across the moor. Annabel glanced back once more. His image had melted into the darkness.

❧

Jevan was stunned. Annabel had always been headstrong and unpredictable, but her reaction was completely unexpected, and her spiteful words rang in his head repeatedly. Had he really done such a terrible thing? Did she really hate him that much?

He watched her running across the moors, her figure getting smaller by the second, and soon she would be gone from his view. He saw her turn once, and then she continued on, moving farther away. Although he was in half a mind to run after her, pride would not let him follow. She had wounded him badly and left him in no doubt that she would be impossible to reason with tonight. Besides, after what she had said, he did not feel like forgiving her quite that easily.

The darkness was falling all around, and night was approaching fast. Jevan sat heavily on the ground. It felt as though she had physically pulled his heart from his chest and viciously trampled over it. In fact, he was certain there was a distinct pain, and he was finding it difficult to breathe properly. How could she really believe that he didn't care?

For him, there had only ever been Annabel. From the first moment he had seen her mass of long red curls and looked into curious wide eyes that stared evenly back at him, he had been fascinated. Then, she had only been seven. He doubted that she even recalled that time. A couple of years later, in the schoolroom, it seemed inevitable that she would draw his attention again.

Jevan sighed. The rest was just history. He knew that he and Annabel were too much alike, both hot tempered and stubborn. Even so, he could not remember ever feeling so devastated than with what had passed between them tonight.

"Damn you, mother!" He had never hated her so much as he did in this moment—her and her imaginary illness. He despised her dissatisfaction and her need for a different life. He didn't care what she wanted, only that she was forcing him to be a part of that absurdity. Jevan leaned back against the tree trunk and ran his finger over the fresh scar on his palm. The dried blood had formed a crust, and he scratched at it with his fingernail until new blood seeped from the wound. Annabel's blood was in these veins. Whether she liked it or not, they now remained joined together.

He took the knife from his pocket, turned to the tree, and dug the blade into the wood. He scratched away at the bark, carving mainly by feel and thought alone, as he could barely see anything in the darkness. When he was finished, he ran his hands over the trunk, imagining the words in his head. Satisfied, he whistled to Jess, and the horse whined. Jevan turned and made his way toward the sound until he could make out the animal's shape. Jess tossed his head and advanced a few paces to meet his master, allowing Jevan to bury his face in the long mane for a moment. Then Jevan untied Jess and, together, they made their way through the disordered trees and over the uneven terrain.

Jevan rode to Rookwood, or rather, Jess found his way home as Jevan no longer really cared where his steed went. Sometime later, Jevan walked into the cottage that adjoined the forge. He glanced up as his mother came down the stairs.

"Jevan, where have you been?" Her voice instantly grated on his nerves and he barely acknowledged her. "I needed you to arrange the stage coach. Your father had to go instead," she said reproachfully. "I can't have you disappearing for hours on end, not with so much to do, and where have you been anyway?" Adella glared at him, waiting for a response.

Jevan shrugged indifferently. "On the moors with— Annabel." The name stuck in his throat.

"That girl, she—"

"What about her?" Jevan's eyes glittered dangerously. He hated it when his mother talked about Annabel.

"Lilith should have more control over her. I've always said that she is a bad influence."

Jevan took a step toward his mother, feeling the blood rising in his veins. "Don't you ever talk about her like that. You have—"

"Jevan!"

Jevan turned.

His father stood in the open doorway. "I will not have you be disrespectful to your mother. I don't care how old you are."

Jevan glared at this father and then forced himself to calm down. "Sorry, Mother," he mumbled, glancing in her direction.

He stalked upstairs, banged the bedroom door loudly, and sat heavily on the bed. The whole world felt as if it was falling apart, and his mother's voice echoed vindictively through his head. He felt as though he wanted to kill her. He could quite easily, and he thought back to Aidden. It had been so easy. He was strong and she just weak and feeble, nothing like his beautiful and fiery Annabel. *But she hates you*, he reminded himself bitterly.

Dark thoughts turned again to his mother. She was a poor substitute for a woman, never content and always finding fault. She didn't really give a damn about his father. Jevan looked down at his hands. They were powerful. His long slim fingers could easily squeeze every ounce of life from Adella's body. And then he thought about Jophiel. Could he do that to him too?

The tormented thoughts tumbled through Jevan's mind. He couldn't harm his father. He loved Jophiel, and Jophiel loved Adella. How could Jevan destroy that? He lay down and hoped a miracle might happen, and that Annabel made it home safely.

Chapter 8

Echoes and Amendment

The time that passed seemed unbearable to Annabel. Jevan and she were like the ebb and flow of a river. One could not function without the other, and even though she yearned to see him, anger or just plain stubbornness got in her way, and she avoided him entirely.

Each day before dawn broke she left Honeymead, choosing paths through the woods that she didn't think Jevan would take, telling herself, that the more unfamiliar the territory, the happier she was, and the farther apart they were, the better off she'd be. She rode and walked for miles, trying to find some pleasure in her own company. Once it had been so natural for her to be alone. That contentment was lost. Jevan had ruined it. Even the quietness of mind was elusive, as he continued to invade all her thoughts, and it didn't help that she was deeply ashamed of her spoken words and her reaction. Still, she could not find it in her heart to forgive him either. The void between them was widening.

❧❧❧

Preparations for the journey to London filled Jevan's day. The stagecoach was booked. Rail tickets were going to be purchased at the station. His mother's luggage was already packed, and, in the forge, his work was nearly all completed.

There was nothing else left for him to do, except take Jess out one final time. He rode across the fields toward Honeymead. He did not have to go near the cottage to see into the paddock where April normally grazed. He could see the pony was not there, and Jevan's heart leapt. He looked around, hoping that Annabel may be close. With no sign of her, he turned Jess toward the trees, making for moors beyond and heading for the oak tree. He seldom rode across the terrain with such haste, and it seemed that the landscape was more desolate than ever as he approached the tree and realized she was not there. Jevan changed directions and took familiar paths through the woods, visiting the places, they both knew well, and still there was no sign of her. Finally, he rode to the clapper bridge and, after tethering Jess to the usual tree, he walked across the stones, stopping when he reached the largest clapper.

He stared down at the fast-flowing current, the water mesmerizing him for a few moments. Coming to this place alone, it seemed the accident could have happened yesterday, so vivid was it in his mind. He looked across to the offending boulder and suppressed a shudder, forcing himself to dwell on happier times. Times when they had come here, believing they were alone. He frowned, wondering just how often Aidden had watched them, then shook that thought away. What did it matter? It was the past and there was no going back. Jevan thought about all the conversations here, the times she hung on his every word and looked adoringly into his eyes. She had loved him then. Now, all he could feel was pure emptiness, and he wondered for the hundredth time, if she was more deceptive than he imagined. Perhaps she never loved him at all.

He picked up a small rock and, with full force, sent it hurtling down the stream. The distant explosion in the water startled a duck. Jevan picked up another stone and aimed it at the bird. He missed the target and then felt remorse for his aggression. Thinking about Annabel just made him impulsive and dangerous.

He stared into the trees, and his eyes opened wider in shock as he thought he saw a familiar figure. It appeared to move fast, zig zaging away from him, and without thought, Jevan leapt across the remaining clappers and darted into the woods. He ran blindly through the trees as her laughter echoed all around. Stopping at the water's edge, he spun around. The shape had gone, and there was nothing, just the murmur of the woods. In the distance, he thought he heard another echo. Was it laughter? He couldn't tell and moved forward again.

"Annabel, where are you? Annabel!"

High up in the trees, the crows cackled in response, and then it was as though the whole woodland came to life with sounds. The birds seemed to be mimicking his frantic calls, and the water tumbled noisily over the rocks, drowning out her laughter. Jevan brought his hands to his ears for a moment, convinced he was going mad.

He finally regained his composure, certain it had just been his imagination, and turned back toward the bridge. He walked at a slow pace, and as he walked farther, he got the distinct impression he was not alone. Suspicion entered his mind. What had occurred here was haunting him. It struck him then that perhaps something supernatural was here, stalking him through the woods, a vengeful spirit that could not rest until Jevan had paid for his sin. Mindful of his dark thoughts, he guardedly approached the bridge. The devil was not visible, although he was undoubtedly mocking him.

∽∾∽

The following day, Jevan spent most of his time in the forge with Jophiel. It was an effort for him to utter more than a few words. For his father's sake, he attempted to be civil. Jophiel also felt the tension between them and knew this might be his last chance to talk alone with his son. After a while, he unexpectedly he put his tools down. He sat on a stool just as Jevan struck a piece of metal unnecessarily hard and raised his arm to strike again.

"I know how hard this is for you, Jevan, but it might be for the best."

Jevan stopped, mid-strike, and stared at him coldly.

Jophiel ignored the look and carried on. "You will have an

opportunity to better yourself, to see a bigger place in this world, and I know it doesn't feel like it now, but to be worldly, educated, and informed can be a good thing." He hesitated, noting the contempt on Jevan's face, and then continued regardless. "I know what Annabel means to you, and that you feel she is worth sacrificing everything else for, and to truly love someone is an amazing thing. Although life is never straightforward and opportunities to see new places and experience new things don't happen very often. Perhaps you haven't stopped to think about them before." He paused for a moment. "I'll tell you one thing, Jevan. Life can never stay the same, no matter how hard we wish it would. Things change, times change, discovering a feeling of self-worth and finding satisfaction is a change for the good." Jophiel paused again, trying to find the right words to say. "I only know how to forge metal, because, like you, I was brought up doing it and, given the chance, I would have liked the choice to be able to do something else, even if I choose not to do it.

"This trade is in your blood, but doing it for the rest of your life should be because you've opened your eyes and seen the alternatives, and you decided not to take them, rather than based on the fact that you are incapable of doing anything else."

Jevan's dark eyes stared into his father's. He put the hammer down and sat heavily on the stool opposite his father. He had never heard such a long speech from him before. "I'm afraid," he said reluctantly.

Jophiel was stunned to hear Jevan utter those words. Jevan was not afraid of anything. Jophiel placed his hand on Jevan's arm, squeezing it slightly.

Jevan dropped his gaze. He hated feeling embarrassed and weak by admitting fear to his father. "Afraid that I will get swallowed up in the city, or that I will choke in the degradation and corruption of that existence. It is not where I want to be, Father. It's a lie to believe I could ever be happy there. This is where I belong. I belong here with Annabel."

"The city will not corrupt *you*. Only the weak or stupid allow themselves to be corrupted and you are neither. You know where you have come from and will remember all the good things about your life here." Jophiel sighed. "I know that we expect too much from you," he said, tightening his hold on Jevan's arm, "but if confessions are in order, perhaps I am also afraid."

Jevan's eyes widened and his eyebrows rose.

"Why would you be afraid?"

Jophiel slumped back on the stool. "You know that your mother will go, with or without you. It's inevitable," he said sadly. "The thought of never seeing her again is something I can't bear. Once she moves to London and mixes with that society, I know, she will give little thought to what she left behind."

"Then stop her."

Jophiel shook his head. "If I do, she will resent it. It will make her miserable, and she'll hate me because of it."

Jevan's thoughts flew to Annabel. She hated him for leaving, and he had a good idea how his father felt.

"With *you* there," Jophiel continued, "I know she can't forget me. she just needs time to work out her feelings," he said, trying to convince himself of that more than Jevan. "When she tires with London society, and she will, she might remember how much I still love her, and you will bring her safely home to me again."

Jevan stared at his father's hunched shoulders and listened to the broken and desperate pleading in his voice. He stood up, towering above him and placed his hand on Jophiel's shoulder.

Jophiel was right and, although Jevan could not bring himself to believe that leaving Exmoor or Annabel was the right thing to do, it would give him an opportunity to see beyond the world he grew up in. At the very least, he could appreciate that some time away might just be the thing he needed right now.

"I'll take care of Mother," he said. "I'll remind her of you and the life she should have with you. I'll get an education properly fitting for a gentleman, if that's at all possible. But *I* will come back, because everything I really want is here."

Jophiel looked up and saw the determination in his son's eyes. "I believe you will," he agreed.

ↄﻭↄ

All too quickly, it was the last day. Jevan's trunk did not contain much—a few clothes, a ribbon and lock of Annabel's hair that she had given him the year before. A sudden knock at the cottage door sent a jolt of adrenaline through him. His hopes leapt higher as Josiah opened it and walked into the cottage.

"I just came to wish Adella and Jevan a good journey," he said, smiling at Jophiel and glancing uncomfortably at Jevan, although Jevan barely noticed.

His attention was still on the empty doorway. He muttered a word of thanks and walked out the door. He looked up and down the street and, with no sign of her, his hopes were dashed. Miserably he went into the forge to be alone. It felt like only a few minutes passed before the door of the forge opened.

"I don't know what's happened between you," Josiah said, walking to where he stood, "but I have never seen my daughter so unhappy, and I get the feeling there is more to this than just you leaving."

Jevan shrugged. "She knows where I am," he said indifferently.

Josiah snarled and slammed his fist down on the workbench, startling Jevan completely. "Don't you see? She is just a child, and you have broken her heart!" He glared angrily at Jevan. "Whatever it is, put it right. Don't leave it like this."

Josiah turned and stalked out of the forge.

Jevan stared at the empty doorway in shock. "Her heart? What about mine?" he said fiercely, to the empty space.

It was a shock to learn how blinkered to the truth Josiah was, and that he failed to recognize that Jevan was suffering too. He picked up a hammer, his breath coming fast and furious. How dare Josiah accuse him like that, as if it was his entire fault?

Josiah didn't know just how spiteful his precious daughter was.

Jevan began to work a piece of metal, his temper raging as he hit the metal for all he was worth, banging each tool down with unnecessary force, until finally he threw it across the room so hard that it stuck fast in a piece of timber. He looked at his hands. They were shaking, and he knew he could stand this no longer. His biggest regret was he should not have let her leave him like that on the moors. In the days that followed, he should have banged on that cottage door or broken it down to get to her. It was clear now that he couldn't leave without seeing her one last time. If she really hated him then he would make her tell him to his face.

Jevan rode Jess out of Rookwood and through Gothelstone, still in a fiery temper, with the words he wanted to say spinning around his mind. He could no longer pretend to himself that he didn't care. His longing to see her was a greater persuasion. By the time, he was on the road to Honeymead, that anger subsided. Even though the night was drawing in, the distant light from the cottage guided him.

Chapter 9

The Wooden Scar.

Josiah told Annabel that Jevan and Adella were leaving the next morning. The words spoken aloud made Annabel's heart ache. She shrugged her shoulders, turned, and stared out of the window. She hoped he didn't see the moisture collecting in her eyes. Tomorrow her life would really be over.

"Why don't you go and see him, go and say goodbye?" Lilith urged, after the silence and accompanying tension had become excruciating.

"No," Annabel said haughtily, not meeting her mother's gaze.

She sighed and left the room. Her heart might be broken, but she would be damned if she gave Jevan the satisfaction of running after him like some lovesick adolescent. The day wore on endlessly. She could think of nothing else, and it seemed a genuine possibility that she might never see him again. All the things she had said came back to haunt her. She had wounded him deeply.

She put her fingers to her temples and rubbed slowly, trying to figure out the best thing to do. Jevan had not come near the cottage, and he was never one to back down in a fight. Then again, nor was she.

It was up to him to come to her, she told herself for the hundredth time. He was the cause of all her heartache, and he should have the decency to fix it. It was a bitter thought. After all, if he did come, what could she say? Moreover, he would never forgive her now.

"Damn you, Jevan!" She choked back the tears.

He was too stubborn, and she realized that he might never come. The void between them felt impassable.

Annabel tried for a while to find solace in the garden and orchard. The flowers appeared dull, and even the bees held no delight for her today. They sensed she was upset and rallied around, buzzing around her head. When she sat upon the ground with her head on her knees, they landed on her skin. Their connection with her always brought some comfort, although, today she brushed them aside with barely a thought. She got up and walked slowly back to the cottage, trying to avoid her parents. They were trying to say the right things. She knew what they thought. They assumed it was just an argument. They couldn't possibly understand what she was going through. She went to her room, where at least she could be alone with her sorrow, and that was where she stayed for the next few hours.

Her head hurt, and her stomach felt so tightly knotted that she lay crunched up on the bed as the lump in her chest weighed heavily like a stone. She had not slept properly since they parted, or been able to allow a single piece of food to pass her lips. Her body felt fatigued. She felt defeated. Even if she saw Jevan, he would still leave her. She closed her eyes and sank deeper into the depression.

The light had just begun to fade, and the day was ending, when in the distance Annabel heard the sound of a horse's hooves. She opened her eyes. Her heart jumped up in shock, listening harder as the noise got louder. It sounded like Jess's hooves, at least she hoped it was. She held her breath. Jevan had come. Even though she had wished for this moment, her emotions were peculiar. She wanted to fling the door open, run down the stairs and into his arms, and he would tell her that he was not going away, and that it had all been a big mistake, but a sixth sense insisted that he was here to ease his own conscience, not hers. Her elation of moments ago faded, and she refused to look out of the window. She sat up on the bed and did not move a muscle, straining to pick up the tiniest sound.

≈≈≈

Jevan stood outside the cottage door. He was such a regular visitor to Honeymead that he normally knocked and just opened the door. This night, he could not bring himself to do that. After a moment's hesitation, he banged on the door and waited. Lilith opened the door.

"Hello, Jevan, I've been expecting you."

He forced a weak smile. Lilith always reminded him of Annabel. They had the same eyes. He stepped over the threshold and hid his disappointment that Annabel was not in the room. He looked across to Josiah who sat on a chair.

"You came then," Josiah's voice was strained.

"Can I see Annabel?"

"What time are you leaving?" Lilith asked, trying to ease the noticeable tension.

"In the morning, early."

Josiah got up and walked to the stairs. "Annabel, Jevan is here."

There was silence, a prolonged silence, and the air in the cottage suddenly felt oppressive as Jevan's heart felt as though it stopped. He knew she heard. He could feel her presence at a distance. He felt deflated, so certain had he been that she would have forgiven him and been happy that he had come. He imagined that she would run down the stairs and into his arms, but now the silence was becoming awkward, and he caught the exchange of glances between Lilith and Josiah.

≈≈≈

The moment that Jevan's voice sounded beneath her, Annabel jumped up from the bed. She moved like lightning across the room and pressed her ear against the locked door. She heard her father speak. She heard her name. She heard her mother ask what time they were leaving, and she heard Jevan answer. He was still leaving. The tears ran furiously down her face, her sixth sense had not failed. Jevan was only here because he wanted everyone to know that he had done the right thing, come to say goodbye like a gentleman might do, and a proper young lady was supposed to act graciously and wish him well on his new life ahead. Annabel went back to the bed and sat heavily upon it.

"Annabel!" She heard her father's irritation. He did not normally raise his voice to her, and she was resentful as her temper built quickly. Everyone it seemed was angry with her, and none of this was her doing.

"Tell Jevan that I never want to see him again," Annabel yelled.

Her voice was loud enough so that no one would be in any doubt of her meaning. There was complete silence for a few moments. She put her head in her hands and rocked back and forth on the bed, hating everyone, including herself.

He was hurting her again. It wasn't fair, and she wanted him to feel the way she did, to feel the pain and to be afraid. Her hands were clenched tight, her thoughts concentrated, even if it was only for a few moments. She abruptly stopped rocking. What was she doing? This was Jevan.

❧❧❧

Jevan froze. A part of him wanted to rush up the stairs, break the door down, and shake her until she came to her senses, except Josiah stood in the way. The other part of him wanted to fall to his knees before them, and oddly, his legs felt they might give way at any moment. He stared harder at the staircase, her malice emanating through the stone walls, weakening his body and tormenting his mind. He jumped when Lilith put her hand on his arm and the feeling vanished.

"She is upset, Jevan. She doesn't mean it. Don't allow words spoken in haste and anger to weigh too heavily on your heart."

Jevan tried to swallow the lump in his throat and nodded, shaken by what he was experiencing. "Tell her that I will never forget her." He looked into Lilith's eyes, eyes that were so much like Annabel's it unnerved him. "I will come back," he said, "I promise."

"I know you will. Right now, it's not going to make it any easier for her," Lilith replied cautiously, seeing the fear in his eyes. She smiled in sympathy, knowing too well what Annabel was capable of, and that made her fearful. "Leave now," she said firmly. "It's for the best. I will talk to her."

As Jevan left the cottage, he gazed up at Annabel's window. It was so clear now, he thought, she did hate him.

❧❧❧

Lilith stayed in the doorway and watched Jevan ride away. As she came inside and shut the door, her suspicions were roused as to what could have passed between them. She walked up the stairs and knocked on the bedroom door.

"Annabel, let me in." There was no reaction. "Annabel?"

Reluctantly, Annabel stumbled across the room and unlocked the door. Blinded by tears, she did not even look up and retreated to the bed again. Lilith lingered in the doorway for a few seconds, watching her daughter, then she came into the room and sat beside her.

"You should have said goodbye," she said at length.

"He shouldn't be leaving," Annabel said angrily, choking on the words.

Lilith sighed gently and placed an arm around her shoulder. "I don't think he really has a choice in the matter, does he?" she said sensibly.

Annabel shrugged and Lilith shook her head.

"It's your decision, although, perhaps you should reconsider. You might regret this night for a long time to come." Lilith hesitated for a moment. "Jevan wanted you to know that he won't forget you." She paused again, thinking. "Sometimes pride is the hardest thing to swallow. By doing so, it can also relieve a heavy burden. Be careful, Annabel, don't destroy the things you love most in this life," she said, stroking her hair and pulling it away from the damp skin.

Annabel looked at her and saw the sadness in her smile as she rose from the bed. "He's destroying me."

Lilith looked down at her with some skepticism. "We both know you are much stronger than that. You must learn to keep your gift under control." Annabel stared up at her mother in shock and, on seeing the look, Lilith sighed. "I'm your mother, of course you are like me," she affirmed, as she quietly closed the bedroom door behind her.

Annabel stared at the door. What had she done? Moments ago, she had hated him, wanting to inflict harm, even if deep down that wasn't what she really wanted. She shook her head. She was wicked and even her mother saw it. Annabel buried her face in the pillow to muffle the sobs.

ᑧᑖᑧ

The next morning dawned bright and Annabel was up early. The mists across the moors had almost vanished as she rode April across the undulating terrain, wanting to believe that the crisp morning air might sweep all her sorrow away. She approached the oak tree, her grief lingering heavily as she had dared to hope that Jevan might be here. She was all alone.

Tying April to a sturdy branch, she walked up the little incline, staring skyward, through the sprawling branches that reached out to the heavens, and then out across the wide expanse of ocean. It was a clear day, bar a few dark clouds on the horizon, which looked ominous. She hoped that the tree's natural umbrella would offer her some protection if the heavens opened up. Annabel turned back to the tree and walked around the trunk. She ran her hands lightly over the rough bark and found comfort in its familiarity and solid strength. As her eyes traveled over the surface, she was surprised to see a new scar etched in the wood. She bent to take a closer look.

Annabel and Jevan
Forever Thine

Annabel drew back, stood up too quickly, and struck her

forehead on a jagged branch. She stared harder at the words, ignoring the throbbing pain radiating across her head. Blood ran down her forehead, and she tentatively touched the skin. Her fingers came away stained scarlet. Pulling up the hem of her dress, she rubbed it briskly over the wound. She was not concerned, not when she was haunted by her mother's words. She should have said goodbye.

Her heart pounded heavily in her chest as she ran back to April, quickly un-tethered the reins, jumped on her back, and rode that horse as fast as her legs could gallop. She clasped the reins tightly in her trembling hands, reliving the events of the night before. When Jevan left the cottage, he would have felt the malevolence she directed at him, and if he really believed what she said, then he would leave and truly forget her. He really would never come back.

Her face was bloodstained, her loose hair tangled by the wind, and she arrived in Rookwood like a demented person. At her advance, people scuttled in all directions as she recklessly ploughed April through the busy main street, oblivious to the angry shrieks and shouts left in her wake. When Annabel reached the forge, she leapt from April's back and quickly flung the door open. Everything was quiet. Only Jophiel was sitting by the bench, and his red-rimmed eyes told her she was too late. Tears sprang into her eyes. Jophiel held out his arms, and she ran into them.

"I never said goodbye," she sobbed, soaking his shirt with tears.

"I know," he said quietly. They sat in silence for a few minutes. "He will come back."

"Do you really think so?"

Jophiel nodded with certainty. "Yes, and you should believe that he won't forget you."

❧❧❧

The passing days turned into weeks, and Annabel's sorrow was self-indulgent. Never one to cry much, now it was as though she was making up for lost time. Her eyes were constantly full of moisture. No one could even begin to comfort her, and she avoided all mention of Jevan's name. Even the will to do anything seemed to leave her. She wanted to sleep. Only then could she withdraw deeper into herself. Had it not been for the gentle persuasions of her parents, she would have truly faded away into nothingness.

As weeks turned into months, with still no news of Jevan, she reluctantly emerged into the world again. Although it was a closed and insular world, as she spent most of her time with the bees. In their company, she repented her selfishness. The bees listened to her words of self-condemnation, her regrets, and her love for Jevan. They demonstrated their understanding as they flew about her. She was a permanent focus for them now and, in Annabel's darkest hours, their tiny buzzing vibrations echoed through her head and seemed to converse soothingly with her. They expressed no judgment, only understanding when they tenderly landed upon her skin in the hundreds. Even so, the darkness in Annabel grew all too easily. It gnawed away at her conscience and hovered over her mind, tangling thoughts into twisted sinister meaning. Utter despair engulfed her, and it lured her soul into a terrain of destruction where she felt the only solution was to end her life.

The bees learned of her alarming philosophy as she beckoned them to sting her. With enough venom in her bloodstream, she could die peacefully. They were confused, her beckoning only served to agitate the colony as they flew to and from where she sat. They would not harm her. Instead, they sent whispering vibrations through her ear, as the bees bade her to conceal this terrible darkness for a more appropriate time.

This moment was obscure. It seemed that even her beloved bees could not help her in her most desperate time of need. She complied with their wishes, even if it might only be a temporary respite. Although she believed that animals gauged the general mood of humans, so it seemed did bees. For those bees knew that, without Jevan, her life was ruined. Like death, it was finished and over for good.

Chapter 10

On the Road to Gothelstone

Four Years Later:

I t was a beautiful morning for walking, though Annabel's progress was slowed by the basket she carried, which was heavily laden with beeswax candles and Royal Jelly. She now thought she should have waited as her father suggested. He had almost mended the wheel on the trap. She had been in too much of a hurry to listen to his advice.

"If you fix it quickly, then you can catch me up," she said, walking out the cottage door.

She was too headstrong for her own good, and the basket felt as though it was getting heavier by the minute. She shifted the weight back and forth on alternate arms. Inspiration to quicken her pace happened as the roofs of Gothelstone village came into view. She hoped to get a lift with one of the villagers onward to Rookwood. This was a monthly pilgrimage, and it enabled her to sell her produce, which was more in demand now than at any time before.

After she rounded a little bend in the road, the tower of Gothelstone church came into her line of sight. Annabel's thoughts turned to her mother, clouding her outlook and making the day feel subdued. It felt impossible that three months had already passed since Lilith's death. Annabel still expected to see her mother every time she walked into cottage, and it was heartbreaking to realize that she never would. Lilith's passing felt like a huge void that could never be filled again. Annabel had never realized before how her mother's presence had been so integral to life at Honeymead. She regretted bitterly ever taking it for granted. Now, the cottage felt empty, and sadness seemed to hang in the very essence of the building.

Annabel brushed her gloomy thoughts away and put the basket down at the side of the road, glad to be able to relieve her aching arms for a few minutes. She set about picking a small bunch of cowslips and pink larkspur to take to the little cemetery and, quite absorbed in the task, only looked up at the sound of fast-approaching hooves. She expected to see a familiar rider.

The man on horseback did not look familiar. The rider saw her at once and slowed the horse. Annabel glanced around. There was no one else in the vicinity, and a sudden wariness came over her. The rider appeared to be of some good standing, judging by his clothes, the way he carried himself, and how he commanded his horse.

Annabel picked up the basket and placed the flowers inside. The rider was only a few feet away from her now and staring keenly. She moved farther back onto the grass verge to let him pass. He did not pass. Instead, he steered the black stallion in front of her as if to purposely block the way forward. The horse reared a little, and Annabel quickly stepped back. She looked up at him and noted the arrogant smirk on his face.

"What do you have in the basket?" he asked, with an air of superiority.

She did not answer. Alarm bells sounded in her head. His manner was abrupt, and she knew she could not out run him on foot.

"I don't see what it has to do with you," she said at last, with a dismissive air of confidence, side stepping the horse and attempting to carry on walking. The man backed the horse up, blocking her way again. This time she was sufficiently provoked and narrowed her eyes. "Let me pass," she demanded.

"I asked you a question," the man replied icily.

Some inner instinct told her to drop the basket and run. It was the sensible thing to do, but it contained a month's hard work and the contents were too valuable. And she refused to be so easily intimidated. Annabel pursed her lips and stared back at him defiantly, thinking about the best plan of action that would not cause trouble for her or her father.

"Honey," she said at last, the anger in her voice evident. "Now, let me pass."

The man quickly dismounted and came toward her. The alarm bells grew louder. He was tall, expensively dressed, with dark blond collar length hair and dark blue eyes. He looked at her curiously, and she saw his eyes linger longer than necessary on her long hair.

"Red hair and green eyes," he said with interest. "Once they would have been considered the distinction of a witch."

Complete annoyance overtook Annabel's initial fear. He was trying her patience sorely. "Well, mind that I don't put a curse on you then!"

His eyes opened wide at her outburst, and he laughed loudly, as though he found the remark extremely amusing. "You are very outspoken for someone of your means," he answered, shifting his gaze down over her old clothes and tattered shoes.

"And you are less polite than what I would expect a gentleman to be, if that is indeed what you are."

Taken aback by her comment, he raised his eyebrows a fraction. "My apologies, miss, if I offended you. I am Alexander Saltonstall from Gothelstone Manor, but you can call me Alex."

Annabel pulled in her breath sharply and bit her lip. Of all the people she could have chosen to insult. It was of course too late now, and anyway, she had heard many stories of the dubious reputations of the occupants of that house. Her words were probably justified.

"And may I have your name?" he continued.

She hesitated. Even if she refused, he would easily find out. Her coloring was hardly inconspicuous in these parts. Everyone knew who she was.

"Miss Taylor," she said haughtily, side stepping him to continue with her journey.

Alex blocked her path again, this time stepping closer to her, making her afraid of a certain gleam in his eye. She realized that he was not going to be easy to get rid of. At the same time, she feared what she could achieve if she put her mind to it. It took only a moment to consider that it was best not to allow him to rile her unnecessarily.

"What do you want?" she said impatiently.

"I would have thought that was obvious," he said, smiling briefly, and the look faded into determination when he grasped the handle of the basket, as if to take if from her.

She held it firmly. When he grabbed her wrist, she let the basket drop, and brought her other hand up quickly to strike him hard across the face.

"You are mistaken if you think that is going to happen," she spat fiercely. "My fingernails and teeth will leave marks that will scar you for life."

Clearly taken aback, Alex did not expect that kind of reaction from such a slip of a girl. Yet staring into her blazing eyes, he saw that she would put up a considerable fight. Her determination was unmistakable. Although, it was more of a shock to realize that his intimidation had no effect on her.

Annabel felt his grasp on her wrist slacken, but her real relief came at the sound of the approaching pony and trap.

"A real wildcat aren't you," Alex said, as he abruptly released her and took a step back. He hesitated for a moment and then remounted his horse, unwilling to show any indication that this common peasant girl had unnerved him. Even so, his ingrained arrogance had to claw back some dignity. "Of course, you know what happens to wild animals, don't you?"

Annabel did not answer.

"They get tamed," he said threateningly, as the pony and trap came into to view.

Annabel turned and smiled widely at her father. Alex caught the look.

"Ah you're the beekeeper's daughter," he said, with sudden understanding. "Well, that is interesting isn't it," he observed quietly to himself. He moved the horse closer to Annabel and leaned forward so that only she might hear his words. "We shall meet again, very soon," he said quietly before sitting up and saying in a louder voice, "Good day to you, miss." He then turned and rode away.

A few moments later Josiah pulled the trap alongside her. "Wasn't that the Saltonstall boy?" he asked, giving her an enquiring glance.

"Yes," she replied nonchalantly.

"Hardly a boy now," Josiah remarked, watching his daughter.

"Hardly," she said dismissively. "So you fixed the trap then," she said, turning and feigning interest.

∽∾∽

Good to his word, it was not long before Annabel saw Alex again. Two days later, she was walking down the main street of Rookwood and had been diverted in her thoughts by a recent conversation with a shopkeeper, not paying any attention to the figure on horseback until he was alongside her. So it startled her when she looked up and Alex raised his hat a fraction.

"Good day, Miss Taylor." He said her name with an air of infuriating amusement, and then to her dismay, he dismounted. Again, she saw that dangerous glint in his eyes when he spoke. "The day has suddenly become far more interesting."

She glared at him. "That is a matter of opinion."

Alex laughed lightly at her comment. "Are you alone, Miss Taylor?" he asked, looking around for any obvious companions. His very presence aggravated her completely.

"Not that it's any concern of yours, but I left my familiar at home today," she replied, with as much sarcasm as she could muster.

Alex's smile broadened and he regarded her speculatively for a moment. "I can see that I have offended you, yet again." He thought for a moment. "My behavior on the Gothelstone road was deplorable. Please accept my apology and allow me to make amends. Let me escort you back to your little cottage. I can easily borrow another horse for you."

"I already have a horse," she said, picking up her pace. "She is at the blacksmiths."

Alex, not about to be dismissed so easily, quickened his step to match hers. "Then I will walk with you," he announced, as if it were the most normal thing.

Annabel did not want his company, and certainly did not wish to enter into another conversation with him. She stopped walking, turned to him, and drew herself up to her full height, which still fell short of being on eye level.

"Sir, your attentions are not wanted. Perhaps it would be wise for you to divert them elsewhere."

Alex stiffened. Annabel was tired. Already she had a mild headache and, with no intention of continuing any conversation, especially with him, she didn't care that he might take offense. She doubted anyone ever spoke to him so bluntly before. Then again, she did not care what he thought either.

"Are you really ignorant to the fact that my family is the most influential in this area. I am not someone that you should make an enemy of," he retorted coldly. "We own this town and make or break the lives of the people who reside in it," he concluded with an air of authority.

"It's just as well that I don't reside in it, because no one owns me," she replied, furious at his annotations.

Alex's face changed subtly at once. "Perhaps, I have yet to make my intentions clear."

"I think you made your intention very clear on the road the other day, and I already warned you that would not be a prudent undertaking. Besides, if you have to resort to threatening behavior to attract attention, then it is a sure sign of a lack of confidence and an extremely weak character."

Alex's eyes widened. "Perhaps your hostile disposition just brings out the worst in me."

"Then perhaps that is a warning that we should not be in each other's company," Annabel replied and turned to walk away from him.

"On the contrary, Miss Taylor, I would say that the fire in

you rivals my own." He tipped his hat again. "Please accept my sincerest apology for my forwardness." He got up on his horse and, after fixing her with the longest look, he rode away.

Annabel sighed, her first instinct the other day was right—he was going to be difficult to get rid of.

The next day there was a knock at the cottage door. Annabel opened the door to a young messenger with a posy of exotic flowers tied with expensive ribbons and an invitation to the Gothelstone Manor House. Annabel sent the boy away with a firm refusal, annoyed that Alex had the audacity to think that some flowers might endear him to her. The following day she was in the garden when Josiah beckoned to her.

"You have a visitor," he said quietly, giving her a wary look.

She noted his expression with mild concern and thought she had made her feelings clear. Not well enough apparently. Even before she walked into the cottage, she knew that Alex would be inside. He sat at the table and instantly stood when he saw her. "Why did you refuse my invitation?" He sounded a little tense and she looked at him in astonishment.

"You didn't really expect me to accept?" she said, shaking her head. "You really are the most arrogant man I have ever met." She saw Josiah hovering near the doorway and noted his look of shock at her words. "And besides, I cannot be won over with a bunch of flowers."

Alex and Annabel stared at each other for several moments. "Perhaps it is you who has a certain arrogance. You are certainly too outspoken for a girl of your status, and I do not take kindly to insults—"

"And nor do I," she interrupted hotly, "nor intimidation, which I believe is what you have tried to do ever since we first met. Since status seems so important to you, I can't imagine why you would have sent me an invitation in the first place."

He sighed heavily. "Miss Taylor, I did not come here to either insult or intimidate you. It is perhaps true that my intentions are confused in your presence. I want you to know that it is my deepest wish that you dispel any animosity concerning me," he added softly, his brow furrowing. "I know, I behaved badly at our first meeting, and I deeply regret that. Now, I can only humbly beg your forgiveness."

Slightly taken aback by his outburst and, despite her resolve, Annabel warmed to his plight because when he next spoke it seemed a perfectly reasonable request.

"All I ask is that you give me the time of day, Miss Taylor, so that I may attempt to earn your respect, and if I may be so bold, your friendship."

Her head nodded dumbly almost of its own accord, and the previous feelings of mistrust were overshadowed by his heartfelt request for forgiveness Alex had a certain amount of charm, and his warm smile made the stoniness of her heart fade away. Tentatively, she looked across to Josiah.

"I'll be outside." She walked through the cottage door and Alex followed her.

They wandered down the driveway and to the edge of the field, which in recent weeks had turned into a wildflower meadow. She stayed close to the wall, slowly heading in the general direction of the orchard, and wanting to stay close to her father. She was still too conscious of being entirely alone with Alex. She left it up to him to break the silence.

"Your father's bees, are they close?"

There was a curious quiver in his voice and she looked up at him. This was not in keeping with what she would have expected. "Yes, would you like to see them?"

"No," he replied, a little too quickly.

Annabel stared at him in surprise.

His look changed subtly to one of embarrassment. "I am afraid of them."

At his words, a slow and deliberate smile radiated across her face.

Alex saw the look. "It is not an unjustified fear," he explained. "I was stung once as a child and had such a severe reaction that if it had not been for the quick action of my nurse, I would have died." He shrugged lightly. "It has left me with the greatest dread ever since."

Annabel nodded, trying to understand. His fear seemed so strange and, having grown up surrounded by bees, she could never feel anything other than love and understanding for them. She doubted someone like Alex could ever empathize with that. Jevan had understood, perhaps even had the ability to charm bees. Annabel quickly pushed that thought away.

Alex regarded her for a moment, as the smile was still obvious. "You obviously think that I am a coward for entertaining such fear."

"No," she said, choosing her words carefully, still feeling quite delighted at the thought of Alex being so afraid of such tiny creatures. "But your fear, it is difficult to grasp. I can put my hand into a full hive and not think twice about it. I have never been afraid," she said smugly. "Although, bees can sense fear, perhaps that is why you were stung."

She thought for a moment. The revengeful and the malicious part of her wanted to walk through the orchard just to see his reaction, but she hurriedly quashed that suggestion. Alex was trying to make amends, and she should at least behave a little graciously. Apart from that, the truth was hard to admit. She was warming to him. It was strange that once her bristles were down and she was more relaxed, there was a definite appealing quality about him.

He was handsome enough, although it was more than that. she got an odd feeling being with him, something she couldn't quite place her finger on.

"The hives are through the orchard, so perhaps we should walk this way instead," she offered, gesturing to a small path that led in the opposite direction.

She could almost feel Alex's relief as they walked for a few minutes in silence. Annabel stole several sideways glances at him. Alex was beginning to intrigue her.

"I never realized that there was no other cottage around here," he said, interrupting her thoughts. "Do you mind being so isolated, Miss Taylor?"

Annabel laughed and stopped walking. "Please stop calling me Miss Taylor. My name is Annabel, and everyone calls me by it. And I am not isolated," she insisted, as they resumed walking again. "Gothelstone is not *that* far, and I know everyone in the hamlet and most in Rookwood village. I go out and

meet friends, and the villagers play music to dance to. We often exchange stories, remedies, and friendship. They are the
people I have known all my life, people that I went to school
with. It might surprise you, but the village has an active social
life."

He regarded her words with some thought. "It is a very
limited life, though. What about the bigger world? Haven't
you ever wanted to dress in the finest clothes, to mix in society, and attend great balls and galas?" He stopped walking and
looked earnestly into her eyes. "I could easily picture you in a
beautiful silk gown at a society ball. Your eyes are the color of
the purest jade, and your red hair catches every glint of light.
Your beauty would shame any other woman in the room."

Annabel was shocked into silence by these comments. Sufficiently embarrassed, she realized that he had noticed enough
details to give every aspect of her a fine description. "And
what would I talk about at a high society ball?" she said, walking forward again, trying not to appear unsettled by his words.
"You forget, Alex, that I am only the daughter of a beekeeper.
I would not be welcome in such highbrow circles. Society
would not accept me."

Alex smiled briefly. "Society would accept you if you're
well connected and married correctly," he replied casually,
"and I understand that your mother came from a good family."

Annabel stopped dead in her tracks and turned to face him.

"How do you know that?" she said brusquely.

"My father spoke of it."

For once Annabel was lost for words. Cerberus Saltonstall
was not the kind of man who even knew they existed, let alone
knew her family history. Since the encounter at the apothecary, Annabel had seen and observed him a few times. His
disconcerting stare was not only reserved for her. Josiah was
subjected to it as well. In addition, her father's attitude toward
Cerberus Saltonstall was always very hostile. The general village consensus was that most people did not like the master of
Gothelstone Manor.

Alex's words filled her head. She suddenly understood the
wider implication of the suggestion that if she were to marry

someone, like Alex for instance, then all things he spoke of were possible. Annabel was uncomfortable with the direction of this conversation. "What about you? Do you miss society life?"

"Yes and no. Sometimes, it can be stimulating. Mainly, it's full of unremarkable young woman and their pushy mothers trying to marry off their daughters into influential families. Most of them are anything but stimulating. Oh, it's true their daughters are taught to engage in the appropriate conversations. They can play the piano, draw, and present themselves properly." He shook his head. "They leave me cold. They see only how they and their families can benefit from such a match and willingly accept their fate. They are the slaves of society and sold to whomever will give them the best social standing." Alex gazed at her. "They have no fire in them."

"Not like me then," she said cordially.

"They are nothing like you. You are unpretentious and entirely more enjoyable company."

Annabel laughed loudly. "Well, that's a huge change of opinion. Let me see, didn't you call me a witch, a wildcat, arrogant, and outspoken?"

Alex grinned. "Perhaps that's what makes you so intriguing."

She brushed his comment aside. "What about the city? You must miss that?"

"Some things," he agreed. "The general comradeship of friends, the places we visited, the lavish dinners, and conversations over a game of billiards."

"So why are you back here at Gothelstone? Surely, it's a million miles from where you would rather be."

"It was," Alex replied, gazing down at her, "although life in the country suddenly seems far more exciting."

Annabel took a couple of steps back from him. "Alex—" she began, but he did not let her finish.

"I do not tease you, Miss T—Annabel. From that first day on the road when we met, I have thought of nothing else but the outspoken girl with the wild green eyes and dark red hair that slapped me. Perhaps you knocked some sense into me. It does not matter now." His voice was tentative. "Although you undoubtedly bewitched me, and you continue to do so. I have a duty to be here. I will inherit the estate of Gothelstone and have an obligation not only to ensure the success of the estate, but to the farmers and tenants that work the land, so they can continue to earn a living. My father is aging, and I have probably spent too much time enjoying myself. So now I have to learn fast. I am forced to remain, and my incarceration would be all the better to have someone like you by my side."

She shook her head firmly, unnerved by his sincerity. "You make it sound like you have been placed in prison, and you don't know me. We have hardly exchanged a civil word before this day."

Alex stepped a little closer to her. "I know enough, and now that we have been civil, I see something in you that greatly attracts me, and I believe that I no longer see contempt in your eyes." He hesitated for a long moment. "You know your own mind, maybe a little too much, except I tire easily of most people. Even though the city has its charms, in you, I see something altogether more tempting."

Annabel had never heard anyone speak with such an educated tongue before and knew that perhaps she was a little in awe of Alex. He seemed so worldly and knew so many things. He had responsibilities and duties that she could not even begin to comprehend. She had thought him hostile and dangerous. That was before. His compliments today flattered her, enough so that her thoughts altered.

That evening as Annabel lay in bed, her thoughts stayed focused on Alex. He had systematically broken down her barriers, and she'd seen a different side of him today. His intentions were clear, and she was reserved in final judgment, as well as in conflict to her inner feelings.

She closed her eyes and stared into Alex's dark blue ones. His voice penetrated all other thoughts, and she felt herself blush, remembering his words. She fell asleep, thinking of him. He invaded her dreams, and late into the night, those visions became confused. Alex's blue eyes grew darker, almost black, his hair grew longer and wilder, and suddenly, it was

Jevan's image she reached out to touch. She woke suddenly as something touched her.

"Annabel, wake up!" Josiah was holding her by the shoulders and shaking her gently. In the flickering light of the candle, his face looked ashen and she felt her heart racing. "You were screaming out Jevan's name. I thought someone was killing you," he said, letting her go.

She covered her eyes with her hands, attempting to shut out lingering images, before taking Josiah's hands in her own. "It was only a dream, Father. I'm all right."

He did not look convinced, and she smiled to reassure him.

"Shall I leave the candle?" he asked.

"No, I don't need it. But your hands are freezing. Go back to bed."

He cast a worried look in her direction as he went out the door, and the room was plunged into darkness again. Yet she was not at peace. Jevan's voice rang through her head accusingly as she turned on her side and wiped away the tears that had fallen.

Chapter 11

Jophiel's Sorrow

The dream felt like an omen, and it played on her mind as she rode into Rookwood the next day. As was usual, she first visited the forge. After Jevan's departure, Jophiel had become like a second father, and since her mother's death, there were things that were easier to discuss with him rather than her own father. As expected, Josiah had taken Lilith's death extremely badly.

"Ah, Annabel, I thought that sounded like April," Jophiel said, putting his tools down on the bench. "Come into the cottage, and I'll make some tea. I have another letter."

Annabel's heart leapt, as it always did, whenever Jophiel received one of these sporadic letters from his wife. She hoped for news of Jevan, although, Adella's correspondence tended to be self-absorbed, and she mainly talked of society events and places she had visited. Although there were occasionally snippets of news, and Annabel learned that Jevan had gained the education Adella had desired. He had gone on to find employment at a prestigious London printing company that was involved in printing bank notes, newspapers, and periodicals.

Jophiel read aloud the latest development.

"'Jevan has learned to use the new autographic press. It is a wonder, Jophiel. Thousands of copies can be produced from any writing or drawing. The subject is transferred from paper to the surface of a highly polished metal plate and then, being charged with ink, paper is placed upon it and the tympan laid down. Then a wooden scraper is passed over it by hand and a perfect impression is at once obtained.

"'Would you believe it, Jophiel? This simple apparatus has gained considerable attention of merchants and shippers for the colonies and foreign countries, where there is no printer to be found, and Jevan may go to these foreign lands to teach them how to use this portable printing machine.'"

Annabel's heart sank. Jophiel looked up from the letter and did not speak either. Adella had won. She had ensured that Jevan had established himself in the city, thus giving him opportunity to travel to foreign lands, and even farther away from her. Adella had tamed the wildness out of him, and now he would never come home.

Annabel had thought about writing to him many times. Then again, after so much time, a letter out of the blue might not have been welcome. What would she have said? That she regretted the words she had spoken, that they were said out of grief and anger. Although, he had not written to her either.

In fact, she was certain that he had put all thought of her out of his mind completely, and Adella would have helped him forget. She would have been busy lining up potential wives from the daughters of her society friends, and perhaps he was even now engaged to be married. Annabel's heart lurched. *Oh God, Jevan with another*. She didn't think she could stand the idea.

"You know how much I regret letting her go." Jophiel interrupted her thoughts. "But I think she will return soon."

Annabel smiled warmly at him. "Perhaps, Jophiel," she said agreeably, not wishing to dampen his hopes.

She did not share them. From what she read in these letters, Adella was happy, surrounded by the trappings of society and city life. Annabel didn't believe for one moment that she would suddenly long for the simple country life again. In addition, her son was there. He was successful and had good prospects. No, Adella would not leave the city.

"I miss them," he said, handing her a cup of steaming tea.

"I know, Jophiel," she said, feeling emotional all of a sudden. She too wished every day that Jevan would come back.

"Thank goodness, I have you. You are the daughter I should have had. Josiah is a lucky man, and I hope he appreciates just how fortunate he is."

"You know he does." Annabel laughed. "Besides, could you imagine it? A son like Jevan and a daughter like me? We would have driven you to an early grave."

Jophiel laughed too. "You're right there. Together you had so much fire in you, and both so stubborn. There were times when I could have knocked your heads together," he said cordially, remembering their antics. "You know I always believed that you would end up together."

Annabel lowered her eyes contemplating the thought. "What a marriage that would have been," she said, trying not to allow her profound longing to be obvious. She smiled softly. "We would have wound up killing each other."

Jophiel shook his head. "Maybe, when you were very young. Time has a way of taming the reckless and wildness in us all."

She sighed heavily. It was an impossible dream. It had been so long since she had seen him, and the Jevan she knew and loved had gone. Yet even now, she still could not face the reality of that. She quickly swallowed the remaining liquid in her cup and stood up. "I must be going, thanks for the tea."

"He will come back one day, you know that," Jophiel said, giving her a knowing look.

Annabel squeezed his hand in reassurance and walked out the door. Even though Jophiel's comment made her heart flutter, she knew it was merely wishful thinking. She walked away from the blacksmith, determined to let the past lie and concentrate on the future.

☙☙☙

Annabel had an unexpected feeling of excitement at the thought of seeing Alex again, and consequently over the course of the next few weeks, her feelings deepened. There was something of a rebel in Alex and, notably, that something, drew her closer to him. They went for long walks. She impressed him with the names of the flowers, and how she could use them for medicinal purposes. They rode over the moors and the vast estate of Gothelstone Manor or strolled around its vast gardens, filled with fragrant blooms and exotic plant specimens.

One afternoon, Alex plucked a dark pink rose and placed it in Annabel's hand. She sniffed at its delicate fragrance.

"This rose cannot match your beauty," he said, taking a step closer to her.

She felt the color rise in her cheeks and her heart quickened as he brushed his lips against hers and pulled her firmly toward him. Then his kiss became deeper.

Alex was unlike anyone she had ever known, and mindful of that thought, she was aware that he had only ever mixed with women of good breeding, born to become wives to the rich or the gentry. Those women were from influential families with respectable fortunes of their own. They said that opposites attract, and she was confident that he regarded her as more than just a casual interest, but her feelings about that kiss were confused. Alex ignited a spark, a connection rarely encountered in her life. She thought of it as a deep friendship, although it was becoming obvious that Alex wanted more. She couldn't really come to terms with that. She did not want to confront those sorts of feelings. Even after all this time, they still felt raw.

Spending so much time with Alex meant that she had not been in Rookwood for several weeks. Therefore, when she finally visited, she was surprised to find the door to the forge tightly shut. There were no horses waiting to be shod, and the whole place seemed altogether too quiet. She opened the door to the cottage and heard a noise in the kitchen.

"Jophiel," she called, walking forward to greet him, and was startled to find Lydia, a close neighbor, standing by the stove. "Where is Jophiel?" Annabel said in surprise.

Lydia bit her lip and looked at her apologetically. "He is

not well, Annabel. He's taken to his bed for days now."

Annabel stared at her in shock. "Did no one think to ride and tell me or my father!" she said, raising her voice loudly.

"Annabel, we wanted to, we tried, but he wouldn't hear of it." She hesitated. "What with the loss of Lil—your mother—he said, we couldn't burden you both."

Annabel did not wait to hear anymore. She rushed up the stairs and threw open the bedroom door. Jophiel lay on his back. His skin looked deathly white. His cheeks had sunk, and there were dark patches under his eyes. The curtains remained closed and the atmosphere was dismal and gray. Annabel was horrified as Jophiel barely opened his eyes before closing them again

"I thought that was your voice." A hint of a smile touched his lips. "You have to leave me now. There is nothing you can do."

Just then, Lydia walked in the room carrying a bowl of clear broth. "Perhaps you can get him to take something. He hasn't touched anything for days." She put the bowl on the table and clasped her hands together in a prayer-like gesture.

"Leave us," Annabel said.

Although, Lydia looked mildly scandalized, she cast her eyes back to Jophiel and then quietly left the room. Annabel closed the door and sat on the edge of the bed. She picked up Jophiel's thin hand and felt shock all over again at how light and frail it felt in her own.

"Are you in pain?" He did not respond. "Jophiel, you have to eat something," she said in desperation.

He opened his eyes again and stared at her from the vacant depths, then he shook his head sorrowfully. Annabel could sense there was no will to live left. Every sparkle or glimmer of life had just vanished.

"No I don't," he said slowly. "There's no point. She's not coming back."

He reached under the pillow and brought out a creased letter. Annabel unfolded the piece of paper and began to read. The letter was as good as a death warrant for Jophiel. Adella's words had destroyed him when she made it clear that she would never return and wished that he would forget all memories of her.

Annabel could not help the tears that ran down her face. Did this also mean that Jevan wanted her to forget him? She looked back to Jophiel. Her life was already ruined. She wouldn't allow his to cease. She firmly wiped the tears away. "No," she said shaking her head. "I am not going to let you do this. Adella might not need you, but I do, and one day Jevan will need his father. How can you be so selfish?"

Jophiel closed his eyes again. For a moment, she stared helplessly at him. It reminded her of watching her mother fade away to nothing, and another tear rolled down her cheek. She couldn't lose Jophiel as well. He wasn't sick. He was just heartbroken, and she had experience of that feeling well enough.

She took a deep breath and stood up. "No, you are not going to do this, and I am not going to watch you do this," she said with determination and pulled the bedclothes from him. She ignored the startling frail and naked body of a man she had always known to be powerful and strong. "Get up, Jophiel. Adella may not be here, but I am, and you will get better. You have to eat, and I will make sure you do, even if I have to force it down your throat." Her voice was growing louder by the second. "I am not leaving until you get up," she said adamantly."

Jophiel appeared to shrink back even farther into the bed. "Annabel, just leave me alone."

Annabel shook her head and went to the window. She pulled the curtains open as far as they would go, and the sunlight fell across his flesh, making it appear whiter than ever.

"You should know better than to cross me, Jophiel Wenham," she said firmly. "I am not giving up on you, because Jevan will never forgive me if I allowed anything to happen to you. I will not let you ruin his life." She took hold of Jophiel's arms and pulled his body upright, which was quite an achievement, but her strength came from determination and anger. She opened the bedroom door.

"Lydia!" she yelled down the stairs. "Send someone to

fetch my father at once and then please prepare some real food for Jophiel. He *will* eat it."

"Annabel."

She turned back to Jophiel. "Don't waste your breath. I don't want to hear any excuses. I will not listen."

"Annabel, I need some clothes."

She suddenly realized his embarrassment, as he was attempting to cover his nakedness. Annabel hastily grabbed the clothes from a nearby chair and threw them onto the bed then turned her back. "Hurry up," she demanded, "because I am not leaving you alone for one second."

Josiah arrived about forty minutes later, and they helped Jophiel down the stairs. With Josiah's encouragement and Annabel's harassment, Jophiel had no choice but to force some of the food down. They sat with him for several hours, until the color had begun to come back into his cheeks, and they convinced him that life might still be worth living, reminding him that he should be thinking about Jevan. As they were leaving, Annabel told him again that she would be back first thing in the morning, much to Jophiel's bewilderment.

"I am too weak to argue with you, Annabel," he said with defeat in his tone.

"Just as well," she said, "because you know how determined I am to see you well." Thinking for a moment, she turned to her father. "Perhaps I should stay. I could sleep in Jevan's bed."

"No!" Jophiel said at once. "I don't think my poor head can stand any more chastisement tonight. I dare not take to my bed again for fear of what you might do to me." Then he grinned mischievously at her.

True to his word, Jophiel did not take to his bed again and, after a few weeks, he regained all this strength. His attitude improved, and the bond between Annabel and him tightened. All his loss and grief he channeled into his work and an overly protective attitude toward her. She didn't mind and, as a result, spent even more time at the forge. Jophiel reminded her of Jevan in his mannerisms and the phrases he used, and she loved him even more for it.

Chapter 12

Dinner at the Mansion

Cerberus Saltonstall had not been in the county these past few weeks. Therefore, Annabel didn't have to face a meeting while she had been in Alex's company. It was something she secretly dreaded when she learned that he had just returned home. Then the inevitable happened. Alex sent his message boy with a dinner invitation, telling her that they would expect her at Gothelstone mansion at six p.m. the following evening. She tried to think of a plausible explanation as to why she could not attend. As it happened, Annabel saw Alex the same day. Having just visited Jophiel, she was leaving the forge.

"Alex, I am not sure if I can accept this invitation," she announced, as soon as he greeted her. "I have nothing to wear and—"

"I am not interested in what you're wearing. You can come in your oldest clothes, for all I care, but I do want you to meet my father."

"Alex," she began, and then stopped. How could she tell him that she was intimidated at the prospect of dinner with his father?

Alex saw her reluctance. "It's you that my father is eager to meet. He knows who you are, and it was his idea. You don't want to disappoint him, do you?"

Annabel greatly doubted the sincerity of his words, although, she couldn't think of any other reasonable excuse, and the last thing she wanted to do was to hurt Alex's feelings. "No, but your father will not approve of me," she said softly.

Alex smiled triumphantly. "Let me worry about that. The most important thing is that I approve of you, and that's the only thing that really matters."

Annabel was quite late home that evening. Josiah was sitting in the chair when she entered the cottage. She walked over to him and kissed him on the forehead.

"I'm tired. I think I will go straight to bed," she said happily.

Josiah looked up at her. She saw the solemn look in his eyes and assumed that his thoughts had been of her mother.

"Annabel, I want to talk to you before you go," he said, hesitating over the words. Then he dissolved into a coughing fit.

Annabel quickly fetched a glass of water and placed it in his hands. "What is it, are you unwell?" she said, feeling concerned as he drank the water straight down and the spasm subsided.

"It's just a cough," he said dismissively. "It's you that I'm worried about."

"Me?" She sat before him. "I'm fine. You mustn't worry about me."

"My only daughter and you tell your father not to worry," he said with amusement in his voice.

Although he tried to remain cordial, she noted the seriousness in his demeanor. "What is it?"

"You have been seeing a lot of Alex Saltonstall lately."

Annabel sensed the disapproval in his tone and gave him an enquiring look. "Do you object?" She felt a little taken aback as her father had never disapproved of any friends before.

He paused for a long moment. "I just want you to be happy, and I don't want you to make a mistake. I…" His words trailed off.

"What? Tell me what you think." she asked cautiously, feeling puzzled over his hesitancy.

He never usually had a problem coming straight to the point.

Josiah sighed. "I always assumed that you and Jevan would be together."

His words pierced her heart and she caught her breath. She didn't want him to say anymore and, in an effort for self-preservation, she forced a laugh. "So did I, but Jevan's gone. It's been four years, and we have both grown up a lot. He has a new life. Maybe he is even abroad by now." The words left a bad taste in her mouth, but she forced herself to continue. "He's not coming back, *is he*?" Josiah did not speak and, despite her best efforts, it felt as though the next words stuck in her throat. "Besides, if he comes back, he may even be married and have a family of his own, and his feelings would have changed."

Josiah placed his hand on hers. "I don't think yours have, though. Maybe, I am mistaken," he added quickly, seeing her distress. "I have no objection to Alex. He seems to be a good man. My concern is with his father. Cerberus is something entirely different." He shook his head and sighed. "He is a cruel man and disliked by many people. I am not suggesting that that Alex is the same, but you should be careful."

Was it really so obvious? She realized how transparent she must be to him, even though she had tried to push the feelings away, tell herself that time had altered her judgment, and that if Jevan returned, he would be a stranger to her. It was clear that she could deceive herself, but not her father. She looked at him anxiously. "I would give anything to be with Jevan again, but he's not here, and how long should I wait? I live my life, hoping that he will return, and yet, year after year he stays away," she said sorrowfully. "I hurt him badly. I may have been a child, but he won't forget the things I said to him." She paused for a moment, collecting her thoughts. "Alex is different. I like him a lot. He makes me happy when I am with him and, even though we are worlds apart, we think alike in many ways." She sighed. "You shouldn't worry, Father, we are just friends. I know it's an odd friendship, given our class difference, but as you say, his father will probably make Alex see sense and, sooner or later, put an end to it anyway." She frowned for a moment. "Although, Alex has invited me to dinner, and to meet his father, should I refuse the invitation?" She thought she saw a curious shadow pass across her father's face, but perhaps it was just the flickering light of the candles.

"I would not forbid you to go. It is your choice. I share your sentiment, and Cerberus will not want you around his son for long. He may be older now, although he still carries considerable weight around these parts, and it would be wise not to become an enemy of him. I am surprised he has tolerated the situation for this long, I just hope he does not have his own plan."

"What do you mean?"

Jophiel smiled. He didn't want to alarm her unduly. "I just ask that you think long and hard about any decision you make regarding Alex."

Annabel gave him a blank look, not understanding his meaning.

Josiah sighed. "I have seen the way Alex looks at you, Annabel. I see that he regards you with a lot more than just friendship and, sooner or later, I feel that he will ask you to be his wife. It may be without Cerberus's blessing, even so, if he asks me for your hand in marriage, I have to be certain that I am doing the right thing."

"He hasn't asked me," she said in a shocked voice, shaking her head. "He won't ask me."

"It's an odd situation, I agree. Although I can think of no other reason that he would wish you to meet his father in such a formal manner."

⌘

Gothelstone Manor House was foreboding. It felt austere, cheerless, and unfriendly. The mansion, for that was what it was, had been home to many generations of the Saltonstall family, and there had been many strange stories and rumors associated with the property. Annabel had only stepped into the great hall a couple of times, while waiting for Alex. This was where she now stood, after alighting from one of Gothel-stone's impressive carriages. She looked up at the grand staircase and immediately Alex came into view. He ran briskly down the steps to greet her.

"Annabel, you look beautiful," he said, as he reached her side and took her hand.

"Hardly silk or satin," she said, glancing down at her dress.

It was pale green, a square-cut low bodice with accordion pleated chiffon, which followed the curve of her figure perfectly. Her hair was pulled back at the sides and secured by combs, leaving the majority of it to hang loosely down her back.

"You are a picture just as you are," Alex said appreciatively, drawing her hand to his mouth and placing a kiss on it. She tried not to blush, although tonight, Alex's attention was powerful. He led her farther through the great hall and then down a wide passageway where the walls were adorned with portraits of the distant ancestors.

More pictures hung in the dining room. Three table settings were arranged upon the long dining table, reminding Annabel of the difficulties that might come. They walked alongside the portraits, and Alex reeled off their names proudly, even though most had brass name plaques with dates inscribed upon them. The portraits hung in pairs, and he started with the most distant ancestors.

"Lucia and Eliza, then Gabriel and Anne."

She could see a distant resemblance to Alex, but more so in his father, and some of the personages shared startling similarities. She peered closer. It was in the eyes. They looked as though there was something foreboding reflected in them. Their mouths had an illusion of a smile, except beneath the falseness, they were set in thin cruel lines. She looked away before Alex perceived her chill.

"This is Zachariah and his wife Maria," he continued, "and these are my great grandparents, Anael and Elsbeth, and then of course my father Cerberus, and Elizabeth, my mother," Alex concluded quickly.

Despite her discomfort, she could not help than to draw

toward Cerberus's portrait, and the fact that he looked considerably younger and more handsome than the man she knew today. Once they came to the end, she walked backward staring at the portraits again, and she did not linger on the men, as she noticed the women were all breathtakingly beautiful.

"These are all on your father's side, are there no portraits on your mother's side?" she asked, looking back at Alex curiously. "They all had uncommon names, except you."

Alex grinned. "They broke with tradition when I was named. Alexander was my mother's father's name."

He appeared to ignore her other comment. She did not press the matter as they walked through into the drawing room, where the furniture was pleasingly situated and elegant, yet comfortable looking.

"Please take a seat." He indicated a chair. "My father will be here in a few moments."

Annabel sat gingerly at the edge of a couch and looked up at a large fireplace with an impressive detailed over mantle. Alex turned to a desk that was stacked with several sheets of paper. Various quills rested in a silver holder. Out of the top drawer, he took a miniature silver frame and handed it to her. "This is a portrait of my mother as a young girl. There is a lock of her hair in the case on the other side. It's the only thing I have left of her," he said hesitantly. "I thought you might like to see it."

"I am glad to see it. She was really beautiful," Annabel said, handing the frame back to him. She wanted to question him about her, but just then, a cold shiver ran over her skin, and the air felt suddenly chilled, as if something had sensed her next line of questioning and was warning against it. She tried to ignore the feeling, especially as Alex seemed unaware of any eerie sensation in the room

"Where is your father?" she asked instead, looking up at him.

"He is still getting dressed for dinner," Alex replied, noticing her discomfort. "Don't look so worried. Everything will be fine."

Their voices seemed strangely dead in this room. In fact,

none of the rooms had any trace of an echo. The manor was decorated with thick carpets, with the windows draped in heavy fabrics, and even the papered walls further served to deaden any possible reverberation.

Alex walked to the fireplace and picked up a poker. He prodded the dying embers and made a noise of aggravation when nothing sprang to life. He half turned. "Sorry," he murmured with a smile. "It is cold in here, isn't it?" He turned back and pulled on a handle set into the wall at the side of the fireplace. A distant bell sounded far below them. "For summoning the servants," he explained.

Annabel nodded, mildly interested at the network of bells she supposed must run throughout this house, and tried to push the previous nonsensical thoughts from her mind. Although the atmosphere remained oppressive, and she was glad when, a moment later, the door opened and a tall gray-haired man entered. The stiff starched collar he wore gave his head a comical perch.

"You rang, Master Alex."

"Ah, Alfred, Miss Taylor and I would like a fire. Please send the maid up at once."

Alfred tipped his head in acknowledgement and walked out of the room. Annabel was quietly amused. She had never been in a house with servants before, and it seemed strange that their whole life revolved around the wants and needs of their master. Alfred had barely disappeared and closed the door when it opened again.

Cerberus Saltonstall entered the room. His gaze swept over his son in the briefest acknowledgement, and then those cold ice blue eyes rested on her. Instinctively, she got to her feet and stared back at him. She felt tense, especially when his mouth did not rise in the slightest. It was set in a hard, rigid line, just like those portraits. Etiquette reminded her that she should lower her eyes and curtsy. Even so, she struggled to manage that. Thankfully, Alex came to her rescue.

"Father, this is Annabel Taylor."

Released from Cerberus stare for a second, she dropped her eyes and bobbed a fraction. Cerberus eyes swept over her, regarding her with what she took to be a disapproving look, then he seemed to remember that he had to pretend to be civil.

"My son did not exaggerate when he spoke of your beauty, although I have seen you before in the village, haven't I?"

Annabel winced inwardly. "Yes, I believe there was an occasion when I saw you also—in the apothecary," she ventured.

Cerberus eyes displayed no emotion. It seemed a chore for him to even converse with her.

She was determined, for Alex's sake, to be polite. "I understand that you do not come into Rookwood that often."

"No, that is what my servants are for." Hs eyes glittered dangerously as he saw her disdainful expression. "I can sense our way of life and rich vices horrify you," he observed candidly.

"Not at all. it is merely different from how I was raised."

Cerberus smirked. "I understand. After all, I don't suppose a girl of your—upbringing—is accustomed to being around society, or has the necessary skills to be in accomplished company. Do you even play the piano?" he said, giving her a questioning look.

"No," she whispered, feeling suddenly out of her depth, as he gestured to a frame containing an exquisite piece of needlework.

"My mother completed that when she was fifteen."

"It's beautiful," Annabel said admiringly, wondering why Cerberus was drawing her attention to it.

"Can *you* embroider?" There was a noticeable amount of sarcasm.

"No," she said warily.

Clearly he wanted to show Alex, just how unaccomplished his guest was. There followed an awkward silence for a moment. Annabel was shocked by Cerberus's tactics and vividly aware that he didn't care about being civil. Alex, clearly taken aback by his father's blunt approach, jumped to her defense.

"Father, Annabel can do a great many other things," he said. "She is a great story teller. She is a quick learner and can even charm bees."

Cerberus did not speak. He made a noise of contempt and

suppressed the next words out of his mouth, as clearly they would not have been agreeable. He saw that his son would quickly defend her and was mildly annoyed as he moved closer to the non-existent fire. His gaze was not as fixed as before, but he still regarded her with suspicion. To Annabel's way of thinking, he was most likely questioning the dubious nature of her entire existence. When his eyes traveled over her as if she had just crawled out of a gutter, his look made her mindful that her clothes, although her best, were not the fine silks and satins that most ladies of good social standing wore. The oppression of the room pressed harder upon her, even more since Cerberus had entered.

Annabel shivered and Alex muttered under his breath something about, damn servants.

"I'll go and see what the delay is. It's freezing in this room," he said, smiling warmly at her. He must have seen the panic in her eyes, as he added, "I'll be back in a few minutes," and smiled reassuringly at her.

He seemed oblivious to the animosity radiating from Cerberus, although, she caught the prolonged look he gave his father as he walked out the door. Annabel heard him shouting for Alfred and then there were muffled voices. She sat on the couch again, feeling angry with herself that she had even agreed to come here. She felt extremely self-conscious, and it was shockingly apparent that Cerberus must have felt he was on a winning streak and was not about to let her get too comfortable.

"You have certainly made an impression on my son's heart and won his admiration."

"You will have to speak to Alex about that, for it was not my intention."

"No, perhaps not. Sometimes there is no accounting for these things. It comes down to just a matter of taste," he said, frowning and lowering his eyes for a few moments. "I was sorry to learn of your mother's illness. I heard it was influenza."

His tone had softened and, for a brief moment, she sensed genuine sorrow in his voice.

She stared at him with suspicion. "Yes, it was the influenza, and mercifully she did not suffer greatly," she replied, thinking that perhaps he did have an ounce of compassion in him after all. Then a thought struck her. "You knew my mother?" It was difficult to keep her tone even.

Cerberus shrugged indifferently. "I was surprised that, after your mother died, you and your father did not end up in the workhouse," he said, meeting her bewildered gaze with his own stony one.

Annabel bristled with anger, and it was an effort to control the tone of her voice. "We make a very good living from our bees," she said icily, "and the workhouse has never been an option for my family." She felt furious now and had half a mind to leave, although, something inside resolved that she should never let him get the better of her. He was obviously pushing her, testing her limits, trying to invoke something. She realized that she suddenly no longer felt intimidated.

"Ah, the bees." He pressed his lips together and forced a bitter smile. "Personally, I have never seen much use for the damn creatures. Nearly cost Alex his life. If I had my way, I would destroy every last hive."

Annabel narrowed her eyes, and her voice did not waver. "And yet you quite happily use the products that bees produce," she said, gesturing to the several fine beeswax candles around the room. "And I don't suppose you mind taking honey to sweeten your food." She was on a roll, and her voice gained considerable momentum. "I may not be able to play a piano or embroider, but I can read and write." She saw Cerberus's eyes lift a fraction. "And I can cook and take very good care of myself and my father."

"All are useless things for a lady of a house. That's what servants are for," he replied disagreeably. "But for once, I am surprised. I see you have spirit and with your limited knowledge you have taught yourself to understand what you observe. Most are too ignorant to understand anything of the world."

"You are right. I understand very well," she said evenly. "You talk of being accomplished, and your suggestions are indulgent things, useful only in a superficial way. My accomplishments are genuine and valuable in the real world, for I can brew concoctions and cure the sick. I can make remedies and heal with herbs and plants. All are more useful things than playing a piano," she said triumphantly.

Cerberus eyes widened, and he stared at her for a full minute. His expression was like stone and, finally, he spewed the venom. "Another witch. I might have known!"

With that startling observation, Cerberus exited the room, leaving Annabel staring after him in astonishment. Alex returned soon after, accompanied by a servant, who hastily made up the fire.

"Where did my father go?"

Annabel shrugged. "I don't know. He doesn't like me," she said tensely.

"My father doesn't like anyone," Alex remarked bemused. "Don't worry. His bark is far worse than his bite."

Annabel wasn't so sure. There was definite malevolence in Cerberus's words. His dislike of her was obvious, although, his parting words really alarmed her. Exactly what did he know? She couldn't bring herself to discuss it with Alex. Instead, they chatted for a few minutes and, warmed now by the blazing fire, the room took on a far more appealing quality. Annabel was noticeably quiet and subdued, too distracted at the prospect of dinner. Just the thought of having to sit through an entire meal with Cerberus troubled her greatly.

Thankfully, it was not quite as bad as she had imagined, and that had a lot to do with Alex. He talked about interesting places he had visited with his friends. He talked about the garden and asked her opinion on extending the kitchen garden. Cerberus only injected a few words here and there, and Annabel responded simply to anything that he asked of her. She was greatly relieved when dessert was finished and Cerberus announced he was retiring early. She was glad that he barely acknowledged her when he left the room. Alex took one look at her and his face broadened into a wide grin. "Was it really that bad?"

She shook her head. "Much worse." And then she laughed.

"Please don't ask me to dinner again," she said in all seriousness.

Alex merely smiled without answering and then moved his chair closer to hers. "You know, I don't often dine with him. I think these days he prefers his own company. He tends to keep to his own wing of the house."

"This house must be huge," she said, thinking how grand it must have been to grow up in a mansion such as this, compared to her father's humble cottage.

"It is. I think about a hundred and seven rooms. But we don't use many of them now, and some are left just the way they were when my mother left." It was odd to hear Alex talk of his mother, and it reminded Annabel that Cerberus had been married. That detail seemed strange. Annabel couldn't imagine what kind of woman had loved Cerberus, for his heart was frozen.

"What happened to your mother, Alex?"

He betrayed a faint touch of pain when he spoke. "I was very young. She was sick." He caught her questioning look. "You know, ill in the head, madness, they said. My memory of her is...confused. I don't remember her sickness, but I was just a child. As I got older, the servants would make comments when they thought I wasn't in the vicinity. I believe she heard voices and saw things."

Annabel felt a shiver run down her spine and looked up at the portraits. Their cold staring eyes did nothing to improve her perception. "Alex, do you mind if we go back to the drawing room? It is a little cold in here," she asked, feeling like she should offer some explanation.

Alex immediately stood. "You should have said before," he said, offering her his arm.

The rest of the evening wore on, and they casually chatted about the house and servants, and what it was like to grow up in this house.

Annabel looked up at the mantle clock as it began to chime. The hands showed that it was eleven o'clock. She had not realized it was so late. "I should be going home," she said, "my father will be worried."

"I'll call a carriage and escort you home."

"No, you don't have to," she assured him hurriedly. "I am quite capable of riding in a carriage alone."

"Nonsense, you have accused me several times now of not behaving like a gentleman, so tonight I firmly mean to prove you wrong."

Chapter 13

The Proposal

In the following week, affairs of the estate kept Alex and her apart. In his absence, Annabel was happy enough. His way of life was not something that she was altogether comfortable with, even if it was easy to be impressed with the grandeur of the mansion. It was, after all, the most imposing house she had ever set foot in, and if she was being honest with herself, she found the whole idea of being waited upon distasteful, and both the building and a certain occupant completely disagreeable. Even she had to admit that it had been fun for a while to dress in her best clothes and pretend that she was accustomed to riding in expensive carriages or eating from exquisite fine china. When she had asked Alex not to invite her to dinner again, it wasn't entirely all to do with Cerberus.

She and Alex were worlds apart. Annabel knew that well enough, and Alex was not stupid. Deep down he knew it, too. Whatever her father believed Alex might have asked of her, she knew he was wrong.

She was perhaps nothing more than an interesting interlude in Alex's life, and one day soon, he would remember that fact. Cerberus would remind him. If he hadn't already done so, he would declare she was not suitable company and certainly not a potential daughter-in-law. Besides that, her father's senses served him well, and his perception haunted her.

If she was that easy to read, could Alex see that too?

One morning when Annabel was up to her elbows in flour, there was a knock at the cottage door. Josiah was out in the fields and she felt flustered as she realized the mess she had created. She called out anyway. "The door's open."

The door opened and Alex's figure allowed a perfect halo of light to surround him as he stepped from the bright morning into the cottage. His mouth widened into a grin as he saw her clothes were peppered with bread mixture and streaks of flour smeared down one side of her face.

"We really need to get you a cook," he said, stepping closer to her and plucking a large crumb from her hair.

"I don't need one. I am more than capable," Annabel said, a little affronted by his remark and the fact that he had caught her in such a state.

He smiled, brushed an invisible crumb from a nearby chair, and sat down. "I am certain you are very capable. It's your methods that are a little unconventional," he said with a knowing expression.

"And since when did you know so much about bread making?"

"Actually, nothing. I didn't come here to talk about bread." He paused. "I have thought about you all week," he said, waiting for a response.

Annabel did not answer. She finished putting the bread into its tin and placed it in the oven before she turned back to Alex.

"Where have you been, anyway?"

"I've been in Bath and attending tedious meetings with lawyers." He shrugged his shoulders. "Concerning lands on the estate, nothing that would interest you," he said dismissively, settling back on the chair and gazing toward the window. "It's such a beautiful morning, and I thought you might like to ride with me."

"The bread won't be ready for a while and I can't leave yet," she replied a little curtly.

"Then I'll wait, and, in the meantime you can tell me just how much you have missed me this past week."

Annabel could not keep from laughing. "How do you know

I missed you at all? And to be honest, I've been very busy myself."

Alex's eyes narrowed. "With what?"

"The bees, general business matters, nothing that would interest you," she said, meeting his look straight on.

Alex's mouth turned up in a smile as he stood up. Annabel
did not move as he stepped close to her, and she did not resist
as he kissed her lightly on the lips.

"Are you trying to tell me that you didn't miss me one little
bit?"

She deliberately took her time in answering the question.
"Maybe just a little," she said, smiling.

Alex, satisfied with her answer, pulled her close to him,
unconcerned as flour migrated from her skin to his dark riding
jacket.

She pulled back. "Sorry, I have to go and change, look at
your clothes."

Alex looked down and lightly brushed the flour from him.
"Perhaps you should," he said, noticeably warming to that
thought.

Annabel ran up the staircase and into her bedroom. She
quickly stepped out of the spoiled dress and ran a brush
through the tangled mass of hair that concealed even more
mixture. She splashed water over her face and scrubbed her
hands and nails with soap. Then she selected a pale blue dress
that was flattering to her figure and pleasing against her coloring. She smiled in satisfaction at her reflection and went to
join Alex.

ოჳოჳ

It was late in the afternoon by the time they reached the
river. They tethered the horses and walked toward a Rowan
tree situated on the riverbank. Its bright red berries reflected
perfectly in the dark water below them, and the tree offered
welcome shade from the sun's blinding rays. Annabel sat on
the grass and watched as the horses gulped noisily from the
river. She removed her shoes and lowered her feet into the

cool water. Alex sat down bedside her. He had long since removed his jacket and rolled his shirtsleeves up past his elbows. She thought that he looked much more relaxed now as
he turned toward her.

"You haven't yet told me what you thought of my house,"
he remarked casually.

She caught a note of anxiety and bit her lip, thinking of the
most tactful words to use. "It's an impressive house."

"But did you like it?"

She took a deep breath. There really was no getting around
this. "Do you want me to be honest?" she said staring at him.

"Of course," he answered with a certain amount of wariness in his voice.

"I thought that it was cold. It felt unfriendly and perhaps a
little frightening."

Alex laughed. His previous tension seemed to have vanished. "I can see how a first impression can be deceiving, and
I know that my father did not help matters. He can be difficult.
Gothelstone is an amazing house, and you are just not used to
such vast rooms. The trouble is, it is not used as it should be,
and we no longer live in it properly. Once it was filled with
people. In past generations, great galas and lavish parties were
held, and it was filled with music and laughter—"

"Not in your lifetime surely?" Annabel interrupted. She did
not think that Cerberus could be capable of such frivolity.

"No that's true," Alex agreed. "Stories have been handed
down. I have seen old records of the sumptuous meals they
served, and the important guest lists. The house was alive
once, and it could happen again." He paused for a long moment. "All it needs is the right woman's touch."

Annabel had been gazing at the waters reflection. Now she
turned. As Alex's eyes settled on her, she blinked, making the
obvious connections. Her throat was dry and the day seemed
warmer than ever.

"Annabel, I am certain you know how I feel about you. I
believe that being in my company also makes you happy."

Annabel froze, and a flicker of panic crossed her mind. Josiah's observations had been correct. She instantly dropped

her gaze back to the water. Her instinct was to jump up and run far away. She did not want to hear these words. She also could not block them out. She felt paralyzed, unable to utter a sound.

"You and I we make a perfect match," he continued, "and I have loved you from that very first day." He picked up her hand. She was compelled to look again into his eyes. They were intense, shining with eagerness and sincerity. His look only made her feel ten times worse. "Annabel, will you be my wife?"

She stared dumbly, masking the panic. She did like him. She liked him a lot and liked being in his company, and she was happy to flirt with him, kiss him even, but anything else was going too far. She hated to think that she had caused him to believe marriage could even be an option. After all, any relationship with him was doomed. He must see that, she thought, he wasn't stupid. It was forbidden by society. Certainly, it would not be tolerated by Cerberus, which when she thought about it, saying yes had a dangerous appeal, a way of getting back at Alex's father. However, she could not be that cruel to Alex. He did not make her heart soar or make her tremble inside. She did not long for his touch. He did not make her feel the way Jevan had.

She knew that most marriages were not like her own parents. They had really loved each other. Most were just compatible, some happy, some just convenient, but there were not many that were intense enough that you would kill or die for that other person. As charming as Alex could be, she could never have those feelings for him.

Alex was still waiting for her response, and she wished herself miles away, anywhere, other than sitting on this riverbank with him.

"Alex, you do make me happy when I am with you." She swallowed nervously. "But we are not a perfect match, far from it," she said, shaking her head. "You don't know me, not really. No, don't deny it," she scolded gently, as he started to speak. "You must understand that I could not fit into your world any more than you could fit into mine. Besides all of that, I am not ready for marriage." She felt his grip tighten on her and saw a flash of resentment lurking in his eyes. She tried to pull her hand away. He did not surrender it. "I can't, Alex, you must see that."

"You're wrong. You could fit into my world, and I am offering you a wonderful prospect, an opportunity to elevate yourself," he said, with a slight edge to his voice. "Most girls, far better bred than you, would jump at this offer."

This time Annabel snatched her hand away and instantly sprang to her feet. "Then go and ask one of them!" she said hotly, turning from him.

Alex was already on his feet and caught her arm "Annabel, I'm sorry. I didn't mean it to come out like that. You have always confused my thoughts. I can't always articulate clearly when I am with you, and I only know one thing for certain. I want you to be my wife. I love you, Annabel, and I cannot imagine being with any other now that I have met you," he said, with a brief smile, "although I am not blind to the fact that you do not feel quite the same way about me. But you will," he said confidently, nodding his head. "You will come to really love me."

Annabel felt sad to see the sincerity in his eyes and hear his heartfelt plea. Deep down she knew he loved her. She wished now she had not allowed their friendship to blossom. She knew she should have rebuked him at every meeting, for now it had become an impossible situation. "Don't you see, Alex? Your life is so different from mine," she said softly. "We are worlds apart, and you need a wife who has been groomed to be a lady, someone capable of entertaining and being the perfect hostess, someone to impress your father and your friends. If I married you, your father would ridicule me. I wouldn't know the correct things to say and couldn't possibly give orders to an army of servants, or expect them to wait on me hand and foot." She paused to catch her breath. "Alex, you know that's not in my nature, and it's not the person I want to be either."

Her refusal appeared forgotten as Alex's face softened.

"I am not asking you to change. I know the prospect must

be daunting, and I don't want you to change. This girl standing in front of me right now is the Annabel I love. What is wrong with broadening your skills a little, or dressing in fine clothes, and having servants to attend to your every need? You see servitude as something terrible. It's not. My servants are treated well, they have a roof over their head, and they have good food in their stomachs. They do not have to go into the fields to labor and earn barely enough to keep themselves from starvation. They have a good life, better than most in their class."

"That's just it, Alex, class. You judge them by their class. As I will be judged, and everyone will question your choice. You will be laughed at and I will be shunned."

"That won't happen," he said adamantly. "Say yes, Annabel," he urged, "I will treat you like a queen and so will everybody else."

Annabel stared at him in disbelief. "Even Cerberus?"

Alex nodded. "Even he will show you the respect you deserve when you are my wife. We can be happy together. I will make you happy, I promise."

She turned slightly. She really didn't want to hurt him, but he had left her with no other choice. "Alex, you mean a lot to me, you really do. I cannot say, yes," she said, taking his hand and hoping that he didn't hate her too much. "Please understand." She didn't often cry. Even so, at this moment she had to will the tears not to fall, as the pain she was inflicting was evident in his eyes and in the tremble of his hand as his finger ran across the scar on her palm.

"You never told me what happened to your hand?"

She looked down at the scar and caught her breath. It struck a chord in her heart and hardened her heart against him. She shrugged lightly. "It got caught on a bramble, when I was a child."

Alex stared at the scar for a moment longer. "It's deep, it must have really hurt."

Annabel pulled her hand away. The scar was just another reminder of why she could not say yes.

Alex's eyes rose to meet hers. He saw her determination, a look which mirrored his own. "I always get what I want Annabel," he said firmly, his voice assured. "You can be certain of it."

She stared at him, a little taken aback. It sounded like a threat, even if his eyes were sparkling and his smile was warm. "And I know my own mind," she said icily.

"Ah, but your mind will change, one way or another."

Chapter 14

The Homecoming

In the weeks that followed, Annabel could not help notice the marked difference in Alex. At first, she wondered if he was tiring of her company and sadly thought that might be for the best, although, on the surface, he seemed as attentive as ever. She guessed he contemplated a great deal, and that the affairs of the Gothelstone estate were often on his mind.

The estate was sectioned into various farms, a water mill, and several hundred acres of land that was worked by the tenants who lived in the cottages of Gothelstone Village, along with neighboring Rookwood. There was also a quarry, where the distinctive red stone was extracted. It was then sold farther afield. Alex rarely discussed the business side of things with her, and she did not like to pry into what was, after all, none of her business.

Then again, after refusing his proposal, she was happy that he had so many other things to occupy his mind. And still mindful of his ominous words, she tried not to let the resentment show. But that was beginning to prove difficult. Alex believed the answer she had given was merely a temporarily glitch and behaved with an arrogant certainty that a change of mind was merely a matter of time. Yet she knew Cerberus would never consent to such an arrangement, and Alex was a fool to believe otherwise.

Another day brought Alex to the cottage again. Josiah was

away for the day and Annabel was carefully pouring wax into candle molds. Alex sat and watched her for a while. He drummed his fingers on the table, and she sensed his impatience. She readied herself for another proposal. This time she would not be caught off guard. She would be adamant that her mind could not be swayed. And, although she had never witnessed Alex's temper, her own determination was more powerful. She bided her time, waiting for him to try to broach the subject and was mildly surprised when he suddenly asked:

"How long has your father owned Honeymead?"

Annabel looked up from the candles. "My great grandfather brought the land, and my grandfather built the cottage. Why?"

"I was just wondering."

Annabel raised her eyebrow, sensing some other reason. Alex shifted uncomfortably and stopped drumming. "I was wondering if your father would like to sell."

Annabel stared at him for a long moment, startled by the unexpected question. "Are you serious?" she said, half hoping he would smile or indicate that it was some sort of joke. She could not imagine where this train of thought might lead.

"Of course." There was no smile.

Annabel shook her head. "Why do you think he would consider selling? This is our home."

"I would make a good offer, and he could live out the rest of his life here, and eventually the property would revert back to the estate."

Annabel felt her heartbeat quicken. She narrowed her eyes and tried not to feel panic at Alex's words. "What do you need more land for? You already have hundreds of acres."

"True," he agreed, "then again, if I bought Honeymead, we would own all the land up to the coast. I would not have to worry about easements rights in the future."

At Annabel's puzzled look, he continued. "Perhaps you don't know that an easement was granted many years ago which allowed access to this property. That right of way runs over the Gothelstone estate lands and, on talking to the estate manager, it seems prudent to reunite Gothelstone with all its original lands." He paused for a moment. "Honeymead is the only thing that stands in the way. Besides, it would make things a lot simpler for the future."

"I don't see that there's a problem," Annabel said defensively. "It's never been a problem in my father's lifetime. Our few acres don't even affect the estate or the work you do."

Alex sighed. "It's a legal matter that I don't expect you to understand. I am only trying to secure your father's future and relieve him of any worries of what may happen to this property after his death. Don't look like that, Annabel, I am thinking of your future too."

"You mean the future of Mrs. Annabel Saltonstall?"

"Well, it is inevitable, isn't it?"

Annabel banged the bottle she was holding on the table, spilling the contents. Her eyes blazing, she ignored the liquid that ran onto the floor. "No it isn't, Alex. How can you be so arrogant? I said no, remember?"

Alex stood abruptly. "Sometimes you are so difficult!" he said coldly. "You know I want to build a new road over the estate, one that doesn't come this far, and I could eradicate the old one. I could quite easily do it."

Annabel felt the blood run to her face as the heat flushed over her skin. Her eyes flashed with anger. "You can't deny us access to our own property, no matter how influential your father is or you think you are. There are laws in this country."

"Yes, there are, and it's people like my father who know how to influence the lawmakers in this county as well," he said smugly.

Annabel suppressed the urge to tell him to leave. Her mind was stretched too far, because the implications were frightening, and Alex was turning on her in the worst possible way.

"I thought, I knew you," she said with contempt. "I believed that, despite your father, deep down you were good, and you really had a care for my feelings." She shook her head in dismay. "Today, I can see your true side. You are willing to use blackmail as a weapon against me and my father, and it is so obvious to me now that, deep down, you are just like Cerberus."

The tension was thick enough to cut with a knife as Alex sprang forward and grasped her shoulders, filling Annabel's heart with dread. "Why can't you see that I will do anything to make you change your mind?"

She stared into his eyes, and he stared back, with a crazed look that she did not recognize.

"Let go of me Alex," she said calmly, and to her surprise, he released her immediately. She stared at him in shock. He was no longer the Alex she had laughed and ridden with, or liked to spend time in his company, today he was different altogether. "Why the urgency?" she said slowly, thinking about the noticeable change in him. "First, when you proposed, it felt like you were driven to get the right answer at all cost, and today you seem overly fraught that I should marry you. Why? I can't believe it's based on love. There is something else."

Alex shook his head and ran his fingers through his hair in agitation. "You are wrong. I do love you, I really do, Annabel," he said, sitting down. He put his head in his hands. He looked vulnerable and as if he had the weight of the world on his shoulders. When he looked up at her, she saw the sincerity in his eyes.

All previous thoughts flew from her mind, her harshness melted away. and she down in a chair close to him. "Alex, you have to tell me the real reason."

He sighed heavily, rubbing his forehead, and then took her hand. "I do love you, truly. From the very first day I first met you, I have never lied about that. I feel a real connection with you." He hesitated for a moment. "And with all my heart I want us to be married. I am not ignorant to the fact that it is a big step for you, and you need time to grow accustomed to the idea, which I can be content with, but what I can be content with others cannot." Alex saw her brow furrow in confusion. "The urgency is because of my father."

Nothing could have surprised Annabel more and her eyes flew open wide in surprise.

"He wants the marriage to happen soon."

Annabel pulled her hand back sharply. "You have told him,

that it's *me* you want to marry." She shook her head. "And he approves?" She couldn't believe those words. Cerberus hated her, and he would not want her married to his only son, let alone actually live under his roof.

"He knows how I feel about you," Alex explained simply. "I told you that his bark is worse than his bite. He will accept my choice. It has been agreed. He is old. He wants to see an heir born before he dies. That's not such a terrible reason, is it? Despite what you may think, he does hold a certain admiration for you."

Annabel stood. Then she sat down again. The enormity of Alex's words had turned her legs to jelly. Cerberus wasn't that old. In fact, he was not much older than her own father. She tried to resist the image of a child, her child, sitting on Cerberus's lap, and a shiver ran through her. Why was that such an ugly thought? Alex's words had little truth to them. Cerberus did not have any admiration for her, only contempt, and she struggled to compose the thoughts in her head. "Alex, you know I won't be pushed into anything against my will. Your attempts to force my hand are posing impossible situations for me to consider. You must see that?" She hesitated for a moment. "Perhaps you are confused in your feelings for me. One minute you are telling me that you love me, and the next blackmailing me. I thought we were friends. How can I even trust you when you behave like that?"

Alex stood, frowning. He readjusted his jacket and then looked back at her. "I am not confused in my feelings for you," he said adamantly. "We are more than just friends. You know that as well as I." He sighed heavily. "Just say yes, Annabel. We are meant to be together. You can deny it all you like, but you must know it's a certainty."

"Why is it a certainty? There is no law that says I have to marry you."

Alex's lip curled into a smile. "Because there is no-one else in your life. Without your father, you have nothing, and I would not see you all alone in this world, struggling to scratch a living, merely a mile from where I live. Perhaps you have not even considered your future. I have. I see the whole picture. My words may anger you, but I speak only out of love, not spite."

Annabel shook her head. "My life is fine, just as it is. I don't need anyone looking out for me, and my father will be around for a long time to come, so that should not concern you either."

"For goodness sake, Annabel, I do not want to fight with you, I want to be with you. I can give you everything, and I can make you happy. Why won't you at least meet me half way?"

"There is no half way, and I am not your responsibility. I'm not easily manipulated and am shocked that you would lower yourself to such underhand tactics."

"You misunderstand, as usual," he growled impatiently.

"No, I don't. And don't treat me like some ignorant child. I am fully aware of what you want. Just when have you stopped to consider what I want?"

Alex turned and leaned against the window. "I do," he said in a clear voice, "all the time." He turned away from the window and walked back to the door. "Please reconsider, Annabel," he said, gazing at her earnestly, "and everything will be all right."

Alex left the cottage and strode away.

Annabel was still reeling from what had just occurred. She wanted to see her father, and she wished he would come home right now. Then she remembered that before he had left, he told her that he would be away most of the day. Instead, she spent the rest of the morning reliving the conversation.

By mid-afternoon, the cottage felt stifling. Her head was in turmoil as she loaded the trap with various bits and pieces she would sell in Rookwood. Even though, her heart wasn't in it, and she didn't really feel like talking to anybody, she forced herself to carry on. With the trap loaded and her onboard, April began trotting patiently toward the village. All the while Annabel voiced her concerns aloud. She wished her horse could talk and offer some reasonable advice. She consoled herself that Jophiel would listen and give her an impartial opinion, better than her father could. In fact, she was certain, by now, that she should not even mention this morning's conversation to Josiah. He would be upset and she convinced herself that Alex had merely been testing the waters to see how far he could push, before she gave in completely. She was certain that most of what he had said were lies. After all, a man like Cerberus could never show admiration to anyone, least of all to someone like her.

Caught up in her own thoughts, she did not realize that April had slowed to barely a walking pace. The trap jerked and the reins tightened in her hand, Annabel saw April's lopsided stance. She pulled up on the reins and jumped down beside her. April was bending her leg as if in pain. When Annabel bent down and attentively touched the favored leg, she felt distinct swelling and heat from the limb.

"I'm so sorry, April. I didn't realize," she said, standing up straighter. The day finally became too much to bear, and she burst into tears. Everything seemed to weigh her down. She buried her head in April's mane, feeling comforted at her closeness to the horse. Eventually she lifted her head and April nuzzled her gently. She patted the horse's head lovingly, reassured her that everything would be all right, and then picked up the reins.

"I know it hurts. Jophiel will know what to do." Annabel walked as slowly as was possible and April leaned toward her with every painful step, but she listened to her mistress's soothing words and did not falter. They were not that far from Rookwood, and little by little, they made their way through the high street and down to the forge.

Annabel tethered April to the side of the forge and fetched the water bucket for her to drink. She could already hear the metal spitting and the hammer crashing into metal as Jophiel worked.

"I'll be back soon," she told April and then walked through the old door. Jophiel was somewhere in the back room. She did not want to interrupt him, so she leaned against the wooden workbench and waited for him to finish. A moment later, everything went quiet. Annabel started to walk toward the door, just as it opened.

"Jophiel, can you look at April?" she began, looking through the gloom.

The figure that emerged from the darkness was not Jophiel. He was taller with longer hair and darker eyes. Annabel's next breath caught in her throat and her heart felt as though it stopped beating.

Jevan came closer, towering over her. Instinctively, she took a step backward.

"I would know that voice anywhere."

His voice was deeper, smoother, and assured, his expression unreadable. He was the same, but at the same time so different from the boy she had known years before. Although his face had matured pleasingly, it was harder, his cheekbones were more prominent, and his eyes disturbed her. There was an intense quality that not only felt as though they saw every thought in her head, his look ignited a charge that forged a powerful longing throughout all her senses, and she trembled in spite of herself.

"You've changed." It was the only thing she could think to say.

"What did you expect?" he answered a little abruptly.

His dark eyes did not release hers as he came unbearably close. Half of her wanted to step back, the other half wanted to move closer still. Her heart pounded heavily in her chest, and she clasped her hands tightly to ease the trembling.

"April's leg—there's something wrong with April's leg," she said for want of something to say that would take his attention away from her.

Jevan's eyes continued to pierce through her head, unnerving her completely for a while longer until finally he dropped his gaze, and she began to breath properly again. Moving past her, he inclined his head so that his face was inches from hers as he ducked lower than necessary under the wooden beam. Annabel's throat went dry, as just a trace of a smile hovered on his lips. Then she was alone in the forge and numbed by the shock of seeing him again. She stood motionless for a few moments, collecting the thoughts that were spinning out of control, then turned and followed him outside.

Jevan was already on his knees before April. His hand was running down the length of the afflicted leg, and Annabel tried not to notice that, in the sunlight, his hair was the color of ebony. It was still long, but less untidy, and she unexpectedly remembered the feel of it against her skin. Jevan stood and turned to her. Out of the forge, he seemed even taller. His physique was powerful and lean and his skin tanned, as if he had spent a lot of time in the sun.

"She is lame. Didn't you notice this before..." His voice was accusing, and it trailed off into silence as he stared down at her.

There was so much to say to him, but she could not think of the right thing to say. She just shook her head.

"Leave her here. She can stay in one of the stables." His mouth was set in a firm line, no hint of a smile now. He turned back to April and began untying the straps that bound her to the trap.

"I have to get these things home," Annabel said, remembering the loaded trap. There was no way she could face selling them today.

Jevan did not speak for a few minutes, and Annabel began to wonder if he was deliberately ignoring her. At a loss for any more words to say to him, she stood in silence. It felt so unnatural to be this uncomfortable around him. Then again, four years might as well have been an eternity, as everything was different. She watched Jevan leading her horse away into the stable and sat down on a stone step.

She looked down at her dusty dress. Her hair was most likely a frightful sight. She ran her fingers through a few tangled strands. She thought about her earlier tears, which had probably left streaks down her face. It was no wonder Jevan couldn't be bothered with her. She wished Jophiel were here. It would be easier with him around. She looked hopefully at the adjoining cottage. There was no sign of him.

There was some movement in the next stable, and Jevan led Jess out. He stared down at her, and she hastily jumped up.

"I am almost finished here. I'll tether Jess to the trap and take you and your things home."

Annabel nodded, feeling a mixture of relief and fear. The thought of being alone and sitting so close to him on the trap suddenly felt daunting. She did not speak, just watched and waited while he moved unhurriedly around, finishing up the one or two things. Everything he did reminded her of past times, and he acted as if he did not even seem to remember that she was present or even care that he made her wait a full hour. By this time, she was certain that all the things he was doing were unnecessary. It suddenly dawned on her that he was just waiting for her to react and say something that he could counter. She knew him too well. Eventually, irritation got the better of her.

"Are you going to take me home or not?" she said sharply.

Jevan shot her the blackest look. "I said I would, didn't I?"

He turned back and readjusted the reins on Jess. Annabel dearly wanted to challenge the necessity of everything he was doing. Instead, she kept her mouth shut and climbed haughtily up onto the trap. Impatience was brimming on the surface as she waited again, knowing she was at his mercy as to when he might take her home. Jevan may have been older and changed somewhat in appearance, but he retained that infuriating air that always provoked her. Anger was her only defense. After all this time, she didn't know what else to feel. After all, she had believed that she would never see him again. Her world had just turned upside down.

A few minutes later, Jevan really couldn't find anything else to delay them, so he climbed up and sat beside her. He reached over to take the reins from her.

"I can steer a trap you know." she snapped, resisting the interference.

"Jess will respond better to me," Jevan said firmly and pulled the reins from her grasp.

She bit her lip and glared at him. Jevan wanted control, and inside Annabel was quietly fuming. She remained silent, biding her time.

Jess set off at a brisk trot, at first a little agitated, as he was not used to pulling a trap, then as Jevan's words of reassurance calmed him, he soon was resigned to the journey ahead.

Annabel was wary that as soon as they were out of Rookwood, Jevan would slow Jess down. The light was rapidly fading, the dark green shadows and gray moorland beyond making the journey seem farther than it really was, and, as dusk turned to darkness, Annabel waited for the accusations, rebuke, or whatever else he had a mind to throw at her. In the steady noise of Jess's hooves and the trap rattling along, she could still hear Jevan breathing. She wished he would speak, even if it were in anger. It would be better than nothing. Jevan did not utter a word.

Then after a while, Annabel sighed, and extended the olive branch. "How was London?"

"Crowded, noisy, and dirty."

"When did you get back?"

"Two days ago."

Two days and no one had even told her! She wondered how many more days would have passed before she would have found out. A sudden thought flashed into her head. Did Alex know? He knew of their friendship. He must have heard their names linked many times and what would he think now? Although, in light of their most recent conversation, she didn't really care.

"Are you happy to be back?" she said, trying to find common ground for them to converse.

"That depends," Jevan said coldly.

"On what?" He did not reply, and before long, Annabel could see the chimneys of Honeymead in the distance. She began to think that Jevan was never going to answer when he suddenly pulled the reins back and brought Jess to a stop.

"Circumstances," he said, turning and looking at her. "You've changed—grown up."

"It's been four years, Jevan. We've both grown up, and I'm surprised you even noticed," she said sarcastically."

Jevan narrowed his eyes. "It seems I'm not the only one. I hear that you have been seeing a lot of Alex Saltonstall. Quite a catch for someone like you, I suppose."

"What exactly does that mean?" Annabel stared at him indignantly, feeling her bristles rising.

Jevan shook his head. His eyes burned into hers. "The girl I remember would never have sold herself for a title," he said, articulating every word to give maximum effect. His words, their meaning cut through her deeply, and she opened her mouth to speak, but Jevan continued. "Perhaps that was always your intention. You always did get bored too easily, and now you can rise well above those you grew up with, a chance for you to show contempt for everyone around you."

Her eyes blazed angrily. "You have no right to accuse me of anything!"

"I have more right than most," he countered and looked down at her worn and travel-dusty clothes. Then his eyes rose and lingered on her mass of long untidy hair. "And I know you better than anyone. He will not make you happy."

"You don't know me anymore. You have been gone too long to know what will or won't make me happy. And why do you think you can come back now and question anything I have done? It was you who left me. I have more reason to be angry with you." She stared straight ahead. She did not want Jevan to see how much his words hurt her.

"Is that what you think? That I have no reason to be angry with you?" The emotion was clearly evident in his voice.

"Are you going to take me home or not?" she said, ignoring the question. She swallowed nervously, Jevan remained staring at her, and reluctantly she turned to him. "It's been a long day, Jevan, I need to get home."

Whatever Jevan might have said, he kept it to himself and clicked the reins to make Jess walk forward again. They did not talk again, and Annabel sensed there was triumph in his words. He had wanted to hurt her, and her upset turned to anger as she thought about what he had just said.

Josiah was waiting at the cottage door as they approached. "Jevan," he called out, "is that really you?"

"Hello, Josiah," Jevan said, jumping down from the trap. He held out his hand to help Annabel down. She shot him her most disdainful look, ignored it, and jumped down.

"I heard a rumor that you were back, but I haven't seen Jophiel these last few days," Josiah said happily.

Annabel ignored her father's joviality and smiling face and he failed to recognize her irritation. "April's gone lame. She's still at the forge," she said and walked passed him into the cottage.

Jevan stared after her and then looked back at Josiah. "She just needs a few day's rest. I have ointment that will ease the swelling and I will bind the leg."

"I already know that she is in the best possible hands," Josiah said, touching him affectionately on the shoulder. "Come inside, Jevan," he said, much to Annabel's dismay.

Jevan and her father talked for a while. She busied herself around the cottage and tried not to listen. Despite the feelings of animosity, she could not help but be drawn to Jevan's voice.

Chapter 15

A Puzzling Revelation

"Did you know that Cerberus wants to buy Honey-mead?" Josiah asked, as soon as Annabel came in the next day.

She hung her head, closed the door slowly, and tried to think of the best thing to say. "I didn't want to worry you, Father," she said at length, meeting his gaze. The way in which Josiah's brow furrowed and the long silence that followed did not bode well. She had her suspicions as to how he could have found out so quickly, and that made her worry. "Did Cerberus come here?"

Josiah snorted in disgust. "He wouldn't dare," he answered abruptly, shaking his head. "The correspondence came from a solicitor in London." He pointed to the formal looking letter on the table.

Tentatively, she picked it up, dreading what it might say and knowing that to have put her father in such a bad mood, the contents could not be welcoming. Annabel skimmed over the words. There was a lot of legal jargon and unfamiliar long words, with an intention to confuse the reader, and it appeared the relevant matter of the letter was that their fertile lands were needed for orchards. *So much for easement rights*, she thought bitterly. "They already have huge orchards." She paused for a moment's consideration "And you know it's not the real reason, don't you?" she said pointedly.

Josiah nodded solemnly. "I know that. He also knows that there is more than one way to make me sell," he added with resignation, slumping backward in his seat.

Annabel caught her breath. "You are not actually considering selling!" she cried and felt like an icy hand had slid down her back.

Honeymead was her life, the only home she had ever known, and there were far too many precious memories secreted in every corner. Just the thought of ever selling angered her to the core.

Josiah sighed. "He has offered a fair price."

"What for, me or the land?" she said sharply.

Josiah's eyes widened immediately. "Don't ever think that," he said, just as abruptly. "I would never allow you to be manipulated in that way, and this concerns me more than you anyway." The bitterness was evident in his voice. "He has bided his time, but I knew that one day he would make my life difficult, and with you to think about, I am powerless to do anything." Josiah hesitated for a moment, knowing that what he was about to say would not be received well at all. "I have been thinking that if we were to sell Honeymead, it would give us the money to move far away and start again."

Annabel stared at him in disbelief. She felt sick to her stomach, and of course, this was about her. Why did Josiah think differently? "Has he threatened you?" she said, sickness giving way to anger.

"Not yet." Josiah hesitated again. "But there is something that you don't know."

"What?" she said. Her legs felt suddenly weak, and she sat heavily next to her father.

Josiah avoided her eyes. He didn't want to see the shock. "Some time before you were born, Cerberus took more than a casual interest in your mother." Annabel's eyes grew wide with amazement. "She, of course, dismissed all his attentions, although her refusals had little effect. Cerberus was not a man you said no to. Things got worse when his own wife disappeared mysteriously." He shrugged his shoulders. "I never did find out what happened to her, whether she died, moved away or—something else." He fell silent.

Annabel felt the hairs on her arm stand on end. "Something else? Such as? Do you think he killed her?"

"I don't know," Josiah, said, shaking his head. "There was talk about the village, but as I said, it was all very mysterious. Although nothing he did would have surprised me."

Annabel's mind was in a whirl. Cerberus was difficult, and she had felt the animosity from him. Even so, was he really a murderer? If that was the truth, how could he look his son in the eye, day after day, knowing that he had killed his mother? Annabel pushed that notion away, and thought back to their recent dinner. He had been difficult and demonstrated his intolerance while in her company, but was he really that deranged?

Josiah interrupted her thoughts. "The consequence was awful. It meant that Lilith became his sole focus of attention." He hesitated and closed his eyes for a moment. "No, it was more than that. She was his obsession. I was young and very different back then. We were already married, so I was understandably enraged. I was not about to let anyone take my wife away from me. Not that she was even interested," he added quickly. "I confronted Cerberus, out of my mind with rage, and I threatened to kill him. If it had not been for several stable hands who restrained me, I swear, I would have done it."

Annabel gasped in horror, realizing the terrible implications. "What did he do?"

There was a stony silence as Josiah fought with memories he clearly wished to forget. Then, at length, he turned to Annabel. "He had me thrown in jail. Not just any cell, no, I had something *very* special." Her father's voice was heavy with bitterness. "An airless flea pit, crawling with rats and the stench of corpses that had gone before, and that was to be my fate." Annabel stared at her father in horror as he continued. "People didn't cross Cerberus Saltonstall. Everyone was afraid to confront him, for fear of similar retribution." Josiah lip curled up into a slight smile. "All, except one," he said gazing at his daughter, and Annabel got the distinct impression it was someone else he was seeing. "Later Cerberus took great pleasure in relating that your mother had begged him whilst down on her hands and knees." He shook his head. "I knew my wife better than that. She was like you when she was younger, full of fire, I doubt she begged him."

"What did she do?" Annabel gently prompted.

"I don't know. She never wanted to talk about what went on, and he arranged my release a few days later." Josiah's eyes glazed over, clearly haunted by the memory. "Cerberus knew it would be even more of a torment to think that my wife had to go any ask him for anything," he said, shaking his head and rubbing his temples, as if it would relieve the burden.

Annabel sensed there was something he was keeping back. She swallowed apprehensively. "Did she and him…you know?" she said, not wanting to say the words.

Josiah looked at her in disbelief. "No, she didn't. Your mother had great dignity! Lilith was a clever woman and, when she wanted something, she got it. She knew how to manipulate a situation without resorting to what ordinary woman might have to do. You know that."

Annabel stared at him. She had never heard her father talk like this before. When she was very young, she had realized her mother wasn't the same as other people. As Annabel grew, it seemed the normal way of things, and something she never talked about. It came now as a shock to realize that of course her father knew. Annabel had questions, many questions, and she wanted to wring every detail from him, but upset by what he told her, she didn't think it was the right time to press him further. It was clearly an awful memory and he had related it with great dignity.

"Things were bad for a while," Josiah continued. "We steered clear of him as much as possible and lived more or less like hermits, only going into the village when it was absolutely necessary. It was a little easier when Lilith was carrying you. The bigger she got, the better it got. It was then he seemed to lose interest in her, and our life became normal again. Cerberus and I haven't spoken since that time, although the hatred between us has festered for years," Josiah said bleakly. "To his twisted mind, I was the only thing that stood in his way, and then you came along." His voice lightened. "You are the image of your mother, only your coloring is more striking. He paused for a moment. "I imagine when he looks at you, it's Lilith he sees, but you are an innocent in this matter and you don't deserve his wrath."

Annabel shivered. "He hates me because I am your daughter."

"Yes." Josiah smiled sadly. "And now it seems he wants to punish you as well."

"This doesn't make sense." she said, shaking her head. "He has shown me nothing but contempt and yet Alex would have me believe differently." She looked at her father, feeling suddenly nervous. "You were right. Alex asked me to marry him, and he more or less told me that Cerberus is eager for us to marry soon."

Josiah's eyebrows shot up as he turned his head and stared fully at her.

"I told Alex no," she added quickly, "but I don't understand. If Alex is speaking the truth, and, with what you have told me today, why would Cerberus want that?" She saw the frown on her father's forehead and his eyes expressed deep concern. She took his hand and squeezed it lightly in reassurance.

"He is trying to get back at me," Josiah said in disgust. "He could not have my wife, so now he wants my daughter. He knows that losing you is the one thing that would cause me the greatest agony."

"I'm not going to marry Alex," Annabel said quickly. "I don't have those sorts of feelings. I never have." She thought for a long moment. "My mother would not be manipulated, and neither will I. We will never sell Honeymead. She would turn in her grave if she ever thought that could happen, and as long as I live, it will remain ours. They can threaten all they like, but both Cerberus and Alex will soon see that we will not bow down to their demands."

"Annabel—" Josiah was unable to finish the sentence as he lapsed into a fit of coughing that wracked his whole body.

Annabel was already making a mental note that these spasms were getting more frequent and she was alarmed. She jumped up and ran to get a glass of water and her own remedy of honey and sage. Josiah drank the water and the remedy.

His breath was significantly weaker when he next spoke. "I wish I still had your fire, my love," he said quietly.

Annabel sighed and kissed his cheek. "You don't need it. I have enough fire for the both of us," she said, grabbing her shawl and the letter. "You just need to rest and I will be back soon."

"Annabel, please be careful."

Josiah's words echoed in her head as she set off across the fields toward Gothelstone. The revelations were going over and over in her mind as to what exactly had her mother done to ensure her father's release. Manipulation and influence was one thing. Gut instinct was something else. Of course, Lilith would have never revealed what had really gone on to her husband. Then again, perhaps she was wrong. Maybe Lilith had been stronger and more capable than she ever believed. Annabel wished her mother was still alive and felt suddenly angry that she had kept all these things from her. Surely she had a right to know her parents' past, all of their past.

When she reached the mansion, her frustration and anger was still at the forefront of her mind, and she was a little dismayed to see that Alex was in the front courtyard talking to the stable boy. He looked up with surprise at her approach and smiled. She did not let that fact faze her and marched straight up to him.

"Where is your father?"

"Inside," he said, the smile changing instantly. He was mystified, if not at the question, then her obvious fury. "Why?"

"I want to see him," she replied, ignoring his look, and walked past him to push open the heavy front door. Alex caught up with her in an instant and took hold of her arm. She swung around to face him. "Let go of me. It's your father I want to see, and I am not leaving until I do!"

Stunned by her entire manner, Alex could see she was very

angry and he was somewhat glad not to be the cause, as the sheer determination emanating from her was impressive. Although, he knew that a confrontation with his father was never a good idea, he released her arm and moved between her and the entrance.

"What's happened?"

She shook her head. "This is between me and him."

"Whatever concerns my father, concerns me as well."

"Oh, I know it does," she snapped. "This little pact you have going between you, it's quite touching, but I'm not falling for it."

Alex drew back from her, a little stunned at the accusation. She triumphantly stepped across the threshold.

"What are you talking about?"

Annabel looked back at him with disdain and had opened her mouth to speak, when a voice echoed down the stairs.

"What does the girl want?"

Annabel and Alex both looked up. Cerberus was moving swiftly down the staircase. His cold eyes penetrated hers.

She stood her ground, anger taking precedence over any fear. "This," she said, thrusting the letter before him, "is nothing more than intimidation. I came here tell you that we will never sell, and all your fancy legal letters and threats don't make a blind bit of difference to me." She stomped her foot. "Easement rights," she said, casting Alex a disdainful glance, "or more orchards. I don't care whatever nonsense you both scheme up together. We will not be threatened." She felt on a roll, adrenaline pushing her further as she leaned a little closer to Cerberus. "And I also came to warn you that I know what has gone on in the past, and if you do anything to harm my father, then I will destroy you."

Both Alex and Cerberus stiffened, and then Cerberus's eyes narrowed briefly, as he met her challenge and drew even closer to her.

"I doubt you really know what's happened in the past, Lilith would never have told you," he said, with an air of conceit, "and I could have you arrested and publicly beaten for that threat."

Annabel's heartbeat was already rapid, although, the adrenaline flooded through her body. "Just like you did with my father?" she challenged.

Cerberus's stony look pierced her retinas and the air around her felt stifling. It didn't concern her, as anger was overriding everything else, and she stared at him in repulsion. She began to tremble as her heart beat quickened and she battled another urge.

"Father, she is upset," Alex said hastily, sensing that Annabel was not going to back down. In fact, she looked as though she might even strike his father. "Let me talk to her."

"Don't make excuses for her. You are beguiled by her beauty, but I see through it." Cerberus stepped closer to Annabel. Instinctively, she moved backward against the door. His face was close to hers, so close that she could feel his breath on her skin. Her throat went dry as his voice rose dramatically.

"Do you really believe that you can threaten me? You have no idea who I am, do you?" he said, displaying a grotesquely sinister smile.

Annabel stared defiantly at him. Of course, she knew who he was, and what he was capable of. Did he really think she was so stupid?

She did not get a chance to answer, as Cerberus continued his venomous spew. "For I see something in you, which you cannot see."

Annabel narrowed her eyes. There was an underlying message, a reference to something, her mother perhaps, and a feeling of utter loathing flashed through her mind.

Cerberus stared at her a moment longer, then he drew back. He looked at Alex. "My son's happiness is of great importance, and out of all the eligible women he could have married, you are the one he has chosen." He turned to Annabel again. "You should consider yourself fortunate that he favors you above all others, and I suggest that you think long and hard about his offer. A positive response will motivate me to leave the estate lands unchanged and Honeymead will remain in Josiah's ownership until his death."

Annabel caught her breath, and the words on the tip of her

tongue disappeared. Alex hadn't lied. Cerberus wanted the marriage. His half sneer turned into an expression of victory when he saw the impact on her face. Annabel was stunned. A deep gnawing sensation began in her stomach, and all her thoughts collected suspiciously.

"Why?" Her voice was barely there.

"Annabel, I think we all need to calm down, leave it for now," Alex said, catching her eye and taking her arm.

"No, I want to know," she said, pulling her arm away roughly. "Why do you want this marriage when you hate me so much. Why would you agree to that?"

Cerberus did not answer. His face was expressionless and he went to turn away from her.

"He doesn't hate you, Annabel. Do you, Father? Let's go and get some fresh air," Alex said, in a feeble effort to distract her.

"No," she said and stepped in front of Cerberus, forcing him to look at her. "Answer me," she demanded, and his cold eyes rested on her again.

"You should listen to Alex," he said evenly. "I don't hate you. How could I? You are so vital to the Saltonstall legacy." He sidestepped her and walked away.

Annabel stared after him and then glanced at Alex. "What does he mean?"

"I don't know," Alex replied, suppressing the urge to call after his father and ask the question himself.

Annabel's world no longer made any sense. The life she knew was in danger of slipping away and she could not imagine why she was so important to the Saltonstall legacy. What did it really have to do with her? It was clear that Cerberus was forcing this marriage, not Alex. She had misjudged him. Perhaps, Alex was merely a pawn in this charade. She allowed herself to be led into the drawing room, still in a state of shock. She did not know what to say to Alex now, and felt a little ashamed at her hostility toward him.

Alex ordered the maid to bring a glass of water. "You look pale. You should sit for a while," he said, making every effort to act as normal as possible.

She sat and he took a seat beside her on the couch. For some time he didn't move or speak, and it was a welcome intrusion when the maid returned with the water. Annabel gratefully took the glass and thanked the girl. Then they were alone again in the quietness of the room.

"You should try not to anger him. He can be strangely irrational at times."

Annabel shifted her gaze to Alex. He really didn't look that much like his father, his blue eyes were darker, but friendlier, not the ice-cold ones that she had seen her shocked face reflected in. That thought sent another chill up her spine. "What is the Saltonstall Legacy?"

"The estate, the money, lands, tenants, the same as any other wealthy landowner."

"There has to be more to it than that. Why am I so vital? and don't you think that was a peculiar turn of phrase?" Alex looked trapped, although he didn't speak, and she softened her voice, her grievance wasn't with him. "He hates me, Alex. You know he does, and yet he is willing to do almost anything to ensure I marry you. Is he just doing it to get back at my father, or is there something else?"

Alex sighed heavily. "Did he really do that to your father?"

"Yes, you don't know?"

Alex shook his head. "Annabel, I'm sorry for what has gone on in the past. I had no idea, but it must have happened a long time ago."

Annabel nodded. "Before I was born."

Alex visibly relaxed. "You know people do wild things when they are young. Tempers get riled easily. People are more passionate above love and revenge. I take it that you have only just found out about this, or I am sure you would have taken it out me long before this?" he said, with a small smile.

That remark made Annabel feel like she had wronged him yet again, and she met his smile with a grimace of regret. "I'm really not that bad, am I?"

"Just a little headstrong," he said cordially. "You know it's all water under the bridge, and whatever happened in the past is just that—the past. You cannot change what happened and it was probably before I was born too, so I am innocent in this as well."

"Sins of the Father," she said mockingly and sighed. "Sorry, it's not you I'm angry at."

"I know," he said sympathetically. "My father knows that I love you, he may disapprove of your outspokenness, the way you dress or conduct yourself, but ultimately he knows that only you will make me happy."

Annabel shook her head. "Alex, I don't think I can make you happy. The thing that drew you to me was my bluntness and independence. I like my life and I don't want to be a mistress of a huge mansion. I want to live at Honeymead and, besides, how could I live under your father's roof. He will make my life miserable. He will make sure that every ounce of my spirit would be worn away until all that was left would be an empty shell."

Alex smiled. "That wouldn't happen, you have too strong a character, and I wouldn't let it happen. My father may have his own agenda, not me," he said with sincerity, "I love you, and together we will resist his interference. He won't live forever Annabel. Besides would it really be such a terrible sacrifice to be married to me?"

Annabel looked at him sadly. Her old Alex was back, the one that she had ridden with, laughed with, and happily kissed. He was her friend again and she hated to hurt him.

"Alex, I don't love you."

If she had slapped him, the effect would have been subtler. His expression betrayed the sting of those words, and he closed his eyes for a few moments. "I know that. I have tried to tell myself that it doesn't matter, even if the truth is harder to bear. The knowledge hurts me deeply." He shrugged and sighed. "But it changes nothing, because together we will save Honeymead and your father's future. And what you feel for me makes no difference. It is what I feel for you that will make you happy, and I can give you everything you ever wanted." He kissed her lightly on the cheek and put his arms around her.

She felt terrible. His suffering was so obvious. But he was badly mistaken. He could not give her the one thing she really wanted. Nevertheless, she allowed him to comfort her and tried to imagine what it might be like to lay in his arms night after night.

e/ɔe/ɔ

The next day Annabel went to the forge to check on April, at least she gave that excuse to her father. As she drew near, her head filled with the previous day's events. If Jevan had not come back, perhaps her thoughts would be clearer, and, given enough time, it was possible that she could have put the past behind her completely. Perhaps, she might have even found a degree of happiness with Alex. But Jevan *had* come back and, at this moment, every doubt she ever had multiplied.

Jevan was with April when she entered the stable. He was on his knees tending the afflicted leg. He looked up at her but did not speak. She walked up to April who was oblivious to the sudden electricity in the air. Annabel smiled, happy to see her horse was no worse for the injury and contentedly eating fresh hay. April nuzzled against her mistress and snuffled her nose into Annabel's hand to see if there was anything for her. She shook her head in disappointment when she found nothing.

"Sorry, April, I'll bring something tomorrow," Annabel murmured softly, feeling strangely nervous, and her heart beat faster when Jevan got up from the floor.

He picked up a stone jar, which she recognized as some sort of ointment, and walked toward the back of the building. Annabel patted April, ran her hand lightly down the leg and over the newly applied bandage, and was relieved to find that there was less swelling. She heard Jevan come back. She did not turn or look at him, convinced that if she did, she might behave like a lovesick fool. His nearness was excruciating. She could feel him, even though he wasn't touching her. She sensed his eyes boring into the back of her head, and a sudden memory of that day so long ago in the schoolroom flashed through her mind. Again, she was waiting for something to happen. Taking a deep breath, she turned and looked up at him.

"Jevan—"

Whatever she had been about to say flew from her mind as his mouth covered hers and stifled the words. His kiss was powerful, and he clasped her so tightly to him that she could scarcely breathe. It did not matter. She didn't need to breathe. She threw her arms around his neck, pulling him even closer, while her heart and head said yes, this was right. This was everything she wanted. This was who she loved and always would.

Eventually, Jevan slackened his hold, and their lips parted. She breathed again as his dark eyes looked into hers.

"I came back for you."

"I was so frightened that I would never see you again," she said breathlessly, "that you hated me. I thought that you would have married and—"

"Shh," he said, silencing her again as he brushed his lips across hers, mildly entertained by the suggestion. "I could never marry another. I have only ever loved you," he said, pushing back a strand of hair from her face

"All the things I said to you," she said, remembering and shaking her head, "my words were hateful, and I thought that, after I refused to see you that last evening, I'd lost you forever."

"We were young, both far too stubborn. I *was* mad at you for weeks and for too many long months. Your words haunted me, and I did believe them for a while, but perhaps because of that I threw myself into a new life, and that opened my eyes to new possibilities. I tried to forget you. And as much as I tried, it never worked. Without you, I am not complete."

"Why didn't you write to me?"

"What, and have my letters thrown into a fire?" He almost laughed. "Or worse still you might have written back and laid it down in black and white that you never wanted to see me again. That would have destroyed me, a tangible reminder of your feelings." He shook his head. "No, I preferred to hold on to the possibility that one day I would see you again, and it would be different."

Inwardly Annabel breathed a sigh of relief. "You've haunted my dreams, Jevan, even my waking hours, every time I have thought about putting the past to rest permanently, something reminds me of why I cannot."

Jevan smiled and placed a kiss on her forehead. "Well, now that I'm back, things will be different, and I won't leave you again."

ഗഗഗ

It was late in the afternoon when she left forge cottage. She and Jophiel spent the afternoon listening to Jevan talk about city life. He spoke little of his mother and, instead, elaborated on foreign travels. His tales seemed exotic and fantastical to Annabel as he described animals and natives that heightened her imagination, then he also talked of long sea voyages, the diseases that ravaged the passengers, and the bouts of seasickness he had endured. To her it seemed there were unimaginable dangers of visiting faraway lands. Jevan walked her to Josiah's horse, a feisty pony that he only brought two weeks before.

"Are you going to be all right?" Jevan said, as the pony reared a little when Annabel pulled on the rein.

"Don't worry, I'll be fine. Storm will soon calm down. He just wants to run," she said reaching her hand down and patting the pony.

Jevan took her hand and kissed it. "I'll see you tomorrow," he said.

She smiled, reluctantly pulled on the rein, and turned from him. She looked up. A carriage had just passed by, and she recognized that it belonged to Gothelstone Mansion. She gave a fleeting thought to her problem. She had not yet plucked up the courage to tell Jevan, as after his jealous comment last night, she wondered about just how much he already knew. One thing was for sure, if she told him everything that had gone on, he would be furious and there would be a confrontation. He would jump to defend her with little regard of the cost to himself. She thought back to Aidden. It suddenly felt as though a gray veil fell upon her and marred the perfect bright day. She shivered, knowing that Cerberus and Alex were far more dangerous to cross. It was only a passing thought. Today, Annabel was happier than any other day she could remember.

Jevan stayed in the doorway, watching her ride into the distance until she finally disappeared from sight. He frowned slightly, thinking of the idle talk being bandied about since his return. He knew rumors could easily get out of hand, then again, he also knew that there was often more than a grain of truth running through them.

⁊ʒ⁊

Storm was feisty and it took all of Annabel's strength to pull him back. He was nothing like her docile April. After his initial energetic maneuvers, he calmed and cantered happily along. Annabel's thoughts were not really with the horse. Jevan had been her sole focus, but now her attention turned back to Alex. She could never marry Alex, despite any threat or consequence.

She was always meant to be with Jevan, and she wondered at her own recklessness and how she could have ever entertained any notion, even being friends with Alex, let alone anything more serious, although she and her father could be in real danger of losing Honeymead. It seemed that her only option was to seek some legal advice, and she did not know the first thing about such things. Alex would know, though she could hardly ask him, he being at the root of her problem, and she doubted he would ever cross his father.

There was no getting away from reality. She would have to tell Jevan. He had been in the city. He had probably met important people, perhaps even legal people. He might even know of a solicitor. The anxious feeling returned, and she pondered again just how much Jevan already knew.

When she arrived home, she sat with Josiah for a while and

told him of her plan. Saying the words aloud better convinced her it was the only option. Josiah seemed a little skeptical.

"Finding someone to even represent us might be harder than you think. After all, they would have to go up against Cerberus. Think of the cost. It might take everything we have."

"Father, we have no choice in the matter," she replied adamantly. "We have to stand up for our rights, and any decent court of law would see that we have a good case."

Josiah huffed and looked unconvinced. "Since when did that make any difference against the likes of Cerberus?"

Annabel would not be swayed and collected her thoughts rationally. "I won't make any rash decisions. I will seek proper advice."

"What does Jevan say? Does he have any contacts in London?"

"I haven't told him yet. I will," she added quickly. "I'll tell him tomorrow."

୧୬୧

Early the next day, Alex arrived at Honeymead. Annabel thought that his manner was unusually abrupt as he walked into the cottage and greeted her, and it wasn't long before she realized the reason for such an early morning visit. He sat at the table, his eyes following her suspiciously, as she rearranged freshly washed crockery onto the dresser.

"Tell me about the blacksmith's son?"

Annabel's heart lurched. "You mean Jevan," she said nonchalantly, not meeting his gaze."

"What was he to you?"

Her back was turned and he didn't see the small smile that passed her lips. What a question. Jevan was wild, sullen, and definitely intolerable at times. He was infuriating difficult and arrogant, but he was also a free spirit. A wild creature that made her heart leap up with joy and her breath quicken every time he looked into her eyes.

Years had passed, and he was still all that, and much more.

He was still everything to her. Alex was watching her closely as she turned toward him.

"We grew up together, sort of like brother and sister, I suppose." she replied, trying to remain indifferent, even though she felt the color rise in her cheeks. She wanted to tell him the truth. The words were on the tip of her tongue, although, there was something about the way he spoke Jevan's name. It made her uneasy.

"I don't like the way he looks at you," Alex replied. "He seems far too familiar with you."

Annabel laughed lightly, her face flushed deeply as she realized Alex had been in the carriage last night and had seen the exchange between them. "He is only concerned for my welfare."

"I see more to it than that," Alex said darkly.

"Then you see something that isn't there," she said, brushing the comment aside casually, and turned back to the job she had started. She hoped that her tone did not reveal the sinking feeling in the pit of her stomach, as she realized that things could easily get more complicated than she could have first imagined.

Chapter 16

In Sanity's Shadow

Later that day, Jevan arrived at Honeymead. Alex had long since departed and Annabel was no-where to be seen. He opened the door and called up the stairs. There was no reply, and the cottage was empty. He frowned and, closing the door again, looked toward the meadow. Storm was alone. Jevan walked through to the orchard and toward the skeps. He found Josiah.

Josiah's face immediately lit up as he approached, and then Josiah waved his hand, gesturing in slow motion for Jevan to stay back.

"Don't get too close, they seem especially agitated today."

Unfazed by the remark, Jevan drew closer. "Is Annabel here?" he asked as the bees flew around his head.

He stood perfectly still and several landed on his bare arms. One landed on his cheek. Josiah held his breath, feeling uncharacteristically uneasy. If they were to swarm suddenly, Jevan would get severely stung, and, suddenly, there seemed to be even more bees around them both.

"It's all right, Josiah," Jevan assured him. "They won't hurt me."

Josiah was skeptical. He knew that it only took one false move, and if they had a mind to, the bees would attack. Before he could voice any opinion, Jevan slowly stretched his arms forward. He closed his eyes and, moments later, the bees flew from him. They rose into the air in a swirling mass. Josiah gazed at him in wonder, mesmerized by what he had witnessed. Jevan had the gift too.

"They must remember you," he remarked, astonished.

Jevan smiled faintly at his expression.

"She said she was going out to clear her head," Josiah continued, answering the earlier question, and his brow furrowed. "They sense it, you know." He nodded at the bees swarmed into the air. "They know when she's upset."

Jevan felt his stomach lurch, and Josiah caught his bleak expression. "Not because of you," he said unreservedly. "She is very happy that you have come home, we both are," he added, "but things have changed while you've been gone." He paused for a long moment, thinking that he really should let Annabel tell Jevan the whole story.

"I know about her and Alex Saltonstall," Jevan said pointedly. "I'll soon fix that."

Josiah heard the determination in Jevan's voice and nodded uncomfortably.

"Did she mention where she was going?" Jevan asked, watching Josiah closely and getting the distinct feeling that there was more than one thing that Josiah was trying to conceal.

"Up on the moors, to sit under a tree and think," Josiah said, remembering his daughter's words. "I think that's what she said. I don't know where, though. She was a bit vague, and, in fact, she could be anywhere."

Jevan smiled. Not anywhere. he knew exactly where she would be. "I'll find her," he said, and he left Josiah still trying to coax the bees back to their skeps.

Jevan rode Jess hard across the moors, only slowing down to navigate the woodlands that ran along the coastline. The years of his absence melted away, and he knew this terrain well. Nothing had changed. The air was heavy with moisture as the clouds steadily lowered from the changeable sky, causing dark green shadows down into the wooded combes.

Jevan knew the dense sea mist would cover the landscape before the day was out. Just as he reached the edge of the tree

line, the cool wind hit him with force. The sea was in turmoil
and brown sedges were being blown horizontally. He dismounted when he came upon Storm tethered to a small rowan
tree. He tied Jess alongside and the horses readily nuzzled
each other.

Annabel was standing on the edge of the cliff, staring out
across the ocean and listening only to the wave's crash against
the rocky shoreline. The wind had gained momentum, and it
blew her hair out in a backward stream. It was wild day, the
brutal force of nature causing an electrical energy in the air
around her.

A sudden noise made her turn. Jevan stood several feet
away. Their eyes locked, and the wind whipped her hair
around, blinding her for a second. She blinked and looked
again. In the dim light, with the insubstantial mist between
them, his face looked gray, and he appeared to be so still that
he could have been carved of stone. She jumped when he
spoke.

"Come here."

His voice sounded clear and sharp, and she went. He drew
her against him. She laid her head upon his chest and listened
to the steady echo of his heartbeat, as his arms tightened protectively around her. She trembled as his lips caressed her
neck, and reluctantly she looked up at him, dreading the moment. If she hesitated, her nerve would be gone.

"There's something I have to tell you," she began and her
throat went dry as he ran his hand down her back. The goose
bumps tingled as he exerted more pressure on her spine.

"Hush," he said. "I already know."

Annabel caught her breath. A little surprised and somewhat
relieved, she wondered what exactly he knew.

Jevan reached down and clasped her scarred palm against
his own. "You will always belong to me." His voice was no
more than a whisper. "We are alike, bound by blood. No one
will get in the way of that."

His kiss was a powerful enough persuasion. She had no resistance as he pulled her to the ground, lulled by his obvious
desire, and seduced by his continuous touch. The buttons on

her dress released one by one. The material fell away, exposing her skin to the elements, but she was not cold for long. Jevan pressed his body against hers, and his warm powerful hands stroked and warmed her flesh. She pressed her palm against his.

"Not just bound by blood," she whispered, pulling him closer.

The urgency with which their bodies joined made her cry out, and then she was silenced by his deepest kiss. The years apart seemed to melt away. The words that had been spoken in anger and grief vanished into the mists of time. In their embrace, they found the completeness denied to them for such a long while. After a time, they grew still, watching the lowering mists. In the dusk, the outline of the branches above them slowly disappeared. The insanity of the world vanished, and they were enveloped in the shadows. Nothing had significance, no one else mattered, and even their consciousness took flight into the swirling blanketing landscape.

Much later, darkness fully descended and the clammy fog was thicker and colder than ever. They had completely lost track of time when they mounted the horses and headed across the moors to Honeymead. Jess guided Storm and seemed undaunted by the atmosphere.

Annabel's happiness gave way to uneasiness as she cleared her throat and began to tell Jevan the full account of recent events. Throughout her conversation, he remained mostly silent. She stole several anxious glances at him, and, even though his face was in deep shadow, she could just see that his lips pressed tightly together. Then she mentioned Alex's proposal.

"What was your answer?" Jevan said abruptly, narrowing his eyes a fraction.

"I said no, Jevan," she replied bluntly. "But it's not that simple anymore," she added, meeting his gaze. "Cerberus is determined to see this marriage take place at any costs, and Alex won't take my answer as final." She sighed. "It's all such a mess."

"You must have encouraged him."

Annabel eyes widened indignantly. "It wasn't like that. Though, I'm not going to lie or pretend that I didn't like his attention or company—and that sometimes I still do."

Jevan swore and made a noise of anger in the back of his throat.

"You weren't here, and Alex was," she said haughtily.

Suddenly Jevan pulled hard on the Jess's rein, at the same time he also grabbed Storm's rein from her grasp. "What are you telling me?" His eyes were full of fury. Even if his voice made her jump, his demeanor really frightened her. "Did you lay with him?"

Annabel snatched the rein back, her own annoyance brimming. "No, I didn't. I liked him, like a friend or brother."

Jevan shook his head. "He is neither one of those things, and you better make it perfectly clear that there will be no marriage. Or I will."

That warning left her in no doubt that he would not hesitate to confront Alex. "No, you won't. I will do it, and you can't get involved in this."

"I am involved, if it concerns you," he said, with a note of sharpness.

Annabel bit her lip. She didn't want to argue with him. She knew what she had to do. They rode forward in silence.

"I know someone that may be able to help with your easement rights," Jevan said at length. "An acquaintance in London," he continued, seeing her enquiring look. "Francis Miles did some work for the printers I worked for. I am certain that he is familiar with land contracts." Jevan paused for a few minutes. "There is something I was going to tell you. It feels unimportant now, considering what you have just said."

"Tell me what?"

"I'm going to set up a printing press in Rookwood," he said, the enthusiasm evident in his voice. "I have the skill and experience, and right now most newspapers and pamphlets have to come from a distance away. I can also print broadsheets and letters, whatever people want. Rookwood is growing fast, and it could be a lucrative business."

"What about the forge?"

"I will still help my father when he needs it, but you know as well as I, he is a very capable blacksmith, and I don't see him retiring any time soon." He thought for a moment. "In London, my eyes were opened to endless possibilities, and you and I need a secure future."

Annabel was mildly surprised. Being unaccustomed to hearing him talk of such things, she felt his excitement and had her own reservations. "Everything's changing so fast." She looked at him. "I wish sometimes that everything was how it used to be."

Jevan smiled, understanding her reluctance. "Your world has always been safe and secure, and your life confined to the villages and moors around you. Times change, progress is happening all around, Annabel, and there are so many new things and inventions that you can't begin to imagine," he said enthusiastically. "I used to believe that I didn't need anything. I longed to be free to do what I wanted. And now I see that you're only really free if you have control of your life. A proper business in the community will earn me respect. It will bring in a good income, and wealth gives you power over your destiny."

Annabel stared at him. His sentiment was so unfamiliar, and she could almost hear Alex's voice, because the words could have come straight out of his mouth. "You don't even sound like the person I once knew," she said sadly.

"I haven't changed, Annabel. I just understand how the world works now."

When they reached Honeymead, Jevan kissed her good-night, holding on to her tighter than necessary before he fixed her with a penetrating stare. "Don't forget what I said." His face changed subtly, betraying his emotions. "Put this right, or I will."

Annabel shivered at the thought, and nodded compliantly. "I'll do it tomorrow."

Jevan frowned.

"I should be with you."

"No," she said at once. "I don't want this getting out of hand. Let me do it alone. Alex would regard you as a threat."

Jevan smirked. "That could be a good thing. He won't argue with me."

Annabel shook her head. "He won't argue with me either. I owe it to him to tell him myself."

Jevan's eyes stayed fixed on her face. He wasn't happy about this situation at all. It angered him to know that she liked being in Alex's company, and he was suspicious as to what she had not told him. He tried his hardest not to let it rile him, and that was proving to be too difficult. He thought for a few minutes as to the next plan of action.

"Tomorrow," he continued. "At first light, I will travel to London. I'll speak with Francis and return the day after tomorrow."

Chapter 17

Past Times Revealed

Annabel sat in the drawing room at Gothelstone Manor House, waiting for Alex. Alfred having just informed her that he would be along in a few minutes, she clasped her hands together to keep from fidgeting, even if her insides were quivering. She had gone over and over the words, but now sitting alone in his house, they didn't seem wholly appropriate. It was best to be blunt, she thought, save Alex the effort of trying to pry information from her and thus prolonging the agony for both of them. It made sense, she told herself, even if she wasn't confident of her ability to be quite that heartless.

A voice in the distance made her fearful, and, as it moved closer, her worst suspicion was confirmed. She clearly heard Cerberus's voice. She held her breath, not daring to move, and prayed that he would not open the door. Confronting Alex was one thing, but today of all days, she did not wish to encounter Cerberus even for a few seconds.

It felt as though her prayer was answered, when the door opened and Alex entered alone. He firmly closed it behind him. He was smiling. Annabel clasped her hands even tighter and took a deep breath. It was only when he crossed the room to where she sat that his smile faded.

"What is it? You look as though you have just seen a ghost."

She managed a weak smile. "No ghosts, I'm all right." She hesitated, willing herself to get on with it. "I had to speak with you, I have to tell you that—" This was even harder than she had imagined, and she drew another deep breath. "That I have decided that I'm not going to see you anymore."

Alex frowned and made a movement to speak.

She quickly stood up and faced him. "Please don't waste your breath trying to convince me otherwise. I've made up my mind. It's really for the best, and I have more than one reason—" She paused. "—your awareness the other day was correct." Another deep breath. "Jevan does mean something to me, more than I revealed to you, and as much as I like you, Alex, I don't feel for you, what I do for him."

She'd said it, and although the words gave her a sense of relief, Alex's expression was disquieting.

He stared at her for a long moment. "Are you mad?" he snapped coldly. "I have offered you all this—" His arms rose in gesture. "—a chance to see your father live in comfort and security for the rest of his days. Yet you throw it back in my face, and then insult me by telling me that you prefer a *black-smith*." He laughed nastily. "And not even a proper one at that. He's only an assistant and works when his father is feeling charitable. *He* will barely be able to feed you, let alone put clothes on your back," he said, looking down at her dress, and shook his head in disbelief. "You can't be serious, Annabel, you can't be that stupid." His laugh was both disturbing and maddening, his words and insults screamed in her head. He was still laughing.

"How dare you?" she said bitterly. "You don't know anything about us."

Alex's face changed immediately. "That's just where you're wrong," he said spitefully. "What? Did you think I wouldn't know about your past? In Rookwood, your name is linked with Jevan every way I turn." He saw her bewildered look and sneered. "Oh, yes, people talk about you," he said staring at her contemptuously. "The rebellious wild children that spent their lives on the moors, and the scandalous love affair of *peasant* adolescents. He didn't love you enough, did he? Because *he* left you."

"I'm not listening to this!" she said furiously and rushed to the door.

Alex was faster. He was already in front of it. "Don't you want to hear the truth? Because I am the only person that will ever tell you the truth. Nobody else wants to upset you. They all know what your temper is like. Tell me, Annabel, when he hurt you, did you find that exciting?" he said maliciously. "Did you like the pain?"

"Get out of my way." she cried angrily, trying to push past him.

Alex grabbed her roughly by the shoulders and shook her. "Perhaps I should abuse you like he did. Would it make you love me more? In fact, I find that thought quite enticing."

"Stop it, Alex!" she screamed. "He never abused me!"

Alex was taken aback by the intensity of her eyes blazing into his. The sheer energy she produced stunned him fleetingly. Physical pain shot through his skin, and he let go of her as if she had stung him.

He shook his head to dislodge the shock he felt, while at the same tried to calm his feelings. Her power had vanished and he wondered if he had just imagined it. His hands were shaking, his body felt in shock. "That's not what I heard," he said more quietly. "People talk of how you were always covered in bruises."

Annabel looked at him with disappointment. "You shouldn't listen to gossip. We were children. It doesn't matter what you think or try to shame me into believing, only Jevan and I know what happened between us, and it's none of your business, because I will not marry you. My reputation is my concern alone and let this be the end of it." She thought for a moment. "You and your father can make up ridiculous stories about land easement rights and orchards, but I will fight it every step of the way. And not just me, but I know legal people, and if you keep up this harassment, then it's them that you will be dealing with."

Alex's look of anger turned to amusement. "You have never left this place. How do you know anything about legal matters?"

"Jevan does, and he has already left for London," she said triumphantly. "Now let me leave. I want to go."

She caught his sharp intake of breath and he stared at her for several moments, before he stepped from the doorway.

"Leave then. You will be back soon enough." His words had a bitter edge to them and she glanced at him disdainfully.

"I doubt that," she said and hurried to the front door.

Just as she reached it, the drawing room door slammed with extreme force. The reverberation bounced off the walls of the great hall and echoed back to her in a serious of rapid beats. Alex's words had cast a shadow, and only when she stepped outside did the gloom lift. Everything he said was out of spite, and that was all behind her. She had done it. This was the end and she was free to be with Jevan.

When Annabel reached Honeymead, she did not go into the cottage. She went to the bees. Today they were calm. They flew around her harmoniously and landed on her skin. They felt her elation and buzzed happily about her. "When Jevan returns, everything will be different. I will declare my love for him to everyone, and no one will ever get in our way now," she promised them, feeling elated as a surge of power swept over her.

The bees felt her energy building. The sky had been clear, moments before. Now, billowing clouds started to gather. She stared harder, focusing her thoughts, summoning the basic elements, and the clouds began to race toward her. When enough had gathered, she held up her arms to the darkening heavens. Then the lightness in her voice vanished. "I summon the elements to do my bidding. Rain down upon the Estate of Gothelstone. Send torrents of water down onto the land to open the streams, channels, and ditches. Let it flow uninterrupted through the courtyard to lap the doorways and seep into the fabric like a beast wanting to enter."

She spread out her fingers and stretched them upward. The rain began to fall. Annabel gazed toward the mansion and saw the rain falling. At first, it was heavy and then it came down as if buckets were being poured out of the sky. "I'll teach you to threaten me, Cerberus," she said darkly. "And rather than throw insults at me, Alex, let's give *you* something else to think about for a while."

She pressed her lips together in a bitter smile. The bees clung to her skin, feeding off her energy. They felt the dark element rising and hummed in unison. Her power was undeniable.

e/ce/ɔ

Vicious rains pelted the mansion. Anybody caught outside ran for cover and watched in wonder at the sudden deluge. Alex heard the heavy raindrops against the glass and walked to the window, watching the sky as it seemed to open up and tip its entire contents onto the countryside. Then he was staring at a wall of water, and, with some alarm, he noticed that the bombardment of the torrent was causing wide cracks to appear in the ground. Hearing frantic movement in the hallway, he went to see what was happening and was dismayed to see the servants with brooms and bundles of sacking, trying to hold back the steady stream that seeped under the main door.

Cerberus also came into the great hall, and Alex saw the deep frown on his brow.

"It's okay, Father, I have it under control," Alex said more confidently than he felt, knowing that if it didn't stop soon, the whole ground floor might flood.

Cerberus nodded and went up the staircase to his private rooms. He crossed the main bedroom and threw open the window. The rain drove inward, drenching him instantly. He threw back his head, a thunderous expression darkening his features, and muttered a series of words under his breath. His eyes shifted up toward the slate gray sky as he concentrated his thoughts on wholly defying the wrath of nature. He knew that this was no ordinary storm. This was a powerful enchantment.

e/ce/ɔ

The worst of the weather eased, although, the storm lasted all afternoon and well into the night. Annabel felt exhilarated by it. She stayed in the cottage doorway and watched the rolling clouds rain down sweeping showers. The thunder roared overhead, and the lightning strikes forked across the land. The wind lashed the trees and whipped the countryside. The cottage was spared the worst of the storm. Only a few raindrops touched the windows and, in the immediate vicinity, the weather was relatively calm.

The next day Annabel was restless. She busied herself, washing the windows, sweeping the floors, and cleaning the cottage until it shone.

"Strange storm last night," Josiah said, watching his daughter closely.

"Was it? I didn't really notice," she said cordially.

"I haven't seen a storm like that since…"

Annabel looked at him.

"…since, Lilith was here," he said quietly.

Annabel didn't say anything. She looked back at the table and began polishing it again.

"Someone is certainly having a positive influence on you," Josiah said, smiling at his daughter's efforts.

"Don't get too used to it." She laughed. "It's only because I can't wait to see him. And if I don't keep myself busy, I'll go mad."

Josiah went to her and kissed her on the forehead. "Let's hope he has some good news for us. I'm glad to see you so happy again."

She smiled at him. "I am so happy, Father."

Chapter 18

The Day after Tomorrow

The sunshine and cloudless sky promised a beautiful day, and Annabel filled the morning hours by extracting honey from the hives and picking soft fruits in the garden. She tried not keep checking how high the sun was in the sky, and told herself to be patient. She would see Jevan soon enough. Early afternoon came and, in her bedroom, she took time getting ready, slipping on her newest dress. It was made of surah and was one of her more expensive purchases. The tight-fitting bodice was boldly patterned with narrow stripes of bronze and crimson, which continued down to its fashionable flounced skirt. She took extra time over her hair, piling half of it up and leaving a few ringlets to frame her face, while some cascaded down her back. Satisfied with her appearance, she walked down the stairs as Josiah walked into the cottage. He ran his eye over her appreciatively.

"You look beautiful," he said. "Don't you think it's a bit elegant to go riding over the moors?"

The small smile she gave him spread across her face. "I am not going to be riding a horse, Father. I'm taking the trap into Rookwood to meet Jevan. He will be back very soon."

Minutes later, she kissed her father and climbed into the trap. Storm set off at a walking pace, and Annabel was in no hurry. She was early and would have time to spend with Jophiel before Jevan returned. It seemed strange to think he had only been back a few days, and her whole life had changed around because of it. Her mindset had completely altered, and he was the focus of it, just as he had always been in the past.

The road to Gothelstone was empty, save for, in the distance she spied two children, a boy and girl, running through the oat field. She watched as they pushed each other playfully until the girl fell then quickly got up, laughing. They began running farther into the distance. The hands of time rewound, for they were similar in looks, and certainly behaved like she and Jevan once had. Her memories were as clear today as they had ever been, and she thought back to the schoolroom incident. Even after all this time, Miss Gatchell and the ink staining Jevan's face was just as vivid in Annabel's mind as if it had happened yesterday. She smiled to herself, thinking how strange life was, for so much time had passed since that day, and her life had literally come full circle. She and Jevan were back together, and the hands of time—or any other obstacle, for that matter—could not destroy their unbreakable bond.

When Annabel reached Rookwood, she reflected that it was unusually quiet, and when she smiled at familiar faces, she could not dismiss their returning watery smiles. People didn't talk. They whispered. She wondered if she was imagining it and if, perhaps, she really was dressed too elaborately for the day. It was only a passing thought. Their blinkered view would not dampen her spirits. And, to her, only Jevan's opinion mattered, anyway.

She parked the trap at the side of the forge and climbed down. It was even stranger that everything seemed quiet at the forge also. It was almost as if someone had died. Her heart nearly stopped, as that indeed could be a possibility. She cried out Jophiel's name, and to her immediate relief, he emerged from the cottage. That relief was short lived when she saw his grave expression and his brow deeply furrowed by a frown.

"Annabel."

He didn't look that pleased to see her, and there was something about the way he said her name. It gave her the terrible premonition.

Jophiel wrung his hands. The words he was about to say

sticking in his throat, and her breath stifled in an anguished gasp.

"Oh God, Jevan's dead," she cried.

Her dress felt tighter than ever, squeezing her ribcage. She was unable to breathe, and her knees buckled.

Jophiel leapt forward and caught her as she fell. "No—no, Annabel, he's not dead. It's all right. It's not that," he said, picking her up and carrying her into the cottage. The light-headedness made her close her eyes and cling to Jophiel. He carefully placed her on the settle and, after a few moments, she opened her eyes. "It's all right. He's not dead," he repeated and nodded, reassuring her further.

"I had this strangest feeling—and your face, I thought something terrible had happened."

"Rest for a few minutes," he said and patted her on the shoulder. "I'll get you some water."

He took his time and was unusually quiet when he handed her the glass. Annabel breathed more evenly, the shock giving way to relief. Even so, there was something else on Jophiel's mind. He sat beside her and waited until she had taken a few sips before he spoke.

"Something has happened." Jophiel's eyes rose to meet hers and Annabel felt the blood drain from her skin. "Jevan's been arrested," he said.

She sighed and breathed easier. She could deal with arrested, having already dreaded something much worse.

Jophiel saw her palpable relief. "It's serious, Annabel. He was arrested for stealing horses."

She opened her mouth to speak, and the words never came. She stared at Jophiel in disbelief and he shook his head.

"I know. I don't believe it either."

She felt afraid, and terrible thoughts ran through her head. Horse stealing was a crime that still carried the death penalty. "Whose horses?" she said faintly.

Jophiel met her look straight on. "Whose do you think?"

It felt as though someone had punched her in the stomach. "No, he can't," she said sitting straight up. "Not even Cerberus Saltonstall can accuse someone without evidence."

"He has evidence, apparently," Jophiel growled. "And I'd like to get my hands on him." He closed his eyes briefly. "What use would that be?" he asked, shaking his head. "He has too much power and can do what he likes around these parts."

He was angry, and Annabel could not recall ever seeing him this troubled before.

"His evidence is wrong. Jevan would never steal a horse." Annabel sprang to her feet. "This is all because of me!" she said starting to pace around the room. "I have to do something." She looked at Jophiel. "And I will," she said fervently. "I'll go to the Gothelstone Manor right now, and put an end to this nonsense once and for all."

"Annabel, you don't know what Cerberus is like," Jophiel said, standing and blocking the cottage door.

"Oh, I think I have a fair idea. Besides, I know what his son is like," she said bitterly, thinking for a moment. "Where was he arrested? Is Jevan still in London?"

"No, here in Rookwood, the dungeons under the town hall. He is being kept in Cerberus's private prison cells." He sneered. "Many innocent men have found themselves locked in those terrible rooms."

"Why didn't you say so before?" Annabel said, pushing past him and reaching her hand out to open the cottage door.

"Don't bother trying to see him. You won't even get near the place, and they won't let you see him. The justice was adamant. No one sees him, not even family."

"You spoke to the justice?"

"Spoke, begged, pleaded. It didn't make any difference. I was talking to deaf ears."

"I need to borrow a fast horse. One way or another, I will get Jevan freed, and if Cerberus is at home, then that's where I'm going. Don't try and stop me."

Jophiel wanted to refuse her. He hated the thought of her placing herself in danger, but he knew her far too well. She would steal a horse herself if she had to. Reluctantly, Jophiel nodded. "Be careful, Annabel. Don't rile him or get yourself arrested."

She gave him a cursory glance and went out to the stable. Jess whined happily as she walked up to him. She hurriedly untethered him, hitched up her skirts, and climbed upon his back.

"Let's go, Jess," she said firmly.

Jess, sensing the urgency in her voice, sprang into action. At once, they set off at breakneck speed toward Gothelstone Manor.

၏ပ၏

Jevan wiped the blood from his head. His shirt was already soaked, and he sat on the filthy floor in a dazed stupor as he struggled to remember the night before.

He had been sleeping soundly. Then from out of the darkness, something grabbed him. He fought the attacker, at first, believing it to be a terrifying nightmare. Then he rose up from the bed and lashed out at the dark shadows, but the dream came to life, when a blow to his head made him lose his balance and then consciousness.

He woke some hours later to find himself bundled into a corner of a fast moving carriage, bound at the ankles and wrists. His two captors talked in low voices, their words oddly muffled from the caked blood that filled his ears. He watched them quietly for several minutes. One was stocky with dark hair. His cheekbone looked distorted as if it had been broken. The other man was leaner with lighter coloring and an earring that shone red in the moving light.

"Lucan, he's awake." The man with the earring turned and grabbed a handful of Jevan's hair, forcing his head backward. A cup was pressed against Jevan's lips and water tipped down his throat. Jevan gagged and then choked. Lucan hit him hard on the back.

He laughed nastily. "We can't have you dying on us before we get paid."

That laughter echoed through Jevan's head as he gradually slipped back into the blackness.

Jevan moved uncomfortably. He was no longer bound by

rope. Instead, a metal cuff was attached to his ankle and a chain tethered him to the stone wall. His breath felt heavy. He placed his hand on his rib cage and pressed down.

He shrieked loudly as the pain shot through his whole body. Nausea overwhelmed him. What was left of the contents of his stomach emptied onto the floor beside him. Shock swept over him as the pain of vomiting seared through him, burning his chest. Nothing felt natural anymore. After a time, he placed his hand again on his ribs, and gingerly felt the two broken ones. Jevan groaned and closed his eyes.

"Horse thief."

The words danced maliciously through his head, but he could not remember why anyone said those words to him.

He saw a face, a fleeting glance of the justice, and realized that he must be in Rookwood. Why was the justice reading to him? Jevan brought his hands to his forehead and pressed his temples.

A conviction was read out, and Jevan struggled to make sense of the words: Frederick Thomas—a prime witness. Stealing horses—illegal trade to the colonies. The words jumbled in his head, then his mind suddenly gained clarity when the justice stood before him.

"Is it not true you recently returned from abroad? Isn't it true that you recently returned to Rookwood, and you are the ringleader for this illegal trade? Don't shake your head in denial. Frederick Thomas, one of your own men, has already identified you. He has already confessed his part in this crime."

That name again. Jevan was certain that he had never met a Frederick Thomas. He began to tell that to the justice, but the broken-cheekbone ruffian from the carriage sent him sprawling to the ground. As he lay face down in the dirt, with excruciating pain searing through his chest, he heard the words.

"There is only one penalty for this crime. You will be hung by the neck until dead."

Jevan tried to sit up straighter, but everything hurt. He leaned his head back against the wall and thought of Annabel. The pain suddenly felt unbearable. He had left her again, and she would be waiting for him. This time he would not be coming back.

೧৩৩

Annabel rode Jess fast as he would gallop, blinking tears from her eyes. The blinding rage began to take over her whole being. Cerberus knew just how to get what he wanted. Was this all because she had defied him, questioned him, and threatened him. She pulled on the reins to slow down, her thoughts turning to her mother. What would she have done, when Cerberus threatened her father? She knew why Josiah said that Lilith would never beg. She would not either. She had more power than that.

Annabel stared up at the sky, her thoughts tumbling around her head. Her stare became focused. Her power increased as the wind picked up, and she watched the swirling clouds gathering, the sky grew darker by the second.

"I curse you, Cerberus," she cried. "And I curse you, Wilfred Preston, Justice of the Peace, for carrying out his demands." She threw back her head, concentrating her thoughts, feeling the power build within her and pass down the length of her body. Jess felt it too. He stamped his feet and whined as she cried out, "I invoke my defenders, by all the power and force I have given you, obey me now. Listen only to my command. Destroy those that would harm him and let my own justice be done!"

The energy flooded through the fields, parting the grasses. It reached far and wide, shaking everything in its wake. The overhead clouds raced through the sky and in the direction of where she had come. In the distance, the rain began to fall over Rookwood, which turned into great torrents, beating hard against the town hall. Jess reared and Annabel clutched at the reins, smiling.

"Whoa, Jess. They deserve what's coming to them," she said darkly and watched the turbulent skies for a few moments, thrilled by the energy all around.

She pulled firmly on the left rein to turn Jess and then continued on to Gothelstone Manor, navigating their way through the deep puddles left on the road from the storm the previous day. She felt a small amount of satisfaction that the fields closest to the mansion were still underwater. Yet, her achievements were forgotten, once she reached the front courtyard. She jumped from Jess's back and ran to the door. She banged loudly and, then after a few seconds more, banged again, louder and longer. The door suddenly swung open and Alfred stood before her.

"Is the master in?" she said, pushing her way past, not waiting for an answer.

There was a dampness to the whole area. She saw evidence of a flood in the wet patches all over the floor. Alfred followed her eye.

"Sorry, miss, the whole downstairs flooded, and the floor is still very wet in places."

Annabel ignored his apologies. She didn't care what state the house was in. "I asked you a question," she said haughtily. "Is he here?"

"The—the master is away on business."

Annabel turned back and glared at Alfred impatiently, not a little disappointed to learn that Cerberus was not writhing in agony anywhere in the vicinity.

"I mean Alex. Is Alex here?"

"I will tell Master Alex that you are here, miss," he began.

"No need, Alfred."

Annabel looked up to the balcony.

Alex was standing on the balcony watching her. He moved to the top of the staircase. "Changed your mind already?" he said mockingly, as he began to walk down the stairs toward her.

Annabel ignored the sarcasm. "Alex, you have to help me."

"Why, what have you done now?" he said, remaining indifferent.

"It's not me, it's your father." She paused, as the worst thought possible entered her head, and glared suspiciously at him. "Just maybe I am wrong, maybe it is you," she said, narrowing her eyes. "Would you do such a thing for revenge?"

Alex sighed impatiently and shook his head. "What are you talking about?"

"Jevan's been arrested."

There seemed to be genuine astonishment on Alex's face. "And what exactly has that got to do with me? Although I must say I am not surprised."

Annabel frowned. Her first instinct was right. It was Cerberus's doing. "It's got everything to do with you, Cerberus had him arrested," she said impatiently. "I need you to release him. Alex, you can't let this happen. They will hang him if he is convicted."

She hesitated, even though she hoped Cerberus was out of the picture for good, Alex couldn't suspect anything. "You have to reason with your father," she added tactfully."

Alex pursed his lips. "What exactly is he accused of?"

"Stealing horses," she replied, watching him carefully. "He didn't do it," she added quickly.

Alex looked doubtful as he came to where she stood and closed the door behind her. "That is a serious crime, Annabel, and I am not at liberty to interfere in my father's decisions."

Annabel stared at him in disbelief. "Jevan would never do that, and you are not the man I thought you were, if you can stand by and watch an innocent man hang."

"I don't know that he's innocent," Alex said, "and my father must have good reason to accuse him."

A shocking thought entered Annabel's mind, making her tremble. What if Alex was bound by law to carry out Cerberus last wishes if he was already dead? Suddenly, her plan was taking a very wrong turn.

She tried not to let the tears fall. Even so as much as she tried, she could not control them.

Alex moved closer to her. "Don't cry."

She shook her head. "You won't help me. What do you want me to do, Alex?" All self-respect went out of the window. She didn't care what she had to do to see Jevan free. "Do you want me to get down on my knees and beg for his life?"

He took her hands in his own and held them tight. "No," he said softly, "I don't want you to beg me."

"But you won't help me. You won't get him released," she said, pulling her hands away from him.

"I didn't say that either, and my father is not here." He paused for a moment, watching her closely. "I can help you and I will, but there has to be one condition."

Annabel looked up at him, puzzled as to what his price was.

"His life for your hand in marriage," Alex concluded firmly.

She stared at him in disbelief, and her heart sank. Nothing would ever be right with the world again if she said yes. She could see Alex was determined, and she knew if he did not help her, then there was no alternative. Cerberus was too powerful. She would do anything to save Jevan's life, even give her own.

On the other hand, agreeing to marry anyone other than Jevan felt worse than dying. She was unable to contemplate how she could even begin to fulfill that obligation with Alex, not while Jevan still lived. She drew in her breath, blinked away new tears, and with a quiver in her voice, she replied, "You're leaving me with no other choice. It's nothing short of blackmail."

Alex smiled fractionally. "Don't be so dramatic. I am merely turning an unfortunate situation to my best advantage. It's called bargaining," he said, with all seriousness. "My father will listen to me, whether Jevan is innocent or not."

"He is innocent."

"So you say. I don't know the facts yet." He wiped away the last of her tears tenderly. "Give me your answer, Annabel."

As uncertain as she was, the alternative was unthinkable. She thought for only a moment then answered with resignation. "Jevan has to get a full unconditional pardon. There can be no reproach, and he will be left alone to work in any trade he wishes."

Alex knitted his eyebrows for a second. "You have my word."

"What about Cerberus's word?"

"For you, I will move heaven and earth to make sure he changes his mind."

Annabel closed her eyes briefly. If Cerberus was away, her manipulation might not extend that far, and at the same time, she felt deflated to know he could, at any moment, walk back in the door, totally unscathed. She opened her eyes and gazed at Alex. There was triumph in his look. She felt like a rat caught in the tightest trap, and Jevan would hate her for it. She sighed. There were no other words to say, other than exactly what Alex wanted to hear.

"I will agree to your terms, Alex."

Chapter 19

Commotion at the Town Hall

Wilfred Preston sat in his office, counting out the money. He lit a cigar and sat back in his chair contentedly, dismissing the twinge of guilt. It was a small price to pay. After all, he wasn't overly concerned with Jevan Wenham, and he reasoned that he hardly knew him. On the other hand, his conscious pricked when he thought about Jevan's father.

Jophiel was a different story. Wilfred had known him for many years and Jophiel was always his blacksmith of choice, as well as a good man. Wilfred moved uncomfortably as he thought about how Jophiel begged him, then offered him a paltry sum of money to release Jevan, and then shouted at him trying to appeal to his sense of honor.

"Just imagine, Wilfred, if this was your son!" Jophiel had implored.

Wilfred had merely turned his back and allowed staff to deal with the commotion. In any case, he reassured himself, there was no need to worry. Cerberus had promised that there would be no loose ends, and nothing would implicate him in what occurred afterward. After all, there was a believable witness and a network of ruffians loyal to Cerberus, and if Wilfred believed Cerberus, then the master of Gothelstone Manor would be in his debt. Not that he particularly believed those words. Cerberus was manipulative and powerful, and even if Wilfred wanted to, he could not have refused him.

Wilfred was mildly concerned at being on Cerberus's payroll now, although even that came as a welcome solution to all his gambling debts. He reminded himself that he had his own family to think of. His sons would benefit from the education Wilfred could now afford. He would be able to pay his creditors off, and the distasteful business of the blacksmith's son would resolve itself.

The rain began to fall outside. Wilfred got up from the chair and walked to the window. He stared out into the street. The day had become suddenly stormy, and many people caught off guard were rushing around, trying to take cover from the rapidly approaching curtain of rain. The atmosphere felt odd, as the wind whistled down the street and thunder bellowed overhead.

Wilfred pulled the window in a little. The air was humid, but he felt unusually exhilarated by the approaching storm, or maybe it was just elation at the sight of the pile of money before him. He sat back down and leaned his head back, taking a long draw on the cigar, and slowly exhaled, watching as the smoke rose into the air.

Tonight, he would tell his wife, Elena, that they could go to Bath this season, after all. He would tell her that she would have the finest dresses for the occasion, and he made up his mind to leave early today, impatient to see her reaction to the news. A small hum made him look toward the window where a solitary bee had flown into the room to take shelter. It rested on the windowpane.

Wilfred stared at the bee for a few seconds. "Don't get too comfortable. As soon as the rain stops, you're going out," he announced and placed the cigar back in his mouth.

He closed his eyes. In Bath, he would introduce his sons into society this year. They would attend dinner engagements and accompany him to private billiard games. Behind closed doors, they would drink and play cards with Bath's elite, the backbone to how important connections were made. He had to plan for their futures now.

The incessant humming from the bee invaded his thoughts,

and he opened his eyes to find the room considerably darker. He looked at the window where he could see only tiny dots of daylight amongst the blanket of writhing yellow and black bodies. Wilfred dropped the cigar, which fell into his lap and instantly burned through the fabric of his trousers. He leapt up with a yelp, staring wide-eyed at the window. Slowly he backed away toward the door. All of a sudden, the humming increased tenfold and all the bees left the window.

His scream choked as they flew into his mouth and down his throat, and his body fell to the floor. He writhed in agony for several seconds. The shock and venom surging through his veins immobilized him quickly. Then the bees simultaneously left him, ripping their bodies away from their stingers as, one by one, they propelled themselves out through the gap in the window and fell to the ground in a spent heap. Shouts came from down the corridor, and then a single scream as a clerk found the contorted body of Wilfred Preston. Someone summoned the doctor immediately, but Wilfred Preston had already been dead for several minutes.

☙❧☙

Annabel left Alex a little later that day and went back to the forge. Her anguish so plainly etched on her face that she could not keep the news from Jophiel. He was clearly horrified at her words.

"You can't marry him. What about Jevan?"

"Jevan will die, if I don't," she said matter-of-factly, even though her insides felt as though they were being torn apart.

Jophiel sat with his head in his hands for several minutes, the enormity of what she said going repeatedly through his mind. "There must be another way."

"No," she said, feeling defeated, "there isn't." Her voice was barely audible.

Jophiel looked up at her. He stood and put his arms around her, wishing there was something useful to say. In his arms, she felt comforted and safe for a few moments. Then the reality of what she agreed to made her very afraid. "If Jevan is released, I think he will kill Alex. Then he will be tried and hung for sure." She sighed sorrowfully and shook her head. "I don't know what to do."

"I know," he said grimly, "the same thought crossed my mind."

❧❧❧

The situation was desperate. What else could she have done? She reasoned that there was still time and hoped that there might still be a way out of this mess, something she hadn't thought of. She was dreading telling her father the news, and before she walked into the cottage, she ran through the orchard to the hives. One by one, she inspected her bees. They were safe and all accounted for. She frowned.

"Didn't you hear my call?"

The bees didn't respond. She sighed wearily. Perhaps she was losing her touch. Feeling completely despondent, she walked slowly back to the cottage to find her father.

❧❧❧

The next day Alex sent a carriage for her. When she arrived at the mansion, Alex was waiting. She was impatient for news of Jevan and bided her time while he spoke of some wedding preparations. She tried not to cringe at the thought.

Then he mentioned the strange way in which the justice died. Her attention came back with a jolt.

"Does that mean Jevan can't be held anymore?" she said, a little too quickly.

"No," Alex replied, watching her closely. "The crime still stands." He hesitated for a moment. "I made you a promise, and I will keep it. I have arranged that Jevan will be released—on our wedding day."

Annabel stared at him in horror. "You can't leave him in that place until we marry! It could be weeks."

"On the contrary, the wedding will happen as soon as it is possible, and then Jevan will go free."

"You know he's innocent. Why can't you arrange it sooner?"

Alex raised his eyebrows a fraction. "I love you," he said wearily, "but I am not stupid, Annabel. Call it my insurance policy. I wouldn't want my bride changing her mind, would I?"

Annabel made a noise of anger in her throat. She knew she was beaten, and Alex was no fool. She suddenly realized how trapped she was.

"You should help with the arrangements, it will take your mind off other things," Alex said, with a hint of irritation at her obvious disappointment.

But, in truth, Alex had acted quickly, all matters were in hand and there was not much for her to do. Only her dress was to be her decision. Alex led her up to a distant bedroom and, to her surprise, a dressmaker waited for her. The woman laid swatches of fabric out in front of her, and a book of designs was open on the dressing table. After Alex left, her measurements were taken, and she was fitted for a suitable gown. Annabel took no pleasure in deciding on a style of dress. She merely played her part and was glad when the dressmaker left her alone.

Eventually, Annabel also left the bedroom. The corridor was empty, and so she made her way to the staircase. A maid walked up the stairs carrying fresh linens.

"Where is the master, Alex?" she asked the girl.

"I don't know, ma'am. I haven't seen him. Can I get you anything?" the maid asked, smiling timidly.

Annabel instantly smiled back. The girl was the first friendly face she'd seen all day. "What is your name?"

"Edith, ma'am."

"Please bring me tea, Edith, and I'll take it in the drawing room."

Annabel made her way to the drawing room. She sat on the couch, and her mind wandered back to the words that Alex said that morning.

She thought about those bees. Where had they come from? Had she really summoned them from the underworld, or were they the only ones within the vicinity of her power yesterday?

The maid interrupted her contemplation. She placed the china teacup on the side table and left the room. Annabel sipped it slowly. Several minutes later and much to her dismay, Cerberus walked into the room. Even more disheartening was that he looked completely healthy and un-traumatized.

"I see that you have finally come to your senses."

She didn't answer. She sipped uneasily.

Cerberus walked across the room to the fireplace, and she tried not to be distracted by his nearness, especially when she felt him turn and stare at her. She dearly wanted to accuse him of the hateful thing he'd done. It would not solve any problem, better that she remain quiet.

"Don't think you can use your witchcraft against me!"

It felt as every drop of blood left her body, and an icy hand slid down her back. She twisted her head and looked up at him horrified. "What?"

"It doesn't work against me."

She swallowed the lump in her throat. "What—what are you talking about?"

"Ah, I think you know."

She nervously shook her head. Cerberus stared at her for a long moment, his mouth moved as if he might speak. He didn't, and the lack of words unnerved her more. She was unable to tare her eyes from him. There was something in his look, which confounded her completely.

"You are like me," he said at last. "You seek to destroy those who would get in your way. But be careful, because I am watching. You are not as powerful as me, and I will make the most terrible enemy."

There was a gleam of menace in his eye as he glowered at her for a moment before he left the room. The tea turned to acid in her stomach. She felt sick. How did he know? How could he know? Unless he was the devil himself.

Chapter 20

The Wedding

The dress was white satin and lace, with deep box pleats and pleated panniers. The heavily embroidered bodice was tight fitting and the elbow-length sleeves ended in ruffles. Her scalp felt tight. The maid, having combed and coaxed all trace of wildness from her hair, laid it in a long red coil on her neck. A fine silk sheer veil reached the ground behind.

Annabel looked at her reflection in the mirror. This was not what she wanted. Somewhere in the back of her mind, she always believed it really wouldn't come to this. She'd hoped there would have been a way out, a way to get Jevan released. She took a deep breath, stretching her neck to ease the soreness of her scalp. Despair settled over her like a gray cloud.

Jevan still languished in Cerberus's dungeon. In all her imaginings, she should be marrying Jevan. All she had ever wanted was a simple dress and a bouquet of wild flowers to compliment the ones tied in her hair. Instead, she felt stifled. She looked artificial, like some mannequin out of a fashion brochure.

Annabel sighed, feeling defeated. This day was going to be one of the longest. She reluctantly glanced at her reflection again and opened the bedroom door. As she made her way down the stairs, her legs felt weak as though they might fail at any moment.

"You can do this, you can do this for Jevan," she told herself again and wondered what it would take for her to believe those words.

Annabel stepped from the cottage into the brilliant sunshine and looked toward the road. One of the best Saltonstall carriages waited for her, along with her father dressed in his finest clothes.

She walked slowly, clutching at a quantity of fabric as to not trip over the dress. Her focus was on Josiah, and when he raised his head, she met his smile with her own. There was concern behind his expression.

Jophiel stood beside her father. They had been deep in conversation, and he took a step forward as she neared.

"You look beautiful," Jophiel said positively, although she noted the sadness in his tone.

"You do," agreed her father, nodding his head, and then he hesitated. His voice was tinged with sadness. "We both know this is going to be a difficult day for you, but—"

She looked from her father to Jophiel. "Is Jevan free yet?" she interrupted, not wanting to be distracted from her own thoughts.

Josiah shook his head slowly. "I went to the court house first thing," he, replied somberly. "He can't be released, not until you are married."

Annabel felt her stomach lurch at the words, suppressing an urge to scream in frustration. She turned to her father. "Before I enter that church you have to see Alex. You must tell him that Jevan has to be released, before I will marry him."

Josiah looked skeptical. "Don't you think it will be better—"

"No, I don't," she said, shaking her head, not caring what he was going to say. "That's my condition, and I won't see Alex until I am inside the church, so you have to do this for me."

Josiah thought about dissuading her, but her look was determined, and he knew she was not about to be swayed.

"And I am not stepping one foot out of the carriage, until I know Jevan is freed," Annabel continued unwaveringly.

Jophiel and Josiah exchanged glances. "All right, if that is what you want," Josiah agreed hesitantly.

"It is," she replied, accepting her father's hand, and stepped up into the carriage. Once seated she leaned forward to see Jophiel better. "Will you ride in the carriage with us?"

"I'm not family," he began.

"You are more than family to me. Please, I want you both with me."

Jophiel smiled faintly and nodded. The conversation in the carriage on the way to Gothelstone church was subdued. Annabel knew that Jevan knew about the wedding. Alex had subtly told her that, although, she suspected he didn't know the true reason. She knew him far too well. He would be livid, and she couldn't begin to imagine what would be going through his mind at this moment. The only thing for certain was that he would do something reckless. That knowledge terrified her.

Annabel fidgeted with the dress, feeling more irritated by the minute. Jophiel's mind was also elsewhere. Forbidden from seeing his son for close to three long weeks since Jevan was placed in that hellhole, he felt out of his mind with worry. Jevan would not accept this situation. His rage was not something Jophiel was easily able to contend with. He played out the imminent scene in his mind. He had to make Jevan see sense, and, for everybody's sake, Jevan had to accept the decision Annabel made.

Annabel clasped her hands together and then clutched at her dress again. Too anxious about the wedding, and the consequences, she longed for Jevan to be free, although, now the fear of seeing him again made her heart race. How could she could ever again look into his eyes, because she was too afraid of what she might find in their depths?

Josiah was very quiet. He dreaded speaking to Alex, and he had no other choice. Annabel was resolute, and no one would force her into this marriage if she thought Jevan was not free.

He sat close enough to her that he could feel how rigid her body was. Her whole demeanor was understandably tense. He took her hand, to stop her from wearing a hole through the fabric of her dress, and smiled, trying to give her some courage. Josiah was only glad that Lilith was not here to see this travesty. Wedding's should be happy occasions, he thought sadly, not fraught with danger as this one promised to be.

The carriage eventually arrived at the church. Both Josiah and Jophiel got out, and Annabel leaned back in the seat. Josiah glanced again at his daughter, vaguely hoping that she might have reconsidered. She stared back at him expectantly. Making no comment, he turned from her, took a deep breath, and hurried into the church. After a few moments, Annabel leaned forward, enabling her to get a better look out of the window.

"Jophiel, go with him," she said anxiously. "Make sure everything is all right."

"What about you? I don't want to leave you alone."

Annabel laughed. "What are they going to do, kidnap me? It's taken them long enough to get me here. I think today of all days, I may have a little leverage." Jophiel cast a concerned look back at her, and she smiled. "Go on, I will be fine."

She watched Jophiel follow her father's footsteps and walk into the church. She didn't feel fine. She was upsetting the apple cart again, and Alex would be furious. *I don't care*, she thought, *let him rant and rave all he likes, Cerberus too.*

Several minutes passed, and her eyes remained glued to the doorway of the church. She wished she could see and hear what was happening. Suddenly Cerberus appeared. He strode toward the carriage with purpose, and Annabel sensed his annoyance even before he reached her.

"Come into the church, Annabel, Alex is waiting," he said evenly and held out his hand for her to accept.

She gazed at him steadily and shook her head. "No," she said with some defiance. "Jevan goes free now, or there will be no marriage."

Cerberus made a noise of contempt in his throat. His eyes glittered dangerously, even if his voice was calm when he spoke. "The blacksmith already has the signed release."

Annabel looked past Cerberus. Jophiel and her father had just left the church and were coming toward the carriage.

"Do you really have it?" she called over Cerberus's head, ignoring his piercing stare.

"Yes," Jophiel said, waving an official looking document. "I will go right now."

Annabel could not disguise her expression of relief, and she looked at Cerberus again. His lips were set in a thin line, and he held out his hand for her to take again.

"You look very beautiful."

His compliment was unexpected and out of the ordinary. Annabel stared at him, her surprise evident. She thought there was a softening in his steely eyes, but only for a moment, and looked down at his hand in confusion. "I should take my father's hand into the church," she said, meeting his gaze again.

An odd look passed across Cerberus's face. He continued to stare at her for a long moment, then he lowered his arm and stepped aside. Josiah helped her out of the carriage.

She smiled at her father. "Jevan will be free," she said quietly.

"Yes," he said happily, giving Cerberus a long look of disdain.

Cerberus did not react. He merely turned and walked before them into the church. Annabel made slow progress, deliberately stopping several times to adjust her dress, although, it was when she crossed the threshold into the church that the stress of the day seemed to hit her with full force. She felt her knees buckle and stumbled awkwardly against Josiah.

"I don't know if I can do this," she said faintly.

Josiah took a firm hold around her waist and held her tight for a few moments. "It's just nerves. You can do this for Jevan," he said confidently.

Annabel closed her eyes for a moment. "You really think so?" she said, opening them and looking up at him.

"Yes," he said without hesitation. "You will make this work to your best advantage." He dropped his arm from her waist and held it out to lean on. As they took the first few steps forward, Josiah looked at her again. "Sometimes we all have to do things that will have the best outcome, not because it's what our heart desires."

His eyes betrayed the pain of what he was encouraging her to do.

"Jevan will not accept this, you know," she said, afraid again, of what Jevan was capable of, and Josiah nodded bleakly.

"I know that no one will keep you apart. And that is extremely dangerous knowledge," he said grimly.

Walking up the aisle felt like one of the most tortuous journeys Annabel had ever made. The sight of Alex waiting at the end made her tremble, although, he didn't look furious as she supposed he might. Instead, he smiled as she reached him. Josiah placed her wavering hand in his, and Alex squeezed it in reassurance. Annabel looked up into his dark blue eyes, and her doubts multiplied.

If Jevan walked into the church right now, she would leave with him and hang the consequences. She was doing the wrong thing. In her heart, she knew it. She nervously looked over her shoulder and caught Cerberus's eye. Alex had a firm hold on her, and everyone else was staring at her. There was no escape.

Thoughts tumbled mercilessly around her head. Alex had kept his promise. Jevan was free, and she was grateful at least. Then again was gratitude really enough of a reason to marry him? It was far more complicated than she could have imagined. If she said no, if she backed out now, what was to stop Cerberus having Jevan arrested again? There really was no choice. Annabel stared into the disapproving eyes of the priest.

With a sudden jolt, she realized he had asked her a question. The whole church was in silence, and Alex had tightened his grip, squeezing her hand enough that it started to hurt. In his grip, she knew there was no getting away. She looked back at her father. Josiah nodded his head.

She turned back to face the priest. "Yes," she said, "I do."

Ͼ∕ᴔϾ∕ᴔ

Jophiel reached the courthouse at eleven fifty-five. He gazed up at the town clock face. Five more minutes remained before Annabel would be married. Jophiel wanted to see Jevan more than anything else, only that want was marred. He did not want to see his son's pain and was still ill prepared for his anger. He took a deep breath, walked into the main lobby, and handed the papers over to the clerk.

"Wait here," the clerk, instructed curtly.

Jophiel paced back and forth. He visibly jumped when he heard the clock strike twelve and felt a surge of bitter pain. That was it. The deed was done. Then he heard his son's voice.

"Father."

Jophiel spun around and stifled a gasp. Jevan stood across the room. He had lost weight, his face was gaunt, his hair lank, and his clothes filthy. The dark circles under his eyes made him look sinister and even more wretched. Jophiel forced a smile

Jevan saw straight through the look. He recognized shock in his father's eyes. He knew he must look terrible. His chest was still painful when he breathed, but there was only one thing that concerned him.

"Where is she?"

Jophiel went to his son. He lifted his arms to embrace him, and Jevan backed away.

"Where is she, Father?"

Jophiel froze. He heard the dark undercurrent in Jevan's voice, and he saw the malice in his eyes. "She—she's married."

Jevan's eyes grew darker. "Not for long," he said venomously, shaking his head, "I am going to kill her!" He pushed passed his father and flung open the courthouse door.

"Wait, Jevan!" Jophiel ran out into the street after his son.

Jevan was moving fast, already half way down the street and heading for the forge. Jophiel ran after him, stunned by the viciousness of his remark. He caught up with him at the stables where Jevan was untying Jess, and saw that Jevan moved with some difficulty.

"There's something you need to know," Jophiel said firmly, walking closer.

"No there isn't. I already know that she betrayed me." Jevan turned his head and stared at Jophiel. "She was the only one who knew where I was going and where I'd be." Jevan made a noise of disgust. "She wanted to marry Alex all along. I am a fool, for she as much as told me how much she liked him when we were up on the moors. This is just her idea of entertainment." Jevan went to climb up on to the horses back, but Jophiel pulled him back. "Get out of my way, my argument is not with you."

"No, not until you listen, Jevan."

Jevan grabbed hold of Jophiel's lapels and pushed him hard against the wall. "I said get out of my way."

Jophiel saw the dangerous madness in his son's eyes; even so, he would not back down. "She was not the only one who knew. Cerberus knew, Alex knew, and she has married him to save your life."

Jevan stared at his father and sneered. "She has you wrapped so tightly around her little finger that you cannot see how toxic she is."

Jophiel's eyes opened wide. "You don't believe that!" he snapped aggressively. "Being in that awful place has poisoned your thoughts and your mind. You love her as much as she loves you. Deep down, you know that her hand has been forced."

"Annabel would not be forced into anything," Jevan said, taking his hands from his father.

"Where you're concerned, she would."

Jevan stared at Jophiel. "Then I would rather hang than see her married to him," he answered fervently.

"She wouldn't see you hang. That's the only reason for this marriage. Think of her, Jevan, and what she's done for you."

Suddenly, Jevan felt lightheaded and nauseated. His strength suddenly drained, his stamina sapped by what he endured over the past few weeks, and it was a struggle to remain upright. Adrenaline initially drove him and his rage, but now it was gone. He stumbled slightly against Jess.

Jophiel leapt forward and grabbed his son's arm, fearful that he would pass out. He became more alarmed as Jevan started wheezing and clutched at his ribcage. "What have they done to you?" he said in horror.

"Only broken bones, Father, they'll mend."

Josiah shook his head. "Bastards, they'll pay for this!" He supported Jevan as best as he could and staggered into the cottage. He lowered him gently to an armchair. "Let's get you a bath and some clean clothes. You need to sleep, and you don't look like you've eaten in weeks."

"Don't fuss, Father," Jevan said weakly.

Jophiel ignored him and began to unbutton Jevan's soiled shirt. He stopped when he saw the deep purple bruises across his chest and Jevan winced again.

"I'm going for the doctor," Jophiel said at once. "You need to be bound." He made for the door, but stopped before he reached it and turned back. Jevan was extremely pale, his eyelids fluttering as if he were slipping in and out of consciousness. "Jevan, you will stay here? You know that you can't go near them, or Cerberus will have you locked up again. The sacrifice Annabel has made will have been for nothing."

"Is it really a sacrifice on her part? Or merely a better choice."

"You don't really believe that?"

Jevan reached his hands up to his temples. "What am I going to do?"

"Right now, you're going to rest here, and I will fetch the doctor—Jevan?"

The pain in Jevan's ribs seared through him again. It felt as though his chest where on fire, and then the pain heightened. He was vaguely aware of Jophiel saying his name, somewhere in the distance. He tried to respond, and black spots danced before his eyes. Then he felt a numbing sensation before the blissful darkness.

ↄ৵ↄ৵

No expense spared, Cerberus made certain the reception party was a lavish affair. The guests were mainly business contacts and people from farther a field that Annabel had never seen before. Her father was clearly uncomfortable being in Cerberus's house. Cerberus, however was polite enough to Annabel and officially welcomed her to the family. As soon as the attention shifted from her, she went to find her father. He stood in the corner of the great hall, casually chatting with one of the grooms as the estate workers were allowed inside to toast the bride and groom.

Annabel smiled at the groom she knew as Mark and accepted his best wishes. He tactfully excused himself and left her alone with Josiah.

"I'm sorry this is just as miserable for you," she said sympathetically.

"I think I should leave, Annabel. You know that Cerberus hates me and doesn't want me here."

She laughed nervously. "I wouldn't take it personally. He hates everyone, especially me." Her face became serious and she nodded. "I understand. Go, I will see you tomorrow before I leave. I don't suppose you have seen anything of Jophiel?" she added hopefully.

Josiah shook his head. "No, I suspect he has his hands full."

"I want to see Jevan, I cannot bear to think what he has gone through. I should be with him!" she suddenly burst out, and Josiah stared at his daughter in disbelief.

"It's your wedding day! You can't. Think of the risk."

"Some wedding, an arranged, forced marriage," she said contemptuously.

"You may be a married woman, Annabel, but I am still your father, and I forbid you to try and see Jevan," he said, in a very low but firm voice, and took her hand. "I think you are trying to send me to an early grave, my love," he added softly. "It would be extremely inappropriate, and the last thing Jevan needs is to see you right now. Besides that, have some consideration for Alex. After all, given what you have told me in the past, Cerberus has manipulated him too in this arrangement. Although, I really do believe that he loves you," he added tactfully.

Annabel kissed her father on the cheek. She nodded, trying

to hide her disappointment, He was wrong. Jevan would want to see her. Her father was right, though, she should give some thought to Alex.

"Will you at least make sure Jevan is all right and—that—" She stopped unable to go on.

"I'm sure he is all right," Josiah said in reassurance.

"I can't bear the thought that he hates me, Father" she said. "You have to tell him that I love him."

"Shh," Josiah hissed abruptly. "Someone might hear. You cannot harbor these thoughts. You have to think before you speak. Your thoughts are too dangerous."

A little while later, Josiah expressed his happiness to Alex and acknowledged Cerberus with a curt nod. Soon after, he left the reception with a dark shadow hanging over him. His daughter's thoughts disturbed him deeply.

The party went on until late. Annabel smiled and feigned interest in their guests and tedious conversations, even if her thoughts were far away. Alex had stayed by her side most of the evening, and she was grateful that he mostly spoke for her. When the last guest had departed, he turned to her.

"I'm as glad as you that it's over with."

She looked up at him in surprise. The day had been a strain on him also, and she felt a sudden compassion for him. As he bent his head to hers, she closed her eyes, and they pressed together silently. She allowed the intimacy of the kiss to stir her passion. This was her husband now, and there was no prolonging the inevitable. They walked up the stairs toward their bedroom suite. As they reached the door, Alex unexpectedly swung her up in his arms and pushed the door open. Then a few moments later, he set her down inches from the bed.

"I have waited so long for you, Annabel," he said huskily, reached up, and one by one, pulled the pins from her head. Her hair tumbled down her back and framed her face. "My wild gypsy," he whispered and brushed his lips against hers.

Suddenly the panic hit her. What was she doing? Did Alex even realize that she had lain with Jevan, and that she was no longer a virgin? She didn't want this. She didn't want to be here. Most of all, she no longer knew how to respond to him.

Alex felt her trembling and he saw the fear in her eyes.

"It's all right. Everything will be all right now."

He kissed her neck and unfastened her buttons. The dress fell to the floor, quickly followed by the silk chemise. Alex murmured in satisfaction and ran his hands over her body. Annabel closed her eyes and thought of Jevan. She didn't react when he pushed her gently to the bed. She pictured Jevan and stopped trembling. With her eyes closed, she could respond to his attention to a point.

❧❦❧

Alex's lovemaking was sedate. That was the only word she could think of. there was nothing particularly bad or wrong, and she played her part with no particular enthusiasm, feeling more like a mechanical toy than a deeply passionate lover.

She tried to block Jevan's image from her mind, but it refused to fade. Two tears ran down her cheek and then a steady trickle followed. Alex, thinking he had hurt her, at once kissed her.

"It will be better next time," he said, clasping her tightly to him, then within a few minutes he was asleep, and his arms still embraced her. The weight was heavy across her stomach, and she tried to move away from him. At the disturbance, he pulled her closer and held her tighter.

Annabel closed her eyes and waited for sleep to come. Jevan's image danced before her eyes. His accusing words would not allow her any peace, and she turned her head into the pillow. Soon, tears she could not control, even if it muffled the sobs she could not stifle, soaked it.

Annabel eventually did sleep, exhausted by the day's events. When she woke the next morning, Alex was already awake.

He was propped on the pillow watching her. "Good morning, Mrs. Saltonstall."

Annabel stared up at him, feeling reassured of his presence in this wholly unfamiliar place, and at the same time unnerved by his appearance. He reminded her of something, yet, she couldn't quite imagine what. Alex kissed her and she surrendered to his desire once more, not even bothering to protest. She knew it was pretense, just a ritual her body partook in, even though her mind was somewhere else. Their lovemaking was a repeat of the previous night, a little more familiar, but no more endearing than the first time. Alex was her husband, and that fact did not make up for the strangeness of the feeling she got.

"It's because I don't love him," she told herself, as she ran the brush through her hair. Maybe he was just too different from Jevan. She stared at the mirror. "What am I to do?" she asked the reflection quietly.

Jevan stirred her passion intently. He only had to look at her. Alex was lukewarm in comparison. Guilt plagued her. Jevan would hate her for this, despite the fact she'd had no choice. He would still not forgive her. She suddenly felt very afraid.

"Are you ready yet?" Alex said happily, walking into the room.

Annabel turned to him and smiled warily. "Yes."

Cerberus was waiting in the hall. His demeanor was visibly relaxed, "Good morning, Annabel, I trust you slept well?"

"Thank you, yes," she said politely.

Cerberus turned to Alex. "How long will you stay in Bath?"

"Three weeks, no more. I want to show off my beautiful wife to society, and as Annabel's never left Exmoor before, she probably won't even want to come back," he said, winking playfully at her.

"I am sure that will not be the case," she said firmly.

The carriage was to stop at Honeymead so that she could see her father, but it was to be a very short visit, as Alex was eager to begin their journey. He did not leave her side, except when she went to see the bees. Then he stood to the back of the orchard with Josiah.

"Be quick, my love," he called. "We don't have much time." He gazed down at the silver watch fob and then turned to Josiah. "I wish she wouldn't go there unprotected. If she gets stung—"

Josiah made a noise of amusement in his throat. "She has never been stung. She understands them and they her. It's the way it's always been."

Alex frowned. "I can't pretend to understand why both of you like the creatures so much. They are so dangerous. Look at what happened to the justice."

Josiah pursed his lips and bit his tongue. He didn't want to argue with his son-in-law and chose his next words carefully. "Perhaps he disturbed a swarm."

"In his office!" Alex said disbelievingly.

Josiah shook his head. "I don't know. It's a bit of a mystery. I've been a beekeeper all my life, and bees don't normally attack like that. Something must have provoked them."

Just then, Annabel came back. "What are you two looking so serious about?"

"Bees," said Josiah, and Annabel laughed.

"Has Alex been telling you how dangerous they are?" she said, bemused, "and how we are going to get attacked in our beds by killer swarms."

Alex was clearly irritated. "I am just concerned with your safety."

"There's no need where the bees are concerned," she said then added more thoughtfully, "You should stay in the cottage with my father, if it distresses you so."

They walked back to the cottage, and Alex spoke about their journey ahead with Josiah. It was only when his back was turned that Annabel was able to whisper to her father.

"Any news?"

Josiah could not respond straight away, and, a short time later, they were ready to leave. Alex bid him good day, and Josiah put his arms around Annabel.

"I am going to miss you," he said with heartfelt emotion. He looked at Alex beseechingly for a moment.

"I will take good care of her."

Josiah pulled out his handkerchief.

"Father, I will be back in three weeks, don't fret. I will come and see you straight away." Annabel looked at Alex. "Can I have a moment alone?"

Alex nodded and walked outside.

He didn't go far and Josiah had to whisper quickly. "He is well. He will stay with Jophiel. I will go and talk with him and make sure he stays away from you."

Annabel's eyes blazed with outrage.

"Be sensible, he cannot come near you, you know that," he added in a whisper as he led her toward the door.

Once seated in the carriage, Alex waved to Josiah, and Annabel gave her father a watery smile. She watched Honeymead getting smaller and smaller, feeling a tug at her heartstrings and then a strange sort of emptiness as it finally disappeared from sight.

Chapter 21

In the Company of Society

They made good progress on the journey, stopping only to allow the sleek black horses to rest and drink. Even though Annabel's thoughts were mainly of Jevan, her attention began to focus on the changing scenery beyond the carriage window. She could not fail to feel impressed by the Georgian architecture in a city that was so beautiful and elegant, or the overall environment, which felt invigorated by general hustle and bustle of daily life.

Alex had already arranged lodgings at the stunning Royal Crescent. On arrival, and never having seen such uniformity in buildings before, Annabel could only gaze in awe as she stepped from the carriage and walked up the stone steps. After the stuffiness of the carriage, the interior of the building felt pleasingly cool and airy. The proprietor promptly showed them to their accommodations, and after a quick inspection of the luxurious apartment, Annabel walked to the window, eager to take in more of the delightful aspects of the city. Her fascination fixed upon the aristocratic-looking gentlemen and the elaborately dressed ladies that stepped from newly arrived carriages.

Alex joined her at the window. "No doubt they have just returned from the Pump Room," he observed, following her gaze. "It is the social heart of Bath. They go to take the waters."

"They look so elegant."

"We are in an extremely fashionable part of Bath," he replied. "Regardless of their fine clothes, none of them can match your beauty," he said, putting his arms around her. "And we can easily rectify your attire," he remarked, looking down at her travel dress. "I have already booked an appointment at Mrs. Eaton's. It is a fine establishment that caters exclusively to Bath's elite."

After lunch, they left their apartment and strolled around the curve of the crescent, attracting inquisitive glances. Several gentlemen spoke as they tipped their hats, and Alex bade them good afternoon with a similar gesture. Annabel felt foreign and uncertain in this place. The women they passed scrutinized her curiously, and she caught their questioning whispers as they passed by. These women were immaculately groomed, with their hair pinned and fastened in neat styles, while many wore hats and feathers. Their dresses were made of chintz and cretonne, their tunics trimmed with fringe or ruching, and many ladies wore a Polonaise, the fashionable bodice with Basques in front and short behind or with detached tunics that were puffed behind. Outfits that Annabel had only seen in fashion brochures. By contrast, her simple day dress was considerably out of fashion, plainer with no fancy ruffles or edging, only a little embroidery on the bodice. Her hair was mostly loose, apart from the two hair combs that swept it up at the sides.

She could well imagine the whispers: *What is a girl like that doing with such a gentleman?* Although Annabel did not have time to dwell on what others thought. She and Alex arrived at an ornate door with large glass panels, and he held it open.

"Good morning, Mrs. Eaton," Alex said to the smiling proprietor who met them as they entered the boutique. "I am Alex Saltonstall. I have an appointment."

"Mr. Saltonstall, I am so happy to make your acquaintance, and that of your wife—Mrs. Saltonstall."

The pause was only minor, but Annabel noticed. She stared back at the woman whose look was full of speculation. There was no time to wonder or even care what the woman thought.

Alex was already asking to be shown a suitable dress for the evening.

Annabel gazed around the Aladdin's cave. It was large room with a vaulted ceiling, and great swathes of material arranged in rows on carved wooden shelving racks. A chandelier hung from the ceiling and hundreds of crystals adorned it. Ribbons and bows were evenly displayed in various cases, and through a curtained archway, dresses hung on rails while dressmaker's mannequins displayed others.

One such dress, immediately took Annabel's breath away. It was pale blue satin with an overskirt of blue gauze, its bodice of ivory pure corded silk and tiny-ribboned bows on the shoulders. It looked as though it belonged in a fairy tale. Never had she seen such a beautiful dress. Alex had been watching closely and saw her expression. She heard him enquire the price, and Annabel's eyes widened when she heard the answer and then even wider when Alex said to Mrs. Eaton, "My wife would like to try it on."

Annabel turned to him. "There's no need to go to such great expense," she said in a low voice.

"Nonsense," Alex said sharply. "You are married to the heir of the Saltonstall fortune. It is only fitting that you outshine everybody else."

Mrs. Eaton helped Annabel into the dress, and even though it was too big, she assured Alex that it could be altered quickly to suit, after which it would be delivered to their lodgings. Within minutes, two younger ladies appeared out of a back room, and Annabel was measured in no time at all. Then the garment was whisked away into the back room. More material was chosen and a book of designs was laid out to pore over, which was done more by Alex than Annabel. He finally decided on six elaborate day dress patterns.

"The French gray will complement the green in your eyes," Mrs. Eaton remarked, warming to her, as she placed the fabric in her hands. "And with that red hair, it will set off the burnished coppery gold in this design. You have such beautiful skin, my dear, I doubt there's a color that you could not wear."

Annabel thanked her for her compliment. Alex settled the

financial account, and Mrs. Eaton promised delivery of the evening dress by six-thirty that afternoon. When they left the boutique, Annabel's mind was a whirl. It was wonderful to be flattered. To have attention lavished, as well as being able to buy beautiful dresses. It fueled her vanity.

Later that evening, with the help of the maid, she put on the fairy tale dress. They were attending a grand ball, an invitation by a family of some importance, which Alex was well acquainted with.

Annabel felt splendid in the dress. The ladies had altered it to perfection, and all eyes were upon her as they made their entrance. Many introductions were made, and Alex was soon deep in conversation with a whiskered older gentleman, named Jeffrey Carleton. Annabel was closely seized up by his wife Catherine, and surprisingly Catherine seemed begrudgingly interested in her and her background.

Reluctantly, Annabel spoke of Rookwood and the moors. She didn't want to share that with any of these people, although, in an effort to be polite, she persevered. Even so, the more she thought about it, the more homesick she felt. Her thoughts turned to Jevan, which left a bad taste in her mouth. She wondered what he was doing, what he was thinking, and how much he hated her. Annabel stopped talking, fearing she would give her emotions away.

Catherine hardly noticed, and Annabel looked around for Alex. He had disappeared from her side. Quite suddenly, she felt ensnared and longed to be out of the stuffy room that was filled with dozens of people, all of whom were complete strangers, but intent on gazing at her, as she was, no doubt, the foremost object of their gossip.

"It sounds terribly dull, my dear," Catherine said, interrupting her thoughts. "I could imagine that you could go out of your mind with the boredom."

Annabel stared at her, flummoxed by the comment. Before she had time to answer, Catherine had spotted someone across the room.

"You must come and meet my youngest daughter, Lucy Ann. She has a love of such things."

Catherine turned and Annabel had no choice but to follow, or be left alone. They made their way to the other side of the room, to where a girl about the same age as herself was giggling happily at a young blond man. Catherine turned to look at her.

"Mrs. Saltonstall, I would like to introduce you to my daughter, Lucy Ann, and my nephew, Gabriel Bayliss."

Annabel smiled at the young couple. She had already seen the looks that passed between them. They were more than just cousins.

Catherine suddenly gushed about making the acquaintance of a fine-looking couple that had just entered the room, and she left Annabel with Lucy Ann and Gabriel. As soon as Catherine was out of earshot, Annabel breathed a sigh of relief and looked from one to the other of the couple.

"Please call me Annabel. I am not used to all this formality."

"I am not surprised," Lucy Ann said warmly. "Mother was most put out when she learned that Alexander Saltonstall had married. He was considered extremely eligible for a potential son-in-law." She laughed lightly and there was an obvious curiosity in her tone. "And she was even more offended when she found out that his wife did not come from a family of, what she considered, suitable background, but I can see why he chose you," she added quickly. "You are very beautiful."

"Lucy!" Gabriel sounded scandalized. "You must excuse my cousin, Mrs. S—Annabel, she is very direct and outspoken."

Annabel shook her head and smiled at them both. "Don't apologize. I can't abide falseness, and, for all its beauty and sophistication, I haven't found that much sincerity in Bath, as I have in the last few minutes talking to you."

Gabriel smiled back at her. He was classically handsome and radiated sincere warmth.

"So correct me if I am wrong," Annabel continued, "but when are you planning to tell Catherine about your relationship?"

Lucy Ann's immaculately pinned blonde curls bobbed up

in surprise, and her china blue eyes widened and stared at her in alarm.

"I also speak my mind," Annabel said, seeing their shock.

"No one knows. Catherine will be outraged," Gabriel said quietly and then raised his eyebrows a fraction. "How did you know?"

"I can see it, by the way you look at each other," she said simply.

Lucy Ann's face lit up in a delighted smile. "I think we are going to be great friends," she said, taking Annabel's arm. "Come, Gabriel, let's get out of here and take a walk in the garden. It's such a beautiful evening."

Suddenly Annabel felt happier than she had all day.

❧❧❧

The rest of the time in Bath was spent taking the waters at the Pump Room, which was regarded as the social heart of the city. Although Annabel couldn't really see what all the fuss was about, the cool clear waters of an Exmoor stream seemed far more enticing than the strange smelling waters of Bath. She couldn't think why they were reputed to be so healthy, but she kept her opinions to herself as they would have been clearly seen as criticism. She and Alex attended the royal theatre, walked through Victoria Park, and rode over Pulteney and Parade Bridge. Annabel was fascinated to see the new horse-drawn trams that ran through the city center. She took tea several times with Lucy Ann and Catherine at their luxury accommodations, Number One Royal Crescent. At first, she had marveled at the paintings and textiles in the apartments, but after the first two visits, they seemed just a normal part of the decorations.

As her time in Bath was ending, she attended one final invitation from Catherine. It felt like a chore to be in her company, as Catherine had remained indifferent and aloof. Annabel did her best to be polite and gracious, as it was Lucy Ann she really wanted to see.

After tea and the formalities were out of the way, the two

girls took their leave to walk around the crescent. For Annabel, it felt strange to have such a friend. They were from such different backgrounds, and yet Lucy Ann seemed to be completely in tune with her way of thinking. They chatted casually for a few minutes, and then suddenly the other girl slowed her pace.

"Annabel, you may think this is none of my concern. I cannot help thinking that for someone who has just gotten married, you don't seem that happy, as I would expect a new bride to be." She looked anxiously at Annabel. "Is that a very inappropriate thing to ask?"

Quite taken aback at her perception, Annabel shook her head. "Not at all." She hesitated for a few moments, wondering just how much to reveal. "The marriage was arranged, I—" She stopped herself.

Lucy Ann saw that her friend was near to tears. She clasped her hand and led Annabel off the main thoroughfare. "Let's sit a while under that tree, there is a small bench."

They soon reached the seat and Annabel brushed the imaginary creases from her dress as she sat.

Lucy Ann sat close to her. "Whatever you tell me, I promise you faithfully that it will go no further. I am not a gossip and cannot abide those that do. I won't even tell Gabriel, if that's what you want."

Annabel gazed at her friend gratefully, and closed her eyes for a moment. "Where do I begin?" she said, clasping her hands together. "I like Alex a lot, and I believe he does love me. But—but there is another. Someone I have loved all my life. And when I see how you and Gabriel look at each other, it reminds me of him, and how we should be." She sighed unhappily. "Now it's a forbidden love, something totally unattainable and dangerous for us both, but I will love him until I die." Annabel miserably looked down at her lap. "I feel torn between them. That is the truth of the matter. I don't want to hurt Alex, and so I am trapped in this marriage, and I am unhappy, because whatever Alex does, he can't give me what I want." She looked up into Lucy Ann's china blue eyes and was surprised to see pools of collected tears. "Don't you think it's scandalous, that your friend could have such thoughts?"

Lucy Ann clasped Annabel's hand tightly. "No I don't. I hear the truth in your words and know that you must love this other man very much." She thought for a moment. "I just wonder how you will manage to maintain this deception. I'm not that strong. If I was forced to part company from Gabriel, I don't know what I would do."

Annabel's eyes stayed fixed on her face. "Lucy, I'm not that strong either. I too cannot stay away from him."

⁊⁊⁊

On the last day in Bath, Annabel invited Lucy Ann and Gabriel to tea. Even Alex was cordial, and they enjoyed a happy afternoon in each other's company. Alex left before they did. He had previously arranged to play cards one last time with an old friend before their departure. Annabel was glad to have her friends all alone for a time.

"It is not fair that now we have found you, you are going back to Exmoor tomorrow," Lucy Ann declared as they were leaving.

"I will write," Annabel promised, "and you must come and see me."

"I would love to see the mansion and Honeymead the charming cottage and meet your father," Lucy Ann gushed. "But mother will not hear of such things this year. She has my calendar all sewn up. Still," she added in a low voice, "when Gabriel and I are married, things will be different. Who knows? We might even move to Exmoor," she said, with a mischievous smile.

"Are you going to tell her then?"

Lucy Ann laughed and looked at Gabriel.

"We are trying to find the right moment," he answered for her. "Goodbye, Annabel," he said, taking her hand and kissing it lightly. "We will meet again, I am sure of it."

Lucy Ann was not so formal. She threw her arms around Annabel's neck and the two girls embraced tightly

"Don't forget to write," Lucy Ann said. "I will think of you often, and hope that there can be a resolve," she added in a whisper.

Chapter 22

In the Graveyard

In the three weeks that had passed, Jevan's appearance had improved significantly, and his bruises had mostly disappeared. The pressure of the binding had helped knit the ribs together, and he no longer felt that he had to walk hunched over. Even so, there was still pain when he moved too quickly, although each day, that too, got a little easier. His skin had filled out evenly and the hollowness in his cheeks was gone, which was mainly due to Jophiel's care and extra-large helpings at every mealtime.

Josiah visited the forge a few days after Annabel departed for Bath. The three men talked long into the night, and on the face of it, Jevan appeared controlled and calm. He was planning ahead, focusing his attention on a printing business. Josiah was happy to see that Jevan was behaving rationally that night and astonished to learn that, only two weeks later, premises had been acquired in Rookwood and printing presses had already been purchased. He would have liked nothing better than Jevan for a son-in-law and regretted this terrible business wholeheartedly. Although he didn't believe for one moment, that Annabel and Jevan's relationship would simply fade away. He knew that Jophiel shared his concern, but neither man wanted to dig too deeply, and, anyway, Jevan seemed detached from any emotion, unable or unwilling to discuss anything that had occurred.

It was when Jevan was alone that the poison festered in his soul. He wanted to tear her heart apart, as she had his. He wanted to kill Alex and Cerberus and dreamed up ways of achieving that ambition. Although, whatever he thought up, the outcome was always the same, and he would hang. His fury heightened when he thought of Annabel lying in another man's bed, night after night. Could he ever forgive her for that? His thoughts were dark. They made his heart bitter, and he imagined killing her too, but as disturbing as all his feelings were, he was also beset with a need to hold and touch her again. Sanity reminded him that she was his, long before Alex came along. Despite what she had done to save him, he couldn't help seeing it as a betrayal. He knew her better than anyone, and he couldn't quite believe that was her only choice. He believed that if she had set her mind to it, then the outcome could have been different.

As much as Jevan tried to curb his feelings, deep down he knew that once he saw her again, it would take every ounce of will-power not to hurt her. Their relationship had often been volatile, and right now he wanted to shake every last breath out of her body.

❧❧❧

Although, Annabel found Bath more agreeable than she first imagined, she was ecstatic to be home. Even if it was not Honeymead, just being in such a familiar landscape gave her renewed hope for the future. She soon discovered that from the uppermost windows in the mansion, she could see the stone chimneys of the cottage in the distance.

The air was unstifled and the countryside beckoned, so on the day after they arrived back on Exmoor, Annabel found Alex in the drawing room, reading some papers. She hovered for a moment by his side, until he looked up at her with a smile.

"I am going to see my father," she said cordially.

Alex's smile faded. "I'll get Mark to take you in the carriage."

"There's no need," she insisted, walking toward the door. "I am going to walk, it's a lovely day."

"Annabel." His tone was sharp. She turned and stared at him in surprise. "You are married to me now, and I don't want you cavorting about the countryside like some wild thing as you used to do." He paused for a moment. "There are standards to be maintained. You have household staff, many of the villagers are on our payroll, and you cannot earn their respect when you behave as they would."

Annabel was stunned into silence by his words, then shock gave way to anger. "Since when did walking become a pastime for only the lower classes?" She turned and stormed out of the door, slamming it behind her.

By the time she reached the front door, Alex had caught up with her. "Perhaps I didn't make myself clear, I forbid you to go," he said firmly.

"Forbid me to what? See my father? I am going to put flowers on my mother's grave. Do you forbid that also?" She was shouting at him now, and Alex looked uncertain.

"Don't raise your voice to me," he said bluntly.

"I will take a horse, if I am so high and mighty now, that I can't be seen to walk alone."

"Where else are you going?" he said, suspicion springing to mind.

"To see my father and go to the graveyard. I may be your wife, but I am not your prisoner. You can't keep me locked up in this place."

"I can do anything I want," he retorted angrily. The withering look she gave him made him shake his head in exasperation. "I don't want to fight with you, Annabel. Take a horse, see your father and the grave, just don't be long," he said, with a distinct warning, and turned his back on her.

Annabel walked out into the courtyard and round to the stable block, where she found Mark. He quickly saddled a horse for her. She thanked him curtly, still fuming at the altercation she had just had with Alex. How dare he try to forbid her to do anything?

ഇരു

Alex went back to the drawing room and sat heavily on the couch. In Bath, he had Annabel's full attention, apart from a few afternoons spent with the Carlton's daughter and nephew, and he had not begrudged her their friendship. In fact, he was happy that she had found suitable companions while there. Since their return to Gothelstone, he was overly fraught with anxiety. The demands of the house weighed upon him. His father's moods grew more unpredictable, and the affairs of the estate had pretty much been left in his absence. Cerberus was growing ever distant. Alex sighed. Then again, he had always been that way. It wasn't his father or the estate that truly played on his mind. It was his wife and her love interest not so many miles away.

The thought of her seeing Jevan again made his heart pound. She was his now, and if she betrayed him he would kill her. He sighed heavily. No, he wouldn't do that either. He would kill Jevan, though, and there was no doubt in his mind about that. He loved Annabel. She was a part of him, a missing link in his life. It was true that their lovemaking was not what he had imagined. She was nothing like the women he had laid with previously. Annabel was something more meaningful. Yet at the same time, there was something so intimate and familiar with her that he couldn't quite place the feeling. He pondered his feelings further and then the words that Cerberus said only yesterday.

"Give me a grandchild."

Annabel's wildness would calm, and even Jevan would not figure that greatly, if she had a child's future to worry about. Alex picked up his papers again and smiled at the thought.

ℭℴℭℴ

It didn't take long for Annabel to reach Honeymead on horseback. She greeted her father happily and related all the stories about Bath, making no mention of the mornings happenings. She was more eager to hear of news of Jevan. She heard the hesitation in his voice as he spoke.

"He is well, trying to move on with his life."

Annabel felt a stab of pain. Move on with his life, a life where she no longer figured. Bile rose in her throat, and what had seemed like a perfectly happy morning in her father's company just turned sour.

"I know what's on your mind, Annabel, although, for his sake, you must stay away from the forge."

There was a warning in Josiah's voice and his words were appropriate. She knew that being seen with Jevan was a recipe for disaster, and that only made her want even greater. She smiled reassuringly at Josiah and changed the course of the conversation, asking after the bees.

"They have not produced these past weeks," Josiah began, grateful for the change of subject, "the whole swarm just seems lethargic." He thought for a moment. "I do believe they knew you were gone and are pining for you?"

"I will go and see them at once," she said, standing up and heading for the door.

It didn't take long for Annabel's presence to calm the bees, and they did appear to rally around and come back to life after her words of encouragement. They left their hives en masse and followed as she walked through the orchard. They stayed very close, as she picked an armful of flowers, and swarmed over an old tree stump. Then, before she left, she ran her fingers through the collective mass, reassuring them that it was time to resume their normal behavior. The bees rose into the air, and, one by one, descended down onto the nectar rich wildflowers surrounding them.

Back at the cottage, she bade her father goodbye. Promising to return on Wednesday, she headed toward Gothelstone graveyard.

❧❧❧

Jevan had been out walking. With premises newly acquired that week, for once his mind had been on the refit. It was only a modest building. Although, it suited his needs and consisted of a large room that would house all the printing equipment and presses, a reception area for his customers and a small office to the side. Upstairs were two rooms—one to be used for storage and the other had been used for a simple accommodation. It had a small ornate fireplace and just about fitted a bed, a table, and a chair.

This past week the entire place was cleaned, and the presses were to arrive tomorrow. His confidence boosted further after speaking to various people in the town, as the general opinion was that Rookwood badly needed a printer. Jevan carried on walking alongside the hedgerows and across the fields. The tower of Gothelstone church rose above the trees in the distance, and he absently headed in that direction. He passed by the few stone cottages with their thatched roofs and pretty flower stocked front gardens. He nodded to a couple of people in their gardens, but he did not stop to talk, as the church felt like a magnet drawing him closer. Opening the gate to the graveyard, he walked around several of the graves, trying not to notice or to remember the grave that Aidden lay in. He stopped only to linger at Lilith's gravestone.

"Would things have been so different, had you lived?" he said sadly.

The bleating of a sheep in a neighboring field was the only sound that disturbed the quietness of the deserted graveyard. Jevan gradually made his way to the old stone building. Once inside the cool church, he walked up the aisle, his footsteps sounding loud on the tile as they bounced soft echoes off the walls. He sat on a pew and remembered the times as children he and Annabel had come here. Back then, they had lain on the seats and stared up at the ceiling, puzzling over the meanings depicted in the carvings. He looked up, admiring the familiar shapes and faces. Then he looked lower and began to read the various inscriptions set into the plaques on the wall. He knew most of them by heart. When he was small, and his mother could still force him to church of a Sunday, he would while away the time by reading and deciphering their meanings.

After a while, he'd had enough of these subdued memories. He got up and made his way to the back of the church. He opened the small arched gothic door that led up the narrow spiral staircase, and to the tower. Jevan ducked under the low doorframe and carefully made his way up the claustrophobic stairwell. It had been years since he climbed these stairs. They were extremely narrow and uneven, in parts crumbling completely.

Once he reached the bell tower, he looked out of the arched window. It was narrower than he remembered, his view restricted by the grime on the outside. He looked around and saw the small ladder to reach the trapdoor was still here. Jevan climbed up and pushed open the wooden door. It opened directly on to the flat roof. He climbed out and leaned over the stone parapet, thinking back to the time when Annabel had told him that witches danced on top of this roof at Samhain, in order to mark the end of the witches' year.

The hairs suddenly rose on his neck, and he looked behind him, as though he might see one now. There was nothing. Jevan let out a deep sigh while a hint of a smile touched his lips, as he thought about her Pagan beliefs. So convincing were they, that he had often been troubled when passing the church tower of an evening. His trepidation was reasonable as, on occasion, if only for a split second, he had seen a figure up on this high roof. Then, in the blink of an eye, it had vanished.

He closed his eyes for a brief moment, remembering so many things from their past. His mind was plagued with them. When he opened them again, he looked across to the horizon and slowly brought into focus a horse and rider in the distance. The horse was moving fast. It was large and black, and the rider's long hair streamed behind her, its red glints caught by the sun's rays. Jevan froze as Annabel turned the horse in his general direction and slowed to a walking pace. When they reached the road, she turned and headed toward the church.

Jevan's senses sprang to life. He jumped through the trapdoor and quickly made his way back down the narrow stairwell. In his haste, he forgot to duck and banged his head on the doorframe. He cursed loudly, ignored the pain, and rushed out of the church. They were already close. He could hear the horse's hooves and quickly made his way to the yew tree that bordered the dense woodlands. He pushed his way through the undergrowth, trying to conceal himself. Then he turned and waited.

Annabel dismounted and secured the horse to the iron railing that ran along the far side of the graveyard. She pushed open the old gate that groaned with age and walked among the gravestones to find her mother's. It was in a quiet part of the graveyard under a rowan tree. She smiled. Lilith would have liked that. Discarding the dead flowers from the old vase, she replaced the water in the earthenware jug from a nearby pitcher. She spent a moment spent arranging the new flowers, before she knelt by the grave, tracing her finger over the carved inscription.

"I wish you were here," she declared sadly. "I wish you could tell me what to do."

All of a sudden, an odd sensation crept over her skin. Someone was watching her. Fear seized her emotions and, instinctively, she looked up to the church tower. There was nothing. Even so, the perception grew stronger. Positive now, that she was not alone, her gaze drew to the far side of the graveyard. Beyond the yew tree, a figure stood on the edge of the woodland, partially obscured and shielded by dark shadow. It was difficult to see any distinct form or features. Fear paralyzed her. Only the hairs on the back of her neck stood at attention.

Afraid that it could be a stranger, even more afraid that it could be Jevan, she had to move. There was no one else around. She stood slowly, his presence disconcerting, even at a distance. His eyes felt as though they pierced her skin, and she tossed her hair back nervously.

Of course, it was Jevan. Only he could have this effect. Fear marred her need to run to him, even if her legs seemed to move of their own accord. He wanted to kill her. She had no illusions about that, but even that knowledge did not stop her. Only when she was close enough to see his face, did her steps falter. He had not moved at all. His lack of action was unnerving as was his paleness, highlighted by the dappled shadows around them. His expression was unreadable, but it didn't matter. His eyes belied damnation and fixed rigidly on hers.

"Jevan?" she said, breaking the silence.

"Why, Annabel?" His voice was sharp and made her jump. "Why did you do this to us? Why did you marry *him*?"

"You must know why!" she answered, as her heart leap up in shock.

Surely, he knew why. Jevan narrowed his eyes and stepped out from the undergrowth. He appeared leaner, and his presence disturbing, as darkness hung over his whole demeanor.

She could not begin to imagine what prison had done to him, and what horror he endured. As he walked to where she stood, he seemed taller and more dangerous than ever before, more so, as he stared down at her, his hostility evident.

"Was it the only reason? Because as much as I want to believe what my father and Josiah told me, a voice keeps nagging at me." His voice was bitter, sending a chill throughout her body. "It reminds me of our conversation that night on the moors." He narrowed his eyes, studying her puzzled expression. "You told me you liked his company and he was your friend. And something doesn't quite add up," he said, his voice full of resentment as he leaned closer. "You were the only one that knew I was going to London."

"No," she said at once, "I wasn't. I told Alex," she said hoarsely, frightened by his nearness, and of what he was going to do.

Jevan's eyes opened wide in disbelief. "Why on earth did you tell him!" he shouted, struggling to bring his dangerous thoughts under control as he grabbed hold of her roughly, his brutality bursting through every pore in his skin as his eyes brimmed with jealously and madness. His nails dug viciously into her arms as he tightened his grip. "Tell me, Annabel, why would you do that?" he demanded, glaring at her in disbelief.

The force of strength he exerted made her blood burn hot. He gripped her arms so tightly that she thought her bones might snap, and her eyes were wide with fright as she cried out in pain.

"I went to tell him that I wouldn't see him anymore," she blurted the words out, "Let go!"

"You told him when I was going to London," he asked accusingly, ignoring her protest and shaking her firmly, frustration getting the better of him.

"Yes," she said catching a sob in her throat. "I told him that."

"And betrayed me!"

"No! I didn't know what his father was going to do," she said, horrified. "If I could have given my life, then I would have, mine for yours. They would not release you, not until I was married, that was the agreement," she said wretchedly, as tears began to roll down her cheeks. "But it's all a lie. I don't love him. I don't want him. You know, Jevan, that it's always been you."

"Stop crying. You don't know what you've done to me—to us," he said, rage pulsing through his body and taking an even firmer hold over his mind. He stared into her eyes, trying to pry the truth from her mind. "If you're lying to me, Annabel, I swear I'll kill you right now.

"I'm not, Jevan," she said, blinded by her tears, her voice betraying her fear. "There was no other way, I swear. I swear it to you, there was no other way. The marriage took place at twelve o'clock, and they would not release you before midday. They knew that I would not condemn you to death by refusing."

Jevan watched her closely, his anger giving way to anguish, and he released his grip a little. He saw she was distraught, and as much as he wanted to punish her, he could not lose control. She was fragile against him, and he could destroy her so easily.

"For God's sake, Annabel, how can we live like this?"

She shook her head miserably. "I didn't know what else I could have done. I couldn't see you, or talk to you," she replied. "And there's more tied up in this than just you and me. There is my father and Honeymead to consider, you know that."

He released her abruptly. "And what? We have to make sacrifices so everyone else has an easy life." He ran his fingers through his hair, still trembling from emotion. "Is your marriage really such a sacrifice?"

"Yes," she said without hesitation.

"If I hadn't come back, would it have been such a hardship for you to marry Alex, anyway?"

She paused for a moment, distracted by the question.

"I thought so," he said distastefully.

"No, you're wrong," she countered. "It's you that I love."

She put her hand on his arm. Jevan was in no mood to be appeased and roughly pushed her away. She fell so hard against the tree that it took a moment to recover from the assault. Steadying herself, she watched him closely. She had never seen him like this and for what she had done to him, shame burned in her cheeks.

"Don't touch me. You're married, remember?" he said with marked vehemence. His words cut deeply, making her eyes flash with resentment.

"I'm still me! I'm still the girl that is a part of you. My blood is still bound with yours, and my marriage means nothing."

She stared at him for a long moment, rubbing her arm. It was clear he viewed her differently now, and that made her more fearful. She could feel, even see his torment, and knew her words were meaningless to him. He blamed her completely for what had happened. Desperation filled her up, promising that unless she put this right, her life may as well be over. She refused to live without him, adamant that she would not. Warily she stepped closer to him again. His dark eyes penetrated hers with such a disturbing intensity, that it made her voice quiver.

"I don't care what has happened. I care about you, and that's all."

"I care what's happened," he replied angrily, unconvinced by her words.

"If there had been any other way than you ending up dead, I would have taken it. You know me better than anyone, and I can't work out why you so eager to believe I would have betrayed you," she demanded, drawing a deep breath. "I made a mistake. I told Alex where you would be, not to betray you, but because I was mad at him. You have to believe me."

Jevan shook his head. "What am I meant to do, Annabel? Tell me? Live my life on the edge of yours, knowing you are only a mile or so away from me. Am I never to have peace of mind again, knowing that you are bound to him. Is that what you want?"

"I will never be bound to him!" Cold dread banished her fear of him as she placed her hands on his chest. "You know that's not want I want. I've never played by the rules, nor have you," She gazed up into his eyes, willing him to hear the sincerity in her words. "This heart—" She pressed harder on his chest and felt the rapid succession of heart beats against her palm. "—moves in time with mine. I will always be yours."

Jevan's expression was bleak as he stared down at her. Forgiveness was still a long way off, and as much as logic told him he should, he was unable to walk away from her. He took her hands in his and pressed them tight against his chest. "You're going to be the death of me."

Her blood ran cold at his words, and then her breath stilled as he bent his head toward her. His lips touched hers, lightly at first, then their frustration and anger turned into a fiercely passionate kiss, heavily tinged with pain. His hands moved down her body, and she ran her hands down the slope of his back. The danger in this union fueled their desire tenfold.

The sound of an approaching carriage suddenly drew their attention, and they sprang apart. Annabel's face flushed, and her heart beat wildly. She stared through the trees and saw that it was a Saltonstall carriage.

"I have to go," she said breathlessly, catching Jevan's eye. "I am going to Honeymead on Wednesday, and I will be on the moors."

Jevan didn't answer. He was already shrinking back into the trees.

Chapter 23

Wednesday

How was your father?" Alex asked, over dinner that same evening.

"Happy to see me," Annabel replied, giving him a weak smile.

Alex studied her face, for a few moments and sensed that something troubled her.

"What else happened?"

With her skin growing warmer by the second, she put down her fork and looked at Alex, with what she hoped was convincing concern. "He has not been well. He has had a bad cough for a while. It seems like it's getting worse, and I really am concerned about him, and—" She paused for effect. "—ever since my mother's death, he hasn't seemed as robust as he used to be."

"Losing your mother was bound to have some effect on his general wellbeing. We will get a doctor to take a look at him," Alex answered agreeably.

"If he will consent." She laughed lightly. "He is as stubborn as a mule when it comes to seeing doctors. He has never believed in them—my mother's influence, no doubt," She hesitated, thinking about her mother, and a sudden melancholia came over her. "She was far more adept than most physicians."

"I will talk to my own doctor and I'm sure we can sort

something out," Alex said thoughtfully, sensing her mood was improving.

"Thank you," she replied graciously.

She was genuinely concerned by her father's health, and his cough had become worse, although she could not feel guilty telling Alex a small white lie. Josiah was as strong as ever. Her real concern was Jevan, and her thoughts filled with the meeting in the graveyard. Already she longed to see him again, and with a bit of careful planning, her father's affliction could be the perfect alibi.

"I promised that I would see him on Wednesday," she said, looking hopefully at Alex. "I think he is missing me quite a lot. I would like to stay for the afternoon to keep him company." She placed her hand on Alex's. "And I also want to spend some time with the bees. My father tells me that these last few weeks they haven't been producing at all. I have neglected them, what with the wedding and going to Bath. You could come with me," she added tactfully, hoping her ploy would work. "I'm sure my father would be pleased with the company."

Alex thought about refusing her, but only for a moment. Her request was reasonable and she seemed unusually concerned about her father. *After all*, he reasoned, *she will be safe enough at Josiah's cottage*. As for Alex visiting, he had far too much work to do. Besides he had no desire to be anywhere near the bees. "I am busy on Wednesday. You can go for the afternoon, just be back before evening falls."

ควร

Annabel could not wait for the next day to be over. She sent a boy with a message to her father, informing him about her arrangements. There was going to be no way around telling him that she was going onto the moors. He would not be happy about that, and he was not stupid. The minute she said the words, he would know that she was meeting Jevan.

Wednesday dawned dark and drizzly, but even the weather could not dampen her spirits. she dressed quickly, took a basket from the kitchen, and filled it with fruit, cake, and ale. Alex caught up with her just as she was leaving.

"Wish your father well for me," he said, looking in the basket.

"I will," she said happily and turned.

Alex caught her arm, and she looked up at him in surprise. He unexpectedly bent and kissed her on the lips.

"I love you," he murmured.

"I know," she said uncomfortably, forcing a smile, "I'll see you later." She went to pull away from him, and he did not let go.

"Can you find it in your heart to ever feel the same way about me?" he asked, the note of pain obvious.

"I do, Alex, it's just different," she said, taken aback at the sadness in his voice. He sighed heavily and let go of her. She smiled more tenderly at him, feeling a huge pang of guilt. "I'll see you later," she said, and hurried out of the door.

She rode to Honeymead, thinking about Alex's words. He was a fool to love a woman whose heart had already been taken. He knew that. Despite her feelings of remorse, her marriage was a lie. She could not love Alex in that way, even if Jevan had never returned. Those feelings were never there. Determinedly, she pushed all thoughts of Alex away. Today was not about Alex and their marriage. It was about her and Jevan, and nothing was going to spoil that.

Annabel reached Honeymead at eleven o'clock. The clouds had parted to reveal a few rays of weak sunshine, and she spent just over an hour with her father, collecting honey and walking in the gardens. Josiah was happy to have his daughter home, and somewhat entertained her by relating local gossip. He finally turned to her.

"What is it, Annabel? You have been on edge and fidgeting from the moment you got here."

She looked cautiously at her father and took a deep breath. "I am not asking for your approval, and I can't listen to any advice you may want to express."

Josiah sighed wearily. "It's Jevan, isn't it?"

He suddenly felt very old and took a seat on the wooden

bench outside the back door. He had suspected from the moment she had arrived that there was another agenda for her visit. She was going to take a terrible risk. He knew it before she said the words. He was also aware there was little he could do to prevent it.

"Father, I am going up to the moors—please don't hate me."

He stared up at her in surprise. "How could I hate my own daughter? But I wish you hadn't told me."

Annabel shrugged. "My life has become a lie. I don't want to have to lie to you as well." She paused and thought for a moment. "Although, if anyone comes looking, then I am collecting wild flowers in the woodlands to take back to the mansion."

"Is anyone going to come looking?"

"I don't know," she said, shaking her head, "Alex is a little paranoid."

"You can hardly blame him!"

She felt some resentment toward her father for that remark. He should be on her side. After all, he was a part of the reason she was in this situation. She frowned at him. "You know I won't be forced into a corner. I will just find another way out. Alex knows I don't love him. *This marriage*," she said with contempt, "won't keep me away from Jevan."

"Am I wasting my breath if I try to convince you not to do this?" Josiah said despairingly.

"You are," she said firmly and hesitated for a moment. "Can I take Storm?" Josiah nodded his head, and Annabel bent down and kissed him. "Don't worry so much. I won't be that long," she said brightly and left him sitting on the wooden bench.

Josiah was no match for her sheer determination. Any words he might have spoken would have fallen on deaf ears. *'Don't worry,'* she had said, but that was all he did these days. She was stubborn and willful. She would not stay away from Jevan, no matter what he might have threatened. Although, Josiah wondered just how long she could keep up this deception.

Then there was Jevan to consider. Just how long could be put up with this situation? His devotion to Annabel had always been clear and he'd never let anything stand in the way of that. But when pushed, Jevan had a violent temper, and Josiah thought about the fight between Aidden and Jevan a few years back. He remembered how passersby had intervened for fear of Jevan actually killing Aidden, all because of a slight to Annabel, Josiah was told later. Then there was the terrible business with Aidden drowning. A shiver passed over him. Josiah quickly quashed a deep-rooted fear that perhaps it was no accident, after all.

That was all in the past. Common sense reminded him that Annabel and Jevan were playing with fire, and eventually Alex would find out. Then the consequences would be terrible. The clouds had gathered again. The light drizzle drove him from the bench, and he walked into the cottage with a heavy heart.

෨෧෨෧

Within half an hour, Annabel reached the oak tree, and was overjoyed to find Jess already tethered. Jess and Storm greeted each other with enthusiasm. Annabel dismounted quickly and ran up the incline. Jevan was sitting beneath the tree and stood the moment he saw her. She ran into his arms and, in his tight embrace, she felt secure and reckless. Their kiss was long and passionate, and his desire and urgency matched her own as Jevan pushed her to the ground. His roughness was unexpected. The pressure he exerted on her was painful, and she protested loudly. Her objection was stifled, as his kiss was powerful and took her breath away. She breathed easier as his lips moved down to her throat, then her neck. His touch on her skin ignited a familiar thrill, and she felt his teeth graze her skin and then bite deeper.

"Don't, Alex will see that!"

Jevan jumped as if she had burnt him. He held her away from him, his eyes black and furious. He should not have come. This was a mistake. She was another man's wife and she had just rubbed salt into that very raw wound. His breathing grew shallower as he reckoned himself mad or perhaps he had just not had enough punishment. Bitterness was brimming to boiling point as he saw how manipulative she had become.

"I have to be careful," she began as he let go of her and got up, glaring angrily.

"Damn you, Annabel, are you completely indifferent to my feelings? Is your heart so cold, because you are ripping mine to pieces!"

"Indifferent? I am not," she said hotly, "I am realistic. How can I go back to Alex with such marks on my skin?" The drizzle became heavier, her skin was wet and she was becoming cold, she quickly stood up facing Jevan. His hair and clothes becoming wetter by the minute. He didn't seem to notice the soaking raindrops and she tried to blink the water out of her eyes. "What do you want me to do, Jevan?"

"Leave him!" Jevan shook his head to dislodge the water. "Leave Honeymead and Exmoor. You would have done it for me once. Do it now."

She opened her mouth to speak, but the impact of his words rendered her speechless. His expression was unwavering.

"Jevan, I can't."

"Then what do you want me to do?" he snapped, taking a step menacingly toward her and grasped her wrist tightly. "Tell me, what am I supposed to do?"

She didn't answer, she couldn't answer, she didn't know what answer to give him.

He narrowed his eyes, and they were full of contempt. "You come here to tempt me and you know I won't resist, but I am always to be second best. What do you think that knowledge does to me?" he said abruptly, narrowing his eyes. "It's him you will go home to, to lie in his bed, and that makes you no better than a whore!"

Annabel's anger was instant and she struck him hard across the face, Jevan reacted immediately and grabbed her other wrist tightly.

"How dare you?" she cried, still reeling from his words.

"Oh, I dare," he snapped. "I know you better than anyone." He tightened his grip painfully. "You know sometimes I think I should kill you. Always you have had such a hold over me, and I long to be free of it."

Annabel sneered at him. "I'm not stopping you!" she challenged darkly.

Jevan's eyes widened and he shook his head. "I don't know what's more disturbing. Listening to you say that to me or just how appealing that invitation sounds right now."

"A crime of passion? You're not capable," she said callously, "and you're not half as dangerous as you like to think, Jevan," she goaded, trying to pull away from him.

Jevan shot her a look of incredulity. He felt as if he might explode with frustration as he stared into her eyes. His breathing became deep, and blood surged through his veins and into his heart making it pound heavily.

"We both know how capable I am," he retorted and making up his mind, he seized her body and threw her to the ground.

Annabel screamed. The weight of his body pressed down on her, making it difficult to breathe. At the same time, she was numbed by shock as her head hit the ground and pain pulsated through her skull. She tried to fight him, to claw his skin through the clothes on his back, but he was stronger. She forced another scream. He savagely covered her mouth with his own and his fingernails dug painfully into her skin. She squirmed and writhed, but pinned against the hard ground, it had little effect. She finally managed to free her arm and grabbed his hair, wrapping it around her fingers, before yanking it hard.

Jevan made a noise of anger and tore her hand away from his head so that she ripped hair from his scalp, and he struck her hard across the face. Surprise and shock pulsated through her, the smarting of her skin was instantaneous, and she stared into eyes that were dark and unfathomable.

"Bastard! I'll never forgive you for that."

"Do I look like I care?" he said brutally before he tore the dress from her shoulders. Annabel screamed and fought, finding it fruitless against Jevan's overpowering strength as, fueled by anger, he lost all sense of restraint. He forced her body into submission and crushed beneath him. Her protests were feeble, as her breath grew shallower, the pain of her flesh dulled. She finally stopped struggling and became still and quiet.

Jevan felt her body go limp as all his rage, anger, and frustration released. He lifted his crushing weight from her. Shock tinged all his senses. Panic seared through him until she finally gasped when a rush of air entered her lungs. She spluttered and coughed violently. He pulled his body away from hers, staring at her battered and bruised flesh. His mind was numb for a few moments, and when it gained clarity, he felt nauseated by the sight. With a trembling hand, he pulled her dress down to cover her nakedness.

He did not want to look at her, then again, he was unable to take his eyes from her, and totally unnerved by her lack of response. He expected her rage and reproach. He deserved it and wished she would at least say something. She lay so still. Her swollen eyes were closed. Her face was unusually pale, apart from the angry red mark he had left on her cheek. He cleared his throat, horrified at what he had done.

"I shouldn't have struck you—Annabel? Say something," he said, feeling desperate as her eyes opened and she gazed at him dispassionately.

"There are a lot of things you shouldn't have done." She forced herself into a sitting position, wondering if she was going to be sick as her head throbbed painfully.

With a slow movement, she rubbed her sore arms and stared at the marks. The bruises would come later. She pulled the fabric of her dress tightly to her body, feeling cold, and still shaking from shock and grief. Somehow her trembling hands managed to tie the shredded scraps of material together to resemble something decent.

Jevan could watch no longer. He stood and adjusted his own clothes. Then he walked to the edge of the cliff and stared out at the vast expanse of ocean. His tears came soundlessly. He was glad his back was toward her. He felt empty and had done an appalling thing. It had been unkind and unjust, and he felt as though he were truly damned. It no longer mattered to him if Alex found out or not, because one way or another, he would pay severely for what he had done.

Their love was destroying them. It drove him to insanity and her to distraction. She was the woman he loved, the girl he had loved since she was a child, and today because of his uncontrollable jealously, he had all, but destroyed her. Jevan watched the ominous black clouds rolling in from the west. He made up his mind that there was nothing else to do, other than leave her alone for good.

He wiped the moisture from his eyes and turned to find that she was still sitting on the ground, her knees drawn up with her head resting on her arms. She looked so fragile, battered, and forlorn, he felt terrible. He could not touch her again, even in comfort.

"Goodbye, Annabel," he said as he went to walk away. She looked up. His words were uttered with such finality that they made her heart pound. Despite her discomfort, she sprang up.

"Goodbye?" she reiterated, knitting her eyebrows and feeling confused. A large gust of wind made her catch the sob in her throat. "What does that mean?"

"You know full well what I am saying, just don't make this any harder." Jevan paused for several moments, their eyes locked in emotion. His voice sounded as callous and cruel as he could manage. "I am not here for your entertainment. I am not something you can cast aside when it suits you and then expect me to come running when you call, and to make sure you are in no doubt, I'll spell it out for you. Your attention, Annabel, is no longer needed." He turned from her. "Go home to your husband!"

He was glad that she could not see his eyes, they would have betrayed him in an instant, and he moved briskly away from her, down the incline to where the horses were tethered. Annabel couldn't move. Fresh shock waves pulsated through her, and tears flowed down her face, as she watched him move farther away. She shook her head and the paralysis left her.

"No!" She screamed out his name and started after him.

He turned before she reached him. "Don't! Don't come near me."

Annabel stopped dead as if an arrow had struck her. Hatred surged through her body as the meaning of his words hit her, and she watched helplessly as he mounted Jess and turned to leave.

"I should have let you hang!" she cried venomously.

Jevan's head spun around and his eyes fixed on her face. "Well, why didn't you? At least I would be at peace now," he answered and rode furiously away from her.

Annabel's knees buckled and she collapsed onto the ground, sobbing. The black clouds were overhead and the sky opened up fully. Great pouring torrents drenched her body and thunder bellowed all around as lightning strikes streaked across the landscape, and rolling waves crashed deafeningly against the shoreline.

Chapter 24

A Promise

Annabel's eyes were tired and swollen. She wasn't certain how much more punishment her body could take as she got to her feet, shivering violently. The rain had soaked through every scrap of fabric on her body, and it seemed that wasn't possible to be any wetter. She stumbled down the slope to Storm and clamored up onto the horse's back, throwing her arms around his neck, trying to leach some of the warmth from his body. He was as wet as she was, but a small amount of warmth radiated from him. She clung to him and guided the horse over the moors. The temperature had plummeted, and the freezing rain felt like tiny daggers hammering against her already chilled skin. She wished she might die. There was nothing left for her anymore.

Sometime later, Annabel pushed open the cottage door. Josiah looked up from the book he had been reading, glad that she had come back before anyone had inquired about her whereabouts. His initial relief turned to horror. The blood drained from his face as he stood up and rushed toward her. She fell into his arms. Shock and alarm pulsated through him. he held her tight, trying to quieten her trembling and warm her skin, which was shockingly cold. She was drenched and a small puddle soon formed at their feet. Josiah pushed the door shut with one hand and, with the other, carefully undid the buttons on her dress, noting that several were missing.

"You have to get out of these clothes—Annabel?"

She was unresponsive, refusing to meet his eyes. He lowered the dress over her shoulders, and saw the garment was badly torn. Realization hit him, and the suggestion in his mind filled him with anger. He pulled a patterned throw from the settle, wrapped it about her shoulders, and pulled it tightly around her, covering her exposed and bruised body.

Josiah led her to the sofa and sat, cradling her in his arms. "What's happened? Tell me," he said, fearing the worst.

She tried to quieten her mind and focus her thoughts, but Jevan's words rang through her head, and she could not stop the tears from falling. Worse still, being soothed and comforted by her father made everything seem bleaker. She didn't want him to know. She didn't want anyone to know.

"Hush, don't cry," Josiah said, clasping her tighter. He rocked her backward and forward as he used to do when she was a child. "It's all right, it will be all right."

"No, it won't," she said miserably. "Jevan doesn't want me, he hates me."

Josiah suppressed his anger and resisted any critical observation as his eyes focused on the clock. It was nearly six o'clock, and Alex would be wondering where she was. He could not allow Alex to see her in this state and wracked his brains to think of a plausible reason for her appearance.

Her hair was damp on his shoulder. He tenderly pulled it away from her neck, some of it stuck fast, and saw the red angry indentations where the skin had been broken. The blood had congealed and several strands of hair were embedded in the wound.

"Did Jevan do that?" he said sharply, already knowing the answer.

Annabel felt afraid as she looked into her father's outraged eyes. "No, Father, it's not what you think."

"Like hell, it's not!" he said, staring at his daughter. "I know what he has done to you. I'll kill him for that!"

"Please—Father—" she stammered. "It's my fault. I thought Jevan would understand. I told him to be careful because I had to go home to Alex. It—it just got out of hand."

Josiah looked appalled. "Are you mad?" he said, shaking his head. "You're both playing a lethal game." He paused for a moment to bring his own distress under control. "And don't make excuses for what he has done."

"I'm not," she said without hesitation. "Jevan and I—"

Josiah had heard enough. "Don't you have any self-respect?" he said, raising his voice. "For God's sake, Annabel, you are another man's wife, and Jevan should know better than to go anywhere near you!"

She saw the fury in her father's eyes and heard the anger in his voice. Even so, her mind was fraught with his underlying accusations. She shook her head and covered her neck with the throw. "That's just it—no one has ever understood us. I hated him with all my heart this afternoon, and he wanted to kill me. I thought he was going to, but he couldn't. He cannot stay away from me, any more than I can from him. We are drawn together. It's always been that way, and no matter how much we fight, we are bound to each other."

"You are bound to your husband."

"No," she said at once. "I am not. That is a contract, and he bought me with blackmail and threats. He has no part of my heart. Because that and every breath in my body is entwined with Jevan." She looked sadly into her father's eyes. "You know Jevan wants me to leave with him, but how can we? I cannot leave Honeymead, or you and the bees. We belong to this place. All the while Jevan was away, he thought of the moors, the place he grew up. It was a magnet, drawing him back, and now to think of leaving makes my heart break." She was quiet for a while. "He may think he can say goodbye to me. He can't," she said, shaking her head. "Jevan and I belong here together."

Josiah heard the folly in his daughter's words. Her sentiments were beyond dangerous, and although he was furious with Jevan, he knew the hold she had over him. She was a beautiful girl, she understood things that ordinary people didn't, she was independent, outspoken, and willful—definitely her mother's daughter. Jevan was as bewitched by her, as Josiah had been by Lilith. Annabel was far more reckless than Lilith was, he reminded himself. A moment ago, he had wanted to kill Jevan, now his thoughts softened a little. Jevan was like a son, and although what he had done was unforgivable, Josiah knew that his daughter was capable of provoking the violence in him.

There was truth in her words. Ever since they were children, they had lived apart from others. They were different, and only in each other had they found a reason to exist. He told himself that his protectiveness was justified. She was his daughter. It was, after all, his parental obligation, even if it was difficult to admit to himself that he was reluctant to come between them. There was something about them, which you just couldn't figure. Thinking back, he realized that their whole relationship had been volatile. Even now, despite what Jevan had done, Annabel defended him as though her life depended on it.

Josiah thought back to all the other times, times when he had seen scratches and bite marks on Jevan's skin and how he always shrugged them off, if anyone enquired about their cause. Lilith had understood them better, and Josiah remembered her firm belief that the strands of their soul were entwined. That they were one entity in two bodies. No one would get between them, for if they did, dark and powerful forces would rain down. "They have to be together," she had said adamantly, "because they are too dangerous for anyone else to love."

Josiah's thoughts turned to Alex. Was he really in danger from them? Josiah couldn't see how, but looking at his daughter now, despite being delicate and pale, she radiated an inner strength whenever she spoke of Jevan. No matter what had occurred, he was her light in this world. Josiah knew he couldn't let her destroy that, because ultimately she would destroy herself. He reached down and took her hand in his own, glad that it felt warmer than before.

"Don't you understand?" he said gravely. "You will get Jevan killed."

She stared at him wide eyed. "No!"

"Yes," he persisted. "If Alex finds out, Jevan will be arrested, and this time you have no bargaining power. He will be hung, Annabel."

"Then I will hang too!"

"Brave words, my love, but I will not let that happen, not as long as I'm alive." He paused for a moment. "Do you really think that Jevan is the only one who loves you?"

She saw the deep sorrow in his eyes and shook her head.

"Be sensible," he continued, "be careful and have a feeling for what Alex might do, and a care for Jevan's heart also. Don't you think it would rip his soul in two, to know that you would die also?"

Annabel's mind felt numb. The shock of her father's words silenced her. Josiah glanced at the clock again.

"It's late, if he hasn't already, then Alex will send a carriage for you soon, or worse he may come himself."

Annabel felt suddenly afraid of that possibility and glanced nervously at the door. "What shall I do?"

"Go upstairs and change. You still have a few old clothes hanging up," he said sensibly. "Wash your face, brush your hair and then we will sort out that mark on your neck."

Annabel heeded her father's wishes. When she came back down the stairs, with her face scrubbed she looked and felt a little better. She saw that her father held the blade of a knife over a naked candle flame.

"Pull your hair aside," he instructed, removing the knife from the flame.

"I don't want to go, Father. I want to stay here."

"You don't have a choice, my love. You are his wife. He has the right to take you away, and he will. We will tell him that you fell from the horse, which will at least account for some of the bruises."

She laughed weakly. "I have never fallen from a horse."

"Well, today you did," Josiah said firmly and brought the knife closer to her skin. "The horse was spooked by the thunder and lightning and reared. You fell on several sharp rocks. That's what you will tell him."

Annabel nodded.

"It will look convincing enough as long as I disguise the teeth marks."

She swallowed nervously and nodded again, this time with more apprehension. Josiah's hand shook a little as he placed the tip of the blade at his daughter's neck and wished there was another way.

Annabel saw his hesitation. "Just do it and be quick. I think I can hear horses' hooves."

෧෨෧

Jevan walked upstairs to the small room above his premises. The sign outside squeaked intermittently as the wind caught it and rocked it back and forth on its mount. He pushed open the door, threw himself down on the small bed that occupied this room, and stared up at the ceiling. He was angry and ashamed of what he had done. For a few awful moments, he had wanted to punish her, kill her, and put an end to his misery. Now, he just felt desperate. He thought back to Aidden's death, and how easily it happened. What if he had killed her? He squeezed his eyes shut. Then his world would have just ended.

He took a deep breath. His death was to happen soon enough. When Alex discovered what had happened, for Annabel couldn't conceal all those marks from him, this time he was certain to hang. Jevan thought briefly about fleeing, but where would he go? He was weary, his heart felt frozen, and he tried to convince himself that he should just accept his fate, as death would be a welcome release from her image that hovered over his mind. It would quieten her screams that were still ringing in his ears. He raised his hands in front of his face. Her blood was under his fingernails, a reminder of how much he had hurt her. When he had told her goodbye, he had really meant it. Riding over the moors, he had been determined that was the end. Now, all he could think of was her.

The next day, Jevan started work early. He had little enthusiasm, but had to do something to pass the time while he waited for the justice to come. He forced himself to concentrate on completing his first two orders. He tried to focus and occupy his mind with the job, but fear of what the day would bring and how much he had hurt Annabel constantly invaded these thoughts. About ten o'clock, the bell on the front door sounded, and Jevan's throat went dry. His heart raced frantically in his chest. This was it. They had come for him. He took a deep breath, closed the press, and went out into the main reception room. He was surprised to find Josiah standing at the counter. Josiah's dark expression, revealed what he knew. Uneasiness followed the initial relief as Jevan crossed the room.

Josiah was remarkably calm as he began to speak. "From this day on, you're going to stay away from her."

His words were cold and abrupt.

Jevan nodded. "I will." His words were barely there and he cleared his throat. "Josiah—"

"Jevan, I don't want to hear excuses. What you did was inexcusable." Josiah's nerves were strung tight as he stepped around the counter closer to him. All of a sudden, he grabbed Jevan's jacket lapels. "If you ever touch her again, I will kill you myself!"

Jevan flinched. His eyes snapped wide open in surprise. He stared down at Josiah feeling the obvious animosity. "I won't," he said, more out of reflex than fear.

"Promise me that!"

Jevan was silent for a while, Josiah's eyes were fixed on his face, and his face grew darker.

"If you love her, promise me that!"

"I promise you," Jevan agreed bitterly.

Josiah reluctantly let go of him. "Then we have nothing more to speak of," he said as he turned, walked through the door, and slammed it behind him, making the bell ring violently.

At twenty to eleven that same morning, Jophiel stormed into Rookwood Printers. Jevan looked up startled from the invoice he had been filling out, half expecting to see the justice and a lynch mob.

What he saw was the thunderous expression on his father's face and knew that Josiah had been to see him.

"Is it true?" he bellowed, "what Josiah tells me? Did you do that?"

The sunlight fell in streaks across the room, shinning in his horrified eyes. Jevan instinctively took a step back as Jophiel shook with raw emotion and moved closer to him.

"Father, I don't want to hurt you," he warned, taking another step back.

Jophiel laughed cynically. "*You* hurt me?" His face changed subtly at once. "Damn you, Jevan!" Jophiel launched himself at his son, striking Jevan hard on the jaw, which sent him sprawling to the ground. Jevan's head bounced off the wall and he bit down hard on his tongue. "She loves you out of all people, and you abuse that love. How could you do that to her?"

Jevan tried to sit up. The room was spinning. He tasted the metal in his mouth and spat out the blood on the floor. Then he looked up at Jophiel who posed a threatening presence over him still.

"You disgust me," Jophiel continued angrily. "We should have let you rot in that prison cell!"

Jevan came to his senses as the room became still. He struggled to his knees and laughed resentfully at his father. "You have never understood. And it's none of your business," he said, staring Jophiel straight in the eye.

"Of course it's my business!" Jophiel cried in fury. "You are my son, and she has been more than a daughter to me. I care a great deal about her and what happens." He shook his head, exasperated that Jevan would think otherwise. "But I'll tell you one thing, Jevan, I won't let you destroy her!"

Jevan's eyes flew open wide. "Will you let her destroy me?"

"What's that supposed to mean?"

"It means, Father, that it works both ways." Jevan shrugged impatiently. "Don't you think Alex and his hired ruffians are on their way here now?"

Jophiel stared at his son. He really believed the world was against him. "No, they are not. Alex doesn't know."

Jevan cast his father a sharp disbelieving glance.

"Josiah has covered for you. Annabel told Alex that her horse reared, and she was thrown from it. She has saved your skin again," he said contemptuously. "It's not all about you." He paused for a moment, seeing Jevan's stunned look. "You promised Josiah that you would not go near her again. Is that a promise you can keep?"

Jevan shrugged and met his father's eyes again. "I can't say if she'll stay away from me," he said with a note of satisfaction.

Jophiel banged his fist on the counter, making Jevan jump. "Neither of you are stupid," he snapped, his anger rising again. "But neither of you can carry on like this! We should have separated you both years ago," he said with a note of regret.

"That wouldn't have stopped us and you know it." Jevan's voice was sharp. "There is only one thing keeping us apart."

Jophiel stared at Jevan.

"Alex Saltonstall."

Jophiel heard the coldness as Jevan spoke the name. He saw the dangerous glint in the depth of his dark eyes, and he stiffened as he drew a deep breath. He was afraid of what was on Jevan's mind.

"Jevan, for God's sake don't—"

"Father," Jevan said abruptly, wiping the blood from his mouth. "I am busy, and if there's nothing else, then I have work to do," he concluded defiantly, before he bent his head and resumed writing out the invoice.

Chapter 25

Estrangement

A week had passed since Wednesday. Alex still could not work out why she would have chosen to ride Josiah's horse through such a storm. She was out of control, and he was still shocked from seeing her body in such a state. Even if the marks seemed consistent with her story, there were scratches on her skin that made him wonder. She shrugged them off, a consequence of falling into gorse bushes. Even so, to his eyes they looked far too even, far too straight.

Then there was the curious injury on her neck. It was a deep ragged cut, and he could not imagine that a rock would make an injury like that. A sixth sense warned him there was something else, an explanation that he did not want to hear. He could wait, he decided. He would find out. Right now, he had to rein her in, keep her close so that he could watch and have every movement accounted for.

Even if Annabel had a mind to do something else, Josiah's warning made her keep away from Rookwood and Jevan. When she visited her father the following week, a coachman accompanied her. He waited outside, and his strict orders determined that she would only visit for an hour. Alex laid down that stipulation the night before, and Annabel did not protest or utter a word to the contrary. He also told her that a servant would accompany her on all further outings. In truth, she felt numb, and the world it seemed was against them. Even her father had told her to focus on making her husband happy by being compliant and hope he did not have any real suspicions.

Through her father, she heard that Jevan's printing business was now operational. She learned that her father had confronted Jevan, but Josiah would not tell her what had taken place between them, and he seemed satisfied with Jevan's promise not to go near her again. Those words that made Annabel's heart ache.

At the mansion, she tried to be more compliant and involve herself in the running of the house. It soon became clear that her input was not needed. It already ran as smoothly as a well-oiled machine. The butler made sure that all the servants knew their place, and completed their duties efficiently.

In desperation, Annabel found some embroidery silks and picked them up with all good intention. As the needle went in and out of the fabric, her mind wandered. She stared at her handiwork. It looked clumsy, as if sewn by a child, and it reminded her that she hated sewing. She put the silks away. This was never going to work. There was no inherent desire to sew or play the piano, and she wandered out of the room. She walked around the great house, trying to suppress the feeling of loneliness. It was an unknown sensation, never having felt lonely in her life before.

Determined more than ever to lift her spirits, she attempted to familiarize herself with the mansion's vastness. It was easy to lose her way in some unfamiliar corridor, or open door after door and not recognize which room she had entered. Many did not appear to be in use, although there was not any conspicuous neglect. Everything was polished and dusted and kept as though the vast majority of the family might return at any moment and bring the house to life.

Alex had given her the grand tour, as soon as they were married. He led her through room after room, and she had realized just how enormous her new home was. Even now, she had still not seen all of it.

It was when they came to a large carved oak door that Alex warned her. "Do not enter into these rooms. They are my father's. He would see your presence as an intrusion. He has a private set of stairs that leads out to the courtyard by the stables."

"So you don't know if he is in the house or not?"

Alex shrugged lightly. "No, not always. He has always been a little reclusive, likes to keep to himself."

That warning played on her mind. Even now the house felt very still, unnaturally so. Maybe it was that just there was never any laughter or light voices, save the servants. But above stairs, they tended to talk in hushed tones. Exploring now, her perception heightened. The ticks of the clocks seemed muted and often absent, as they frequently went unwound. She remembered that Cerberus would not allow any servant to touch them, and he would habitually forget. Annabel found this quietness unnerving. It made her all the more homesick for Honeymead. The cottage always was full of noise, the windows left open in warmer months, and bird song resonated through.

In contrast, the windows at Gothelstone were fastened shut. Some even had nails driven through so that they could not be opened at all. No one was ever allowed to open a window any wider that a crack for fear of bees.

When Alex had first told her that regulation, she laughed aloud, believing he was joking and only stopped when his eyes narrowed and she caught his disapproving expression. He related again his childhood trauma of being stung by a bee and nearly dying. His quick-thinking nurse had placed a tourniquet on his arm, immediately applied ice so that the spread of the poison had slowed and not killed him. Annabel never realized just how highly allergic he was to bee stings, and she could make the color literally drain from his face when she spoke in detail about the bees at Honeymead. Before this moment, she even toyed with the idea of asking Alex about keeping a few skeps in the gardens. That was never going to happen.

"They are so dangerous, Annabel," he would say, much to her amusement, and then the more Annabel observed her husband, the more she saw that he had an unhealthy hatred for all insects.

Alex became fastidious about the bed, checking between

the covers, and then the walls and crevices around the room before he could relax and sleep.

Over the weeks that followed, Annabel's bruises healed. She did try to enjoy being in Alex's company again and spent more time with him, trying to convince herself that he could make her happy, and it was the best she could hope for. Occasionally, when he wasn't tied up with the estate, they went riding through the countryside and fields that surrounded the mansion. Alex was mildly entertained, not only that she wanted to gather so many wild plants, but also with her stories of the simple country remedies to cure numerous ailments that had been handed down to her from her mother. He knew nothing of the simpler things, having grown up in a man's world filled with hunting and business, and Annabel brought a gentler side to him. She collected wild flowers, poppies, cowslips, and armfuls of flowers that looked like lace doilies.

"Queen Ann's lace," she told him, handing him the delicate filigree flower head. "Do you see the tiny red flower at the center?"

Alex, humoring her, peered at the flower. "I suppose you are going to tell me some special significance of that," he said a little sarcastically.

She ignored his scorn. "Legend says that when Queen Anne came to the throne, she pricked her finger while making lace. A red flower blossomed at the center of these otherwise pure white flowers, and symbolizes the single drop of royal blood. They have grown that way ever since."

Alex laughed. "I suppose you believe that. Next, you'll be telling me that it has magical healing powers."

Annabel didn't answer; she merely turned to pick more flowers.

Alex's teasing was not far from the truth, and her mouth turned up a fraction into a small smile. These flowers did have magical properties, and every wise country girl knew that by crushing the seeds and ingesting a spoonful after coitus, pregnancy was preventable. She may have had her hand forced in marriage, but they would not be able to force her into child bearing.

They walked a little farther.

Suddenly, Alex froze. "Let's get out of here," he said. "There are a lot of bees!"

Annabel looked around. "They are only wasps, not bees," she corrected, unconcerned by his panic.

"Wasps, bees, I don't care, I hate them all!" he exclaimed.

Annabel gave him a look of incredulity. "They won't hurt you if you stand still."

Alex didn't listen. He picked up an old stick and was brandishing it around, beating the flower heads violently, sending both petals and creatures into the air.

"Stop it, you will only make them angry!"

He spun around, his aggression obvious. "You talk about them as though they have feelings. They are only damn insects. If I had my way, I would eradicate them all from the earth!"

She stared at him wide eyed. He was behaving like a mad man, a character trait she caught a glimpse of before. That lunacy manifested itself much later, when they were back at the house. During dinner, she noticed that Alex consumed several glasses of wine. His curt remarks made her think that someone had put the idea of her and Jevan in his mind. She felt nervous. Idle gossip no doubt, but something that could prove dangerous.

After dinner, she went up to the bedroom to fetch a book she had been reading. Alex entered the room a minute later. He came straight up to her and grasped her tightly around the waist. His kiss was demanding and rough, the smell of alcohol sweet and sickly on his breath. She went to push him away. He just held her tighter.

"What is the matter with you, Alex?" she said, exerting more pressure, to little avail.

He pulled back a little and looked at her rather oddly. "Shouldn't you be with child by now?"

She stopped struggling, bewildered by his words and the reproach she saw lurking in his eyes. "I am not ready for children," she said cautiously.

He pushed her from him, so that she fell onto the bed, her

hair falling backward, revealing the scar on her neck. Alex stared at it, and Annabel saw his grimace. She swallowed nervously. He was suspicious, after all. His eyes locked with hers, and she readied herself for the interrogation, which was surely to come. Only Alex just stared at her for a long moment.

"It's not about what you want," he said callously, unfastening his clothes. "After all, what use are you if you can't give me a child?"

ભજભ

After that night, she felt like nothing more than an object for his use in order to serve another purpose. She did not conceal the coldness she felt toward him. His sudden change in personality was deeply disturbing, and she no longer welcomed any of his attention. She wished that he might take a mistress and leave her in peace. That thought was unlikely to happen, as he seemed adamant on her producing an heir soon. Although, remnants of the old Alex were often present, and he was not overly cruel. Without alcohol in his system, which only brought out the worst in him, more often than not he accepted her rejection.

The worst thing for Annabel was he insisted he loved her. It would have been easier to hate him, save for those three words and the belief that shone out of his eyes and reminded her that for him it was a certainty.

Days moved into weeks, and she never felt so unhappy, not even wanting to look at him unless she really had to. Alex felt her resentment, but it was when she sat at the dressing table, brushing her hair, that the real extent of their estrangement became obvious.

He placed his hand on her shoulder, and she immediately cringed under his touch. He made a noise of anger in his throat and stared at her reflection. He loved her, although even he was becoming more and more intolerant to her behavior, especially after making enquiries to the exact whereabouts of Jevan on that Wednesday weeks ago. Spies reported to him that no one had seen Jevan that day. They concluded by telling him that when he was next seen, his skin displayed marks of violence, the sort of marks left by a woman. Of course, it could have been any woman, but Alex wasn't stupid. Annabel's skin had grown colder as Alex's eyes remained fixed on her face.

"What happened to the girl I married and spent three wonderful weeks in Bath with?" he said at last. "She was unlike any other, a bit wild yes, but there was a part of her that loved me." He paused, pursing his lips. Annabel lowered her eyes and focused on herself in the mirror. She felt like a caged animal that had resigned itself to defeat. "Now," he continued, "you are duty bound to give me a child, an heir."

Annabel's eyes opened wider and nausea rose up in her throat. He went to turn away then stopped himself and her eyes rose to meet his again. "And I need a wife that is compliant with my needs, capable of keeping my passion aroused," he said menacingly.

"Is that a threat?" she countered angrily.

"A wise suggestion," he remarked and left the room.

Chapter 26

A Disturbance in the Night

This latest revelation was the final straw. Annabel was adamant that there would be no child. She was even more certain that she had to get out of this marriage, regardless of the cost. Determination filled her thoughts and kept her awake into the early hours. Alex did not come to bed until even later. When he climbed in beside her, she kept her breathing even and steady, feigning sleep. He asked if she were awake. She did not make a sound. He sighed and turned his back to her. She lay motionless, her limbs rigid, in case she gave herself away. After a while, she heard Alex's steady breathing, allowing herself to relax and fall into an uneasy sleep.

Someone murmured her name and touched her arm, making her wake with a jump. At first, she thought it was Alex, but the rhythm of his breathing was even, and he still faced away from her. She held her breath, now fearfully alert. Afraid to move, she forced herself to stare into the darkness, listening for the sound to come again. Perhaps she was dreaming. There was no one by her bed. She breathed easier. It had sounded so close and so real. A click from the other side of the room sent a shot of adrenaline through her body. She was not imagining things. She sprang into a sitting position and turned her head toward the door, the dark making her disorientated.

Alex was perfectly still, emitting slow rhythmic breaths.

He appeared to be sound asleep. Annabel's shock subsided a little. Her eyes adjusted quickly to the dismal aspect of the room, and she peered at the clock. It was already half past three, even though she felt as though she had only been asleep for five minutes. Carefully, she threw back the bedclothes and slowly got out of bed, so as not to wake Alex.

Annabel hurriedly put on her dressing robe and pulled it close to her body. She was in two minds whether to wake Alex. She was certain he would tell her that she was dreaming, and now uncertainly was creeping into her mind. Perhaps it was a dream, and a passing draught might have pushed the door shut. Logic reminded her, she heard Alex close the door before he got into bed. She shivered, remembering the cold flesh had that caressed her bare arm.

She stole across the room and glanced back at Alex. He had not moved at all. Watching him carefully, she turned the handle slowly and pulled the door open, peering down the empty hallway. The play of shadows made the large tapestries and statues look abstract and unfamiliar. Annabel hesitated for a moment, debating the wisdom of any excursion.

She was wide-awake now, and sleep would be impossible until her mind was eased. Making up her mind quickly, she stepped into the hallway and closed the door behind her. The house was quieter than ever. It was too early for any of the servants to be up, and intuition drew her toward the small staircase that led up to the attic rooms.

What if it was Cerberus? The thought made the hairs on the back of her neck stand on end, and she pulled her robe even tighter. Meeting him at any time was disturbing enough, but in the dark and the dead of night, that was truly frightening. *I should go back*, she told herself and was just about to turn around, when a door latch unfastened directly above her head. Rooted to the spot, she looked upward. It was the attic door. They were the only rooms above her. With apprehension mounting, she stared up the dark staircase, lit only by the moonlight from a small side window, and considered that it might be one of the servants, after all. Cerberus wouldn't go up there. What reason would he have?

She contemplated ignoring the noise, wanting to go back to her room and feeling torn as what to do for the best. If there was a servant sneaking around, it was better that she find them before Alex or Cerberus did. She could at least save them from any punishment. Her mind was quite convinced of this supposition, and she breathed easier. Although with wandering around on her own in the dark, the adrenaline kept her senses alert. She tiptoed up the stairs, and when she reached the top, she saw that the attic door was ajar. Moving quietly across the landing, she tentatively pushed it farther open. Two windows let in enough moonlight to flood the room with a ghostly luminosity, making dark curious shadows stretch out of all proportion, and into the corners. The various shapes were mostly unrecognizable, as they were draped with old dustsheets.

"Who's in here?" Her unsteady voice sliced loudly through the air, and she took a few cautionary steps into the room. "Show yourself. I know you are here."

Suddenly, out of the corner of her eye, she saw movement. Her heart pounded heavily, and she spun around to face it. She caught her breath, but initial shock subsided. She was staring at herself in a long mirror. It wasn't the only one. There were many other mirrors, various empty frames, and life-sized portraits. Dozens of eyes gazed unnervingly back at her. Her reflection moved fluidly with her, and her focus came to rest on a life-sized glass. She studied the shadowy image for no more than a moment, then the image moved. She had not.

Every sense in Annabel froze. It was no mirror. There was a girl staring back at her—a maid, after all, was a fleeting thought. That impression immediately disappeared when the girl stepped out from the shadow of the empty frame. Her hair was long and dark, her clothes were strange, and she was oddly striking, even if that beauty was contorted with a grimace of viciousness and hatred. Her eyes were obscure by the dim light. All Annabel saw was dark pools in the whiteness of her face. She felt their intensity, even if she could not see their detail. Struck by horror, Annabel stepped backward, and, at the same time, the moonlight picked up the brilliance of the silver dagger the girl held in her hand.

The girl's face changed subtly at once. Her figure shifted frighteningly fast and, bringing the dagger up above her head, she leapt forward. Annabel's piercing scream cut through the air and reverberated down through the corridors. She spun around, catching her foot in the fold of a dustsheet. She stumbled and clutched wildly at a quantity of material, to stop herself from falling. It dropped over her, enveloping her as she fell heavily to the ground. She screamed again desperate to get away. Something collided with her, and then she felt the dagger plunging into her flesh. Her blood flowed out in a great river, and she fought wildly for her life as her terrifying screams echoed through the house.

There were voices in the distance, which came closer, and then light flooded through the fabric. The sheet, roughly torn from her and the old lamp which fell on her, was thrown aside. Alex was on his knees before her, his face ashen in the flickering lamp light. In panic, she looked down to her disheveled nightclothes. There was no slit in her skin, no river of blood. Only Alex's voice brought back some sense of reality

"For God's sake what is it, Annabel?"

Annabel's wild eyes stared at him for a few seconds, and then she threw her arms around his neck and clung to him tightly, trembling all over.

"My God, what in hell happened?" he said, clearly shaken.

"A woman—" She was sobbing now. "—with a dagger."

By this time, the room was full of servants. Alex picked her up.

"She tried to kill me," she managed in between sobs, and Alex ordered a search of the attic at once.

All the dustsheets were pulled from their places. Servants looked in chests and moved every single piece of furniture in that room and then the adjoining one, but the search brought forth no evidence to substantiate her claim.

"Go back to bed everyone," Alex said at last. He sat Annabel down on a convenient chair and knelt before her. He stared up at her in confusion. "It was just a nightmare, Annabel," he assured her, as the servants made their way to the door.

"No, it wasn't. She was real," she insisted.

"Not in front of the servants!" he hissed quickly.

Annabel stared at him in disbelief as he waited until the last servant left the room.

"I didn't imagine it," she said, shaking her head. "And why not in front of the servants? If there is a mad woman in this house, then none of us are safe. They have a right to know."

Alex stared gravely at her. She didn't like that look one little bit. Alex shifted his gaze above her head, and she glanced over her shoulder. Cerberus had been standing in the doorway watching them. He stared down at Annabel with cold unfeeling eyes, and then said to Alex. "Just the same as the others." His voice was filled with contempt.

Alex caught his father's eye. "She will be fine, Father," he said with authority.

Annabel turned, looking directly at Cerberus. "What do you mean?"

"It means we have another mad woman in this house," he said icily.

"Another? Who is the other?" she said first to Cerberus and then Alex.

Alex just pulled her upward and lifted her into his arms. He did not speak as he walked down the stairs and back to their room. He put her down on the bed, and sat beside her. She searched his face for some clue.

"Alex, tell me what Cerberus meant."

"Nothing," Alex replied all too quickly. "It's a joke, just his sense of humor." He frowned, seeing how frightened she looked and sighed heavily. "My mother was insane, Annabel, but you just had a bad nightmare."

༒

The next day, she speculated for the hundredth time on just who the girl could be. Alex did not explain anything and avoided her questions about the implication that his mother might have been insane, which resolved nothing in her mind. Annabel knew there were asylums filled with supposedly insane women. That did not necessarily mean they were mad, more likely they had become a burden, an embarrassment, or their husbands just wanted rid of them.

It was one of the harsh injustices in today's society. Annabel had never much thought about it before this time. She was however, quite convinced that the girl was not a figment of her imagination, and she had never seen that person before in her life. Surely, a dream or nightmare would manifest itself into something she recognized.

Annabel found Alex in the estate office. He was busy writing in a large ledger.

Looking up he smiled faintly when she entered the room. "Did you get any sleep at all?"

She nodded. "Some." She hesitated for a moment. "Alex, I need to get out of this house and clear my head." He looked relieved that she appeared to have let the subject drop and nodded sympathetically. "I would like to go into Rookwood." Alex's face-hardened at once. She dropped her gaze and continued anyway. "I want to go to the shops and just do something normal…" Her words trailed off.

Alex did not answer straight away. He would have preferred to keep her away from Rookwood. Although, even he thought that it would do her some good to get out of the house for a while. He was worried about her. She was extremely pale and clearly shaken from the night before.

"You can go into Rookwood," he said at last, standing up. He pulled her toward him and kissed her on the forehead. "But Agnes will accompany you. And I don't expect you to visit any establishment that would displease me."

Alex fought hard to bury his disapproval at the thought.

Annabel shook her head, and looked coyly up at him. "Don't worry, you have chosen a good spy."

Alex drew in his breath sharply. "Don't you think that it pains me to know I cannot trust my own wife?" he said watching her closely.

Annabel's expression changed into one of hurt. She tried to be careful not to rouse any suspicion. "I will make you trust me," she said earnestly and placed a kiss on his cheek.

Alex nodded, even if he didn't look convinced. Annabel

walked out of the office, feeling better at once. She knew just how to keep Agnes occupied for a while.

An hour later, Annabel and Agnes arrived in Rookwood. They stepped from the carriage directly outside the confectioner's shop. Annabel walked with an air of confidence and cheerfully greeted Samuel, the shop owner, as they entered. They chatted for a moment or two, as Annabel watched Agnes closely. Her maid's eyes lit up in delight as she looked longingly at the multicolored confections. She already knew that the girl had a weakness for sweet things. Annabel turned to her.

"I know you would like some and I would like to give you a present. You must sample the sweets and choose a selection."

"Milady, I couldn't possibly—"

"Nonsense, I insist." Annabel smiled warmly. "Take your time. I will go any buy some ribbon next door and catch up with some gossip while I'm there."

Agnes looked dismayed. "Milady, I am not allowed to leave you." Embarrassed, Agnes looked down. "That was the master's orders."

Annabel laughed. "Well, we won't tell him, will we, Samuel?" She drew closer to the girl and whispered, "It will be our secret and you can have whatever you want."

Agnes was clearly in a dilemma. She gazed at Annabel for a moment and then nodded happily.

"Make certain she tries one of everything," Annabel said to Samuel.

"I will," he said, with a wink. "I am glad to see you in Rookwood again."

Annabel looked back at the maid. Agnes was already bent over the trays of confection. Annabel had known Samuel since she was a child. He always talked fondly of her mother, especially as Lilith had been so kind to his wife before she died two years ago. More importantly, Annabel could trust him, and he knew she was looking for a distraction.

"I have many new sweets," he said, catching Annabel's eye and nodding toward the side door.

Agnes was oblivious, her hand already outstretched to receive the first confection. Smiling thankfully at Samuel, Annabel slipped out the door and hurried down the alleyway. The print shop was on the main high street and only two doors down. She reached the corner and stopped. The coachman was nowhere to be seen. Cautiously, she looked up and down the street and scanned the doorways on the far side, just to be sure.

When she was confident that no one would really notice her, she left the relative safety of the alleyway and hurried along the high street with her head down. As she reached the print shop, she looked up.

Jevan was leaning against the open doorway. He stood quite still, eyes focused on her, apparently having watched her antics for a couple of minutes. Annabel swallowed nervously and then quickly glanced behind her. She hastily moved to the door, and Jevan took a step back. She rushed past him and the door closed firmly behind her.

Annabel turned and looked up at him. His mouth twitched, and he turned his head a little to the side, fixing her with a penetrating stare.

"I knew you would come," he said. "Everyone has warned me to leave you alone and stay away, but, I knew that *you* wouldn't."

She was a little infuriated by his smugness, although two people passed by the window and Annabel caught her breath and moved back farther into the shop. Jevan twisted the sign in the window to closed and turned the key in the door.

"It's nice," she said, looking back at him, "the premises."

"I don't care about the damn building." He scowled furiously. "What took you so long?"

Annabel stared at him and saw reproach lurking in his eyes. "I am married, remember?"

Jevan flinched, his mouth now set in a firm line.

"I can't just go when I want. Alex watches me like a hawk, and now I have a companion whenever I leave the house. Just how easy do you think it is?" Her voice was high-pitched, and she felt flustered.

Jevan's face softened a little. "Stop screaming at me. I only asked."

Annabel shook her head. "I am not screaming. But I have to go," she said, making up her mind quickly. "It was a mistake to come in here. It's much too risky." She made toward the door, and Jevan caught her arm.

"Not yet," he said, "you haven't seen the rest of the building." His grip was firm and she knew that he would not let her walk out of the door.

"Jevan," she began, with some sharpness.

His lips pressed together tightly. "Don't pretend to me that you want to leave."

"I thought you didn't want to see me again, so what are you going to do now?" she challenged. "Beat me and rape me?"

Jevan's arm fell away immediately. "No," he said evenly. "I won't touch you, if that's what you want."

A surge of emotion rushed through her and she closed her eyes briefly and shook her head.

"That's not what I want. As much as I have hated you, I have to be with you Jevan, just as you knew I would come. I also knew that you wouldn't leave. You couldn't say goodbye to me," she said, shaking her head.

Jevan heard the arrogance in her words. Even so, he couldn't deny them.

"But," she continued, "we can't go on like this forever. I can't live the rest of my life sneaking around, lying, and looking over my shoulder, with a death threat hanging over you if we are seen together." A full minute passed. "I never wanted any of this, Jevan. It is a torment that our lives have turned out this way, for it was never meant to be like this," she said sadly. "Nothing, not even Alex can stand between us."

Jevan's senses tingled. Every word she spoke mirrored his feelings.

"Come upstairs," he said with a faint touch of pain in his voice, and he gestured to the narrow staircase.

"No, I should leave," she said, trying to resist the familiar pull of him.

"I won't let you leave," he said firmly, "not yet."

She thought about protesting, but Jevan moved closer to her, and she didn't want to leave either. She sighed as she turned and walked up the stairs. At the top, Jevan pushed open the door to the larger room. Annabel eyes were instantly drawn to the bed. She tentatively sat down upon it. To her surprise, Jevan did not sit beside her. Instead, he moved a small wooden stool in front of her and sat before her. He took her hands in his own and looked into her eyes.

Any reservations there might have been, disappeared. She knew exactly why she could not stay away. His look reminded her of everything she had always loved. He glanced down at her slender fingers, rubbing his thumb over her gold wedding ring, and frowned.

"We are different from how we were when we were younger." He looked up with a hint of a smile. "You and I, we have been shaped by each other, and deep down we understand the driving force behind the things that we do, terrible things I know, but regardless of the consequence, we cannot stop. On the moors that day, I wanted to kill you, that day and many others before it. There have been times in our lives when I had those feelings, and you always welcomed it. You seemed to revel in my wicked thoughts and lead me further and further from what was right. The fact that you knew I was capable of murder," he said, frowning as he remembered Aidden, "that you could look death so blatantly in the eye, was perhaps what corrupted me. You made me what I am and you were never afraid, except for the last time…" His words trailed off.

"You are wrong," she said, looking down at their clasped hands. "I am afraid, but I don't often allow it to show. I have never believed that you would or could take my life. I understand the darkness in you. It reflects my own, and that exhilarates me. You have power over me and that is frightening, for when I am apart from you, my world is unbalanced. It's always been that way."

"You have power too, enough to bewitch my mind."

She felt the surge of raw emotion and her voice trembled as

she spoke. "I am afraid now, Jevan, afraid of our situation and what will happen. It is I who has the unfathomable darkness inside me. Perhaps I corrupt everyone that comes into contact with me. After all, I can make things, terrible things happen."

Jevan pulled her a little closer, watching her face intently. "I know you can."

She laughed uneasily, certain that the color drained from her face. "You don't know what I am talking about."

"Yes I do." Jevan sighed and closed his eyes briefly. "I have thought about little else these past weeks." He watched her eyes widen in suspicion. "Did you think that *I* wouldn't work it out?"

Annabel felt suddenly afraid, and did not dare to even blink.

"It not just the fact you are a skillful bee charmer and have power over them, but I have seen other things, and I feel it when we are together. You are capable of a lot more than people would believe." He paused, gauging her demeanor. "Perhaps, I should ask about Wilfred Preston, for instance."

That name sent a cold shiver down her back, and her heart skipped a beat. "You knew?" she said incredulously.

"I guessed, but—" He considered for a few moments. "I've been wracking my brains to figure out how you did it."

She swallowed nervously, staring into Jevan's dark eyes. She had never thought that she would have to make a confession. "I don't know." She shook her head and bit her lip anxiously. "I don't understand it myself. Sometimes things happen when I want them to. It's like an energy in me that builds and it becomes all-consuming and powerful. I don't think I can control it." She watched his face closely. "But it doesn't always work. Cerberus was the one I wanted dead, and he—" She shuddered and then her voice quivered. "—and he knew it."

Jevan's eyes snapped wide open and he sat back with a jolt. "What do you mean?"

Annabel shook her head. "He more or less accused me. He just knew," she said, remembering his words. "For the life of me, I can't work it out."

Jevan was silent for some time, watching her wrestle with inner emotions. "Lilith knew," he said at last, as a sudden thought dawned on him. "Didn't you tell me that Cerberus was very interested in your mother, and that she worked at the house at one time?"

Annabel nodded. "Yes."

Jevan was certain the answer to this puzzle was staring him right in the face. He just couldn't make the pieces fit exactly. Then as he watched Annabel, a shocking thought bombarded his mind. He tried to blink the revelation away. Surely, he was wrong.

He suddenly saw something in her that he had never realized before. He ran his hands through his hair and tried to clear his mind.

Annabel did not fail to notice the change in his manner. He acted as if he were battling some inner conflict. "What is it Jevan?" she asked faintly.

"Lilith was a witch, and her gifts no doubt were handed down to her daughter." The other thought on his mind he did not voice. It was too shocking, and he had to be sure. He saw that she was startled by his observation.

Of course, Annabel knew. Deep down she had always known, but foremost Lilith had been her mother, and suddenly she understood what Cerberus meant that first night at the mansion, when he had said "another witch." He had known too.

"My mother understood things," she said, "I am not so adept. If I were, I would understand the strange happenings at the mansion."

Jevan raised his eyebrows, and she wished she had not spoken. She didn't want to burden Jevan with her concerns.

"Tell me," he insisted.

"I think he is keeping a woman locked up, maybe his mistress," she said reluctantly, "but she's insane."

"You're joking!"

"No, I'm not. I saw her last night. She's not local, and I don't know who she is."

They sat in silence for a few minutes and then reluctantly

Annabel got up. "I have to leave, before they send out a search party and raid this place."

Jevan stood too and drew her against him. "Do you forgive me?"

"Don't I always?" she said and lifted her head to him.

Jevan smiled and kissed her tenderly, wishing he could keep her with him. After a moment, she drew back from him. She willed herself to walk away, even though her resolve was melting. She knew that a few minutes more and she would not be able to leave.

Annabel quickly walked down the stairs. Jevan followed. They peered around the corner of the doorway. There didn't appear to be anyone directly outside.

"Wait," Jevan said, as she began to move forward. "There is a back door. Leave that way and walk up the alleyway. I will leave by the front and go to visit my father at the forge. If anyone is watching, they will follow me."

Annabel nodded and Jevan unbolted the back door. She rose up on her tiptoes, kissed him again, and remembered something they used to do as children. "Do you remember the gap in the hedge, which leads to the old pavilion in the woodland garden?"

"Yes."

"Meet me tomorrow after four o'clock," she said, slipping out of the door.

Chapter 27

The Far Pavilion

Agnes sweet tooth proved to be a useful affliction. She did not breathe a word regarding Annabel's little excursion, to Alex. Alex's manner was cordial in the evening, and Annabel felt relieved that no one else had reported anything that would displease him.

After lunch the next day, Annabel made her way down to the library to replace a book she had borrowed earlier in the week. The house was silent. Her footsteps were lost in the deep pile of the carpets and the heavy fabrics of the curtains and tapestries dampened any echoes. The library was an impressive room, made even more interesting because of the several hundred books that filled the oak cases. There were dozens of identical bound volumes written in Latin. They were of no interest. Everything else was in English, on subjects from botany and art, to those of local interest. Annabel was especially taken with an old book that was brimming with concise ink drawings, all of Exmoor, and depicting the landscapes she knew. Her real passion, though, was for novels. They transported her into the lives of daring heroines in exotic and faraway places. She devoured these stories, since returning from Bath. It was an escape from the complexity of what her life had become. She replaced her book, trying to decide which title captured her imagination the most.

Annabel walked back and forth along the bookcases. No

matter how often she did this, it appeared there was always something new. Something she had not noticed before. Today was no exception. She picked out a book and then replaced it as another caught her eye, although, unable to decide what she really felt like reading.

Emily Bronte evoked thoughts of a Yorkshire moor. Barren, cold, and windswept, and yet with a feeling so different from her beloved Exmoor. Jane Austin promised to lift her mood with the prospect of a rambling old house and a spirited young woman, making an excursion to the town of Bath. A situation comparable to her own, although Annabel predicted it would be a lot less complicated. She chose Jane Austin after all.

"Annabel."

It was a pronounced whisper. Every hair stood to attention as she spun around, surprised that she wasn't alone. The room was empty. That was more of a shock. Annabel held her breath, straining her ears, unable to repress a shudder. The room felt noticeably colder than before. She shook her head; convinced her mind was playing tricks. She listened harder, waiting for the slightest odd sound, and when nothing came, she shrugged and turned back to the bookcase. Her peace of mind instantly shattered. A hideous sound penetrated her ears. It sounded as if long fingernails slowly scratched down the wooden bookcase. It was close to her. She could not move, glued to the spot as terror stalked her mind. Her heart pounded, her stomach tied itself in a knot as she shifted her eyes to the side. Fear kept her senses alert, as the noise grew fainter. Forcing herself, she stepped backward, and moved her gaze over the entire bookcase.

Someone was trying to frighten her, that was obvious. So far, they were doing a great job, as she half expected a hand to reach out from the bookcase. Even so, there were no gaps, and every book was accounted for. Never one to run away at adversity, her fright quickly gave way to realization and then fury. She did not intend to stand for this. Annabel was certain it was the girl in the attic, trying to terrorize her, and she was adamant she would not rest until she found and confronted her. That way, neither Alex nor Cerberus would be able to deny her presence. Especially, not when Annabel dragged her by that long dark hair to stand in front of them. She had a single reservation. The girl might still have the dagger. Annabel looked around the room and spied the poker by the fireside. Feeling calmer, she began to remove books from the shelves throwing them on a pile at her feet. She cleared shelf after shelf, and there was only solid wood. She tried higher up, but still nothing.

"Annabel."

She stifled the gasp and moved toward the voice. Farther along the case, she hurled more books from their positions, determination taking a firm hold of her senses. After all, this time she was ready to face this deranged woman. Suddenly, she saw a metal lever, recessed into the back of the shelf.

Annabel took a deep breath. She seized the poker with one hand and, with the other, pulled on the lever. All at once, the case clicked open. Grasping the edge, she pulled it toward. her. To her surprise, there was a small door. She pushed and it creaked open. Annabel gripped the poker tightly, half expecting to see the girl with the dagger. What she saw was an empty passageway, lit by a small window at the far end. As her eyes adjusted to the subdued light, she cautiously looked up at the high ceiling and the cobwebs that shivered as she walked forward.

After a few steps, she was standing next to a recess that had three stone steps leading up to an arch-top door. She hesitated, summoning some courage, and then reached forward and pushed the door wide. She stood back, expecting something to happen. There was silence. Annabel wished that her heart would not beat so fast and that her hands did not feel as damp as she clasped the poker tightly. She stepped forward. The chamber was small and dimly lit from the small amount of light shining through the open doorway. The room was furnished sparsely with a desk and chair. Annabel edged forward and raised the poker. She quickly rounded on the doorway. There was no one there either.

She breathed easier and turned to the desk. One by one, she

opened the drawers. They were all empty. In fact, the room held no fascination at all, but she looked around for some clue as to who could have used this room. The gray stone walls were unadorned. There was only one anomaly. A small-hinged wooden disk, no bigger than a one-penny piece, was positioned halfway up one wall. Curiously, Annabel stepped closer. She saw there was a tiny hinge. It looked like a tiny door. Sliding her nail under the disk, she flipped it open. Light shone from beyond and she pressed her eye against the hole.

Below her was the library. From her perspective, she was somewhere near the over mantle, although just a little to the left of the fireplace. The spy hole was set with convex glass, which magnified and gave a bird's eye view of the whole room.

Annabel returned the cover to its original position and turned away. This was how the girl knew she was there. She watched her. An unnerving revelation. Just how many other times had she been observed without knowing? She repressed the shiver and left the room, eyeing the corridor with some apprehension. She had expected a room, a corridor even, although not this big. She moved farther along the passage until it dead-ended at a small stone spiral staircase. Eying the heavily worn treads, Annabel looked up, debating whether to follow.

She stepped onto the lowest stair and then paused. Listening carefully, she urged herself to continue. As quiet as a mouse, she stepped up each stair, her eyes searching for the slightest movement or shadow.

"Mine—this is my house."

The whisper echoed through Annabel's head. It paralyzed her with a spine-tingling shiver. Her eyes riveted on the empty staircase ahead. She felt the danger. She sensed the girl was luring her deeper and deeper into a trap. All thoughts of a confrontation deserted her, and in fright, she let out a sharp cry, dropping the poker at the same time. It clattered loudly down the staircase, the noise echoing off the corridor walls. Annabel spun around and, taking the stairs two at a time, ran after it, scooped it up, and fled back the way she had come.

Moments later, she reached the library. Once through the doorway, she pushed it shut and pulled bookcase back into position. Her heart raced, her emotions in turmoil, as she grabbed armfuls of books and hurriedly stuffed them back onto the shelves. Once done, she glanced nervously at the over mantle and ran from the room. She fled up the main staircase to her room, and once inside, locked the door soundly.

Alex had already left. She didn't know what to do, or who to confide in. She couldn't tell the servants and wouldn't tell Cerberus. Collecting her thoughts, she calmed a little. It was now a reality. Someone else, someone insane, was living in this house. The revelation and her discovery of the secret passageway made her wonder just how many other secret rooms and spy holes were concealed in this place. She looked at the walls suspiciously, searching for any evidence of another spy hole. While there did not appear to be anything unusual, it did not give any comfort. She no longer felt safe. Questioning the logic of telling Alex, given what had happened the night before last, it would only convince him she was unbalanced. She had no proof. Even if she showed him the secret room and spy hole, there was still no confirmation that anyone was there. She thought about what Alex told her about his mother.

'She heard voices.'

Annabel was now hearing the same voices, and she was not insane. Annabel realized with shocking clarity that Elizabeth Saltonstall had not been insane as Alex believed. Some terrible secret was being kept, not only from her, it had been kept from Alex's mother.

Uncharacteristically on edge, Annabel stayed in her room, which was at least bright and cheerful with its primrose colored walls. The locked door offered her some protection, even though it now felt as if she were a prisoner. She went to the window and longed to breath in the fresh air. She pulled on the nail that held the window fast. It was unyielding. Frustration flooded through her. Her breath felt heavy as if she would suffocate if she didn't get this window open. Inspired by her metal comb lying on the dressing table, she picked it up. With the spine of the comb, she levered it under the raised head of the nail, and little by little working around the nail evenly, she pried it out of the wood.

The sash was difficult to open, having been nailed shut for so long. Annabel used all her strength to jerk it up so she could breathe in the fresh air. It was pleasing, laced with the heady sent of jasmine that reached to just below her window. She instantly felt better, freer of the house and its confinement. She lifted the sash higher and leaned out, taking in the view. She willed the time to pass quickly so that she could go and meet Jevan. At least with him she could forget what horrors might be lurking in this house, even if it was only for a short time.

Later that afternoon, Annabel changed into a dark gray dress. She hoped the color would conceal her through the trees, in case anyone should be watching from the windows of the mansion. At ten to four, she made her way downstairs and walked out onto the terrace. Walking in the gardens was nothing out of the ordinary, and at this time of year, the gardeners were busy in the vegetable gardens and orchards closest to the mansion.

By contrast, the pavilion was in one of the farthest gardens. Long neglected, it was surrounded by overgrown high hedges and only reached through an expansive woodland garden, or if you knew the secret way in, from the dense undergrowth and woodlands beyond. It was a secluded place. The roof leaked, the benches were rough and splintered and had not been used by the family for generations. It had been used by Annabel and Jevan, when they used to steal into the gardens as children. It became one of their favorite haunts.

Annabel made her way down the stone steps that led from the terrace. Weaving her way haphazardly through the formal gardens, she exchanged pleasantries with the head gardener and walked casually down to the shrubbery then across the lawns. Once under the canopy of large trees, she kept to the shadows and approached the crumbling ruin of an old folly.

At this point, she was no longer visible from the mansion and quickly made her way through the woodland gardens. The domed top of the pavilion came into view over tall hedges, and she hurried along the perimeter to find the opening. She ducked under the arched wooden doorway and entered into the intimate pavilion garden. It was far more neglected than she remembered. Squeezing past overgrown brambles at the entrance of the structure, she squinted and turned her head as the low sunlight blinded her.

Sensing she was not alone, she looked up. The light touched Jevan's face in streaks. He reached out and pulled her back into the shadow of the pavilion. His hair brushed her skin as he moved his hands to tip her face toward him. He kissed her, tangling his fingers in her hair and then slid them lower down her back.

Their embrace ignited a mutual obsession. His continuing caress brought all her senses to life, as Jevan uttered words of endearment. Annabel's dress puddled at her feet and, she stepped from it as she pulled Jevan's shirt down his back. Closing her eyes, she luxuriated in the sensation of his naked skin against her own.

ⅇ⁓ⅇ⁓

Alex returned home early that day, he went from room to room, calling her name. There was evidence that Annabel had been in the library, although what she had been doing, he could not guess. The books were strewn irregularly across the shelves. He ordered the maid to rearrange them and ran up the staircase. In the bedroom, there was a dress discarded on the floor. She must have changed recently or the maid would have already picked it up. He ran back down the staircase, questioning servants on the way. No one appeared to have seen her for some time. They were certain that she left the house and was in the gardens. Alex did not miss the cautious tone in their answers.

Alex heard Cerberus come in the front door, and he quickly moved into the drawing room. A confrontation with his father this afternoon was best avoided. Cerberus would ask where Annabel was. He had already made it plain that Alex allowed her too much freedom.

"Rein her in, Alex, keep her on a tighter leash." His father's words echoed in his ears.

Alex moved to the door. Cerberus disappeared down into the kitchen passageway. Alex began pacing about the room.

What was she doing in the gardens at this time of day? The light would be fading soon, and why had she changed her dress? Now, he came to think about it, yesterday the coachman reported that she had spent nearly an hour in the confectioners.

It hadn't really crossed his mind until now that it seemed odd. Annabel wasn't even that keen on sweet things. The more Alex thought about these things, the more suspicious be became, and it wasn't exactly a like a slap in the face, just more of a gradual realization that he was being taken for a complete fool.

There was only one reason she would spend so long in the confectioners. It was the same reason she came home battered and bruised, having supposedly fallen from a horse, and now only one reason she would change her clothes to walk in the gardens.

"Damn you, Annabel!" he roared and stormed out of the front door. He knew she was cunning, and she would not linger in the formal or vegetable gardens that were overlooked, but in the neglected wilderness of the woodlands and the far pavilion. The light was beginning to fade as he crossed the lawns, past the shrubbery and the old ruin, just as he was hurrying through the woodlands; he heard laughter, her laughter. Incensed, he ran.

ᘓᘏᘓ

"I have to go," she said, laughing and adjusting her clothes. Jevan kissed her again and reluctantly let go of her.

"I'll see you tomorrow," he said, placing a final kiss on her forehead.

She watched him squeeze through the gap in the hedge and disappear. Happily, she turned and walked in the opposite direction, excited already at the prospect of tomorrow. She rounded the corner of the hedge, ducked under the archway, and her heart leapt up in shock.

"Alex!" The color rushed into her cheeks. There was a thunderous look on his face, and her heart beat violently.

"Where is he?" Alex demanded with unexpected ferocity, as he grasped her arm painfully and pulled her back under the arch toward the pavilion.

"Who—who are you talking about?" she said faintly.

Alex rounded on her in disgust. "Don't take me for a fool. You're a liar, a cheating liar!"

She stared at him, wide eyed. His hostility was startling as was the resentment in his eyes. He was incensed with rage.

Keep calm; she told herself, *he doesn't know anything.* She feigned a look of surprise. "I have been walking in the garden," she said, trying to keep her voice even and free herself from his tightened grip.

Alex glared at her, breath heavy with emotion. "I heard you!" he said, through clenched teeth.

She shook her head frantically, trying to keep the feeling of panic at bay.

"I was alone,"

Alex's eyes glowed with fury and he sneered. "The confidence with which you lie confounds me. I only have to look at you to know the truth," he said in revulsion. "Look at your clothes, crumpled and disheveled, and I can see it in your eyes." He leaned closer, his face inches from hers. "I can smell him on your skin. You disgust me. Did you really believe I wouldn't find out about your sordid secret?"

Annabel stared at him, horrified as he continued.

"I will have him arrested, you can be certain of that. And you—" He looked at her as if she were something repulsive that he had stepped in. "—I will deal with you accordingly; after all, adultery is a crime, Annabel."

Josiah's words sprang maliciously into her head. *'You will get Jevan killed.'* Alex's arrogant expression riled her. She was terrified of his threat, even if his words provoked her.

"Sordid secret?" she reiterated. "And what about yours?"

Alex eyes showed an element of surprise and his eyes widened.

"You and your father. I also am not a fool. Let's talk about that girl you have kept locked up in the house." She looked at him with scorn. "Who is she, your father's mistress, yours even?"

Alex let go of her and shook his head. "I have heard enough! There is no other woman." He pointed a finger sharply on her temple. "It's all in your head."

They stared at each other for several moments, the tension between them concentrated as they both fought with their own rage.

"I have tried to be patient with you, Annabel. God knows I have given you every chance to consider your disgraceful conduct, but you can be certain of one thing. I will not tolerate your behavior anymore," he threatened, clutching her again and pulling her after him.

"Let go of me!" she yelled.

"No," he roared back as they reached the ruin. "I will never let you go. You are my wife and you will behave!"

Annabel spat at him "You are a fool," she said, tearing at his arm with her fingernails.

He snatched her hand away and twisted her arm painfully, digging his nails into her flesh.

"And I want a divorce!" she shouted as Alex pulled her round to face him.

He saw the hatred in her eyes, and at that moment, it mirrored his own. He wanted to kill her and shook with emotion.

"You can't divorce me!"

"I can and I will," she said with loathing. "I'll go home to my father and find a lawyer, and I don't care about reputation or slander, let the lawyers sort it out in a court of law," she concluded triumphantly.

"You're only a woman. It's not possible, and I'll not stand for it," he snarled fiercely. "And even if you could, I'll never let you divorce me. Do you understand!" he said, shaking her so hard that it made her feel dizzy.

He faltered, shocked by his own violence. He sized her roughly again.

Too shocked and frightened to think clearly, Annabel pressed her body against the wall and held her breath, expecting more aggression.

Alex just stared at her for a few moments. "Don't you dare think about crossing me ever again," he said bitterly, "or I'll destroy everything you hold dear!" And with those terrifying words, he dragged her back to the house.

Chapter 28

Waking the Bees

Alex left her alone for the remainder of the day. He took the key to the bedroom and locked the door. It was only opened again when a maid brought up a tray with a light supper, but Annabel could not touch a single morsel. Her imaginings were too graphic of what Alex might do, and even the intermittent footsteps, in the attic above her head, seemed of little importance now.

The door was unlocked the next morning, and Alfred escorted her to breakfast. Alex was already seated, but he barely acknowledged her. She sat away from him and refused all food, only accepting tea when it was offered. After a few moments silence, Cerberus came into the room. Annabel stiffened, waiting for his reprimand.

Much to her surprise, Cerberus's mood was cheerful. He only talked of the guests that were due to arrive later that day, his unusual jovial countenance made her feel all the more despondent. Guests were the last thing she wanted to think about, and playing the perfect hostess was not something she was cut out for, and by no means, in the mood for. She sipped her tea slowly and did not interject a single word, as she wondered if she could perhaps convince them of a malady, although she was as robust as ever. She might look distressed, but an illness would be hard to fake. She sighed inwardly, knowing it would be impossible for her to see Jevan today, and that made her feel ten times worse. Alex and his father conversed on for a while. Eventually, Cerberus rose from his chair, and walked to Annabel's side. She looked up at him apprehensively and was surprised when he placed his hand lightly over hers.

"Your constitution is far too delicate. You should eat something, my dear. I am getting worried about you." And then he smiled at her for a brief moment. "You are very important to this family."

His gesture and words were so out of character that she smiled back. In that instant, she felt an overwhelming connection with him. Her heart pounded, the smile froze. The longer his hand rested on hers, the stronger their connection grew. A powerful flow of energy rushed through her body, frightening and exciting.

Cerberus lifted his hand and the bond was broken. He turned and nodded to Alex. Annabel stared after him, partly fearful, partly curious, as he left the room. She cast a quick glance at Alex. His eyes were downcast. He had not been aware of the exchange. It took a few minutes to recover from the shock of Cerberus's touch. The only time she had felt a similar sort of power before had been with her mother. Before she could speculate any further, Alex spoke.

"Annabel." He said her name coldly.

Her head jerked up, and she did not give him time to finish his thought. "Alex, please forgive me," she begged earnestly. "I will be the perfect wife. I will do everything you ask of me, just please forget about yesterday."

"And what about all the other times?" he said icily.

She swallowed the lump in her throat and shook her head miserably. "You knew that marrying me was going to be difficult. Given the circumstances of that union, you knew this would be no easy match," she said sadly, "and I did warn you."

Alex made a noise of contempt in his throat. "I loved you, Annabel, and that love has been thrown shamefully back in my face!"

She lowered her eyes, as she did not want to see the accusation in his.

"Like it or not, *you* are my wife, and I demand respect from you. I will not tolerate the blatant disregard of my feelings any longer, and an example has to be made." Her eyes met his again.

"I don't disregard..." Her words failed as his sank in, and she saw the spitefulness in his expression. "What are you going to do?" she whispered uneasily.

A doubt crept into Alex's mind, but it was only briefly there. "I haven't decided yet," he said rising from the table and fixing her with an angry stare.

He flung his chair away and left the room. Long after the echoing clatter of the chair on the flagstones died away, Annabel remained. She didn't know what to do for the best anymore. She knew that trying to reason with Alex was the most sensible option. At the moment, he was extremely angry, and she could not bring herself to go and find him. Although, playing more heavily on her mind was the peculiar feeling she got when Cerberus touched her. Deep down, she felt something sinister in that touch, something terrible, evil even.

The day wore on endlessly, and Annabel was not permitted to leave the house. Servants were everywhere. It seemed they had all been instructed to polish the furniture in whatever part of the house she moved to. After lunch, she joined Alex in the library. He barely acknowledged her. He seemed to be busy writing, so she sat on the couch and stared at the over mantle. Her eyes focused up to where the spy hole was situated, and she was glad there was no feeling that anyone was watching today. She had just about plucked up the courage to speak when there was a knock on the door.

"Come," Alex, said, looking up from the desk. Alfred entered.

"Yes, Alfred?"

Alfred looked oddly uncomfortable and briefly glanced at Annabel, before addressing Alex. "Jophiel Wenham is in the hall, asking to speak to the mistress. He said, it was urgent."

Annabel stifled a gasp. For Jophiel to come here, it must be about Jevan. She jumped up and, ignoring Alex's protest ringing in her ears, ran down the corridor to the hall. Jophiel's face was white, and her heart missed a beat. He stood nervously twisting the cap in his hand. He smiled for a moment when he saw her, but Annabel caught the odd expression on his face.

"Jophiel!" she cried, "what is it?"

"Annabel, my dear, you must come—it's your father."

Inwardly, she sighed in relief, but it was short lived as dread hit her. "What's—what's wrong with him?"

"We—we just left him. Jevan has already gone to fetch the doctor," he said, trying to reassure her and catching Alex's sour expression.

Annabel went white at the words, and Jophiel put his arm out to steady her. Alex immediately stepped closer and placed his arm firmly around her waist.

Jophiel quickly withdrew and stepped back, sensing the hostility. "From what I can gather," he continued, "he fell last night. He is not able to speak much and his breathing is worsening. That cough of his weakens him every day. You must go to him," he urged.

Annabel nodded. She felt Alex stiffen and tighten his hold. Her emotions were in a whirl, and she tried to move away from him, as he held on to her. She turned toward him. "You are not going to stop me from seeing my father!"

"I have no intention of doing that," he said, a little surprised at her animosity toward him, "but you will go by carriage," he said firmly. Alex looked back at Jophiel. "Thank you for telling us. Please make certain that the doctor comes at once."

Suspiciously, Annabel looked at Alex. Even though he was polite, he was dismissing Jophiel in a cold and calculating manner. Jophiel cast a worried glance at Annabel.

"Don't worry the doctor will be there soon, I'll make certain," he said, looking from one to the other and then hurried out the door.

"Don't distress yourself so, Annabel, I am sure everything will be all right," Alex said calmly as he released her and walked to the front door.

"He is all the family I have, I have good cause to be distressed," she said irately, annoyed by the unnecessary comment.

Alex turned back.

"I am your family too, Annabel," he said pointedly. She shook her head.

"I don't have time for this, Alex. I must go to him, it will be quicker if I go by horse, and there are no carriages ready."

"No, I will go and you will follow in the carriage," he said determinedly.

"I can ride with you."

Alex looked down at her with contempt. "Just like a couple of gypsies! I don't think so, Annabel." He walked out the door heading toward the stable block.

A little stunned by his words and their meaning, Annabel could not waste time arguing. She ran up the stairs into her bedroom, threw on her outdoor shoes, and then almost flew down the staircase and raced out of the front door.

To her dismay, Jophiel was nowhere to be seen. She cast a wary glance at the stable block, and then ran as fast as she could in the other direction. The shortest route was across the fields and by horse. On foot the hedgerows and long grasses would hinder her progress, so she kept to the road. As she reached the end of the carriageway, she saw Alex on his black stallion galloping at full speed across the field. She was surprised that he appeared so concerned for her father after all, for he was clearly eager to reach Honeymead in all haste. She felt a surge of gratitude.

After several minutes, she slowed her pace to catch her breath and, ignoring the painful stitch in her side, continued hurrying along the road. It took several more minutes for her to reach the boundary walls of the orchard. Yet, as she approached the cottage, she saw Alex in the doorway, leaning casually against the doorpost, watching her. A cold shiver passed over her.

The scene was wrong. Alex should be inside with her father. Annabel rushed through the garden gate and hurried to Alex, although his body blocked the doorway to the cottage.

"It's too late. He is already dead." His words had no feeling, and Annabel's eyes widened in disbelief.

"No!"

Alex grasped her firmly, and she reacted instantly and tried to shake herself free.

"Let go! I don't believe you!" She stared at him wildly, as the tears spilled down her face, and struggled to push past him. "Let go."

"It's best if you don't see him," Alex said evenly.

She stopped dead and stared at him in disbelief. "Neither you or anybody else has any right to stop me seeing him!"

"I am thinking of you, and I will decide what you will or won't do!"

Annabel shook her arm free and brought it up with such force that it connected sharply with his face and then raked her nails down the softest part of his cheek. Alex cried out in pain and pushed her hard against the doorframe. She gasped from the sharp pain in her back. "You have no right!"

"I have every right," he said, eyes blazing in anger. He touched his cheek, withdrew his hand, and stared at the blood-stained fingers. "Damn you, Annabel, you will pay for that!"

Just then, the sound of galloping horse's hooves could be heard on the road, and in the distance, Annabel recognized Jevan, Jophiel, and the doctor. "They won't stand by and allow this," she said triumphantly.

Reluctantly, Alex let go of her. She ran up the stairs and into the bedroom, her eyes instantly drawn to her father, who lay on the bed so unnaturally still. His eyes were glazed over, no breath came from him, and any feeling of existence had long since left the room. Annabel sank down into the chair at his bedside and clutched his hand. Trembling, she brought it to her lips and kissed his warm skin.

The jolt of shock hit her with full force. He had only just died. She blinked away the tears, as the realization dawned on her. She searched his face in disbelief. It was contorted with distress. His death had not been peaceful. She stood and shifted her eyes over the state of the crumpled bedclothes and the freshly plumped pillow beside him.

A noise made her turn to the doorway. The wariness that crept into Alex's eyes made her stomach turn. Annabel shook her head. She would not have believed him to be capable of such wickedness. The truth was plain to see in the dead face of her father. Blood coursed through her veins, accusations roared in her head.

"You killed him!"

Alex's expression changed subtly, and he caught his breath. Her gaze was intense, and he could barely breathe from the malice emanating from her. With every fiber of her body, she directed all her hatred toward him. Alex clutched at his throat which was closing. He was choking but, as she heard the others enter the cottage, her hypnotic gaze left him, Alex reeled backward. At this moment, there was evil in the room. His spitefulness was out of self-preservation. He had to retain control.

"You are hysterical, and delusional. I am the injured party here," he said, thankful the constriction had stopped. He brought his hand up to the welts on his face, reluctant to anger her again, but he had not yet played his hand. He displayed a chilling smile. "Perhaps I would be justified in having you locked away for a while, for what you have done."

Blood froze in her veins. Only the sound of footsteps on the stairs broke the tension. Jevan, Jophiel, and the doctor entered into the room. Jevan looked at Annabel and then Josiah. She caught his strange expression, and the withering look he gave Alex as he moved closer to her. Jevan felt her bristling hostility, even though it was not directed at him. Even the air felt electrified. Annabel sat in the chair again and watched the doctor, who conducted a quick examination and pronounced the death due to heart failure.

"He suffocated," she said, looking at the doctor.

The doctor turned to her as if he were about to question her observation, until Alex stepped forward.

"My wife—" He empathized the word, taking his gaze briefly to Jevan. "—is too distressed. She cannot deal with this matter."

Annabel stood up at once. "Distressed is not a word I

would use. I will deal with all my father's affairs," she said indignantly, giving Alex her most disdainful look. "I don't want you anywhere near him or his things," she added through clenched teeth as her eyes locked with Alex's again.

"I will go and write the death certificate," said the doctor, attempting to diffuse the strain that everyone seemed to be under. He cleared his throat, "But I do need a witness."

"I will witness it, Annabel," Jophiel said.

She looked at him gratefully and nodded. He and the doctor went back down the stairs, leaving Annabel standing between Jevan and Alex. She sensed the intense hatred that each man harbored against the other, and if looks alone could have indeed caused death, then there would have been three dead bodies in that room with her. Alex grasped hold of her wrist "Let's go," he said, half turning toward the door.

"No!" she said, shaking him from her and stared defiantly up at him.

Jevan did not miss the opportunity and took a step closer to Alex. "Don't touch her!"

Alex laughed coldly. "She is *my* wife, and I can do anything I please with her."

Annabel saw the brutality in Jevan's eyes, as he moved toward Alex. She could not let Jevan get in the way.

"No Jevan," she said, imploring him, as his gaze was fixed on Alex.

His fury was obvious, and she feared he would kill him.

"You and I have unfinished business," Jevan threatened, ignoring her plea.

Alex sneered. "Don't make me laugh. I will destroy you and your father, and she will still be mine."

Jevan was sufficiently provoked. He moved fast. Faster still was Annabel. She pushed both of them from her with all the strength she had. "No!" she cried loudly.

They both stared at her.

"Have you no respect? This is not the time." She turned to Alex. "I am not leaving yet. I want a few minutes with my father, and I have to wake the bees."

"What?" he asked impatiently, staring at her intently.

"I have to wake the bees," she repeated, "otherwise they too will perish or swarm, now that their master is dead."

Alex stared at her for a few moments as if she were truly mad. "Superstitious nonsense," he said at last. "You will do no such thing."

Annabel would have liked nothing better than to throw all consequence to the wind, claw the other side of his face, and allow Jevan to do his worst.

Jevan spoke. Now his voice was calmer, as if he remembered the precarious situation she was in. The moment of vengeance seemed to have passed. "I will take care of the arrangements," he said. "Josiah meant a lot to me, too."

Alex stared at Jevan contemptuously for a few seconds and then turned to Annabel. "You are not even needed here, but I would not deny you a few minutes alone with your father."

He looked expectantly at Jevan, but Jevan stared back at him, not moving an inch.

"Alex." Annabel sighed. "I *will* be down in a minute. I want to grieve, nothing more."

Alex paused at the doorway. "Just make sure you say goodbye," he said, with a sinister connotation and stalked down the stairs.

Annabel was relieved to be alone with her father and Jevan. She sat on the edge of the bed, staring at Josiah, unable to stop fresh tears from falling. Jevan placed his hand on her shoulder and she immediately covered it with her own. She looked up at him through blurred vision. "He was murdered—Alex—" The words stuck in her throat.

"I know," Jevan replied, squeezing her shoulder and she felt him tremble. "I will take care of him," he said, placing his hand over Josiah's eyelids to shut them.

"I know you will," she said, standing up.

Jevan was so close to her that she could feel his breath on her skin. She wanted him to put his arms around her, hold her tight, and never let go. Jevan wiped away a fresh tear from her face and moved closer. His face was inches from hers. She went to close her eyes.

"Annabel!"

Alex's sharp call broke her trance and, by instinct, she jumped back.

Jevan took a deep breath "You must go."

She glanced at her father and then at Jevan. "Wake the bees," she urged. Jevan's expression turned into a grin. She also felt a lightening of the terrible day. "I know it's superstitious, but my father believed it, and so do I."

"I promise I will wake them all," he said as she turned to go. Suddenly he caught her arm and swung her around to face him, bent his head, and kissed her quickly. "I don't care about consequences," he said with a mischievous glint. "I will wait for you. We will find a way."

Alex shouted again and Annabel looked back at Jevan.

"I'll be there if I can," she said under her breath and ran down the stairs.

She pulled down a small quantity of black crepe from a shelf laden with different fabrics. Just as Jevan reached the foot of the stairs, she thrust it into his arms and hurried outside.

Alex was standing by his horse. "You took your time."

"I was saying goodbye."

"Don't play games with me, Annabel." He thought for a moment. "And I hope you said your last goodbyes to more than one person in that room."

Jevan came out of the cottage and walked up to Jophiel, who was leaning against the stone wall. He suddenly remembered something and looked toward Annabel.

"I need the key to the cottage."

"I don't have it," she said worriedly.

"I have it," Alex said, retrieving the key from his coat, and held it out to Jevan. Jevan opened his hand to take it. Alex's eyes narrowed a fraction. "That's a curious mark you have on your palm," he said, looking Jevan square in the eyes.

Annabel felt her heart lurch. Jevan merely shrugged. "Just on old scar," he said, taking the key and avoiding Annabel's eyes.

She felt Alex's eyes boring into her. She would not meet his look or lift her head as he approached her. Alex lifted her onto his horse and swung adeptly up behind her. He put his arm tightly around her waist and turned the horse. "A word of caution, Jevan," he said, looking back then shifting his gaze to Jophiel. "Stay away from my wife or both of you will regret it." He yanked on the reins, and the stallion broke into a gallop. "I am the only family you have left now," he hissed in her ear. "Your fate is entirely in my hands."

Jevan watched them ride into the distance. He felt so much hatred for Alex, but the threat was real. He felt powerless against him, unless he placed both his, his father, and Annabel's life in grave danger. He turned to Jophiel and saw that his father's eyes were moist. He placed his arm about his shoulder. "You should go home."

"No," Jophiel said at once. "He was my friend, and you can't do all this on your own. For Annabel's sake, let me help. She would want it that way."

Jevan nodded thoughtfully. "I have to go to the bees."

Jophiel turned solemnly back to the cottage. "I know."

Jevan made his way through the orchard, his thoughts in turmoil. This could not go on. He had to change things for both their sakes. He would not have thought Alex was capable of such a wicked act, although, the evidence was clear. The thought of Annabel spending one more day with him churned Jevan's stomach. He needed a plan, something that looked like an accident, and Alex would not be easily lured by him. And if Alex turned up dead anywhere, all suspicion would fall on him. He had to be cleverer than that.

Jevan reached the skeps and approached each in turn, knocking three times on their roofs with the cottage key.

"Bees, bees, bees, your master is dead." He hesitated, whom should he name? Annabel wasn't here anymore. "Now you will work for Jevan Wenham, your new master."

The bees listened. There was silence. Then a low humming began. It grew in pitch as Jevan ripped the black crepe into strips and adorned each skep with the fabric. The humming continued harmoniously for a while, and then it died away. The bees had consented to stay.

🙰🙰

Annabel felt numb. She did not utter a word as they rode back to Gothelstone mansion. Even the horror of what Alex had done felt distant, and the countryside passed by in a haze. They reached the mansion and dismounted.

Alex pulled her round to face him. "You look a dreadful sight. Go and get yourself cleaned up. Don't forget we are expecting guests in less than three hours."

She stared at him in amazement. "You can't seriously expect me to entertain your guests! My father has just died!"

His hand was on her bare arm. "That's exactly what I expect, now go. And, besides, it will take your mind off that business."

"No, it won't. How can it? Have you no compassion?" All her hatred and venom built rapidly, and she looked down at his hands, "No, I don't think you do."

When she looked up into his eyes, Alex saw they were full of loathing. Warily he stepped back.

"Are you going to kill me too?" she said menacingly and leaned toward him.

Suddenly, Alex's skin felt electrified, a stinging sensation where her flesh touched his. He jumped as though stung, astonished at her bitter smile. A shiver ran down his spine, and his heart raced. He was confounded as to her ability to render him so afraid.

"W—wear the green d—dress," he stuttered, letting go of her.

Annabel turned, walked into the mansion, and climbed the staircase, listening to Alex shouting at a servant in the background.

Chapter 29

The Saltonstall Legacy

Five minutes later, Alex stormed up the stairs, along the passageway to the intricate carved oak doorway. he didn't bother to knock as he burst into the room.

Cerberus was sitting at his desk and looked up, startled.

"What the hell are you playing at?" Alex cried, exasperated.

Cerberus stood quickly and faced his son.

"What happened?"

"He wasn't dead. I had to finish him myself!"

Cerberus made a noise of irritation. "They told me that he wouldn't last the night."

"Well, he did, and right into the afternoon. When she got there, he was still warm, for God's sake." Alex put his head in his hands. "What have I done?" A feeling of horror overwhelmed him. "She is driving me to madness, knowing she's been with him, and all her talk of divorce. Even now, this very afternoon, I saw the way they looked at each other." He shook his head, his thoughts growing darker and mood more despairing. "It sickens me. She is my wife and yet it's him that she is devoted to You were right," he admitted, looking into the cold blue steel of his father's gaze. "I should have kept her on a tighter rein."

Cerberus crossed the room toward Alex. "It won't always be this way."

"Won't it?" Alex said, shaking his head, his mind full of accusations. "A child you said, and she would forget him, but there is no child. She is not capable of giving me a child, and if I kill Jevan, she will hate me forever." He shook his head. "I couldn't bear that. You didn't see the way she looked at me this afternoon." He paused, wondering if his father would think him mad if he voiced his concerns, even though, he had to tell someone. It was eating him up inside. He had to get the words out. "She has this strange energy. I really think she could kill me with it, if she wanted to."

"You did kill her father," Cerberus reminded him coldly, oddly calm, given what Alex just said.

Alex's eyes glowered with distain as he stared at his father. "*We* killed her father." He shifted his eyes to the fireplace, feeling the regret. "In spite of everything, even though, I know there to be something wicked in her, I love her so much. She has this way of bringing out the worst in me..." His voice trailed off into silence.

"Sit down, Alex."

Alex hesitated for a moment, wishing he could turn back time and start this day over, wishing he'd had another choice. He took a deep breath and sat down in the opposite chair.

"She has power," Cerberus said, "but she can't control it."

"How do you know what she can and can't do?" Alex said wearily.

"You know it, you feel it. You just admitted it. Lilith was a powerful woman and a powerful witch, and Annabel is just like her, with you being the last of the Saltonstall line, your child will inherit the same powers."

Alex shook his head in disbelief. "Father, this is nonsense."

"No, Alex, it is not nonsense. You don't have the gift, so it is hard for you to grasp. Lilith did, and her daughter does too." Cerberus pursed his lips. "This house carries a secret, a dangerous secret," he said, looking at him a little oddly, and Alex skin tingled as goose bumps rose on his flesh. "There is a spirit here," Cerberus continued, "it cannot rest. Your grandmother and mother saw it. As a consequence, it took their sanity."

Alex raised his eyebrows a fraction, wondering whether to humor him. "How do you know that?"

Cerberus shook his head. "I don't see it. I feel the spirit, and I know that it must be summoned for it to have form, and only the most powerful witch can do that."

Alex's eyes narrowed. "Annabel?"

"Yes," Cerberus nodded. "The consciousness of this spirit must be raised and brought under control."

"What is it?" Alex swallowed nervously, not liking the direction the conversation was heading. "Are you talking about the Devil?"

Cerberus laughed. "The Devil and God, what are they? Demons and Angels. I am not talking about religious fairy stories. I talk of great universal energies. It can't be named. It's too strong, too extraordinary. It is dark magic."

"Black magic, Father," Alex said warily. The realization hit him and he leapt to his feet. "Just why are you so adamant you want a child? What for, a sacrifice?"

Cerberus sighed impatiently. "Have you not been listening?" He drew up his knees and sat forward. "I would not sacrifice my grandchild. It's so much simpler than that. I am a pureblood, born from generations of Saltonstall and, like Annabel, I have power. Your child would ensure an heir to this legacy." He fixed Alex with a rigid gaze, and his lips pressed together in a chilling smile. "Annabel has a more pressing and important destiny. The spirit is possessed by a demon, only she can summon it."

"I don't understand," Alex, said, rubbing his temple. "How could she do that?" He watched his father warily. "You know too much power is not a good thing. It leads men into darkness. Besides, you don't need Annabel, and you just need a priest to exorcise this ghost of yours."

"I don't want an exorcism," Cerberus cried. "The spirit has to be summoned. Annabel is strong and the perfect vessel to be used." There was a sudden concentrated darkness in his eyes. "For what better incentive for the spirit, than to be summoned by her own daughter."

Alex's face contorted with horror, the penny dropped, and Cerberus nodded his head.

"Yes, Lilith."

∽∾∽

Agnes came hurrying in to the bedroom. "I am sorry to rush you, milady. It's just the master insists that you look your best tonight," she said apologetically. "I—I'm sorry to hear about your father. It must be very difficult for you."

Annabel smiled weakly and sat upon the dressing table stool. "Thank you, Agnes." She stared at the reflection in the mirror—eyes red and swollen, pallor alarmingly pale. She doubted that Agnes could improve her appearance. All she wanted to do was close her eyes and shut out the entire world. That was not an option. Alex made that very clear. She couldn't believe how heartless he was. She could never have believed that he was capable of such a terrible thing or that he'd changed so much over the past few weeks. Guilt flittered through her mind. Had she made him behave this way. She'd lied to him, deceived him in the worst possible way. Even so, it was not a good enough reason for him to seek such terrible vengeance. She hung her head and sat perfectly still, while Agnes fussed over her make-up and hair.

When she looked back at the reflection a while later, a life size doll stared out of the mirror. Powder rouge and lipstick were carefully applied, the green dress was becoming, and her hair was pinned up perfectly in a fashionable elegant style. Annabel stared harder at the stranger in the looking glass. Who exactly was this person? It wasn't her. It was a perfect representation of what Alex expected tonight.

A single tear ran down her face, followed by another, and soon tracks appeared through the perfect make up. Agnes finished putting the last pin in her hair and glanced in the mirror to admire her work. The two women's eyes locked.

"Milady, you mustn't cry. The master will be angry."

Her words made Annabel's tears fall faster, and she turned around to face her, clutching at her maid for some comfort.

Agnes brought her arms around Annabel's shoulders and held her tight. "It's all right, milady" she soothed. She caressed and comforted for a few minutes then, as much as she was loath to be harsh, Agnes could not allow her to remain this way. "That's enough. Now we must get you ready."

"I'm sorry, Agnes," Annabel mumbled.

Agnes smiled warmly. "It's no trouble, milady," she said, wiping Annabel's face, and began to apply more white powder. Agnes worked quickly and, within ten minutes, Annabel was ready again, only the puffiness around her eyes betrayed her grief.

Annabel stood up and looked down at the dress. She hated this dress, even more so since Alex picked it out. "Agnes, I don't want to wear this dress. Bring me the red one."

Agnes hesitated. "Milady," she said cautiously, "don't you think it a little inappropriate?"

"On the contrary, I think a tasteless outfit is most fitting for the occasion."

The scarlet red dress bodice was cut low at the back with a V cut at the front. It exposed a daring amount of cleavage that would be considered vulgar. The single skirt had a sheer scarf drapery, lightly embroidered with silver thread. A dress that got attention. Annabel pulled a few pins from her head, which allowed her red hair to tumble down in long ringlets, and she stared back at her reflection again. Far more like the Annabel she remembered.

એન્ડ

"No," Alex said for the third time. "What you're suggesting cannot be true. What you say goes against all sense of reason."

Cerberus leapt to his feet. "You cannot be weak or frightened. This spirit is evil. It has invaded Lilith's soul. By bringing it into form, I can release Lilith from its clutches and bring her back to me."

"No!" Alex cried, horrified, his face now inches from Cerberus. "Spirits are not evil. They cannot harm us once they have passed. What you talk of goes against God and reason. Resurrection is not something mortal man can do. You are mistaken, Father."

"This one is evil. She has been here for centuries. She roams the grounds and churchyard. Lilith knew she was here, and now she has taken Lilith's soul. Lilith was taken too soon. She can be brought back. It's not impossible."

Alex was afraid of the madness he heard in his father's words and his unshakable belief in these frightening ideas. "Father," Alex said, in a calmer voice, "that night in the attic, Annabel said she saw a woman, even though we saw no one. The rooms were empty. We searched the house from top to bottom, yet if Lilith had somehow become this spirit, don't you think Annabel would have recognized her own mother?"

"No, the spirit is clever. Lilith would have a different form."

"No, there was nothing there," Alex said, shaking his head. "It was all in her mind, just like Mother." He wanted to say, just like you too, but restrained himself. "Didn't you tell me that she saw things and heard voices behind the walls?"

Cerberus looked at him as if he was dealing with a feeble-minded individual. "Don't you see," he articulated slowly, "that was Lilith. She was your mother's maid, remember? She was the one who bewitched her and sent her mad, because Lilith loved me as much as I loved her."

Alex stared at his father in shock. "So you want me to help you bring back someone who sent my own mother insane? I can't listen to this anymore," he said, needing to get out of his father's presence as soon as possible. "We are expecting guests, and I have to get changed."

Alex strode across the room and slammed the door loudly behind him, thankful to be out of the room and his father's company. On the landing, he stood still, composing his thoughts and trying to make sense of the words Cerberus said. Nothing made sense. His father was mad, that was the shocking truth.

Alex knew his father was brutal and many innocent men were killed on his order. It was a shocking realization to see that he was in danger of becoming just like him, having played a horrifying part in Cerberus's latest plot. Alex shivered, his conscience in turmoil. Things had changed. He never understood before just how disturbing his father's beliefs were. His suggestions of what he was doing was dangerous, dabbling with the dark arts. Didn't that make him a witch too?

Cerberus had just about admitted that fact. Alex wanted to laugh—if it were not for the truly sinister implication that went with it and a nagging doubt.

Annabel did have power. He saw and felt it, and on that account, he knew his father was right. But could the rest even be possible? There was another truth, so clear to him now. Lilith had bewitched his father, just as her daughter enchanted him. Alex thought back. Just look what she had driven him to do. He clasped his cold hands together to stop them trembling. In his mind, he heard Josiah's last strangulated gasps from beneath the pillow.

"It wasn't my fault," he whispered.

She had made him do it. His father might be mad, but his wife was the evil one in this house.

ভৈক্তভ

A door banged loudly from across the landing. A few minutes later, Alex entered the room. His eyes met Annabel's in the mirror's reflection, and then he looked down at her dress. "I told you to wear the green one," he said angrily. "Guests will be arriving soon."

Annabel turned from the mirror. "I am wearing this one," she said defiantly, "and unless you want me to be extremely late, I suggest you let me continue getting ready."

He saw the loathing in her eyes. He heard the coldness in her voice and felt the hateful energy she summoned. It struck a fearful chord through him.

Just like his father said—the power she possessed was alarming. He turned to leave the room.

"Wait, Alex." Her voice had softened, and he turned back to look at her. "Agnes, please leave us." Annabel waited until the maid left the room and closed the door. "There is something I have to know."

Alex swallowed nervously and came a few paces closer to her. "What?"

"Did he suffer?"

Alex saw through the hatred to the inner pain and caught the quiver in her voice before she caught her breath. He remembered the prolonged gasps from beneath the tightly gripped pillow but shook his head. "No."

Annabel breathed again and lowered her gaze. Alex stood motionless. At that moment, he wanted to ask her forgiveness, although the terrible way she looked at him earlier, unnerved him again. He felt as though she was capable of anything— more so now since leaving Cerberus's room. Alex felt as if he were standing on a precipice, waiting for her to draw on her dark magic, waiting for her reaction.

Annabel merely sat back down and looked up at him inquisitively. "Alex, have you heard a woman's voice in this house?"

The question caught him off guard and Alex heart beat faster as his thoughts flew to his father, and then to what he had told him. "Only yours, Annabel," he said cautiously.

"There is someone else."

Inside, Alex was screaming. This was his worst nightmare. She was confirming not only the madness of his father, but her insanity too. He couldn't let this go on. He'd had his fill of all this darkness today. He glanced at the clock. Guests were probably arriving, and he had to maintain calmness for at least a while. "You don't seriously think that I have a mistress concealed in this house?" He laughed cruelly. "Honestly, Annabel, I think that I should get a doctor to look at you."

"Like Cerberus did with your mother, before they took her away?"

Alex's eyes narrowed. "Don't talk of my mother," he said abruptly.

"Why not? Don't you ever wonder what became of her?"

He stiffened. The room suddenly felt oppressive. "I know what became of her," he said, bending closer to her. "She is quite mad, and if she lives, she is still locked away in an asylum in Bristol. Before you ask, no, I don't want to see her. I have quite enough to deal with one deranged woman in my life."

Annabel leaned back. He was clearly angry. She also sensed his nerves.

His eyes bore into hers for a moment, and then he took a step back. "Be thankful that I still love you," he said, moving to the door. His eyes lingered on her for a few moments and then he left the room.

Alone, Annabel did not know what to think of his reaction. He had appeared to be afraid of her. Not only that, his eyes had belied some great suspicion. She closed her eyes for a moment. The day had been terrible enough. Now she had to face this evening. Annabel stood, brought herself up to her full height, lifted her head high, and took a deep breath.

When she descended the staircase, all eyes were upon her. Her smile was fixed. She did not waver as she caught the scandalized whispers when she moved among the assembled guests. She felt as though she moved like a wooden doll and did not utter more than a few words herself. Suddenly, Alex appeared by her side. He expressed concern to their guests that she had been feeling unwell.

A well-rehearsed speech, it made Annabel seethe with anger and, as soon as was convenient, she rose up and hissed in his ear, "Perhaps you should tell the truth, let them know your true character."

Alex seized her arm firmly and led her to the edge of the room. "Don't you dare make a scene," he said through gritted teeth.

"How could I possibly do that?" she said, narrowing her eyes.

"Christ, I am warning you, Annabel," he said under this breath.

"Annabel."

The familiar voice made her turn. Annabel was completely taken aback to find Lucy Ann and Gabriel standing before her.

"I'm very pleased that you could accept the invitation."

It was Alex who spoke and his countenance immediately relaxed. Lucy Ann did not miss her friend's great shock, as she leaned forward and kissed Annabel warmly.

"Alex thought it would be a nice surprise," she said, over-joyed that Annabel was clearly lost for words. "Alex invited us for the weekend," she continued, "and, as you can imagine, mother was thrilled that we would get such an invitation, although a little put out that she was not included," she said, giving Alex a mischievous smile.

"Ah, yes, Catherine was always a social climber. I am certain that you and Gabriel are not displeased that I did not include her," Alex said, returning her smile and Annabel stared at him in wonder.

This morning he had murdered her father, and only a few hours later, he was conversing with her friends as though their lives revolved around a social calendar. Annabel dismissed the thought. This was not the right time. She forced her face to brighten and turned to Alex. "Thank you for inviting them, it is a lovely surprise."

After a few minutes polite conversation, Alex made an excuse and left them alone. Annabel turned back to her friends, and Gabriel leaned forward.

"By the way, I love your dress, very bohemian."

"I wanted to make an impact."

"I think you have done that," Lucy Ann said. "What a bunch of old gossips. I can't believe they are your friends."

"They're not, I hardly know them." Annabel smiled happily. "Oh, Lucy and Gabriel, you cannot imagine how good it is to see you!" she cried.

Lucy's eyebrows knitted together briefly. She did not miss the sorrow in her tone of voice. Then dinner was announced, and they began to make their way through to the dining room,

"Are you all right?" Lucy's voice was full of concern.

Annabel nodded. "We will talk later," she promised.

∞∞∞

Later came the next morning after breakfast, Lucy Ann, Gabriel, and Annabel sat on the back terrace in complete silence after they listened to Annabel's awful news, followed by her account of what had occurred.

"When is the funeral?" Gabriel asked in a gentle voice.

"A few days."

"What can we do to help?" Lucy said.

Annabel shook her head. "I wish you could." She thought for several moments. "Perhaps there is something," she said in a low voice. She looked up and all around to see who else was in the vicinity. Satisfied that they were alone, she leaned forward. "It has to be done in secret."

Lucy Ann clapped her hands. "I love secrets."

"I'm serious, Lucy. This is a dangerous secret, no one can know." Annabel captured their undivided attention. "I need to find the whereabouts of somebody, somebody that has been in an asylum for the past twenty years." She noted the shock on her friends faces. "Will you help me?"

"Of course we will," they said in unison.

Annabel related brief details of her suspicions, and Lucy drew a deep breath. "I am not sure that I will feel that comfortable sleeping in this house tonight," she said.

Gabriel squeezed Lucy's hand in reassurance. "Don't worry. We will lock the doors, and I will stand guard outside your room all night to protect you."

Lucy looked at Annabel. "What about you?"

"Alex will be there," she said confidently.

"Then who is going to protect you from him?"

Chapter 29

The Funeral

Lucy Ann and Gabriel left the next morning. Before they departed, Lucy Ann made a point of saying, in earshot of Alex, that she would send Annabel the latest fashion pamphlets from Bath.

"You must come to stay next year," she said warmly enough to Alex.

Only Annabel heard the strain in her voice.

"I am sure we will do that," he answered kindly.

Gabriel extended his hand. "Thank you for your hospitality. It was good to see you both again."

"The pleasure has been all mine, and it is you, I should be thanking," Alex said, turning to look at Annabel. "You have put some sparkle back into my wife's eyes."

The last of the goodbyes were said and, as their carriage pulled away, Alex turned to Annabel. "They certainly have a positive effect on *you*."

Annabel did not comment. She turned and walked into the house. Cerberus was standing in the hallway and placed a note back on the silver letter tray then looked across at her.

"Ah, Annabel," he said hesitantly. "I have just had word that the funeral will be on Tuesday."

"Where?" she said hoarsely.

"At Gothelstone. That was your request, was it not?"

Annabel caught Alex's eye. He did not speak, only shifted uncomfortably.

"Yes, next to my mother's grave."

Cerberus gave her a longer than necessary look, but did not say anything.

Annabel was relieved that Jevan had not wasted any time, or her request was not denied by either Cerberus or Alex, as she suspected they might. Then again, what reason would they have to upset her further? They had already done enough. She wished she could see Jevan, just to talk to him. But that was impossible. Instead, she consoled herself with the fact that he would be at the funeral.

ぐろぐろ

The day dawned bright and mild. A few clouds hung in the sky, but there was nothing threatening on the horizon. Annabel wore a suitable black dress, her hair left loose. And before she went to the carriage, she wandered around the garden in search of a flower. She picked a single red rose.

In the carriage, she sat between Cerberus and Alex. Neither one spoke, and she was glad. She did not want to have to be nice or have to exchange pleasantries or reveal her feelings to them, and was thankful that it was only a short journey to the church. On arrival, Annabel graciously took Alex's arm when offered, thankful that she did not have to walk into the church alone.

All eyes seemed to turn in her direction when they entered the church. Most of the congregation sat, as Alex led her slowly up the aisle. The last time she had done this, she had been leaning on her father's arm. She stifled the sob and felt Alex's gaze.

"Are you all right?"

She nodded without looking at him and watched the faces of the gathered crowd. They were all here. People she had known all her life—villagers, shopkeepers, and farm workers from neighboring villages. Close to the front sat Jophiel and Jevan together. Hushed voices were all around.

Her sole attention was on the wooden coffin before her. It was closed. Even so, the impact of its presence hit her with full force. She trembled and could not stop the tears as they began to roll down her cheeks. The more she stared at the coffin, the more the reality of the situation hit her, and she clutched the rose tighter in her fingers, not feeling the pain as a thorn dug into her skin.

They reached the front of the church, and she sat. Her eyes remained fixed on the coffin. The priest began to speak. Words were said. They seemed to make no sense, then one or two respectful murmurs rose from the crowd. A hymn was sung, but the melody was muted, and the majority of the service passed by in a haze. Annabel could only think about her father lying in the coffin. She found it impossible to believe that she would never hear his voice or lay eyes on him again.

The congregation rose, and she stood with them. She lifted her eyes and watched as Jevan, Jophiel, Luke, and David— twins, that she had known at school—stepped up to the coffin. Between them, they lifted it from the stand and carried it solemnly out of the church. She followed close behind, touched by sounds of crying and the glistening faces of the people she passed by. Some smiled weakly. Others touched her lightly as she moved through the church.

Outside, the sun warmed her skin, and she gulped a deep breath of fresh air, glad to be out of the stifled and solemn atmosphere of the church. She and Alex followed the pallbearers through the graveyard and, when they reached the far side, they stopped and lowered it next to the freshly dug grave. The following congregation took a few minutes to assemble, and then the coffin was lowered into the hole in the ground as the priest began to talk again. Annabel stepped forward and threw her rose down into the grave.

She moved backward and felt Alex's arm resting lightly around her waist. A chill ran up her spine. She glanced uneasily at Jevan. He stood on the opposite side, and his gaze did not waver from hers. She wanted to smile at him. She couldn't. She felt frozen like a statue, as if all her blood had congealed, and not a single muscle could move. Her mind numbed, only the voice of the priest invaded her thoughts. He talked on and on, and she turned her head and stared at him in contempt.

She wanted to scream at the unfairness and the pretense. Why did he not see that the man standing next to her was her father's murderer? It was unbelievable that everyone was so blind, and he could stand there so calmly, acting like a dutiful husband, mourning his father-in-law like a loving companion to his grieving wife. That was what everyone saw. They did not see the poisoned love, perverse and dangerous. She looked pitifully around at the sea of faces. All were fooled by deceit, and the priest's voice still droned in her head.

"God has taken Josiah from this earth for a purpose."

Annabel shuddered. The priest knew nothing, and she wished he would shut up. Her eyes flew to Jevan again, her heart raced, and adrenaline pumped through her veins.

Jevan watched her closely. He knew something was not right, and his mouth turned up just a fraction, because he saw, he understood.

Annabel's breathing quickened, and she blocked out the priest's words. She closed her eyes. Her eyelids fluttered lightly as the power flowed through her body and the energy built. Several seconds passed, then her eyes flew wide open. She stared into the sky and watched the clouds rolling across the distant moors. They traveled fast, coming closer and closer, blotting out the sunlight and darkening the sky with each second that passed.

A tumultuous thunderclap rang out, followed immediately by another. The priest looked up at the sky. His words were hurried now, and the congregation began to fidget and glance nervously skyward.

"Ashes to ashes, dust to dust, we commit this body—" He did not finish the sentence.

The lightning strike hit the stone statue behind him and split it in two. Terrified screams echoed around the graveyard. People scattered in all directions and ran for cover as the rain pelted down on their heads. The wind howled and whipped the trees, breaking branches and sending them flying through the air. Alex let go of Annabel as a branch hit him in the back.

Someone pulled him from the graveside as the rain, now horizontal, felt like driving daggers and everyone ran for cover. Only Annabel and Jevan did not move.

"Annabel!" It was Alex's voice in the distance, disorientated by the bizarre event. He thought she had moved with him. He was forced to take cover in the church doorway, but she was not by his side as he imagined, and the curtain of rain obscured the other side of the graveyard to where they had stood. People rushed past him, and he grabbed Jophiel's arm as he passed.

"Have you seen Annabel?"

Jophiel looked at him with contempt. "Everyone's in the church," he said frostily, shaking Alex's hand from him as he continued through the door.

Alex turned and followed, convinced now that she had already entered the church. He went to search for her.

Jevan moved closer around the open grave. His hair was plastered to his head and rain ran in streams down his face. Another thunderclap made him jump. Lightning struck another tree. It groaned and split.

"Annabel, stop. It is too much. You will destroy too much!" He took her hands in his, and brought them close to his body.

"Everything I love has been destroyed."

"Not everything," he said, shaking his head. "But it will be, sweetheart. The crops will be ruined, the fields will be flooded, and your bees will drown!"

She stared at him for a moment, a puzzled look on her face. "I can't control it."

Jevan frowned. "Yes, you can, you called it up, and you can send it away. Make it stop, Annabel." But as he spoke, the rain was easing, the black clouds parted, and a glimmer of sunlight fell over them.

Annabel stared into Jevan's eyes. "I didn't do anything," she said, bewildered.

They lifted their gaze toward the church, and then higher up to the church tower. Standing on the parapet was Cerberus. His arms were raised to the sky. He appeared to be chanting and the rain was easing to a drizzle. He lowered his arms and stared down at them. Annabel shivered.

Jevan resisted pulling her toward him. Too many eyes could be watching them. "Go into the church," he ordered, "find a way. I have to see you."

He turned and walked back through the graveyard.

"Look at the state of you!" Alex said a few minutes later. "You could have been drowned. I have never seen so much rain fall out of the sky." She did not speak, and then his eyes searched hers accusingly. "I thought you were with my father, but you were with him."

"Josiah was my father, and he was like a father to Jevan. You cannot forbid us to mourn him," she said coldly.

Her abruptness upset him. "Can't you find it in your heart to love me as you love him, Annabel?" he snapped, anger pulsating through him.

Annabel stared at him in disbelief. "How can you even ask that? Today of all days." She shook her head. "You shouldn't be asking for my love, but my forgiveness." She would have gone on, except, Cerberus walked into the church.

The last of the congregation left. The church was empty now, save for the three of them.

Cerberus gave her a most peculiar look, before shifting his gaze to Alex. "Go and wait in the carriage."

"Why?" Alex's surprise was obvious, and the withering look Cerberus gave him made him regret the question.

"I said, leave us!" he repeated icily. "I need to talk to Annabel."

Alex looked from Cerberus to Annabel. He did not want to leave her alone with him, but his father's determined gaze made him feel as though he should obey.

"I will be right outside," he said and closed the heavy door behind him.

As soon as the door shut, Cerberus stepped closer to Annabel, his eyes steady on hers and his voice low. "What are you doing?"

Annabel didn't answer him. She would not be intimidated by him, not today. Besides, her dress was dripping and she was cold. "I have to get changed," she said, turning toward the door.

Cerberus blocked her way. "Answer the question."

She shook her head defiantly. "I don't know what you are talking about."

"Yes, you do, you called it up."

"What?" she said in a whisper, "what did I call up?"

"The powers of darkness."

She swallowed nervously. "No, I don't do that. It's just a simple manipulation."

Cerberus laughed coldly. "Manipulation! You could have killed everybody today. Your lightning strike missed the priest by a few inches, because you wanted him dead, didn't you? You have some of the darkest powers I have ever seen."

Annabel stared at him uneasily. "What about you?" she challenged, "up on the parapet. I saw you. You had more of a hand in this than me."

"Don't get clever with me, Annabel," Cerberus said fiercely. "Who else has the power to control you?" Annabel drew in her breath sharply as he continued, "You have always known that I am a powerful witch."

She shook her head. "No," she said, appalled. Her skin felt like ice, and she shivered. "What do you what from me, Cerberus?" she said, feeling suddenly afraid.

"Your compliance."

"With what?"

"Your destiny."

"You talk in riddles," she said, sounding braver than she felt. "And I have had enough of this." She went to turn from him, but Cerberus's hand shot out and caught her arm in a tight grip. The mild vibration turned into a powerful energy flowing through her, electrifying her veins. Startled she looked up at him.

"With my guidance, your power can be even greater."

She was picking up the etheric charge of emotional energy, combined with something more powerful still. Something was happening.

A great mass swirled through her mind, shaping her

thoughts. Vivid images were taking shape, and she saw her mother.

"Don't fight it, Annabel. See what I can show you." Cerberus's shape shifted fractionally, his face hardened, his form grew more grotesque, more evil.

She felt the energy flowing through him, pulling her toward his consciousness, his mind melding with hers. The visions were terrifying and, inwardly, she screamed, forcing the power into her body and down her arms, away from him and his manipulation.

Cerberus leapt back from her with a shriek. He looked down at his palm, covered in red welts. His eyes rose to meet hers, and his mouth turned up in a misshapen smile.

"You have the power, and you have always known that power is not given unless there is a use for it. You know what must be done."

Annabel backed away, shaking her head. "No, I don't know."

Cerberus followed, until he was standing close to her again. "You can summon the spirit."

Annabel shook her head, horrified.

"Yes, my dear, the spirit is in the house. She is waiting for you to call her name."

"Don't come near me," she warned, as he moved closer.

"She has summoned you. She has been looking for you."

Annabel was trembling.

"And soon she will be at her strongest. She can cross over."

"Who are you talking about?" Annabel's words were barely there.

"The woman I have spent a lifetime loving."

Instinctively, Annabel knew the name before it was spoken and her heart missed a beat.

"It is Lilith that calls you."

All the tiny hairs on Annabel's neck and arms stood upright, the cold shiver ran down her spine, and she opened her mouth, even though no sound came out. Cerberus reached down and took her hand. She felt the vibration start again.

"You and I have the ability. We can save her soul from damnation. In two weeks' time, the thirteenth moon will be full, and the witch's ladder will be complete, then she can cross over."

Annabel searched his eyes in disbelief. "It's not possible!"

"Yes, it is, and you know it. Our power combined is unstoppable."

He let go of her hand, and watched her terrified expression for a few moments. He stepped back from her and walked toward the church door as if to leave, then he stopped and thought for a moment. "I wouldn't mention this to Alex. He is weak, he frightens too easily."

Chapter 31

An Arrangement

It was the worst day of her life, more awful even than when her mother died. Annabel hardly touched her food at dinner and, much later, when she lay in bed, she was too afraid to close her eyes, fearful of the things that might come out of the darkness. Could Cerberus be right? Every gut feeling told her no—if it wasn't for the fact that he seemed so certain. His disturbing words made her question everything.

Despite these misgivings, she would not fear the spirit of her mother, and she was adamant that the girl in the attic had not been Lilith. It was a shocking truth that the house was cursed, truly cursed. The more she thought about everything, the more she saw a pattern of insanity emerging. More disturbingly, trying to get at the truth was driving her that way too.

Cerberus had shaken her faith in everything she knew to be right. His philosophy was too fantastic. One thing was clear. He was powerful and knew the craft. Perhaps as well as her mother. Annabel had never thought of herself as a witch before. The word alone conjured up the horror stories of persecution and torture, where innocents had been horrifically tried and executed, because of ignorance and hysteria. Now in this time, three witches. What did it all mean, and what was the connection?

Lilith was dead. There was no doubt in Annabel's mind. She had seen her body, kissed her cold white flesh, and duly mourned her. She thought back to the open coffin, and the burial in the churchyard. She had witnessed all these things, so why did Cerberus's words disturb her so much? For as much as she wanted to dismiss every word, something held her back. An element of truth rang through it, and that was the most terrifying thing of all.

✍✍✍

The next day a note came for Annabel, secured inside the promised fashion periodical from Bath. Alex read the enclosed letter but had no interest in the latest women's fashions. Annabel casually thumbed through the pages and waited until Alex left the room, before detaching the note. Later, in her own room, she unfolded the paper.

Lucy Ann and Gabriel's research had turned up several false leads, before recently discovering that Elizabeth Saltonstall was currently a resident at Blackheath House on the outskirts of Bristol. They reported it as being a private sanctuary for genteel women, mainly afflicted with mania and hysteria. A small shiver ran down Annabel's spine as she continued to read Lucy Ann's words

> *Gabriel visited last Tuesday on the pretense that he was considering Blackheath House for his sister's recuperation after a spell of melancholia. Gabriel met with Doctor Heath, who also operates two other sanctuaries within the country. He was told that the inmates were often long-term residents, and Gabriel was assured, the object was to "cure" them, using various methods, which the doctor did not elaborate upon. By his own admission, the cures did not often work. He went on to say "these women's constitutions, by mere default of their sex, tend to get hysterical and respond poorly to new treatments. But purging with tonics is working wonders with some of them, and research into their mental wellbeing is ongoing." In short, Gabriel reported that the women were not permitted to leave the sanc-*

*tuary. Gabriel later confided to me that he would not
have put his dog under the care of Dr. Heath, let alone
a relative. I can only imagine as well as you, dear
friend, how terrible a place it is.*

Lucy Ann ended the note by saying that they would be
happy to assist further if she wished it. Annabel folded the
letter carefully and tucked it into the secret compartment in
her writing desk. She thought about all the possible scenarios
of what to do next. The obvious conclusion was that she
would have to go to the city herself.

Alex was also going to Bristol soon, a meeting with a solicitor regarding Honeymead, and her heart sank when she
thought about it. As his wife, her father's legacy automatically
became his. She had no independent claim or say as to what
was to become of the property. She tried not to dwell on it, but
that meeting was to take place the following week. Alex
would no doubt confine her to the house with instructions that
she be closely watched. But with a bit of careful planning, she
might manage to slip away.

For the next few days, Annabel made a daily pilgrimage to
Gothelstone graveyard, accompanied by Agnes. During these
trips, she confided her heartbreak at losing her father and, in
turn, Agnes related that she had never been comfortable being
Alex's spy, not when her real loyalty was with Annabel, adding that she was fearfully frightened of Cerberus and Alex. It
gladdened Annabel's heart to hear this information, and she
gave her word she would protect Agnes as much as she could.
It also gave her the confidence to ask a favor.

"Agnes, I have to ask something of you," she said, as they
headed for the graveyard again. Agnes looked wide-eyed and
fearful. Annabel did not falter. She had no choice. "I have to
see Jophiel. He was my father's best friend. All my life he has
been like a second father to me, and he is devastated by my
father's death."

Agnes nodded sympathetically. "Yes, milady, I know they
were old friends."

"I feel terrible that I have not been able to see him, and you are aware of the situation, but if I can bring him a small amount of comfort, then my conscience will be eased." They stopped walking and a twinge of doubt crept into her voice. "Do you understand that I cannot rest until I see him?"

Agnes nodded. "You know I will not tell the master," she said reassuringly.

Annabel smiled gratefully at her, and then they picked up the pace and made their way to Rookwood, via fields and hedgerows, and out of sight from any passerby. Thankfully, the forge was located at the edge of town, and Annabel did not have to enter through the main door. She left Agnes sitting on a straw bale in the stable, made her way through the stables, and opened the wooden door that led into the back room of the forge. Jevan looked up, startled to see her, and put down the tool he was holding. Annabel ran to him, and he gathered her in his arms.

"I can't stay long," she said breathlessly, even though his lips were already on hers, sending a tingling sensation down her spine.

His nearness invoked all the old familiar sensations. His hands moved over her shoulders and down her back making her heart pound. She wanted him to whisk her up in his arms and take her to the little room above the print shop, to make love to her slowly and then more passionately, more brutally. She craved the pain of his violence. It would make her feel real again. She dug her nails into the fabric of his shirt, willing herself to resist him. Their lips parted, and he looked down at her, sensing her longing, even though she was trying to pry herself from him.

"I have to see Jophiel," she said, a little sharply.

"Are you all right?"

Annabel nodded, and he placed a kiss tenderly on her forehead, his hold tightening possessively. Just then, Jophiel came through the door, and his eyes widened with obvious surprise. He held out his arms. She left Jevan, rushed across the room, and threw her arms around his neck.

"I wanted to come sooner." Her voice was muffled in his tight embrace.

"I know," he said, "but you're here now."

In his arms, Annabel felt safe. It was like being held by her father, a reassuring warmness without the complication of yearning, radiated through her. Jophiel always made her feel that way, as though no harm could ever befall her in his company. She looked up at him as he moved his arm protectively around her shoulders, concern marked on his face.

"I need your help."

Jophiel nodded his head. "Anything, just ask."

"I need to borrow a horse, tomorrow morning, one that won't be missed."

Jophiel stared at her in surprise.

"What for?"

Jevan spoke brusquely. Annabel bit her lip as she turned back to face him. "Please don't ask me. It's better if you don't know. You can't have any part in this."

His eyes narrowed immediately and his expression hardened. "Tell me what you are going to do," he demanded abruptly, moving closer to her.

"Calm down, Jevan," Jophiel said quickly. "But he has a point. Josiah would have wanted us to protect you at all costs, and you should know well enough by now that you have always been like a daughter to me. I will not knowingly let you put yourself in danger, and I need to know what you are doing tomorrow." Jophiel's tone and determination made her smile briefly. He and Jevan were so alike.

She sighed, defeated. "I have to go to Bristol," she said, catching their exchange of glances.

"On horseback? You can't ride to Bristol," Jevan said, shaking his head.

"Yes, I can, and I will," she said defiantly, ignoring his temper, and turned back to Jophiel. "Please, Jophiel will you let me have a horse?"

Jophiel shook his head. "Jevan's right, Annabel. It's too dangerous for a woman to ride alone that far. Anything could happen to you."

"And I won't let you go, anyway."

She looked back at Jevan. "How are you going to stop me, tie me up?"

"If I have to," he said coldly.

"Enough! The three of us should not argue," Jophiel said, looking at Jevan.

Jevan's anger subsided. He reached out and took Annabel's hand, and she did not resist as he led her across the room. He pulled out a stool from under the bench for her to sit upon and knelt before her, covering her hands with his. His mood may have lightened, but his hands held hers tightly on her lap. Despite the power in his hands, his eyes showed only concern. She looked into the dark depths of his eyes and wished they were alone.

"Tell me what you are planning to do?" he said evenly.

She shook her head. "No, I can't. Please don't ask me," she beseeched him.

"Then I won't let you leave here."

There was determination and an underlying warning in his voice. Jevan was not about to be manipulated. Annabel squirmed uncomfortably beneath both sets of eyes that suspected something terrible. It was Jevan's unyielding grip and determined gaze that steadily broke her resolve.

"I am going to an asylum," she said nervously, anticipating his reaction. Jevan sat back on his haunches, a clear expression of horror registering on his face, as she went on. "I have to find Alex's mother. She's in that place." She looked up at Jophiel, beseechingly. "I have to know what's going on at the house. I have to find out what the Saltonstall legacy really is, and right now, she is about the only person left who can give me any answers."

"No!" Jevan stood abruptly, releasing her. "There is no way I will let you go to a place like that. What were you thinking?" he said, visibly reeling. "A woman can't go into those places alone, and why do you think you will get any sane answers? By my calculation, she's been locked up for many years."

Annabel stood up crossly. "I don't believe that she was ever mad. Cerberus locked her away because of my mother.

With Elizabeth out the way, he believed that Lilith would become his wife. Don't you see?" she implored him. "I have to do this, and I have to find out."

Jevan stared at her. He knew her too well. She would not be swayed, not once she got an idea in her head. He wished that he could take her away from this place and end the torment of her marriage. But unless he murdered Alex—and that temptation was growing greater by the day—there would be no end to this ordeal.

His mood softened. She was seeking to make sense of her life at the mansion, and he trusted that there was something odd happening in that house, for Annabel was not one for fanciful imaginings. Perhaps it would resolve something for her, after all.

"How will we do it?"

"You can't come with me, Jevan!" she gasped, staring at him in horror at the mere idea. "If I go missing for a day, it will be bad enough, but if you are implicated, then Alex will be justified in having you arrested."

"She's right, Jevan," Jophiel said. They turned to look at him. "But you are not going alone. I will go with you." Annabel stared at him in surprise. "It's Jevan that Alex wants rid of. If you are seen with anyone else, it won't be the same. You can think of a reason, and I am an old man. Alex won't be jealous of me," he finished softly.

"You're not old," she said, overwhelmed with gratitude. In another life, in another time, she could have loved Jophiel the way she loved Jevan. She brushed that thought aside and looked back at Jevan. He was watching her, thinking.

"Where will Alex be tomorrow?"

"He leaves for Bristol early in the morning."

"How early?"

"Six or seven."

Jevan thought for a few minutes. Could he arrange something for Alex at this short notice? He might only have an hour to spare. It could be possible. He smiled at Annabel. "Then by eight, go into the garden and to the far pavilion, go out through the other side to the gap in the hedge, and I will be waiting for you. We will meet Father on the road with the small carriage, and I will go back to the print shop." Jevan turned to Jophiel. "I will open the forge and work between the two." He took his gaze back to Annabel. "I know you'll take care of her, but—" he said with a warning, "—don't let her talk you into anything you shouldn't do."

Annabel's indignant look made Jophiel smile, and a shadow passed across his face as he watched his son. "And you have to make yourself prominent, Jevan. Be seen, talk to as many people as possible. There can be no doubt in anyone's mind, that you are not a part of this."

"Thank you," Annabel said, looking from one to the other.

Jophiel looked at her anxiously. "Do you really think her mind will be clear? After all, it's been a very long time."

"I have to try." She sighed heavily. "Something is happening in that house. It's been happening for a long time, and I need answers. Elizabeth was not mad. She saw and heard things, I think they were real. And if I don't find out what's really going on or the secrets that Cerberus has kept, then I too could easily end up like Elizabeth."

Jophiel looked horrified. "Jevan and I will never let you end up in a place like that."

"How would you stop a husband's legal right?" she said sadly.

"I will kill him before that ever happens," Jevan said heatedly.

"Shhh," Jophiel said, alarmed, looking over his shoulder. "There is someone in the stable."

"It's Agnes, don't worry. She is the reason I was able to come here."

"Do you think she heard?" Jevan said, in a low voice.

Annabel shook her head confidently and Jevan visibly relaxed. She rose up and kissed him lightly. Sadness came over her as she touched him. She wanted him to put his arms about her again and stop her from leaving. As if he read her mind, he pulled her firmly toward him and held her tightly.

"I have to leave," she said, willing herself to believe it. She parted her lips to speak, but her mind drifted for a moment.

Then she looked back at Jophiel. "See you tomorrow," she said with a smile and Jevan let go of her.

Annabel had debated whether to tell them what had taken place in the church. Then again, what use would it have been? It was too frightening to contemplate. For as much as she would like to deny it, Cerberus was a witch. She could not ignore his words. Soon the thirteen moons and the witch's ladder would be complete. Samhain was coming closer and closer.

Chapter 32

Blackheath House

Jevan waited in the woods for nearly two hours, the thick branch was cut and tied with rope, the tree cut just enough, so that with one good jerk it would fell completely. At the optimum moment, he would cut the rope, the branch would swing forward and the momentum and weight would knock the rider off his horse. Once on the ground, the falling tree would finish the job. An unfortunate accident on the way to Bristol.

The calculations were perfect. The only flaw was that Jevan did not anticipate that Alex would not ride alone. Alex and his estate manager approached at six-thirty a.m. Jevan nearly made the cut, although, his conscience struggled with the killing of an innocent bystander. His knife hovered. The voice in his head insisted he had to do it, and this would be his only chance. His hand shook as he nicked the rope. His throat parched from fear as he thought back to the horror of Aidden's death. The wind moved through the trees, scattering leaves along the ground, the riders were passing. It was now or never. He moved the knife to make the final cut, then he remembered seeing the estate manager with his wife and young children in Rookwood less a week ago, and he hesitated. The optimum moment passed.

❧❧❧

Annabel's arrangement worked to perfection. By eight o'clock, she was waiting at the gap in the hedge. Before long, Jevan appeared. He seemed pre-occupied and did not say much to her. She assumed he was worried at what they had all planned to do that day. They hurried to a hasty liaison with Jophiel. Jevan left for Rookwood, and Annabel and Jophiel began the journey to Bristol. It was a long way to ride in the small carriage. They felt every bump along the route. Jophiel and Annabel barely noticed, happy to be in each other's company, as it felt like an age had passed since they had last spent any time together. They talked for most of the journey, and Annabel related some of what had recently occurred. She knew Jevan had already spoken to his father about her life at the mansion. She didn't want to distress Jophiel unnecessarily and, after a while, changed the topic. They reminisced over her father and happier times.

As they approached their destination, Jophiel's disposition became graver. Annabel was struck with a sense of regret, as the real object of this journey loomed before them.

"You shouldn't be involved in this. It could be dangerous," Annabel said, gauging his mood, and turned her body so she could see him better.

Jophiel was quiet for a moment, and then he pulled the reins and slowed the horse to a leisurely trot. He turned to meet her gaze. "I haven't been seized by a sudden impulse, and I am old enough to make my own decisions. I would help you, no matter what the consequences are. Jevan would give his life for you, and so would his father."

Too choked to say anything, Annabel squeezed Jophiel's hand and smiled gratefully, forcing back too much emotion. "I hope it won't come to that Jophiel," she said softly.

Jophiel nodded in agreement and brought carriage to a standstill. "We are almost there," he said needlessly, looking at her. "Climb into the back. We can't arrive with you sitting beside me."

Annabel nodded and climbed into the carriage to sit alone as a lady might do.

Blackheath House was located outside the city, separated

from surrounding farmlands by high hedges and a carriageway bordered by large oak trees. Built in the Elizabethan period, the dozens of mullion windows were recessed in brickwork, and that stretched up three stories. Chimneys dominated the rooftop, and spiraling smoke poured out from the largest. Jophiel guided the horse and carriage under the metal arched entrance, which displayed the name *Blackheath House* in tall curved lettering. They came to a standstill in the interior courtyard.

A sudden pang of nervousness hit Annabel. She felt unsure of how to proceed. Having spent so much time considering how she would leave Gothelstone unobserved, she had not thought about how to actually gain access to Elizabeth.

Jophiel was already helping her down from the carriage. "I will do the talking," he said, confidently.

Annabel nodded gratefully. "Don't give your name, only mine, and take this just in case."

She placed several coins in his hand. They walked up the two stone steps and into a covered porch, which concealed the main door. Jophiel pulled the heavy bell cord, and they listened to the echo of the bell ringing inside.

Several moments later, the door was opened by a middle-aged woman dressed in black. Her dark hair was pulled up into a short chignon, but her eyes were not friendly, and Annabel sensed the hostility right away.

"Good morning, madam," Jophiel began. "My mistress has traveled a long way to visit with one of your residents." He bowed fractionally and gestured at Annabel. The woman's gaze fell upon Annabel who stood a few paces away from Jophiel.

"Did you send a letter of this intention? Because this is quite irregular."

Annabel had heard enough. From the woman's tone, it was obvious she was getting ready to refuse their request.

Annabel stepped forward. "Do you have any idea who I am?" she said haughtily, catching the woman off guard. She sighed impatiently. "I thought not. I am the wife of Alexander Saltonstall." She held out her calling card. "My mother-in-law,

Elizabeth Saltonstall, is in residence here, and I want to speak with her." She paused for effect. "And I am not used to being kept waiting like some common peasant!" The woman's body tensed. Annabel eyed her coldly. "I will be certain my husband hears of the cold reception, and perhaps he will reconsider his patronage of this establishment," she finished triumphantly. The woman went to speak, but Annabel interrupted. "And what is your name?" she asked, with general disinterest.

The woman shrank back, her face paler than before. "Mrs. Hardwick—b—but I did—" she stuttered. "I didn't realize, milady. Please come in. Of course, you are welcome."

Annabel caught Jophiel's eye and she shook her head fractionally. "Francis," she said, "wait for me here."

Jophiel nodded submissively and ambled back to the carriage.

Annabel entered, and Mrs. Hardwick closed the door. Annabel felt surprisingly calm as she looked around the outer hallway. The furniture was sparse, and the walls were simply exposed brickwork with a huge fireplace at one end. A large archway cut through the middle of the room, and several doors recessed in the walls were closed. It felt austere, and a mild odor of ammonia hung in the air. Yet the house was silent. There did not seem to be any other staff or residents close to them.

"Please come this way." Mrs. Hardwick indicated that they should enter into the inner hall.

Annabel walked under the large archway to a wide central curving staircase. As they walked upward, she felt Mrs. Hardwick's sidelong glances and noticed she was a little hesitant when she spoke.

"I hope you will understand we were not expecting anyone. Mrs. Saltonstall will not be prepared for any visitors." She paused. "She frequently becomes agitated, and we will have to restrain her for your protection."

Annabel felt a shiver run down her spine. She could not falter now. "Of course," she said indifferently. "I understand."

They reached the second floor and veered off into a long corridor. Mrs. Hardwick opened a door, and an orderly appeared. He was dressed in a white smock coat. He was tall, and his vacant expression did not change as his eyes darted over Annabel.

"We have a visitor," Mrs. Hardwick said pointedly, "for Mrs. Saltonstall."

The orderly removed a key from a wooden pegboard and tipped his head to Annabel. Something about his eyes gave her chills. She pushed the feeling aside. The three of them walked down the corridor. Various muffled sounds could now be heard from behind the closed wooden doors. Annabel saw that each door displayed a small-hinged panel at head height.

She heard the sounds of crying, coughing, and talking, although she could not make out any words, and she felt distraught that Elizabeth was in this place at all. At last, they stopped in front of a door where she read the number thirty-three fashioned out of black painted metal. The orderly opened the small-hinged door and peered inside. Satisfied by what he found, he unlocked the main door and entered.

Annabel followed. At once, the smell of stale urine and damp invaded her nostrils. She resisted the urge to cover her nose, but the smell of the room became insignificant as she stared at a woman who perched on the edge of the bed. A long gray gown covered her body and her bare feet rested on the stone floor, although, she did not appear to notice how cold it was. Annabel's gaze turned to a look of horror as she saw that one wrist was bound in a shackle, and that was on a short chain from the wall. It was shocking to think that she was not bound just because Annabel was visiting. The orderly hadn't known that. Elizabeth was clearly chained all the time. Annabel turned to the orderly.

"Why is she chained to the wall?"

"She suffers from mania," he said, as if it were a standard reply.

He didn't even seem to notice Annabel's contemptuous look. She looked back at Elizabeth, whose head tilted toward them and, despite her age, the features were intact. The same eyes that smiled out of the portrait at Gothelstone mansion still had that same beautiful shape and vivid blue coloring that pierced through the dismal grayness of the room. The orderly produced a chair and placed it in the middle of the room. Mrs. Hardwick gestured for Annabel to sit.

"It is advisable to keep your distance. She can't reach you here."

Annabel turned to her and the orderly, who was now leaning against the doorframe, looking bored. "I require privacy. I will talk with her alone," she said, her eyes in a fixed gaze on Mrs. Hardwick, daring her to protest.

Annabel sensed the woman's inner conflict. She dearly wanted to refuse, to tell her that it was not the policy of the institute, and Annabel could virtually sense her having to bite her tongue. Even so, the Saltonstall name carried a lot of weight, and Mrs. Hardwick turned to the door.

"I will be downstairs, and he will be outside if you need him," she said, indicating for the orderly to leave.

Annabel glanced at him. "Please close the door. I will call you when you are needed."

The couple left the room and, as the door closed, the interior became even darker. It was dismal enough with bare brick walls, and the small window afforded little light. Even that small window to the outside world was heavily barred, and the glass could not be reached. Voices outside grew fainter and then high up on the wall, a single gas light suddenly flickered as it came back to life, and then grew brighter still.

Elizabeth stared at it, as if in a trance, her eyes suddenly alert and wondrous as if she had never seen so much light before. Annabel sat on the chair, watching in dismay. Elizabeth was thin. She looked sick, and there were old stains on her dress, which looked suspiciously like blood. Annabel choked back her emotions and leaned toward her mother-in-law.

"Elizabeth, do you remember your son, Alex?"

Elizabeth's eyes left the gaslight and she gazed blankly at Annabel. She did not speak. Annabel felt her heart sink. Perhaps the woman could not remember anything at all, or her mind was truly broken. Annabel could well imagine, now sitting in this room, that it would not take long to drive all sanity from the strongest of women. Despite her inner struggle with

Elizabeth's plight, she smiled in an effort of reassurance, while she considered how best to approach the subject. Alex was the key, and she had to make the woman remember him.

She tried again. "Elizabeth do you remember Alex, your little boy?"

Something ignited instantly in Elizabeth's eyes, a spark of recognition. Her face changed subtly, and she began to rock slowly back and forth. "Alex is dead." Her voice was light and without feeling.

The words hit Annabel like a punch in the stomach, and an overwhelming feeling of pity gripped her. Just what had Cerberus told her? That Alex had died, perhaps when he was still a child.

"Alex is not dead," she said softly. "He is grown and married."

She hoped that she was doing the right thing, because Elizabeth's face was expressionless.

"No," Elizabeth shook her head firmly. "He died of a bee sting."

Annabel felt the tiny hairs on her arms stand on end. Cerberus made her believe this terrible lie. Annabel wondered if it would be a better kindness to just let her be, let her live with this injustice, for surely it would destroy this poor creature's mind, if Annabel made her believe the truth. Annabel was quiet for a few moments as she wondered what to do for the best. There were other lives at stake now. Elizabeth's life had already been shattered.

Annabel ignored any misgivings and remained resolute. "Elizabeth you have been told a dreadful lie, because Alex lives and I am his wife. We live at Gothelstone Manor House."

At the mention of the house, Elizabeth visibly jumped. She stared at Annabel with wild piercing eyes and, instinctively, Annabel moved back farther in the chair. Elizabeth's rocking grew in intensity. Her breathing became rapid, and Annabel was alarmed that a few words could have such an effect.

"Elizabeth, stop it—Elizabeth!" she pleaded and rose from the chair, no longer afraid. She went to the bed, sat down, and placed her hand on Elizabeth's arm.

The woman flinched and the rocking stopped. Annabel slid her hand down to rest on Elizabeth's and curled her fingers around the other woman's hand. Elizabeth's skin was thin. Annabel could feel the outline of her bones as well as see them.

Elizabeth turned toward her and stared in wonder. "Are you an angel?"

Annabel smiled softly. After the harshness of her life, it was no wonder Elizabeth saw a small kindness as unearthly. "No, I am not. My name is Annabel. I am Alex's wife, and I need your help."

Elizabeth shook her head rapidly. "I can't help you," she said fearfully. "You must leave and never come back."

"You are the only person that can help me, Elizabeth. We need your help. Help me and Alex."

At the mention of his name again, a frown furrowed her brow and then a faint smile touched her lips as she turned and looked inquisitively into Annabel's eyes. "Is he really alive?" Annabel nodded. A single tear rolled down Elizabeth's cheek and she shook her head, as if she was confused, and she stared at Annabel again. "Is he very handsome?" she asked, a new glimmer of trust in her eyes.

Annabel smiled briefly. "Yes, and he is very important, a wealthy landowner." She paused for a moment. "He has your eyes, but his are darker, the darkest blue."

"You are really his wife?" Elizabeth asked, staring intently.

Annabel breathed a sigh of relief, glad to find that Elizabeth still retained some sanity and asked rational questions. "Yes."

Elizabeth sighed. "And Cerberus does he still live?" There was a marked chill to her voice.

"Yes."

Elizabeth closed her eyes for a moment. Then they snapped open. She clutched at Annabel, with her chained hand as if remembering something important. "You're not safe." The seriousness of her demeanor, made Annabel unexpectedly fearful. "Not while Jane Saltonstall is in that house."

Rubbing Elizabeth's cold hand to comfort her, Annabel

tried to remember all the names of the household. "Jane Saltonstall?" she replied at last. "No, there is no one of that name,
and no other woman save the maids." Annabel suspected that
she was confused and was remembering some distant relative.

Elizabeth suddenly let go of her. She rocked back and forth
a couple of times then grew very still. She turned to Annabel,
fixing her with clear and penetrating eyes. "The attic." Her
eyes darted nervously over Annabel's shoulder toward the
door. She nodded her head. "Read the diary."

"What diary?" Annabel whispered.

Elizabeth did not answer and was quiet for some time.

Annabel tried again. "What diary, Elizabeth?"

Suddenly Elizabeth turned her body. Eyes opened wide she
looked over Annabel's shoulder making Annabel feel as
though someone were standing behind her. She kept her nerve
and refused to take her eyes from Elizabeth. Annabel felt the
other woman's terror when she spoke.

"Jane Saltonstall is still there. You know she is." Elizabeth
nodded slowly. "You feel her just as I did, just as we all did."

Annabel felt the shiver run down her spine as Elizabeth
gave an odd sort of knowing smile and lowered her voice.
"She watches closely."

"Why?" Suddenly Annabel felt more frightened than she
had at any other time. "Why does she watch us?"

"Because there can only be one mistress of Gothelstone!"

Then Elizabeth cackled like an old crone, unnerving Annabel completely. She watched in dismay, struggling to take in
Elizabeth's change in demeanor. She felt helpless as she
watched Elizabeth rocking back and forth and then she began
to hum, a low and un-tuneful noise. Annabel felt out of her
depth. She felt so sad at the state of Alex's mother.

Unexpectedly, Elizabeth stopped humming and rolled her
head to the side. "But what do I know? They say I'm mad—
mad, mad Elizabeth," she chanted doggedly.

Annabel stood up wearily. "Where in the attic is the diary?"

Elizabeth looked up at her. "Under the floor. I hid it well."

"Where under the floor, the attic is huge?"

But Elizabeth only hummed.

"Elizabeth, tell me!"

"I don't remember."

Annabel went to turn away, and Elizabeth snatched her arm. She stared up at her with terrified eyes. "Don't turn out the lights, don't close your eyes. She comes out of the darkness!"

"I know," Annabel said softly, and Elizabeth pulled her hand back.

Her terror was clear. Whatever had happened to her in that house destroyed her. Annabel felt sick. She felt confined and trapped and all the things she imagined that Elizabeth endured over the years hit her with full force. She couldn't stay in this room any longer. The oppression was too great. An added feeling of despair grew when Elizabeth put her hand to her head.

"So many needles," she said, grimacing as if in pain.

She ran her hand through her hair, lifting it away from her forehead. Every hair stood up on the back of Annabel's neck as she stared at the swelling and scars of repeated puncture wounds. Tears fell down Annabel's cheek, as Elizabeth turned to the wall.

"Go away. Don't come back, and if you speak the truth, don't ever let my son see me," Elizabeth said quietly.

Annabel was too choked up to reply. She nodded, even though Elizabeth didn't see. She walked to the door, wiped away the tears, and took a deep breath, composing her face and voice. It was the singularly most awful thing she had ever done, leaving Elizabeth in this place, even if her mind was broken. Annabel did not have the authority to release her. Only Cerberus or perhaps Alex could do that. She opened the door and, after a final glance at the forlorn figure on the bed, walked out, and closed it softly behind her.

How could Cerberus have been so cruel? He had allowed her to be subjected to this treatment and left her to such a terrible fate. Alex did not even seem to care. Chilled by more than the dampness of the room, Annabel shivered. The implications of Elizabeth's words were disturbing. There was much more than a grain of truth in them. Annabel could only hope that the diary existed, and that it was not just a figment of poor Elizabeth's troubled mind. After all, she had shown moments of real clarity, except for Jane Saltonstall. Annabel had not heard that name before.

Annabel's relief was overwhelming when she left Blackheath House and saw Jophiel standing by the carriage, waiting for her. She felt as though she could breathe again. Freedom was something she would never take for granted. The burden of what she just witnessed lightened at the sight of the vast open spaces of countryside and the feeling being unconfined. That small taste of repression disturbed her deeply, and her thoughts turned to Jevan and his weeks spent in jail. Then her father and the weeks he must have spent in confinement, although, it was nothing compared to the years of cruelty Elizabeth endured.

As they rode away, Annabel relived the visit, telling Jophiel what had taken place. She confessed that what she had seen there would haunt her for a long time to come. Blackheath House was not a sanctuary. It was a torture chamber.

They rode toward Exmoor as fast as they could. It was very late and dark by the time she reached the mansion. She entered by the kitchen door, Agnes agreed to leave open for her, and by some miracle, she had not been missed. Largely thanks again to Agnes. Even more fortuitous than that, Alex had not come home, as business kept him longer than anticipated. He did return the following day and in a foul mood, although Annabel was elated to learn the reason for that anger.

Unbeknownst to her, her father had left a legal will, drawn up by a solicitor several months ago. In it, he had left Honeymead, not to his only daughter, but to Jevan the son he would have liked. They were his words.

"Sentimental nonsense!" Alex fumed.

"No, my father knew that Jevan would take care of Honeymead and the bees."

Alex shot her a murderous look and stormed out of the room. Annabel smiled. Josiah had hoped that by leaving everything to Jevan, it would someday fall into her hands.

"Thank you, Father," she said quietly.

It had been a long time since she had felt unburdened and happy. This news felt as though dark oppressive clouds had parted, and at last, a ray of hope and sunshine was shining down.

Later in the day, Agnes came to her room and, after closing the door, the maid pulled out a letter from her apron. "Milady," she said nervously, "the blacksmith sent this."

Annabel tore open the seal. The writing was defiantly Jevan's, although Jophiel had signed it for safety's sake.

My Dearest Annabel,

I wanted to let you know that, although Honeymead has been generously left to my family, it will always be yours. Be assured the cottage, lands, and bees will be well looked after.

Jophiel Wenham
A. J.
F. T.

Annabel studied the strange initials and then smiled. She remembered the carving on the oak tree. Then, as reluctant as she was, she burned the letter. There was to be no trace of their communication.

Chapter 33

Annabel was running out of time, with only a few days left until Samhain. The end of the witch's year—a time for the onset of winter, as the leaves began to fall—and it was a time when dead souls came back to life, at least that was Cerberus's prophecy.

Breakfast was a quiet affair, and she was feeling uneasy for no reason. Alex left the room, leaving her alone with Cerberus. She had to find a way to take control of the situation, with no real clue as to what Cerberus planned. She was tired of being constantly on edge with no peace of mind. Even now, he did not utter a single word. She pushed her feelings of contempt for him to the back of her mind and listened to the clock tick for a few minutes. She left her seat and sat in a chair closer to Cerberus. "Tell me about the witch's ladder?"

He did not look up. It was as if he had been expecting her question. Annabel watched as he deliberately took his time placing his cup back on its saucer, and then he turned in his chair to face her. A faint smile touched his lips.

"It is a very powerful tool in the craft. With the witch's ladder, you bind the power of thirteen moons, which opens a doorway to another world."

Annabel frowned. "The underworld."

"I prefer just to think of it as a doorway through which the departed can return."

Fear seized her. What if he really could call back the dead? His eyes were piecing bright blue today. They gleamed with wickedness and madness, but she forced her gaze to remain on him. "My mother died, Cerberus," she said sadly, shaking her head. "She is dead."

"But her soul lives."

"How can it?"

Cerberus stood abruptly, his eyes boring into hers. "Why do you question this? You have heard her. She has called you." His voice was bitter. There was no trace of a smile now.

"I heard someone. It was not her."

"You should trust in my judgment. I see the legacy unraveling before me, the whole picture. You will see that I am right," he said, pushing his chair away.

"You are right. There is something here," she agreed. "Whatever it is, it is dangerous. What if you call up something else, something terrible?" She shook her head firmly. "And I don't want to be a part of it."

"You are a part of it. You coming to this house, living under this roof. You are the reason she will come back," he said furiously. "Don't doubt me, Annabel. You cannot imagine the extent of my power. What you saw in the churchyard was child's play." Annabel took a long deep breath, as Cerberus glared down at her. "Or perhaps you need a reminder," he said, turning swiftly and reaching out to her.

Annabel jumped up quickly and backed away from him. "Don't touch me!" she cried. "Don't you dare touch me."

"Afraid?"

"No, I'm more afraid of what I could do," she said with confidence, meeting his gaze full on, even though her heart leapt in shock at what he might do.

Cerberus smiled coldly. "Do you really think you can harm me?" He didn't wait for her to answer as he turned and walked away.

Annabel stared after him, wondering why she had allowed him to get the upper hand again. She meant to seem compliant and let him think she was playing along. Instead, she had allowed him to draw her anger and made him suspicious. She pushed the chair back toward the table, and picked up a knife from amongst the used cutlery. She pushed it up into her sleeve and thought again about Elizabeth's words. Were they the ravings of a mad woman or the plain truth?

By mid-morning, Cerberus left the house She already spoken to Alex long enough to know that he was also leaving to visit a nearby tenant. At last, she was alone in the mansion, save for the servants. She took morning tea in the drawing room and told the maid, she did not require anything else until lunch. She downed the tea and picked up the walking stick with a silver handle. It felt heavy, and she brandished it about her head to find out if it had any real substance. She felt she could inflict a heavy blow with it and went to the door.

As quietly as was possible, she turned the handle and peered into the hallway. It was empty. Many of the servants were below stairs, in the kitchen. Having cleared away the breakfast things, they were beginning their mid-morning duties. She heard two maids giggling as they laid out the polishing cloths in the dining room.

Annabel made her way up the staircase and along the corridor to the attic stairs. Glancing over her shoulder to make sure she hadn't been seen, she ran up them. She thought briefly about ghosts as she opened the attic door. Nothing stirred. By daylight, the old furniture and chattels were not sinister, and the dust covers posed no particular threat. Even so, she pulled off every sheet and heaped them in a pile on the floor. Then she turned each mirror to face the wall. Now the attic was just an old room. No images would move in the glass, no shapes could shift menacingly. The walking stick remained in her grip, and she looked down at the floorboards. She methodically walked backward and forward across the room, moving pieces of furniture in her way, to see if any floorboards felt loose.

One or two moved and creaked as she stepped upon them. She pulled out the knife from her sleeve and got down on her knees. She jammed the blade between the boards, trying to lever the wood, but it stuck fast. Disappointed, she stood up and walked into the corner of the room. After hitching up her long skirts, she got down on the floor again and crawled along the floorboards, examining each in turn. At one corner, a large chair obscured the end of the board, and she pushed it out of her way. The wood looked rougher. Several deep grooves were gouged along the edge. Annabel felt her heartbeat quicken. This board might have been pried up before.

She pushed the knife blade between the boards and levered the old wood up. It was cut and carefully crafted to appear unaltered, but the two-foot section came away in her hands. Anxiously, she peered into the hole, and her pulse raced. A mixture of relief and excitement swept over her. Elizabeth wasn't that mad, after all.

Annabel retrieved a leather-bound book along with several yellowed documents, all tied together with faded ribbon. They were covered in a layer of dust. She blew lightly over the papers to dislodge the particles, then she leaned back against the wall. She untied the ribbon, unfolded the fragile papers, and stared at the Saltonstall family tree. It was different from the family tree displayed in the library. This one had other names.

The name Jane Saltonstall leapt off of the page and sent a small shiver down Annabel's spine. Jane had been the young wife of Isaiah, born in 1681 and died in 1698, aged seventeen. Annabel thought back to that night in the attic. That girl had looked young, maybe seventeen. Annabel suppressed the shudder and quickly cast a glance around the room. That night was hard to imagine now. The sunlight made it feel warm and bright. Annabel looked back to the paper, following the familiar names down the tree. Lucian and Eliza, Gabriel and Anne, Azaril and Abigail, Zachariah and Maria, and it ended with Anael and Elsbeth, who died in 1827 at only twenty-five. With a jolt, Annabel realized something disturbing, in that there was a pattern. None of these women lived long, many died after the birth of their first child.

Although, mortality in childbearing had always been high, these were women of standing. They would have had access to the best doctors and medicines, and it was alarming that all would have died. Annabel traced her finger down, over the faded ink to Cerberus, and was startled to find another name and notation. Annabel's eyes widened in shock—he had been a twin. His sister, Jessamine, had perished as an infant, and Annabel found this fact strangely disturbing.

Reading this record brought a certain melancholia. This wasn't just a history she was studying. There was something so solemn and sad about this particular tree. So much death happened in Alex's family that it didn't feel normal. Annabel laid the paper to one side and looked at the other documents, they were badly torn and looked as though they had suffered from water damage, as the writing was hard to decipher. She persevered and read the paper.

> *The jurors foro'r Sov'r: Lord and lady the King and Queen present that Jane Louisa Saltonstall wife of Isaiah John Saltonstall of Gothelstone in and upon the third day of March last in the yeare aforesaid and other days and times as well before the certaine detestable arts called witchcraft and sorcerys. Wickedly, melodiously, and feloniously hath use practised and exercised at and in the town of Gothelstone aforesaid in the County of Somerset, upon and against one Agnes Adella Gant of Gothelstone by which said wicked arts after was and tortured, afflicted, wasted, and tormented. Against the peace of our Sov'r lord and lady the King and Queen theire crown and dignity and the forme in the stattue. In that case made and provided.*

The writing and spelling was old-fashioned, the meaning was shockingly clear. Jane Saltonstall had been accused of witchcraft and further documentation recounted that she had been arrested and bodily searched to prove she was suckling a demon familiar and when, asked to recite the Lord's Prayer, she had faltered, thus sealing her fate as a witch. There were also several pamphlets, along with the alleged confession.

> *The confefsion of Jane Louisa Saltonstall March 10, 1698 made before the major and other jurates.*

*She confessed: That the divell about a year agoe did
appeare to her in the shape of a little cat, and bid
her to forsake God. The divell had promised, she
further said, that she gave some of her blood to the
divell who wrote the covenant betwixt them and she
did neele downe upon her knees and make a circle
on the ground and pray unto sathan the cheefe of the
divells. Furthermore, she confesseth having carnall
copulation with the divell and how she bewitched
young men to death. She being brought to the Barre,
was asked guilty or not guilty. She answered guilty.*

Annabel's skin had turned to gooseflesh. Had Jane Saltonstall really been a witch in life, and in death, was she now a
vengeful ghost? Annabel cast a shuddering glance around the
room and picked up the first pamphlet, an account of that
death. The reporter wrote:

*We do not yet know the extent of how terrible
Mistress Saltonstall crimes must be to carry the punishment of a burning, a practice that often takes
place in the barbaric northern lands. For the hanging of a witch seems a kindness, after what I witnessed today. For the flames burnt though the faggot
pile and ravaged the woman's body, catching her
long hair alight. The stench of burning flesh filled
the square and was sickening to the stomach. Except, the witch still cried out:*

*"Heare this, Isaiah Saltonstall and the people of
Gothelstone, I call upon you all to bear witness to
the curse I place upon your heads. Let the Saltonstall legacy begin, your bloodlines will be rendered
insane. I am the only mistress of Gothelstone, and to
those that would accuse me, I will return and see
you all burn in hell."*

*Mistress Saltonstall would have gone on, but fire
overcame her and she screamed in agony. The burning was grotesque, the worst death I have ever seen,*

*and she forced words from her mouth, even though
her whole body was on fire. The villagers all retreated. Only her husband, Isaiah Saltonstall,
watched until only bones and ashes were left.*

Annabel looked up from the paper as though Jane might
appear from out of the lengthening shadows. She pulled the
walking stick close to her and picked up a later pamphlet. It
was dated 1699.

*A terrible blaze ripped through the village of
Gothelstone in the night. Many buildings were destroyed and many of the villagers died in their
homes. Help came from Rookwood, but for many it
was too late. Several eyewitnesses gave a strange
account. They claimed that while the fire blazed, a
young woman with long hair stood watching the
blaze from atop Gothelstone church tower. Fearing
that the young woman would jump from the tower,
several men folk raced up the narrow staircase to
her rescue. The men reached the tower, but the
young woman was never found.*

The floor was becoming uncomfortable and Annabel had
spent a long time in the attic. She knew she would be missed
soon, if not already. Quietly, she replaced the floorboard,
pushed the chair back into position, and took all the documents with her. No one saw her as she made her way to her
room. She locked the papers in the secret drawer in her writing
bureau and, glad to be able to sit on a comfortable chair,
opened the leather-bound book. In neat curling letters were the
words, *The Diary of Elsbeth*

Many pages were ripped from the spine, and others were
blank, although, there were still many that could be read.

*19th October 1826 ~ Madness has long since
cursed this family, for the male heirs inherit the
blight. With each generation, it grows stronger. My*

son already shows cruel and wicked inclinations, sticking pins into insects and torturing the stable cats. I pray for the soul of my beloved daughter Jessamine, and that her murderer is one day held to account. If she had lived, I am certain that this terrible curse would have lifted.

25th October 1826 ~ The demon haunts me constantly, she whispers to me in the darkest hours of the night, wanting me to jump from the highest window. She tries to lure me out on the highest window ledge. She stands by my bedside with her silver dagger. I know what I should do, but however wicked he is, or will become, I cannot spill the blood of my only child.

27th November 1826 ~ Her calls are relentless. I see her shadow in the library and hear her cruel whispers behind the bookcases. She hides there still, watching me. I have tried to get Cerberus out of the house, but the servants guard him constantly. I am no longer allowed time alone with him.

28th November 1826 ~ Today I took all the books from the shelves. One case came crashing to the ground, but Anael has locked me in my few rooms. He will not listen. He cannot hear her and has called for another doctor.

22nd December 1826 ~ The medicines and strange potions keep me weak, and I am unable to leave my room. I can no longer protect Cerberus. She will corrupt him into insanity and fulfil her wicked legacy.

5th January 1827 ~ I have been locked in my room for days now. Anael has a strange power, something I cannot explain. He has been corrupted with madness, and he no longer is the man I once loved. I have tried to warn Cerberus. He is so young, but he understands things beyond his years. I feel a power in him, like his father. Perhaps he can find the strength to defeat the evil in this house.

Date unknown ~ I do not know what day it is any more. Anael called for the priest today. He laid his hands upon me, while the doctor drew my blood, to rid my body of the demon. They won't listen to any of my words. They want to send me from this place so my soul can be saved.

Date unknown ~ I kissed Cerberus for the last time today. The darkness descends. It is the last thing I can control, and the demon has triumphed. I shall not wake, for the poison weaves its deadly path through my body. Already my breath is shallowing, my heartbeat slows, and fatigue chases my thoughts away. I shall write no more.

Chapter 34

Murderous Intentions

Annabel closed the book, unable to repress a shudder. She sat perfectly still for a moment, collecting her thoughts, and then jumped up and rushed out the room and down the stairs. She almost collided with Agnes as she turned the corner.

"Milady—" Agnes began, clearly startled. "We were looking for you." She hesitated for a moment. "Would you like to take lunch in the dining room?"

"I've been resting," Annabel replied hastily. "I don't want anything to eat. I have to go out, and you'd better come with me." And then she added worriedly, "Is the master back?"

Agnes shook her head. "Neither of them have come home yet."

"Good, then get your coat. We need to get to Rookwood."

A short time later, Annabel and Agnes were making their way through the gaps in the hedgerows, over fields, and into the woods, keeping out of sight of any road or passersby.

"Milady, are you sure we should be out, with the master due back at any time?" Agnes said, clearly worried and looking over her shoulder as if she expected them to be fetched back at any moment.

"Yes, we should. It's important," Annabel, said firmly, quickening her step.

They reached the forge unseen, and soon Agnes was sat in

Jophiel's front room, sipping water and recovering from her painful stitch. Annabel stood in the kitchen with Jophiel.

"He's not at the print shop today."

"Where is here?" she said, feeling panicked.

Jophiel was surprised and concerned to see such a troubled expression. "I am sure he is at Honeymead. These days he spends as much time there as possible."

Annabel thought for a few minutes. She had to find Jevan. It was getting late, and she would be missed. She did not relish the thought of getting Agnes into any trouble on her account.

"Can Agnes stay here for a while? I have to see him alone."

Jophiel looked dubious. "Is that wise? How much can you trust this girl?" he said in a whisper, giving a sideways glance into the next room.

"I trust her enough," Annabel, said walking to the back door.

"In the last stall there is a chestnut mare. Take her. She is sturdy and docile. She won't give you any trouble."

Annabel nodded. "Just give me twenty minutes and then tell Agnes to go back to the mansion. If anyone asks, she is to say that we went to the graveyard, and I gave her the slip. She looked for me, but I was too quick for her."

Jophiel nodded and Annabel turned to leave. "Wait," he said, opening a drawer in the dresser. "Take this." He held out a pale blue scarf. "It may help to hide your hair. It is so distinctive, even from a distance."

Annabel took the scarf she had seen Adella wear in the past. "Thanks," she rose up and kissed him on the cheek.

Jophiel held onto her for a few moments longer. "Be careful, Annabel, you're going to be in enough trouble as it is," he said with a warning note.

"I will," she said.

Jophiel watched, feeling helpless as she went through the door.

In the stable, she tied her hair under the scarf and freed the chestnut mare from her tether. Annabel read the name scrawled on the wooden marker. *Cassy.* She patted the horse's head and climbed on her back. Cassy was as docile as Jophiel said, and they rode quietly out of the stable. They made their way along the back lane and then turned into the field.

Annabel kept the horse close to the hedges and trees, keeping her eyes peeled for Alex or Cerberus. She passed only workers in the fields and a few children playing truant from school. No one gave her cause for concern.

She crossed three fields and led the horse into more wooded areas, taking well-trodden deer paths that approached Honeymead from the more forested side. She reluctantly passed the skeps, and wished that she had time to see her bees. There was no time for sentimentality, she reasoned, and left Cassy in the orchard tied to the gate. As she walked, she took the scarf from her head and shook her mane of hair to dislodge the tangles. As she made her way up the path, she heard footsteps coming around from the front of the cottage. She froze on the spot.

Around the corner Jevan appeared. Breathing a sigh of relief, she smiled and ran up to him. He was as surprised as she was shaken, but he swept her up into his arms, squeezing her so tight that she gasped for breath. Jevan slackened his grasp and bent to kiss her. She tangled her fingers tightly in his hair, her skin electrified by his touch.

Jevan drew back and a shadow passed across his face. "What is it? Why are you here?" he said, sensing her tension.

"Don't you want me here?" she said, looking up at him with a deeply hurt expression.

He grinned. "Do you really need to ask me that? I just didn't expect to see you. It was a shock coming around the corner like that."

"I had to see you," she said, smiling and taking his hand.

They went inside the cottage and closed the door. Jevan sensed her nerves. she avoided looking at him directly when she walked around the cottage, picking up and putting down various objects.

"Can I take this?" she said, holding out a glass jar.

"You don't need to ask," he said agreeably. "How long can you stay?"

"Not long. I will be missed," she said, turning to look at him.

He sighed heavily. "It angers me, Annabel—no, that's the wrong word, anger is an understatement to how I really feel, to have to let you go back there."

Annabel sensed his fury and the overwhelming sense of frustration in his tone.

She wanted no more than to stay with him, and she swallowed the lump in her throat.

"You know, Jevan? I half expected to see my father walk around the cottage today. How foolish is that?" she said evenly, removing her coat and sitting on the settle.

Jevan sat close beside her and put his arm around her. "Not foolish at all," he said, calmer now. He picked up her hand and caressed her fingers. "This place holds so many memories for us both." He thought for a moment. "Do you remember how Lilith would show us how to make medicines and remedies, to cure the sick and injured animals we found out on the moor, and how Josiah set the leg of that baby deer that I brought to him?"

"Yes," she nodded, thinking back, "we sat on the floor and stroked and talked to it all night until the candles burned down to nothing."

"And the stories that Lilith told us, of the fairies that lived in her garden in Ireland. She made me believe in magic," he said, smiling.

"I would like to go to Ireland one day. Mother made that land come alive in my mind. An enchanted isle is what she used to call it."

Jevan nodded in agreement. "But she loved Exmoor. It is just as enchanted," he said. "Lilith knew that, because she stayed here. She didn't want to go back to Ireland."

"I know," Annabel murmured.

Jevan saw the single tear that fell down Annabel's cheek, and he gently wiped it away. He drew his fingers down her face, tracing the outline of her bones. "Don't cry, it's a happy memory."

"I know," she said, turning to look at him. "It seems crying is all I do these days, this is just this is how it should be, you and me here at Honeymead."

Jevan nodded. "Did you get my note?"

"Yes," she said quietly.

"Honeymead will always be yours," Jevan said quietly.

Annabel sniffed and fought back more tears. She wished she had time to luxuriate in this moment and their devotion to each other, but the clock was ticking.

"Jevan," she began, "the other day when I went to Bristol—"

"Father told me that you saw Elizabeth in the asylum. He spoke little of what occurred. He said you were distraught when you left."

Annabel nodded, remembering that day. "It is awful, a terrible place. No wonder at times she seemed vague and confused."

"So was it really worth the risk?"

"Yes," she said, looking deep into his eyes. "Elizabeth was not mad, not when they locked her in that place. Now, she lives in one dark room, bare bricks, and chained to the wall. You cannot imagine how dreadful it is, so oppressive, and they have done things to her." Annabel shivered remembering Elizabeth's puncture marks. "I am not certain how sane she may be now, but one thing became clear. She was shut away for all those years because she knows what I do." Annabel paused briefly, "There is something in Gothelstone Manor—a ghost, a spirit—I don't know what it is, but I swear to you on everything that I hold dear, it is not a figment of my imagination, any more than it was Elizabeth's."

Jevan watched Annabel struggle to find the right words. He knew she did not make things up. She would not alarm him unnecessarily. His thoughts slowly amalgamated into something more terrifying as he watched and listened to her.

"Only the women can see and hear the spirit, and so the men come to believe that their wives are demented and their daughters will inherit the same fate. Down the generations, the women have been destroyed or locked away. The male heirs come to believe the curse. That is when its power is the greatest, for sooner or later it's their sanity that leaves them. It is driven away by something, and that is the real legacy," she said, reaching for her coat and pulling Elsbeth's diary out of the pocket. "Here. Read it. I also have other documentation. There is a real threat to any woman who becomes the Mistress of Gothelstone." She paused for a moment. "I think Jane Saltonstall wants her house back."

Jevan's blood ran cold at her words, his face ashen as he stared at the book in his hands. "Where did you get this?"

"Elizabeth told me where to find it. Jane Saltonstall was burned as a witch centuries ago. I believe she is the spirit that won't rest." Annabel shook her head despairingly. "Cerberus grows more psychotic every day. He cannot be reasoned with. In his madness, he believes that my mother, Lilith, is the spirit, and he wants to bring her back to life. I am truly frightened of that intention." Jevan was staring at her in complete horror. Annabel sighed wearily. "I do not fear my mother's ghost. That is not what this thing is. You know that as well as I do. Cerberus has power like me, and I am afraid he might succeed. What if he can bring it into some earthly form? Because I do fear the entity that is Jane Saltonstall."

Jevan ran his fingers through his hair in agitation and bent his head over the diary. He read each page slowly. When he looked up at her, she saw a steely determination. "You can't go back there," he said closing the diary. "I won't let you. You should never have been in that house. I should have not listened to my father when you married, and I should have taken you far away." He shook his head. "I was afraid of what would happen. but I am no longer afraid. If Alex comes here, I will kill him."

"Jevan—" Annabel began.

"Listen to me," he said abruptly. "Haven't you always trusted me? Haven't you always known that I would have done anything for you, done anything to protect you? Haven't I always loved you?" She nodded nervously. "Now, I have to end this before something terrible happens to you."

Annabel shook her head frantically. "No, Jevan,"

"Yes," he said coldly, "I will kill them both!"

Annabel's eyes opened wide in shock. "No!" she said horrified, "I can't let you do that."

"I've made up my mind. I've always known that it would come to this. I thought I had my chance a few days ago." He hesitated. "I planned it. Alex would have been thrown from his horse, and I would have made certain he didn't survive."

She choked down her grief at his revelation.

"But there was someone with him, and I couldn't kill an innocent person."

The heavy regret was obvious in his voice, and a chilled calmness settled over her.

"You are not a murderer, Jevan!" He gave her an odd sort of look. "That was an accident. In your heart, you know it as well as I do."

"I wanted Aidden dead the minute he insulted you. If the rock hadn't been there, I would have killed him anyway."

She shrugged. "That's in the past, a very distant past, but you have to listen to me."

His eyes were the blackest she had ever seen, raw emotion in every crease in his face. "Don't try and talk me 'round," he said bluntly. "It won't work, not this time, Annabel."

"Don't you understand?" she said, sounding surprisingly calm. "All my life, I have had powers. You, of all people, have known that. I never knew what they were for, but now I can use them."

"No, it's too dangerous, and you will put yourself at risk." He stared her down. "We have always been different, us against the world, remember? Even when we were children. No matter what anyone did or thought, it was you and me. No one else ever really mattered."

"I know," she said, shaking her head. "What will our life become? Even if we were able to get away from these shores, we love this place. It's part of us. I am already in danger, but I can destroy them so that no blame can lie with either of us. Trust me and the power I have inherited from my mother. After all, you've seen what she could do."

A realization that hovered uncertainly in his mind suddenly became fact, and Jevan finally understood the enormity of her inherent power. The blood drained from his face as Annabel stood up.

"Keep the diary for me," she said, glancing down at him. "Jevan, what is it?"

"You are not leaving," he said slowly, "because there is something you need to be told."

"What?" she asked faintly, greatly disturbed by his demeanor.

Jevan pulled her back down onto the settle and studied her face for a few moments. "I wish you didn't have to hear these words, but—"

"Tell me—Jevan?" Adrenaline rushed through her body. There was something so disturbing about the way he took hold of her hands and looked deeply into her eyes.

"Don't you realize? Cerberus is your father."

At first, Annabel was startled, paralyzed with shock. Then her mind filled with outrage, and she leapt to her feet. "Of all the terrible things you could ever say to me!" she cried.

Jevan stood promptly and took her firmly by the arms. He swung her around to face the mirror on the wall. "Look at yourself," he demanded, tightening his hold. "You are undoubtedly Lilith's daughter. Where exactly is the resemblance to Josiah?"

"He was my father!" she insisted, searching her face for some spark of recognition. She stared harder and harder, failing to find any. "Josiah was my father!"

"Take a closer look. The line of your jaw, the shape of your nose—the same as Cerberus."

"No!" she said, glowering at Jevan's reflection, and looked again at her own.

Then, as she peered closer, reality hit her. Not only could she see the likeness to Cerberus, but more shockingly to Alex. She let out a loud sob and then opened her mouth to speak. But there were no words. She turned back to Jevan. Her clothes felt as if they had tightened unbearably, and now she was struggling to breathe.

Jevan held her to him tightly. "Breathe slowly," he commanded, and she stared up into his eyes.

The revelation knotted her stomach and caused bile to rise in her throat. She was shaking, her thoughts tumbling about chaotically. All the conversations, the words that had been spoken. Worst of all, the intimate moments she had shared with Alex. Little by little, her natural rhythm came back and the pounding in her chest grew quieter. She dissolved into Jevan's arms, stifling her breath against him, so that she wouldn't scream out. After several minutes, she pulled back from him in a last effort of protest.

"It can't be true. It's just a coincidence. Josiah was my father." Despite her protest, Annabel could no longer believe that.

Jevan brushed away the hair from her eyes and gathered her to him again. "Hush, sweetheart," he said soothingly. "It will be all right."

Annabel drew back from him, blinking away the tears. "Jevan, none of this is all right," she said sadly. "Don't you see? I married my own brother, with my real father's blessing? Why did he do that to me? I hate him, I hate them both." And a sudden shocking thought struck her. "Did Alex know?" She and Jevan stared at each other.

Jevan shook his head. "I don't know, but I wouldn't have thought so, and as much as it pains me to say, I think Alex loves you."

Annabel felt somewhat pacified. At least, it was something, to think that both of them had unwittingly played a part in Cerberus's deplorable arrangement. Alex was just as much a victim. Annabel put her head in her hands. It made perfect sense, the strange connection she had always felt to Alex. She *had* loved him like a brother. She shuddered. She felt unclean, as if she could never wash away the ugly stain that was permanently etched on her body. She looked at Jevan. How could he want her? She felt repulsive. How could he want to even touch her now he knew the truth?

Her vision blurred as she stared at Jevan's form before her. *A good thing*, she thought, *not to be able to see his expression in any real detail*. How could she have been so blind, not have known, not have felt it?

"I'm sorry, Jevan," she said, taking a step back from him. "I am not worthy of you, or to be loved by you. How can you bear to even look at me, let alone touch me, knowing what you know?" The blurry vision shook his head. She felt his hands grasp her firmly.

"Don't ever talk like that. I am bound to you as you are to me. I would die for you, I would kill for you, and, although it rips me apart to think of you with anyone else, I would endure an eternity of hell to be with you in this lifetime. Don't ever think otherwise!" His dark eyes came into focus and glowed with intensity. "Cerberus is powerful and Lilith had a great gift. It stands to reason that they would produce a powerful witch." He drew a deep breath. "We have to destroy them both, Annabel, you know that."

"Yes, I know it."

She took Jevan's hand and looked up at him. She loved him so much. There was so much danger, and he would die to protect her, which was precisely what would happen if he got in Cerberus's way. Samhain was tomorrow. Tomorrow, it would all be done. Jevan only had to be appeased until tomorrow was over.

"You are right. We will end this. Cerberus will not be at home until late on Thursday." She hated lying to him, but she had to buy some time. "It's only two days, we can wait two days, Jevan," she said resolutely. "But you have to let me go back. Cerberus is not an ordinary man. We can't fail. We have to do it right first time."

Jevan shook his head. "No, I will be sick with worry."

She smiled softly. "Haven't I always been able to take care of myself?"

"No, not always, because I have always been there to protect you."

She shrugged. "Friday morning, come early to the mansion, five o'clock, before any of the servants are up, and I will let you in by the kitchen door. How will we do it?"

"I will use a knife. Cerberus first, then Alex, while they are sleeping!"

Annabel saw the malice in his eyes, and knew he would do

it without hesitation. "Too risky, Jevan. I was thinking a better option might be poison the night before. That way, you will just have dead or dying bodies to deal with," she said coldly.

Jevan narrowed his eyes. "I don't know. I want to make sure."

Annabel's mouth twisted into a grin. "Don't you believe a witch can make a potent poison?"

The mood between them lightened.

"Oh, I believe," he said, grinning back at her and pulling her close to him.

Suddenly there was the sound of fast-moving horse hooves and it was steadily growing louder.

Jevan sprang away from Annabel and rushed to the window. "It's Alex!"

"Oh my God!" Annabel grabbed her coat. "He can't find me here!" she gasped, rushing to the kitchen door. "Jevan," she said warningly, "remember our plan. Don't do anything to antagonize him. I will slip away tomorrow evening, I promise, we will figure it out then."

Jevan nodded and sat down at the table as Annabel picked up the glass jar and slipped out the kitchen door. She crouched under the window and listened as the sound of hooves came closer along the path. When the horse stopped, she heard rushing footsteps. Slowly, she moved to the corner of the cottage. The front door opened, then she heard Alex's voice. He was inside the cottage. She tiptoed over the stones and ran through the garden to the orchard.

Annabel untied Cassy and led her through the orchard and down to the skeps. The bees buzzed lazily around. The days were shorter now, and they had less energy. She coaxed a large bee onto her finger. She whispered softly to it as she took out the glass jar and placed the bee inside. She placed a piece of fine muslin on top and secured it with twine. Then she moved up to the woodlands and stood behind an old rowan tree to conceal her body. She wished she could hear what was going on inside the cottage, but it was too far away. Although she caught the occasional voice, no real words were audible. She waited. She had to see Alex ride away from here.

ဆာ

Jevan looked up as Alex threw open the cottage door and stormed inside. "Where is she?"

Jevan stood quickly, rage burning inside him. "Have you forgotten so quickly that this is my house? You have no right to be on my lands. Get out!"

"Not without my wife."

"She is not here."

Alex gave Jevan a scornful look. "Why don't I believe that?" he said, taking a step closer to Jevan.

Jevan was trembling with fury. He could kill him right now. No one would know, and that seemed a favorable option over Annabel's plan of poison. "You can believe whatever the hell you want, but I just told you to get out."

"Perhaps I'll look around before I go," Alex said bitterly, making for the staircase. Jevan blocked his way. Alex brought his fist up sharply and connected with Jevan's jaw, sending Jevan sprawling backward. His shoulder slammed into the wall. Alex sneered. "I wouldn't normally strike a dumb creature, but in your case, I'm happy to make the exception!"

Jevan had already curled his hand into a fist. He punched Alex in the stomach. As Alex reeled back, Jevan grabbed his coat, swung him around, and propelled him through the cottage door. Alex sprawled out on the stones, but for only a moment, before he leapt to his feet and came at Jevan again.

Blow after blow, the men fought each other, equally matched in size, although in strength, Jevan had the upper hand. Blood ran from Alex's mouth. One of Jevan's eyes was half-closed and smarting, and they both still burned with fury.

His onslaught was relentless. Finally, he pinned Alex against the cottage wall. "It wouldn't take much for me to finish this."

Alex struggled against him. He was wheezing hard, certain he had felt a crack in his ribs. "You wouldn't dare," he sneered, spitting the blood out of his mouth.

"Wouldn't I?" Jevan said, seething and shaking with rage and adrenaline.

Alex saw the danger in his dark eyes. he saw the hatred and loathing and, in that instant, he knew Jevan would.

ເ∕ວເ∕ວ

Annabel was horrified. She saw Jevan pummeling Alex into the ground, and then he slammed him up against the wall. Jevan was going to kill him. She couldn't let him do it. It would wreck everything, and their lives would be ruined if it happened this way. Annabel closed her eyes, letting the energy build.

'*Jevan, let him go. Don't do it, not now.*' She summoned all her strength and willed him repeatedly. '*Not like this, let him go.*'

ເ∕ວເ∕ວ

The gust of wind wound its way through the orchard and over the wall to the cottage. It hit Jevan full force, encircling him and distracting him. Then he heard her words in his head. He twisted his head up to the tree line. He couldn't see her. Even so, he felt her. The jolt of energy traveled through his body. He was torn. He could easily finish this, but an oppressive energy invaded his lungs, and then he was struggling to catch his breath. He loosened his hold on Alex and, as the wind continued to bluster and whip his hair across his face, reluctantly he let Alex fall to the ground.

"Get off my property while you still can!"

Alex staggered to his feet, startled. He had believed that Jevan would kill him. He had seen and felt the powerful energy in him. Alex spat more blood out of his mouth and moved quickly to his horse. His body ached, his ribs hurt, and the wheeze was still prominent, but he scrambled on top and, without looking back, turned the horse toward Gothelstone.

Jevan watched him leave before looking at the trees again. He felt nothing now. She was no longer there. He walked inside the cottage and slammed the door behind him.

Chapter 35

Samhain

Annabel rode through the trees, back to Rookwood, the way she had come. The mists had closed around her like a protective blanket, and she thought about her plan. She hoped Jevan had not hurt Alex too much. If he died of his injuries tonight, it would ruin everything.

She tethered Cassy in the stable at the forge and made her way back to Gothelstone. She did not see Jophiel, and was glad of it. She didn't want to talk to anyone. She just needed to think. It was dark as she walked briskly through the mansion's garden. Several windows glowed with lamplight, and she made her way around the side and opened the kitchen door.

Annabel was surprised to see Agnes sitting in the corner on a chair, crying. The red angry mark across her maid's cheek made Annabel suddenly fearful. A shadow moved at her side and Alex awkwardly stood up from the chair he had been sitting on. His eyes glowed with fury. She narrowed her own, waiting for his angry words.

His face was swollen, his lip cut, and bruises were just beginning to emerge. She should be sympathetic and act surprised by the state of him, but she could not bring herself to go anywhere near him.

He stared at her for several moments, perhaps waiting for the reaction. "Where were you?" he snapped at last.

Annabel glanced briefly at Agnes, and her maid moved her

head fractionally to the side. "I was at the graveyard and then went to Rookwood. What has happened?"

"Who were you with?" Alex snarled. "What lies are going to come out of your mouth this time?"

She could only stare at him in disgust and reminded herself that, as far as he was concerned, she was only his rebellious wife. "Jophiel. I went to see him. I knew you wouldn't approve. Is it really such a crime?" she said, moving past him to Agnes's side. "How could you?" she said reproachfully, looking back at him. He didn't answer. "Have you had an accident?" she asked, staring at his bleeding lip.

Alex came closer to her and fixed her with a malevolent gaze. "I fell from a horse," he said bitterly and then walked out of the kitchen.

When he was out of earshot, Agnes looked up sorrowfully. "I'm so sorry, milady, I had to tell him I was at the forge. He made me."

Agnes dissolved in a flood of tears. Annabel raised her hand to her temple. She could feel a headache building. "Agnes, dry your eyes," she said patiently. "It's all right. It's my fault. I should not have asked you to come with me." She pacified Agnes for several minutes, bathed her face in warm water, and rubbed a little royal jelly over the mark. "It will soothe and help with the stinging."

Afterward, Annabel went into the drawing room. She lay down on the couch. She did not dare close her eyes. She dined alone that evening, and Alex went to bed early, too tired to accuse her of anything else. She *almost* felt empathy when, later that night, she climbed into bed beside him. His naked skin was black and blue, and he was sound asleep, exhausted from the assault. Too many thoughts crowded her mind. The dull pain in her head did little to blot out her mental suffering.

"I have a brother," she whispered under her breath as she choked back her tears.

౭৵౭৵

It was barely light when Annabel woke. Alex was breathing evenly, laying on his back with the cover pushed halfway down his torso. Annabel stared at him for several minutes. It was so unnatural to have remorse clouding her judgment. She comforted herself with the knowledge that saving Alex, from the heartache of what she knew, was worth it. She climbed slowly out of bed so as to not wake him. She crossed the room, pushed open the only window that was not nailed shut, and breathed in the fresh air as she pressed her forehead against the glass. The crisp morning air filled her lungs, and she took several gulps to clear her head before leaving the window. Going back to the bed, she reached underneath to find the glass jar. The bee, having been brought out into the light, moved its legs, waved its antenna, and vibrated its body.

Annabel removed the muslin and tipped the bee onto her palm. Their connection was instant. The bee, sensing the air, walked slowly across the surface of Annabel's hand, its tiny feet tickling as it moved unhurriedly onto a finger. Annabel brought the velvety body to her lips and placed a gentle kiss on its back. She then whispered softly to the bee.

The bee hummed. It understood what was being asked of it and vibrated its wings harder, before soaring into the air.

Annabel sighed. Even knowing what she now knew, she had to kill him. Otherwise, Jevan would never be safe. Even if Alex found out she was his sister, he would kill Jevan just for spite. She moved back from the bed and watched. The bee flew to Alex, hovered for a moment, then descended onto his bare chest.

Annabel held her breath and waited as her heart pounded. Nothing happened for a couple of seconds, until Alex roused slightly and sleepily brought his hand up to his chest. All at once, he let out an ear-splitting scream. His whole body leapt a foot into the air, and his eyes were wide with pain and shock.

"What in *hell*?" he roared with rage, clutching at this chest.

He ripped the bee in half and away from his body and stared in disbelief as it fell to the white sheet, leaving the stinger protruding from his skin.

"Oh God!" he screamed. He looked toward Annabel and saw the open window behind her then shot her a withering

look. "You left the bloody window open!" he roared accusingly, as he jumped out of bed and took a couple of threatening
steps toward her.

Suddenly his complexion turned deathly pale. He clutched
at his chest and his breathing quickened. Annabel saw the panic in his eyes as he fell to his knees.

"Quick get me a tourniquet," he gasped.

Annabel shook her head. "You have been stung on the
chest, that won't help."

"Annabel, get it!" he demanded, not thinking rationally.

She did not move. She watched him grower weaker, feeling a tiny pang of regret. She might loathe the fact that he was
her husband, but he was her flesh and blood also, and when he
called her name, she instinctively moved closer.

Alex was now lying on his back. He struggled to breathe,
and it was astonishing and morbidly fascinating to witness the
sting having such a powerful effect. Annabel knelt beside him,
and he suddenly reached up and grasped her wrist, surprising
her with his strength, given the state of him.

He gasped laboriously and then forced the words through
his constricted airways. "I always knew—that you would be
the death of me."

Horrified at his grimace, Annabel instinctively moved
backward. But he was so close to death that she changed her
mind, slid her arm under his head, and cradled it in her lap as
he drew his last breath.

"Forgive me, Alex," she whispered softly.

౭ఎ౭ఎ

She sat there, not moving for several minutes, numbed by
shock, and the reality of what she'd caused. It was a surprise
that her grief for him was considerably stronger that she had
imagined.

She had an awful feeling of remorse as she stroked his hair
back from his forehead. He was gone.

She kissed him lightly, brushed his eyelids shut, and laid
his head gently back on the floor. She got up and dressed

quickly then rushed down stairs, calling for the servants. The house was strangely quiet. Only Alfred was to be found in the kitchen.

"Something terrible has happened," she said breathlessly. "Alex has been stung by a bee, and I fear it is too late to save him."

Alfred rushed up the stairs with her and saw at once that Alex was dead. He bowed and shook his head. "It is too late," he said sorrowfully.

Annabel didn't have to act the part of the grieving widow for Alfred's benefit, but she felt the grief intensely. A part of Alex had loved her, and she had always believed that.

"Where is everybody?" she asked sadly, with a glance at Alfred.

"The master has given all the servants two days leave," he said, distracted from his thoughts. "I was about to depart myself."

The room was chilled enough from the open window, but Annabel went cold with fear. "Where is the master?"

"In his room, milady, he wasn't to be disturbed."

Annabel saw that Alfred was trying to fight back his emotions. He had been very fond of Alex. She patted his arm. "You should still take your leave. First, go into Rookwood and inform the doctor what has happened. We need a death certificate."

Alfred looked at her with concern. "I can't leave you all alone."

"Yes, you can. I will be fine. Cerberus is here."

Ten minutes later, Alfred left by the front door, Annabel watched him walk across the courtyard and left the window. She had to be strong. Everything was going according to plan. The doctor would be here within the hour, and he would confirm that a bee sting killed Alex. She paced about the room for a few minutes. She picked up a bottle on the dressing table, shook the contents, and replaced it.

Then, pulled by a great urge, she knelt beside Alex and held his hand, oddly mesmerized by his face and the features that she had never really seen before. She wondered how she could have been so blind, but their coloring was so different. Perhaps it was only when you looked closely you saw the subtleties of resemblance. It was no wonder she had been drawn to him and, in some ways, even loved him.

"So you finally killed him!"

Annabel jumped, shocked at the sight of Cerberus standing behind her. Fear washed over her and she scrambled to her feet. All she could think of was the truth that Jevan had revealed. She looked at him with contempt, her heart pounding heavily. "Why—why did you do this to us?"

A flash of realization crossed his face, and he tilted his head to one side. His lips pressed together in a bitter smile, and then he laughed coldly. "I thought you would have realized a long time before this. You were never Josiah's daughter. It was your mother's fault. Your mother destroyed me!" There was a faint touch of pain in his voice. "I would have given her anything. I even had my own wife committed to an asylum so that I might be free, but still, she rejected me."

"My mother never loved you and you raped her," Annabel hissed accusingly. "What did you expect?"

Cerberus shook his head. "No, I loved her."

"No, don't you dare talk of love where my mother's concerned. You don't know the meaning of the word!" Annabel wanted to scratch his eyes out, yet she felt herself shrink back from him, in body at least. Her mind was struggling to make sense of him. "In all these years, why did you never try to see me, why was this kept from me?" she demanded bitterly. "I barely knew you existed."

Cerberus looked at her rather oddly and then walked past her into the room. He glanced briefly down at Alex, before shifting his gaze back to her.

"I made a promise to Lilith. That I would stay away from you and conceal the truth. But—" He considered for a moment. "I watched you grow, Annabel. I used to see you and Jevan steal into the gardens and play by the pond. I watched when you climbed the trees in the orchard to steal the fruit." Cerberus's mouth twisted into something like a smile. "I was always in your life, even if you didn't know it."

"So what changed?" she demanded with ferocity. "Why did you break the promise you made to my mother?"

Cerberus stood still, eyes steadily penetrating hers. "When Lilith died, my perspective changed. Your mother could have destroyed me and Alex," he said in all seriousness. "And she threatened as much, if I ever came near you or Josiah. In those months after your mother's death, I tried to put you out of my mind, but it is she that still haunts my dreams, even my waking hours."

Annabel shook her head. "Your son lies dead at your feet, and yet I see no remorse or sadness. It's your conscience that haunts you, not my mother!"

Cerberus made a noise of impatience in his throat. "You are naïve if you don't acknowledge that there are greater forces at work here. Alex was never strong. He was easily influenced, but with his return and subsequent chance meeting with you, I knew then that he would love you. He talked of nothing else for days, constantly asking tiresome questions about your family. I saw that you had already bewitched him. I admit that, at first, I hated the idea. You are so like Lilith, that I couldn't bear to look at you, but as his adoration grew, so did mine. I saw the power you possessed, and I had the perfect plan to have both my children under my roof."

Annabel gave him a look of incredulity, as she reeled from his words. "Alex was my brother! When you urged me to marry him, did you somehow forget that significant detail?"

Cerberus shook his head. "You and Alex would have strengthened the blood line, half brother and sister, your child would have guaranteed the legacy's future."

Annabel could not believe the words she was hearing. "Did you have no care for my feelings at all? You knew I didn't love him, not that way."

"I knew that with your devotion to Jevan, I had the perfect bargaining tool."

Annabel stared at him with loathing. "You are despicable!"

"No, I know how to get what I want. Once you and Alex were safely married, it was a matter of time before there would be an heir. But enough of this," he said dismissively and looked back down at Alex.

He raised his eyebrows a fraction. "A bee sting. Ingenious I must admit. Although, you do know that Alex was never really a threat to you." Annabel didn't move. "Perhaps he was only part of your plan. Tell me, Annabel, was I to be next? Would you murder your own father?" he said bitterly. "And what exactly did you have in mind for me?"

Annabel's thoughts flew to the infusion of belladonna on her dressing table and was alarmed to see that Cerberus also looked in that direction. "You talk nonsense." She was talking now only to distract him. "You're mad. There was no plan, and Alex died in my arms, a terrible accident."

Cerberus shook his head. "I see your true character. I see through your lies, and I see that you are uncharacteristically nervous. But there are more important things to think about today." He stepped closer. "I was going to use Alfred. Alex will be even better," he said, looking down at the body.

Annabel frowned and shook her head, looking back at Alex.

"I've sent Alfred for the doctor—use him for what?"

Cerberus looked down at her. "No one is coming. Alfred never left." He twisted his thin lips into a brief smile. "Only you and I are here."

"Is Alfred—dead?" she stammered, horrified.

"That is not important. Soon Lilith will join us, and we will be the most powerful witches, a coven like no other."

"My mother is dead," Annabel said firmly. "The spirit you speak of is Jane Saltonstall."

"No," he said, knitting his eyebrows. "Who is that? I don't know that name."

"Well, you should," she said, moving closer to him and gaining momentum. "Jane was the girl in the attic, the girl behind the bookcase, the spirit that speaks and terrorizes all the Saltonstall women. My mother is at peace in her grave. This spirit, if that is what she is, has power. She is the root of all evil in this house, even your corruption is down to her."

Cerberus kept his eyes upon her and saw her anger and determination. "You will help me," he said, leaning closer. "I will resurrect Lilith, and you will see just how wrong you are. This demon you talk of—if it exists and is as influential as you think—then we will use its power as well."

"No," Annabel shrieked, recoiling at the thought and the reality of his diabolical idea. "Jane Saltonstall wasn't a powerful witch. She was betrayed by those she trusted. She was an unremarkable woman with no power, and only in death is she vengeful! Her revenge is to render all the Saltonstall males insane. That is the spirit's goal, that's what she does, that's all she does. There is no power or ability to resurrect dead people."

"Annabel, I am your father, and you will help me. Why else do you think you have these powers? You inherited them from me!"

Annabel was stunned to hear him use those words. She was fuming, torn between wanting to kill him, and resisting due to the fact that he was her father. Perhaps she was startled into complacency as she saw the resemblance to herself. Just like Alex, the evidence was clear, once you looked close.

Cerberus, on the other hand, had no such horrors or speculation to hold him back. He grabbed hold of her arm.

All at once she felt the power and resolve in him. "Let go!" she screamed.

"No," he answered angrily and dragged her along the corridor.

She screamed and fought, scratching at his skin, twisting her body away from him, but he was relentless. He picked her up firmly in his arms. His hold was tight, and he was considerably stronger than she had ever imagined. They reached his private rooms, and he threw her through the open door where she fell heavily to the floor. Unfazed, she sprang up immediately and faced him.

The brutality was evident in his eyes, and she would need every ounce of her power to fight him. He stood before the doorway, blocking it. She took a few steps backward. All the furniture was cleared to one side of the room, and she glanced wildly around.

The gasp caught in her throat when she saw the drawing of a large pentagram on the floor. Cerberus came closer, his eyes filled with a terrible darkness. She was full of fierce determination as he came at her again. Her nails raked his flesh as he grabbed handful of her hair and twisted it tightly. She hit him until he restrained her arms and spun her around to the bed, pushing her against the bedpost.

"What are you doing? Let me go, Cerberus, or I will destroy you!" she spat venomously.

He was not fazed by her outrage. He reached up and pulled down a length of cord from the curtain, and, despite her protest and threats, he continued to wrap it tightly around her wrists. She twisted and turned her body, screaming in his ear, but he held her fast and did not flinch as he tied her firmly to the post.

He pushed her onto the bed, pinning her down with his weight as he tied her ankles. Annabel knew something awful was going to happen. She stopped protesting and, instead, fixed him with a shuddering gaze. Cerberus's head shot up, his teeth gritted, his hand shot out, grabbing her throat, closing off her air supply. She gasped and gagged. Her only thought now was of self-preservation.

Cerberus released his grip. "Don't try and use your power against me. I will crush every last breath out of you."

Her breath was rapid now, her head spinning. He left the room and returned moments later, carrying Alex. He put the body on the floor at the center of the pentagram.

Terror made her blood run cold, and her eyes flew to Cerberus. "What are you doing?"

His gaze fixed on her face. "His blood will make our magic stronger."

Annabel shook her head frantically. "Cerberus, don't do this, don't call up this thing."

"I hoped that you would understand, and that you would co-operate," he said regretfully, "I need your power, and to make sure you oblige me, I will have to subdue you a little."

Annabel pulled against the cord that bound her. It was too tight. She grasped it in her teeth and tried to bite it. It was too strong. The hairs stood up on her flesh as Cerberus walked to the dresser and lifted a cup from it. He came back to the bed. The brown liquid inside the cup smelled strongly of herbs as he lifted it to her lips.

She turned her head away. "I won't drink your poison!" She turned and spat at him, her gaze locked with his.

Cerberus's composure didn't falter. "It's not poison, it's just something to make you more agreeable."

"I won't be more agreeable," she said, and pressed her lips together tightly.

All at once, Cerberus grabbed her jaw and squeezed painfully. Prying her mouth open, he tipped the liquid inside. She spluttered and tried to spit it out, but he clamped her mouth shut and pinched her throat to make her gasp for air. The thick liquid ran down her throat, making her gag. Cerberus smiled in satisfaction. She tried to will herself to be sick, but it would not happen.

Cerberus left the room and closed the door behind him.

Annabel frantically curled her fingers back and forth and again pulled on the cord with her teeth. Tears ran down her face. It seemed hopeless. She sat still for a few moments, feeling giddy, and focused on Alex's body. Did she make a mistake? Should she have let Alex live? He would not have stood for this. Then again, Alex would have been no match for Cerberus.

She thought back to Cerberus's reaction earlier. He did not even seem to care that his son was dead. In fact, she firmly believed he would have killed Alex himself had he gotten in his father's way.

Her predicament was terrifying. She did not know the extent of Cerberus's power or insanity, and the substance he had given her was altering her state of consciousness. She felt tired, as if all her energy had drained away. Perhaps Cerberus considered that she was stronger than he was, and he had now stacked the odds in his favor. Whatever despicable plan he had in mind, she could not stop him. More disturbingly, she could unwittingly help him. He would be able to control her.

Annabel closed her eyes for what she thought was a few

seconds, but after opening them again, she found the room inexplicably much darker than she remembered. Her vision would not come into focus properly. Her mouth was dry, and her throat parched.

She called for Cerberus. He did not answer. She closed her eyes again as sickness rose in her throat, and her head throbbed continuously.

๛๛๛

Something touched her leg. A hand ran up her calf. She opened her eyes with a start. Cerberus was untying her ankles. His touch made her cringe. He was looming over her, his face only partly in focus, but he was whispering something. She tried to push against him, but she had no strength. His words were muddled and, when they became audible, she felt only despair and horror.

"We will ensure there is an heir," he said, his eyes gleaming brightly.

Oh, God, he is going to rape me.

She felt his hands over her body. Then her arms and legs were free of cords. He pulled her up to him, and she stumbled against him.

He held her tightly and grabbed her jaw, forcing her to look at him. "With Alex dead, only I can be the father of your child!"

Her eyes betrayed her horror, and he laughed vindictively. "There will be enough time for that later. The time is close now. We must prepare."

He clasped her firmly around the waist and pulled her into the pentagram. He pushed her to the floor so she was sitting before Alex's body. She tried to move back, but her body did not want to respond. Her head was spinning. Cerberus was lighting the candles placed around the pentagram.

Annabel's vision was doubling and tripling. She couldn't tell if there were ten or fifty candles. She felt herself drifting away from her body onto some higher astral plane, no longer afraid, no longer caring what Cerberus was doing.

Then, oddly, he was seated opposite her, with Alex in the middle, between them. She saw Cerberus holding a silver dagger and, although she cried out, she watched in horrific fascination as he placed the blade against Alex's chest, plunged the dagger into the flesh, and chanted—calling forth the blood.

As Alex's chest split open, the blood spilled out over the body and floor, obscuring the lines of the pentagram. The puddle grew bigger. The sticky substance touched her legs and soaked into her clothes. Still, she could not move. Cerberus was holding up a length of dark cord. It appeared to have black feathers tied in knots along its length

"The witch's ladder," he said, holding it before her eyes. Her focus suddenly sharpened. She hadn't realized, but her hands were clasped in Cerberus's and the witch's ladder was entwined in their blooded fingers. He stared deeply into her eyes. "Concentrate, Annabel, I need your power."

She shook her head in defiance and tried to pull her hands away.

"I said concentrate!" he roared.

She felt his power draining her energy. Something was burning hot inside her. It radiated through her legs, up her torso, and into her chest. Her body was shaking. It felt uncontrollable, a burning agony, mounting by the minute. She felt his power, an intense energy that built all around her. It felt immoral, a source of pure evil, as if the gates to hell were opening. Her mind screamed out, but she was unable to resist him. Cerberus's hold grew suddenly tighter, and his low voice cut through the air.

> "Powers of the witch's cord,
> Bow to the witch's word
> Forces of darkness,
> Bound to the witch's knot
> Come, Hecate, bend to my will
> and escort thy witch back from hell."

The candles went out. Annabel felt the energy surge in Cerberus. Her own skin felt as though it were on fire, and she tried again to push herself away. Cerberus did not let go. Her legs pushed under her and slipped on the slick blood puddle.

"No!" she screamed.

"Silence!" Cerberus roared. "It is building, it is happening!"

Annabel felt it too. She twisted her head and looked back. There was movement. Something stirred the air, swirling around like a great black shadow. Annabel shook her head. She could not let this happen. She had to fight, no matter whether or not it was a fight to the death. She closed her eyes and concentrated on her hands, summoning a familiar energy. Despite the evil entering the room, she focused on controlling what she knew. The energy built quickly and radiated through her body, waking her subdued consciousness into alertness. She squeezed Cerberus hands tighter. He had begun chanting again, and his power was weakening her. With all her might, she fought back. Her mind would not be broken. She would not let him.

Then she felt it. Deep rage compressed into a frenzy of tiny connections being made throughout her body. The intensity built, swirling the energy through every part of her being, and the humming, which had started quietly, grew in pitch until it was a deafening noise in her head. With one last mental effort, she forced it from her, and Cerberus screamed in agony.

He leapt up and back from her, staring at the bee stings that covered his hands.

Annabel scrambled clumsily to her feet as he stared at her with contempt. His face changed subtly as he looked past her. Annabel's blood froze in her veins as she turned.

"Lilith, my love!"

Cerberus's voice was behind her. Annabel caught her breath in horror. The demon lived and breathed as she had before, but the girl was not Lilith.

"Jane." Annabel mouthed the word silently and the demon's eyes flew to her.

"You," her cracked voice cried. "You were stronger than the others. This is my house!" Her eyes were the color of ebony, her flesh was white with prominent gray veins that streaked across the pale surface, and her hair was long and dark, although old and ancient looking—as if she had lain in the ground for a very long time.

Annabel stepped back. The demon's mouth turned up in a grotesque smile.

She let out a horrific scream and leapt across the room toward Annabel. "A house full of witches, and thou shalt not suffer a witch to live!"

Triggered by adrenaline, Annabel's senses came to life, and she moved fast. She turned, stumbled, and ran out through the door, slamming it behind her. Her legs felt as though they might buckle at any moment, but she propelled herself forward. The door behind her was ripped from its hinges and came hurtling toward her. She shrieked and ran down the stairs. The demon launched its body over the banister, landing on all fours at the foot of the stairs so she looked up menacingly at Annabel.

Annabel was struck with terror. She could not out run it. She had to think fast. "You are right, Jane," she said, raising her arms and concentrating the energy. This time it built more rapidly, causing the house to shake as she backed up, one step at a time. "I am stronger than all the others. I was born from goodness and evil combined, and that makes me a force to be reckoned with. You said it yourself, stronger than all the others, and the most powerful witch you have ever encountered." The demon started up the stairs, as Annabel continued. "You have manipulated and ruined this family, but your legacy of torment is at an end. Now that you have an earthly form, you can be destroyed. For you, witch, cannot live!"

The demon leapt into the air, at the same time as the glass in the windows shattered. Hundreds of bees flew into the house and descended on the creature.

It shrieked and writhed in agony as the bees covered its form entirely. There was a clear element of the girl, which had once been Jane, in the contortion. Its pitiful cry pulled at the strings of her conscience as Annabel watched the bee-covered demon seemingly run up the wall and across the ceiling, connecting sharply with the gasolier. It pulled on the fitting, shaking it in fury. The gasolier groaned at the onslaught. Annabel concentrated her energy once more to pull the fitting from the ceiling. It fell to the ground with an almighty crash. Flames leapt out in every direction, covering the bees, as the demon shook itself free.

Annabel stared in horror as tiny burning corpses fell through the air.

"My bees!" she cried, turning and racing up the stairs.

Cerberus stood at the top. "No," he cried out to the demon. "Lilith, it's me and your daughter."

Annabel stared at him, bewildered at his unwavering belief. The demon was close to her now, but Cerberus moved in front of her.

"Lilith?" he said, clearly confused,

The demon laughed cruelly. "You fool! Now it's your time to burn."

She launched herself at him. Cerberus fell backward, breaking through the banister. He wildly clutched at the balustrade and caught hold of the demon's ankle. It shrieked with rage and catapulted over the balcony. Cerberus did not release his grip. The balustrade came away, and Cerberus screamed as he flew through the air with the demon shrieking in fury. Together, they hit the burning floor. Even though Annabel's eyes were streaming from the smoke, she could not tear her gaze away as Cerberus's body melted into the flames.

The demon let out a hideous screech as it writhed around in the fiery hell, until at last it dissolved into a swirling black dust that rose through the smoke, building in density. It clung to the walls and raced along the ceiling, searching for a way out. It was making for the glassless window.

Annabel pushed every ounce of her energy toward the swirling black mass. "The heat of the fire will consume every last particle. You will not rise again," she cried fervently, her voice rasping. "I send you back to the underworld from whence you came!"

The billowing smoke changed directions. The flames roared across the window. Annabel was seized by a painful coughing fit as the swirling blackness raced back and forth, trapped by the suffocating black smoke and leaping flames. Finally, it disintegrated, and Annabel could no longer see it. She hoped she had done enough, as she dropped to her knees and crawled along the floor until she reached the bedroom door. She pushed it open and fell inside, where the smoke was still thick. Slamming the door shut, she staggered to her feet and rushed to the window. Her lungs were filled with the choking smoke, and she was gasping for air. She pushed open the window and gulped the clean fresh air.

Close to exhaustion, and overcome with smoke and the effects of whatever drug Cerberus had given her, she was determined that she would not die today. With what little energy she had left, she pulled herself up onto the windowsill and squeezed her body through the opening. She climbed out onto the windowsill and edged along it, trying not to look down. She felt dizzy, sick, and weak as she gingerly placed her foot on a piece of stonework that jutted out only a few inches deep. Clawing at the uneven stonework, she made her way along this tiny ledge. She found a few sturdy branches of an old wisteria tree and held onto them as she made her way downward and onto a lower roof. From there, she lowered herself to the top of a window rim and jumped down to the ground. She staggered farther back, staring at the burning mansion. It looked as though the fire had spread to most of the rooms, as each window opening blazed and glass shattered intermittently.

Her hand was throbbing painfully. She glanced down at a deep gash, which poured blood, and lifted the hem of her skirt to staunch the bleeding. It was damp and heavily stained from Alex's blood. She let out a sob, ripped the skirt from her, and tore a strip of fabric from it before discarding it. The wind picked up and flames fanned into the air above her head as the fire gained intensity. Thunder crashed in the distance and, what was left of her spirit propelled her away from the blazing mansion.

Her goal was to go home, home to Honeymead, home to Jevan. Rain began to fall, light at first, then it grew heavier, making the ground sodden underfoot. She stumbled more than once, staggering into the fields. In the distance, she heard voices ringing across the countryside. She did not turn back. Grief kept her moving until fatigue finally overcame her and, beneath a hedgerow, she sat down. It gave her a little protection from the weather. She wrapped the scrap of material tighter around her cut, feeling extremely lightheaded.

"The witch is dead," she whispered and passed out.

Chapter 36

Honeymead

As night approached, the violence of the wind was enhanced. The rain beat against the windowpanes, and Jevan's uneasiness increased. Upstairs in the cottage, he threw open the window and watched the ominous black clouds rolling in from the west. At a frenzied pace, they raced toward Gothelstone, as the fast-moving current of air whistled eerily all around, sounding like the howling of distant dogs.

Jevan's gaze moved across the blackened fields to where the mansion stood. He was startled to see an indistinct light surrounding it. It appeared shrouded in a gray mist as if covered with low cloud. He had waited for Annabel all evening. She said she would come, and he decided to give her another hour before he went to find her. As his gaze sharpened on the mansion, the mist billowed, just like smoke. Fear besieged him as he leapt down the stairs, two at a time, ran out the door, and darted across to the stable. Jess was already agitated from the storm, and, as Jevan burst through the stable door, the horse backed up fearfully.

"Whoa, Jess, come on, boy," Jevan cried impatiently.

As he swung up onto the horse's back, Jess raced out of the stable. The lightning streaked across the sky, and the horse reared a little. Sensing his master's urgency, he held his nerve. They raced across the fields, going faster and faster, leaping with ease across low hedges and ditches.

Jevan's heart felt as if it would burst with grief as they neared the blazing mansion. Villagers had already gathered, and some were fetching water. Jevan saw that it was useless. This was a fire that would not be put out.

He jumped from Jess's back and pushed through the crowd. "Annabel! Has anyone seen her?" he cried frantically, searching various faces.

People shook their heads, and he stared back at the mansion in horror. To think that she was trapped inside, overcome with smoke, or just unable to get out, made him catch his breath. He ran into the courtyard to find a way in. The thick putrid smoke invaded his lungs. It poured out from each window, and flames lit up every opening. Undeterred, he rushed forward and was immediately hauled backward by hands that held him firmly.

"Let me go!" he roared, twisting and shaking himself free, but only for a moment, because the farm workers restrained him again.

"You cannot go in there. You will be dead within seconds!"

"I have to get her!" he roared.

They held him fast, and Jevan could only watch as the fire consumed the building. He fell to his knees in despair. She couldn't be dead. She couldn't. He shook his head, his eyes blurred from the moisture. He wiped a shaking hand across his face, believing that it would be better to burn with her than to suffer the sorrow. A firm hand rested on his shoulder and he looked up to find Jophiel.

"Father," he cried softly, but couldn't find any other words to say.

Jophiel pulled him to his feet and wrapped his arms around him, unable to conceal his own tears. The wind was changing, and the smoke started to engulf the crowd. The mansion was fully ablaze. Nothing could survive in those flames. The crowd was forced to move farther back toward the fields. They had even stopped fetching water. Everyone could see it was useless. Jophiel tried to pull Jevan back, but Jevan pushed him away.

"Don't!" he cried distraught, his tears breaking Jophiel's heart. Jevan looked again at his father. "I can't live without her—I won't!" he said, shaking his head

"Jevan, I won't let you go in there. I can't lose you as well," Jophiel said wretchedly.

Jevan saw his father's grief. He shook his head and pushed Jophiel from him. "I have to be alone," he said, and reluctantly moved away from the burning building.

Jophiel watched Jevan stumble across the ground. He couldn't leave him alone. He was too afraid of what his son might do. Jophiel followed slowly, choking back the grief.

Jevan staggered toward the fields. Lurid pictures plagued his mind and made his head hurt. Had she been in terrible pain, or was it a quick death? He couldn't bear to think of her suffering, and his imagination conjured up all too easily how horrific it might have been.

Consumed by grief, he didn't pay attention to what caught around his foot. He stumbled clumsily, ripped the rag from his boot, and discarded it. His hand was wet. He glanced down at his blood-stained fingers and caught his breath. His heart was pounding so heavily that he feared it might burst from his rib cage as he turned back and stared at the rag. He was certain that he recognized the material. He quickly scooped it up, alarmed to see that it was not only wet from the rain, but from blood. And the blood looked fresh. He straightened the skirt and saw it was ripped to shreds.

Jophiel came closer and saw it too. Both men looked at each other.

"She's alive!" Jevan said, feeling suddenly lightheaded.

Jophiel nodded and swallowed nervously, "But badly hurt by the look of things. I'll set up a search party," he said, heading back toward the congregation.

Jevan didn't hear. He was already making his way across the field.

There was a partial moon. The rain had almost stopped, and the violence of the earlier storm was nowhere to be seen. Jevan followed a trodden path through the field, noticing that the grass looked flattened in several places, perhaps where she had fallen. The sight of the blood on her clothes terrified him. What, exactly, had happened? Had Alex discovered their plan and tried to kill her? Was he out here, too?

"Annabel!" Jevan cried, through the stillness of the night.

಴಴಴

The air was heavy with the thick scent of smoke, and a cool wind blew across her skin. Something was in the air, beckoning her back from the darkness. In the distance, she heard the calling.

"Annabel."

Her name came again. She recognized the voice and the urgency when her name was repeated. Her eyelids fluttered, and she tried to respond. The air caught in her throat. She coughed, pain shooting through her chest. The penetrating dampness from the ground had numbed her. There were no real senses anymore. Horror flitted through her mind and kept peace at bay. Her mind could not cope. She could no longer respond to anything and retreated into her safe dark world.

಴಴಴

Jevan caught the sound of a stifled cough carried on the wind. He turned at once toward the noise and the hedgerow. As he drew nearer, he saw her body. His initial relief was replaced by apprehension. He was appalled at the sight of her— her clothes covered in blood, her face blackened by smoke and dirt, and she was still. Too still. Jevan eased her body from under the hedge, pulling her slowly toward him. Anxiously, he felt for her pulse. It was weak. At that moment, he heard Jophiel's voice.

"Over here, Father!"

"Where is she hurt?" Jophiel said, his relief turning into fear.

"I don't know," Jevan, said shaking his head. "I can't see any visible wounds apart from her hand. I am afraid to move her, until I am sure." Jevan looked up at his father, swallowing nervously. "She is covered in so much blood." He carefully began to loosen her clothes, dreading that there would be a deep knife wound or something to explain the excessive amount of blood. He carefully tore away the sodden material and slowly ran his hands over her body, feeling for any injury. Reassured, he looked back at Jophiel. "She's not hurt," he said, half relieved, half mystified. "Where has all this blood come from?" He took hold of her shoulders and shook her gently. "Annabel wake up!" he pleaded frantically.

Jophiel had already taken his coat off. "Here," he said, extending his arm. "Wrap her in that. She'll freeze otherwise." He bent down, gathered up all the bloodstained clothes, tied them into a bundle, and glanced at Jevan. "We will burn them," he said. "It's not her blood."

Jevan nodded and pulled Annabel to him. He wrapped the coat around her and swung her carefully up into his arms. Jophiel whistled to Jess, and the horse ambled over to them. Jevan handed Annabel gently to Jophiel while he got up on Jess's back, and then Annabel was placed back in his arms. Jophiel followed with his horse and the bundle of clothes.

They rode steadily back to Honeymead. Jevan carried her upstairs and placed her on the bed. Jophiel fetched warm water and wiped the dirt and dried blood away from her skin.

"Why doesn't she wake?" Jevan said, looking for Jophiel to give him a plausible answer.

Jophiel shook his head. The situation confounded his understanding. Her skin was thoroughly chilled, and they wrapped her in warm blankets. They sat by her side all night, but, by morning, the dark circles around their eyes belied the anxiety. Jevan could take no more. He was beside himself with grief.

"Something is really wrong. I cannot rouse her, and I think she is dying."

Jevan's words caught in his throat as Jophiel took hold of her wrist. "Her pulse seems stronger," he said, giving Jevan a glimmer of hope. "The first light has just come over the horizon. I will ride for the doctor."

Jevan nodded in agreement, and Jophiel left them alone.

Jevan listened to the sound of the horse's hooves moving away from the cottage. His eyes could not leave her face, even for a second, too fearful she might fade away.

"Wake up, Annabel," he pleaded softly. "Don't leave me."

He clasped both arms around her and, even though he could feel her breathing and that was a reassuring sensation, he was fraught with uncertainty. What if she never woke again? Surely fate could not be so cruel. To be spared by the flames, only to die in his arms—

He couldn't bear this agony. Jevan shook his head. He wouldn't let her die. She had to come back to him. "Annabel, you cannot give up now," he demanded. "Use your power, your witchcraft, and come back to me." He thought he saw her eyelids flutter, but he could not be certain. "You are bound to me, remember? Without you, I cannot live. You have to wake up. Please come back."

Jophiel returned with the doctor within the hour. The doctor spent several minutes examining her and then turned to Jevan. "Her throat is raw. She has probably inhaled a lot of smoke, but her breathing is even, and her heart rhythm is strong and normal. There are no visible injuries or broken bones." He hesitated for a moment, staring at her gravely. "There may be trauma in the brain. I cannot tell. Shock can do strange things. She may just need time to heal. Give her peace and quiet, and keep her warm. I will call in and see her tomorrow."

Jophiel thanked the doctor and saw him to the door. Jevan sighed and placed his head in his hands. He felt so fatigued and helpless, and he couldn't do anything for her, only sit, and watch. Wait for her to wake, or for her to die. Raw emotion made his nerves ragged, and he swallowed back the nauseous feeling.

Jophiel returned a few moments later. "Go and get some rest. You need some sleep," he said, coming closer to the bed.

Jevan shook his head. "No, I won't leave her," he said firmly.

Jophiel nodded in understanding. It was no use arguing with Jevan. "I'll get you something to eat. You have to keep up your strength. She will need you when she wakes."

Jevan looked up. "Do you believe she will?" The pain in Jevan's words was shattering.

"Yes," Jophiel said confidently and left the room, hoping with every ounce of his being that he was right.

He couldn't bear to lose Annabel. He felt all the pain as if she had been his own daughter, and he knew without a shadow of a doubt that, if anything happened to her, he would lose Jevan too.

Jevan watched his father leave, and minutes later heard him moving about below in the kitchen. Jevan carefully lay down on the bed next to Annabel. He put his arms around her and leaned his head against hers. Jophiel brought food, but Jevan could not touch it. There was no point in doing anything without her. Nightfall came, and Jophiel took the food away. He lit a candle, which sent flickering shadows around the room. His anxiety was clear, but he made no comment. Jevan was all that Annabel needed right now.

Jevan listened to his father's retreating steps on the stairs and laid his head on the pillow, his eyes barely able to remain open. "What happened to you?" he said softly, as he raised her hand to his mouth and kissed it tenderly. "Forever thine," he said and closed his eyes.

Tired as he was, sleep still eluded him. He listened to her quiet breathing. Hours passed until he finally drifted into blackness.

Jevan woke with a start. The dream had been vivid. The fire burning hot on his skin, the terror so real in his mind, and through it all she called out to him. In the stillness of the room, he slowly gathered his thoughts. Her voice sounded so close but, with no real expectation, he leaned over and looked at her. Her eyes were open. He caught his breath as elation replaced terror and a surge of relief flooded through him.

"I'm here," he said quickly.

Annabel's eyes fluttered as if she were struggling to keep them open. She raised her hand to touch his face. Even in her injured state, and by dim candlelight, she was alarmed by the hollowness and worry lines that cast dark shadows over him.

Her mouth was so dry that, when she tried to speak, her throat hurt and any utterance was torture.

"Water," was the only thing she managed.

The rasping cough felt as though grit was being rubbed against the inside of her throat.

Jevan jumped up and rushed to the top of the stairs. "Father, bring Annabel some water, quick!"

Moments later, Jophiel appeared at her bedside, his face radiating happiness. He sat on the bed beside her. "Annabel my dear, how are you feeling?" he said, tilting her head and lifting the cup to her lips.

She shook her head and sipped the water. The coolness of the liquid was soothing and, although the agony was still there, it eased a little. She wasn't sure how long she had slept. She still felt exhausted and lay back on the pillow. She looked from one to the other of them. Their deep concern was not concealed by their smiling faces. She struggled to speak, but Jevan urged her to drink more. Jophiel fetched some honey and slowly fed her a spoonful to ease the soreness. When she spoke, her voice sounded broken, but gazing into Jevan's eyes, she could not stay silent. She picked up his hand, and his fingers curled around hers.

"You should know me well enough by now," she said with a surge of emotion. "I could never leave you. We are part of one another."

Jevan placed a kiss tenderly on her forehead. Jophiel patted her arm.

"What matters is that you are safe and here at Honeymead." Jevan leaned closer to her. "What happened, Annabel?"

Annabel cringed inwardly. A coldness radiated through her body as the memories flooded through her mind. "I can't remember," she said with a sob, feeling her body go rigid with terror. "I don't want to remember," she corrected, staring intently at Jevan.

Intuitively, he picked up her awful feeling. "It's all right, sweetheart. Tell me when you are feeling stronger." He paused and frowned. "Should we leave? Will they come for you?"

Annabel shook her head. "They are all dead. Alex, Cerberus, and I think Alfred as well. The whole house was alight."

Jevan sat back, stunned, although he hoped he did a good job of hiding the triumphant feeling that overcame him. He had assumed they had gotten out with her, and she escaped them. Now, all he could think of was how she could be so certain—unless she knew they were dead before the fire started. He looked anxiously at his father, and Jophiel's brows knitted together.

"The house is now just a ruin, the fire was so intense, there were no bodies found. That's what I heard," Jophiel said, looking uncomfortably at Annabel.

"The bodies are gone. I saw Cerberus in the flames and Alex—" She broke off, remembering Alex in her arms and then the dagger that Cerberus plunged into his chest.

Jevan clasped her hand tighter.

"It means, Annabel," Jophiel continued, trying to distract her from a clearly traumatic memory, "that you are the only surviving Saltonstall heir."

She stared at him for a few moments, feeling suddenly haunted as she took in the reality of his words. The only remaining Saltonstall, except Elizabeth, and she would have no claim to the Saltonstall legacy, as she was mentally unstable and locked in an asylum. It was true, even if the thought made her shudder. That house had contained evil. No one had ever been happy there, and their suffering was buried for eternity in the ruins and ash. Insanity and sorrow was its real legacy.

"In that case, it will stay as it is," she said directly. "If any ghosts remain, they can haunt that ruin until the end of time, for all I care. My home is here at Honeymead."

Chapter 37

A Point of View

It took several days for Annabel to regain her strength and for her throat to feel something like normal. Her cough persisted, and all the while Jevan hovered around protectively, not allowing her to do anything at all. The doctor examined her again and said that, as far as he could tell, there would be no permanent damage to her lungs or throat. All she needed was time to recuperate.

Since the fire, local reporters had plagued Honeymead. Jevan sent them all away, insisting that she was not well enough to receive any visitors. Only Jophiel was allowed into the cottage.

A week later, Annabel insisted she could not delay any longer and, in order to lay her own ghosts to rest, she agreed to give her account of the events of that terrible night.

❧❧❧

The reporter wrote:

> *Mistress Annabel Saltonstall gave her account of how the devastating fire spread rapidly throughout the Gothelstone Manor House. She reported that her father-in-law, Cerberus Saltonstall, had given the servants time off, and she believed that it was he or*

*Alex, her late husband, who lit the fire in the draw-
ing room. The fire was left unattended whilst they
dined in the grand dining hall. After dinner, Mistress
Saltonstall retired early with a terrible headache,
but sometime later, she was awakened by the smell
of smoke and rushed out onto the upstairs landing.
The downstairs rooms were all engulfed in flames,
and she was overcome with smoke. She called out to
her father-in-law and to her husband, and no one
answered. Mistress Saltonstall believed they were
already dead and, stricken with grief, went back to
her room. She managed to escape by climbing out of
the bedroom window. She fell and cut her hand badly. She persisted in her endeavor to raise the alarm
and fetch help, but in her grief, she became disorientated and overcome with smoke herself. That same
night, she was discovered unconscious in a nearby
field and was bedridden for many days after. Mistress Saltonstall is now convalescing in her family
home. Lawyers have already confirmed that Mistress
Saltonstall is the sole surviving heir to the sizeable
Saltonstall fortune.*

ඏඁඏ

Annabel read the newspaper article with mild amusement.
Her black widow's dress in the photograph made her skin
seem even paler than normal. Being the heir of such a fortune
meant this picture made the front cover of many newspapers
in the country.

Several weeks after, when the gossip finally became old
news, another reporter from Bristol was visiting Rookwood.
He had heard about the terrible tragedy at the mansion and had
a mind to see the ruined house. The charred ruin was visible
from a distance away, its dark sinister presence looming over
bright golden cornfields.

As he neared, his horse suddenly became agitated. It shook
its head and reared sharply, throwing him to the ground. Peas-

ants in a nearby field ran to his assistance. They helped him up
and calmed the horse. The reporter was angry and swore at the
horse, at which one of the men stepped forward.

"It is not the animal, sir, it's the house," the man said. "No
horse will go near the ruin now."

The reporter looked at him curiously. "What do you
mean?"

"They sense something," the man said, "and we don't go
up either, sir, not since the fire." He hesitated. "It's haunted."

The reporter smiled. "A ghost?"

The man shook his head. "I don't know for sure. People
talk of an apparition of a young girl. Maybe it was a servant
girl who died in the fire. Perhaps they didn't realize she was
still in the house."

The reporter felt a cold chill run down his spine. He
thanked them for their assistance, and the men went back to
the field. The reporter stared at the ruined mansion. It would
have been magnificent before it burned. The charred ruin
looked sinister, now he was closer to it, and, unexpectedly, he
felt inexplicably cold, despite the bright sunshine and the
warm day. A feeling of foreboding crept over him, and his
desire to look any closer disappeared. He got back on his
horse, turned around, and headed in the opposite direction.

∽∾∽

Elizabeth Saltonstall was moved to a private residence in
the country, and Annabel employed a nurse and housekeeper,
who were both kind and qualified to be her constant companions. Annabel promised to visit her every few months. She
employed a new estate manager and paid a handsome settle-
ment to all the staff who had worked at Gothelstone manor
house. She ensured that the tenants on the estate still had their
homes and livelihood and, with those business matters taken
care of, she acquired new bees for the skeps in the orchard.

Jevan kept his business and thrived as a successful printer
in Rookwood. With no obstacles in their way, Jevan and Annabel could finally live the life they had so longed for. Once

again, they were inseparable, dividing their time between Rookwood and Honeymead.

For appearance's sake, Annabel wore her widow's dress for five months and then burned it, even though she caused a mild scandal when she appeared in public wearing bright summer clothes. Malicious gossip never bothered Annabel. Much more of a concern were the nights she woke screaming, having been plunged back into the terrible nightmare of Samhain.

Jevan was there to chase away the horrors. He never pushed or insisted that she reveal what really happened at the mansion. He knew when she was ready, she would tell him.

That evening came soon enough. Her story made his blood run cold. At last, he was able to understand the magnitude of those night-time terrors and realized why she had retreated into herself and shut out the entire world, even him.

"So there you have it," she said, as she finished the story, oddly unburdened at having spoken the words aloud.

Jevan was silent for a time. He wondered if her sorrow would ever fade. Their life together was ahead of them. They were already planning a simple wedding at Gothelstone church, and what she really needed was time to heal. Only then, would these terrible thoughts and memories be put behind them. They could and would move on from this devastating chapter in their lives.

Annabel's eyes flickered over him, coming to rest on his intense gaze. "Can you still love a murderer?" she said sharply, emotion running high. "Because that's what I am. I burned the demon that was Jane Saltonstall. I destroyed Cerberus and—"

"You didn't kill Cerberus," Jevan interrupted.

She shrugged indifferently. "What about Alex? I planned it in detail. He was my brother, and I urged the bee to sting him, knowing full well it would kill him. I should feel remorse, but I don't, not one little bit." Annabel sighed sorrowfully. "It's so obvious to me that I inherited the same evil that corrupted Cerberus."

Jevan put his arms tightly around her and kissed her hair.

"You also inherited the goodness of Lilith, you forget that. You forget that you saved me, as I would surely be facing a trial that could only end in my death. I, too, planned their murders in detail, and I would have not been as subtle. You destroyed what had to be destroyed. That is not a sin."

"I killed Alex, as good as plunging a dagger into him."

Jevan looked deeply into her eyes. "Evil is a point of view, and you are not evil. You just did what you knew best." Annabel frowned and looked at him curiously. His mouth turned up a fraction. "You charmed a little bee."

About the Author

Jane Jordan was born in in England and grew up exploring the history and culture of London and surrounding counties. After some time spent in Germany in the 1990s, she immigrated to Detroit, USA, eventually settling in South West Florida. She returned to England, after a fifteen-year absence, to spend six years in the South West of England living on Exmoor. Here, inspired by the atmosphere, beautiful scenery, and the ancient history of the place, she wrote her first novel *Ravens Deep*. The next two books *Blood & Ashes* and *A Memoir of Carl* completed her gothic vampire trilogy.

Jordan is a trained horticulturist, and also spent time working and volunteering for Britain's National Trust at Exmoor's 1000-year-old Dunster Castle. Gaining more insight into the history and mysteries surrounding these ancient places, and having always been intrigued by the supernatural, inspiration came for her fourth novel, *The Beekeeper's Daughter*, combining the age-old struggle between good and evil with the passion and romance of the characters she creates.

Jordan returned to Florida in 2013 and lives in Sarasota with her family.

CPSIA information can be obtained
at www.ICGtesting.com
Printed in the USA
LVOW10s2111181116
513646LV00002B/4/P